W9-CBQ-185

THE SIEGE

STEPHEN WHITE

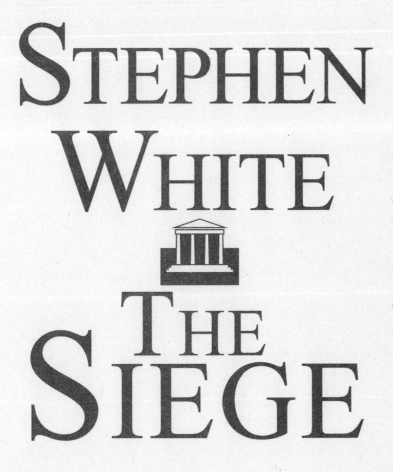

THE SIEGE

DUTTON

DUTTON
Published by Penguin Group (USA) Inc.
375 Hudson Street, New York, New York 10014, U.S.A.
Penguin Group (Canada), 90 Eglinton Avenue East, Suite 700, Toronto, Ontario M4P 2Y3, Canada
(a division of Pearson Penguin Canada Inc.); Penguin Books Ltd, 80 Strand, London WC2R 0RL,
England; Penguin Ireland, 25 St Stephen's Green, Dublin 2, Ireland (a division of Penguin Books Ltd);
Penguin Group (Australia), 250 Camberwell Road, Camberwell, Victoria 3124, Australia (a division of
Pearson Australia Group Pty Ltd); Penguin Books India Pvt Ltd, 11 Community Centre, Panchsheel Park,
New Delhi – 110 017, India; Penguin Group (NZ), 67 Apollo Drive, Rosedale, North Shore 0632,
New Zealand (a division of Pearson New Zealand Ltd); Penguin Books (South Africa) (Pty) Ltd,
24 Sturdee Avenue, Rosebank, Johannesburg 2196, South Africa

Penguin Books Ltd, Registered Offices: 80 Strand, London WC2R 0RL, England

Published by Dutton, a member of Penguin Group (USA) Inc.

First printing, August 2009
1 3 5 7 9 10 8 6 4 2

 REGISTERED TRADEMARK—MARCA REGISTRADA

LIBRARY OF CONGRESS CATALOGING-IN-PUBLICATION DATA

White, Stephen, 1951–
The siege / by Stephen White.
p.   cm.
ISBN 978-0-525-95122-3
1. Yale University—Fiction. 2. Missing persons—Fiction. 3. New Haven (Conn.)—Fiction.
I. Title.
PS3573.H47477S54   2009
813'.54—dc22   2009007586

Photo credit: page iii, Scott Meacham
Cartography/Art credit: page ix, Killeen Hanson

Printed in the United States of America
Set in Sabon
Designed by Leonard Telesca

to Xan

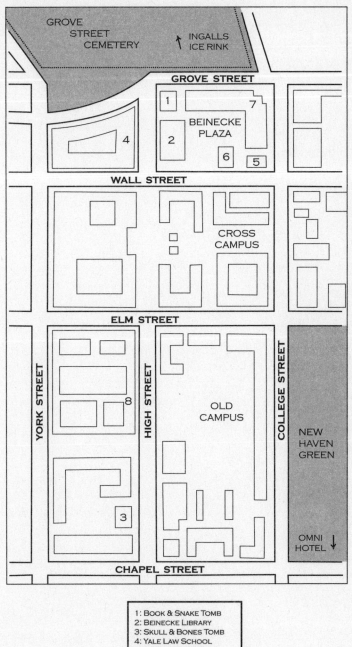

GROVE
STREET
CEMETERY

INGALLS
ICE RINK

GROVE STREET

1

7

BEINECKE
PLAZA

2

6

5

4

WALL STREET

CROSS
CAMPUS

ELM STREET

YORK STREET

HIGH STREET

8

OLD
CAMPUS

COLLEGE STREET

NEW
HAVEN
GREEN

3

OMNI
HOTEL

CHAPEL STREET

1: BOOK & SNAKE TOMB
2: BEINECKE LIBRARY
3: SKULL & BONES TOMB
4: YALE LAW SCHOOL
5: SCROLL & KEY TOMB
6: WOODBRIDGE HALL
7: WOOLSLEY/COMMONS
8: HARKNESS TOWER

But now, God knows,
Anything goes.

—Cole Porter
1934

THE SIEGE

You may be tempted to ignore these words. Do not. You were not chosen to receive this at random.

Do not discard this note. At some point in the near future, you will be desperate to reach me.

Do not share the contents of this message with anyone. I commit to you that the consequences of breaching my trust will be more severe than you wish to endure.

Blue will indicate that I am content. Orange will show my disappointment.

What do I want? I cannot answer that.

What do you have to offer? Give that question some thought.

When the time comes, we will reach an understanding. Despite all appearances, I am a reasonable man.

The building on the edge of campus could be mistaken for a mausoleum erected beyond the boundary of the cemetery across the street.

It's not.

Some assume it is a mock courtroom for the nearby law school.

It's not that either.

Although the structure's Ionic columns suggest the imperial, like a treasury, or evoke the divine, like a temple, the word "tomb" is the tag attached by the community. The building puts out no mat and welcomes no stranger—the classic style was chosen not to invite attention, but rather to feel as familiar to passersby as the profile of the elm tree that shades the marble steps leading up from the street.

The scale is deceptive. The neighboring edifices are large and imposing, with Gothic flourishes or neoclassical grandeur. In comparison, the tomb feels more stout and diminutive than it actually is.

The building's unadorned back is the only face that it reveals to the college. The sides are rectangular planes of marble blocks staggered in a brick pattern from ground to roof. There are no windows. In front, paired entry doors are recessed below a shallow gable at the top of eight stairs. That portal, trimmed in stone, framed by columns, overlooks the ancient plots of a graveyard that counts among its ghosts the remains of Eli Whitney and Noah Webster.

An iron fence, the posts smithed in the form of slithering serpents, separates the building from the public sidewalks on the adjacent streets.

The architecture is symbolic. The few decorative elements are symbolic. The site is symbolic. What happens inside the building is, at least occasionally, symbolic.

This fine spring day, though, the crowds gathering behind the hastily established police lines aren't gawking because of any symbolism.

The curious are gathering because of the rumors of what is going down—that some students might be locked inside the mysterious building.

The spectators don't know it yet, but the reality is they are there because the building is a damn fort.

A door opens and closes rapidly. When the young man emerges in front of the building his sudden appearance seems to have been part of an illusion.

His eyes blink as they adjust to the light. Across the street he sees a crowd contained behind red-and-white saw horse barricades stenciled with the initials of the campus police. At the periphery, on both sides, are television cameras. Nearest to him, cops, lots of cops. Many have just raised their guns.

The young man jerks his head, startled. "Don't shoot! Don't fucking shoot!" he says.

He lifts his arms high before he takes two cautious steps forward. He stops a few feet in front of the row of columns. It is the spot a politician might choose to make a speech.

His eyes close for a moment. When he opens them again, his irises—the same shade of green as the leaves budding out on the elm tree near the curb—are so brilliant they look backlit.

The brilliance is generated by the terror churning in his cells.

Two clusters of cops, one huddled group on each side of the building, begin to edge toward him in measured steps. The police are in full body armor and have raised weapons. Some carry shields.

"No! Don't come forward!" he yells, matching their adrenaline drop for drop. "Don't! Don't! Do not come near me! I am a bomb."

The cops slow at that caution.

The young man is dressed in worn jeans and an untucked striped dress shirt over a T-shirt. He is barefoot. His chin and cheeks are spotted with stubble. Other than the absence of shoes, his appearance is not unlike that of many of his peers on campus.

He lowers his arms before he lifts the front of his shirt. "See that! It's a bomb. I'm a bomb. I . . . am . . . a bomb. Stay where you are."

On his abdomen, below his navel, is a rectangular object the size of a thick paperback book. It is held in place with tape that wraps around his hips. On the tape are handwritten block letters that read, "BOMB."

A few wires are visible at the top of the bulge.

The device appears about as threatening as a burlesque prop.

An officer barks an order. The approaching cops stop in their tracks. A few take a step or two back.

The young man releases his shirt, covering the apparatus at his waist. All eyes are on him. He waits until there is complete silence.

He opens his mouth to speak, but his throat is so dry he coughs. Finally, he manages to say, "I— He wants the . . . cell towers . . . turned back on." The young man's voice catches on the word "back." He pauses, as though to think. "The news cameras stay in place. He says you have five minutes." He lifts his wrist and looks at his watch. "Starting right now."

Near the police barricades two men in suits begin conferring with a woman wearing khaki pants and a simple top. She has a badge clipped to the front of her trousers.

The younger of the two men is telling the woman that they know nothing about a cell tower shutdown.

In an even voice, the woman says, "Then how about somebody finds out?" She takes one step forward.

She has been preparing for this moment for hours. She is thinking, *Finally, let the show begin.*

"Hi," she says, addressing the hostage. "My name is Christine Carmody. I'm a negotiator with the New Haven Police. I know you're scared."

She waits for his eyes to find her. To pick her khaki and pink out of the sea of blue. She is eager for this young man to make her his personal oasis. "I just requested that an order be given to get those towers working."

She is choosing her words carefully, beginning to communicate to the unseen subject that there is an active chain of command, that things will proceed in a certain way, that everything that happens going forward will take time. Mostly, she wants anyone inside the tomb to begin to understand that she is but a conduit, that she doesn't control the world of blue uniforms and blue steel he sees around her.

"Please . . . please tell . . . him? Is that right? . . . It's a him? If he has a name, I'd love to know it, so I know what to call him . . . Five minutes? Please tell him that we can't do it that quickly. Not quite that fast. It's just not possible."

She has no intention of cooperating with this first demand on the hostage taker's timetable. Certainly not *yessir, right away, sir*. One of the initial goals of her business—her business is hostage negotiation—is to make contact with the hostage taker and begin to establish rapport. Talking through this hostage, or any hostage, isn't what she has in mind. Her response to the first demand reflects her underlying strategy. She will use this preliminary request to begin to set the piers for the bridge that will lead to direct discussions with the still-unseen hostage taker.

Sergeant Christine Carmody's African-American father died during the fall of Saigon in 1975. She grew up on Long Island with her Puerto Rican mother. Her life has not been easy; it's been about always being tough enough to take it and about trying to be smart enough not to have to fight about it. She's been talking her way out of tight spots since the day she stepped off her first school bus.

Consonant with her desire to be invisibly obstreperous with the unseen hostage taker, at least at first, her voice is as close to level as she can make it. She makes sure that any lilt in her tone exudes respect and the promise of cooperation and conciliation. She is also trying to make certain that whoever is inside begins to understand that the current situation has real limitations.

Carmody is cognizant of the purported bomb. For the moment, she is thinking about it the way she thinks about God. She is slightly more of a skeptic than a believer.

She says, "Don't get me wrong, I'm not aware of anything that will keep us from working something out about the phones. It must be some kind of technical problem. But we're on that. Nothing makes me think that will turn out to be a big concern. He—you said, 'He,' right?—can . . . call me. We can talk directly. He and I. That's probably the best way to get all this worked out. He and I can begin to solve this problem."

A uniformed officer hands her a scribbled sign. She holds it up so that it is facing the young man. "As soon as we solve the cell tower thing, this is the number that will get through directly to me. Me, personally." She holds her mobile phone aloft so the young man can see it. "Like I said, it shouldn't be an issue. His? . . . It's a he? I have that right?"

The young man does not react to her words. He does not reply to her questions.

"Okay. Like I said, his request is . . . something to discuss. Absolutely. I'm ready to talk about it, explain what's going on at my end, what we can do to solve this. How about a radio that will work until the cell phones are up again? We'll give you one of ours—for him to use to talk to me in the meantime. We will work this out. Absolutely."

She emphasizes "will."

The young man doesn't acknowledge her. He doesn't move.

She waits. The frittering away of seconds doesn't concern her. Time is on her side.

The young man closes his eyes. A good ten seconds pass before he opens them.

"Okay, first things first," she says. Her confidence has grown a tiny measure because her initial entreaties haven't been shot down. She leads with the most basic of offers. "Would he like to come out? We're ready to end this right now, before things go any further."

The hostage doesn't reply.

Always worth a shot, Carmody thinks. "Okay. Is anyone hurt inside? Let's start there. Does anyone need medical attention? I am ready and eager to provide help to anyone who might need it."

The young man raises his head, looks at her. "He . . . ," his voice breaks, "is . . ." Fresh tears make his eyes glisten. He looks down, then back at her one more time. ". . . not here . . ." The young man swallows, then he purses his lips and blows.

A little *whew*.

"He is not here"? What?

Carmody notes that red bands encircle the young man's wrists. The kid has been shackled. *Shit.*

The young man grimaces, squeezing his eyes together in concentration, or consternation. ". . . to negotiate . . . about . . . anything." He chokes back a sob. "Anything. Please."

He is not here to negotiate about anything. Anything.

Carmody glances to her left. In a low voice she says something to the two men five feet behind her. The ones in suits. The men turn their backs, step away, and lift their mobile phones. Behind them, a dozen or more officers maintain their positions. Their weapons remain raised. Aimed.

Carmody checks her own cell. No bars.

"You mean the phones? Well, it turns out that some things just aren't possible," she says. "Not instantly, anyway. Everything takes time. Right? We'll get it done." Despite her self-discipline, she knows that her voice has changed, betraying her fresh, creeping awareness that the circumstances confronting her are different than she anticipated. Minutes earlier she wasn't even convinced that she indeed had a hostage situation. Now? Her pulse is popping on her neck.

She knows that without contact with the subject—the hostage taker—she will be at a significant disadvantage going forward in this negotiation. She needs direct communication. She needs an opportunity to build a relationship.

She needs to feel his anger. To measure his fear. To establish rapport.

She needs the freedom to barter. Phones for hostages. Smokes for hostages. Pizza for hostages. Hope for hostages. Almost anything, for hostages.

She needs the Hostage Negotiator Bazaar to be open for business.

She needs the chance to relieve the short-term pressure of time, to begin to string this event out. She needs minutes to become inconsequential. Hours to accumulate. If it proves necessary, she needs for days to pile up to induce fatigue.

Once, after Christine explained her job as a hostage negotiator to her daughter, the thirteen-year-old concluded that "basically time is your bff, Mom."

Christine thought, *Damn straight.*

Whether the hostage taker knows it or not, time is his mortal enemy.

As time passes, people get hungry. People get tired. As day becomes night, the reality of the predicament they've created takes on a truer focus.

As time's horizon recedes, the hostage taker's adrenaline seeps below the low-tide line.

His initial inflated sense of control begins to lose some of its buoyancy.

In most hostage situations what she just heard from the young man on the steps—*he is not here to negotiate anything*—would present an obstacle to be cleared by the erosion that accompanies persistent negotiation.

But this situation—only minutes old—already feels different to Christine. She senses control slipping away before she ever even gets a grip on it.

She prides herself on her ability to forecast the end game before the opening has been completed. She is finding it difficult to inhale.

This isn't going to end well, she says to herself.

The young man's voice interrupts her musing. He says, "I will . . . die. I . . . will . . . die . . ."

The tip of Sergeant Christine Carmody's tongue wets her upper lip. She is preparing to comfort him, to disagree, to reach out and yank back some control. *You will do no such thing* is what she is thinking.

But before she is able to speak the young man glances at his watch. "In three . . . minutes," he says.

The two men in suits have walked away.

One is the New Haven Police Department lieutenant responsible for managing the crisis. The other is a second sergeant on the hostage negotiation team. Behind their backs, colleagues call them "The Sun" and "The Moon." When the sergeant is blocking access to the lieutenant—which happens more often than not—the troops in blue refer to it as an "eclipse."

Overall authority for the hostage situation is Lieutenant Haden Moody's. Sergeant Christine Carmody is the primary negotiator for the current incident. Her responsibility is direct communication with the hostage taker. The lieutenant will tell her what he thinks she should know. He will withhold information that he doesn't want her to consider while she does her job. He will also withhold any intelligence that he fears she might inadvertently communicate while she is in contact with the hostage taker.

If her experience is any guide, Carmody expects that The Sun will do his communicating through The Moon. The Moon is Jack Lobatini. He is the secondary negotiator on the team. During this incident he will act as Carmody's backup. Her scribe. A third negotiator is functioning as an intel officer, gathering information.

Carmody has been negotiating in pressure situations for the department for seven years. She knows the way things work.

Where Moody and Lobatini are concerned, things don't always work well. She knows that Lobatini sometimes proves to be more interested in keeping Moody happy than he is in assisting his colleague on the front line.

"What is your name?" Carmody calls out to the young man standing in front of the tomb.

He doesn't reply. She is disappointed but not surprised. She is quickly learning the rules of her unseen subject, the man inside the tomb. Apparently one of those rules is that the young man doesn't say anything he hasn't been told to say.

She isn't enamored of the rule. One of her short-term goals in the negotiation will be to change it to her advantage.

"How many . . . people . . . are inside? Students?" she asks. Seven or eight kids are unaccounted for, most with active ATLs. There may be more kids inside than that. On a weekend at a college it's not easy to do a head count. Yale PD is worried that fifteen or sixteen students might be inside the tomb. Caterers? Custodial staff? No one is sure.

Carmody has received estimates from Yale College officials that range all the way from seven or eight hostages to thirty-two.

Thirty-two? God. Carmody doesn't want there to be thirty-two.

The young man is breathing through his mouth. His chest is rising in quick quakes. She no longer really expects him to answer her question aloud, but she is hoping for some extended fingers or a rapid series of eye blinks. Some indication of a number. *Give me something,* she's begging silently. *A clue.*

Nothing.

"Earlier you said, 'He.' Is it only one man in there?"

The young man blinks twice.

Does that mean there are two? She doesn't know.

She waits for the kid to double-blink again, or communicate some other way. Carmody needs confirmation. She doesn't get it.

"What does he want? The man . . . inside? Is there something we can provide?"

The hostage looks down.

The hostage is at least six-three. His hair is already receding on his temples. His ears are too small for his head. But he is a handsome kid. In other circumstances his confidence and presence would probably command a room.

She reminds herself that she doesn't have to be worried about the kid's smarts. To be a student at this college he has already demonstrated that he possesses a few million neurons above the mean.

She watches him rotate his red wrist so the watch face is toward her. He taps it with his finger.

"Two minutes," he says. After the second word his lips continue moving. He extends a finger on each hand for a fleeting second.

She wonders if he is praying.

"We're working on it," she says. "The cell tower thing. We are. As I speak. Everything we can do. We're on it." Her words aren't tactical. They're maternal. Her heart is ripping apart at the boy's clear anguish. She's wondering who the hell had the bright idea to kill the cell towers in the first place. That sure helped her with the whole building-rapport thing. "Apparently, getting them working is not just throwing a switch. Things have to be rebooted. It will all be okay."

Christine has no idea if anything has to be rebooted, or how long it will take somebody to solve the problem and make the local cell towers active again. She is hoping it will not take long.

She risks another quick glance at her mobile. No bars.

A uniformed officer steps into place right behind her. His name is Joseph Blankenship. Everyone on the force calls him Joey Blanks. She knows Joey well. He was a five-year vet when she was a rook. He begins to speak to Christine in his distinctive bass tone. Joey is one of those guys who, when he sings, people stop to listen. And when Joey talks, Joey still sings a little. He can't help it. Even when he whispers, the low notes rumble and his words find melody.

She shakes her head at what she's hearing, disagreeing. Joey Blanks talks some more. Finally, she glances at him and nods reluctantly. "Yes, okay," she says. "Okay, go. Thanks, Joey."

Before she turns back to face the young man in front of the tomb, he again begins to speak.

In a tone full of wonder at his own predicament, the young man says, "I will die in one minute."

Christine is struggling to lock on to his elusive eyes. She feels like she's grasping at air the way she did as a girl in Wantagh when she would try to corral fireflies in her cupped hands. She says, "No, no. You won't. We'll get it done. You'll be— It will be—"

Her words are almost swallowed by the growing commotion behind her, as the assembled cops belatedly mobilize. They start to hurry the crowds away from the perimeter. Retreating spectators scramble as they begin to digest the potential danger. They run down the sidewalks. A few scream. A woman trips and falls.

Other people run past the fallen woman, over her.

The younger of the two men wearing suits—The Moon—taps Carmody on the shoulder. He says, "We think we have an ID. The kid is Jonathan Simmons. A student. You should take cover, Christine. Just in case, you know, it's a real bomb."

Carmody considers the information even as she ignores the suggestion. She consciously plants her feet. "Jonathan," she says to the student. "Can I call you that? Any second. Any second, the cell towers will come back up. Tell him that. The man inside. Tell him that it's all happening. That we're doing what he asked. What he wants. We're showing good faith, Jonathan. Good faith. Give him a signal. Whatever you need to do. Do it now. The phones will be working any second. Hold on. Stay with me. I'm not leaving. Keep your eyes on me. Right here."

She keeps her focus on Jonathan Simmons as she allows Joey Blanks to steer her to cover behind the nearest vehicle—a campus police patrol car parked at the curb. Joey is wiry but no one in the department can beat him at arm wrestling. When Joey puts his big hand on someone's back, people tend to step forward whether they were thinking about stepping forward or not.

The crowds are being pushed even farther away, beyond the street corners. All of the nearby cops have scrambled to shelter. Some are close to Carmody, kneeling behind official vehicles or crouching behind cars parked along the street. Some are in the shadows of buildings. Other officers have taken defensive positions behind the brownstone section of the cemetery wall.

Jonathan Simmons is standing alone at the top of the steps of the building that looks like a Greek temple.

He gazes at his watch once more.

His shoulders drop. He raises his eyes. He blinks rapidly. He mouths, *Mom, I love you.*

*   *   *

The explosion is loud enough and forceful enough, it seems, to stop the world.

A segment of Jonathan Simmons's left hand that includes his entire thumb plops onto the hood of the cruiser in front of Carmody. A six-inch smear of blood shaped like the Nike swoosh tracks the carnage's final path across the sheet metal.

Christine doesn't see or hear the fragment hit the car.

Joey Blanks puts his lips next to her ears. He's holding his cell phone in his hand. "The phones are working. The towers are back up. I have bars," he says.

She can't hear him. She hadn't thought to plug her ears as the clock ticked down. She hadn't allowed herself to believe that the device on the kid's waist was a bomb. Or that the man in the building would really set it off.

The concussion from the blast is reverberating in her brain. The meaning of the explosion isn't even beginning to settle in her consciousness.

Her eyes are darting left and right in desperation.

She is trying to locate a piece of Jonathan Simmons that is large enough to rescue.

Sam Purdy

I thought the plane had landed in the wrong country.

Miami's airport was my first experience with international air travel, and I didn't even have to leave the good old U.S. of A. to do it.

After a ground hold at LAX for fog and an extra hour in the air dodging spring storms that were carpet-bombing most of Texas and Oklahoma with tornados and hail, the plane arrived way late in Miami. I stepped off the Jetway into a concourse brimming with an effervescent energy that almost buckled my damn knees. At first I felt assaulted by the sounds and the smells and the colors and the people and the languages, but by the time I'd meandered past a couple of dozen gates full of travelers flying to or arriving from exotic destinations and finally began to find my bearings on the sidewalk in front of the terminal, the place was beginning to infuse me with something that I had to admit was making me kind of happy.

It was possible that the next four days would be all right. Okay at least, maybe not a disaster.

I had a message waiting on my cell phone. A woman with a gorgeous island voice had apparently been tracking my flight.

I returned the call. She let me know, with a swell of apology in her tone, that if I wanted to make the first party—I didn't, but I was expected to, and this trip was all about meeting expectations—I didn't have time to check into the hotel. I had to go straight to the marina. Did I mind taking a cab?

I mentally counted the twenties in my wallet, and hoped the marina was nearby.

I said, "No problem."

I'm not exactly a marina kind of guy. In my life I've tended to get into boats from a rickety dock near a buddy's crappy summer cabin on the shore of some Lake Noname in Minnesota. Or from a boat ramp. I'd done boat ramps a few times. The boats I've been in were never anything special. Outboards mostly. They held maybe two or three guys—two if the other guy was as big as me—our tackle, and a couple of coolers. One cooler was for our catch, the other was for our beer.

I went waterskiing once in high school. On the Mississippi, of all places. The water was cold. I never quite made it up on the skis.

That's the complete and true history of me and boats.

Oh, I took a ferry once, too. But I didn't get out of my car and spent most of the time sleeping in the backseat. So I don't think that counts.

No marinas. I promise.

The taxi driver was from El Salvador. I gave him the name of the marina. He said, "Sí." Traffic was god-awful the whole way, but he displayed no impatience. He pulled into the marina, stopping the car near a building. He looked at me in the mirror. He said, "Dónde? Aquí?"

I knew both words. He would probably be disappointed to learn that he and I had just covered about thirty percent of my usable Spanish comprehension, excluding nouns related to food and drink, of course.

I said, "Why not?"

He laughed, exposing a set of sad yellow teeth. He said, "Por qué no?"

I laughed with him. I gave him a thirty percent tip and threw in an extra ten bucks that I figured would soon be making a Western Union journey to El Salvador. I watched him drive away.

Almost immediately, I regretted my largesse. I was unemployed and basically broke. *I should have maybe given him an extra five instead,* I thought.

I looked around the marina. There were like a million boats.

Only one had a live band playing thumping Latin music on its spacious stern.

I pulled up the handle of my borrowed carry-on suitcase and began walking toward that one.

It was only April. But it was already hot in Florida.

A tent was set up on the dock beside the boat. A crisp white tent. Two attractive people, both with some Latin blood, sat in the shade at a table with a crisp white tablecloth. The young woman who greeted me was wearing a white skirt and a soft watermelon blouse. The flawless triangle of skin exposed on her chest was the color of a perfectly baked dessert.

"Mr. Purdy?" she said. Her voice was unaccented.

"That'd be me," I said.

We shook hands. She then offered me a choice of a chilled towel or a warm one for my face.

I wondered if this was the first question of a weekend-long etiquette test that I was doomed to fail.

I chose chilled.

The other person who'd been sitting at the table delivered the tightly rolled towel on a silver tray. He looked like a guy who was moonlighting from his night job as a headwaiter. A cool headwaiter—the guy who'd end up owning his own trendy club before he was thirty.

The icy cloth felt great on my travel-grimed face. I didn't, of course, know what to do with the thing when I was done cleaning myself. It seemed rude to give it back, but I could hardly stuff it in my pocket. The young man held out the tray.

Fold it? Plop it? I plopped it. Another failure? I was certain I'd get my grade later, when I was least expecting it.

The young woman said, "We are delighted you could make it in time, Mr. Purdy. Everyone is on board now. I am so sorry about your long flight. The spring weather? It's always so unpredictable, especially in the South. May I take that bag for you? Please? Perhaps you would like to visit a cabin to freshen up a little? Change for the welcoming event? We have a lovely evening planned."

The "welcoming event"?

She took the bag from me and rolled it to a stop under the canopy. I suspected that someone else was charged with actually taking custody of it.

"That would be terrific," I said. "Much appreciated."

I didn't really know about changing. Into what? Or freshening up. I certainly wouldn't admit it if I was back home in Boulder, but I considered freshening up to be a girl thing. The honest truth was that my well-worn Fruit of the Looms had started riding up the crack of my butt shortly after the seat-belt sign went on over the Gulf of Mexico. A private moment to coax them back into position a little farther south of my continental cleft would be a welcome thing indeed.

I would also be more than appreciative of a chance to pee.

The young woman took me by the elbow and led me toward the boat. "Welcome aboard," she said as we climbed the gangway. "Please allow me to escort you to a guest cabin where you can, you know . . . as you wish. I will let the captain know we are ready to sail. Everyone, as you can see, is gathering on the stern."

If I had been paying better attention, I would have realized at that point that her repeated offers to steer me to a cabin were due not only to her graciousness but also to her assumption that I must certainly be planning to switch out my travel attire for something that would be more appropriate to attend the "welcoming event."

Oh well. What I lacked in sartorial sophistication I would have to make up for in charm. Story of my life.

I prepared myself for some novelty. This would be my first boat with a captain. Or a cabin, for that matter. Or a method of relieving myself on board that didn't involve fighting to keep my balance and worrying about the direction of the wind.

At the top of the gangway, the young lady handed me a name tag that read, "Samuel Purdy," in calligraphy that appeared to have been scrolled by a pirate. Or his secretary.

My name's not Samuel. It's Sam. Just Sam. My parents were simple people who didn't want to burden their offspring with extraneous syllables. I kept that news to myself.

At the top of the gangway a waiter, well, waited with a tray balanced on his manicured fingertips. On the tray rested a frosty, solitary glass of champagne. The champagne bubbled vigorously. He said, "Sir?"

I made good eye contact with him and said, "Got a beer maybe?"

He nodded, briefly closed his eyes, and said, "Cerveza, sí," before he added, "Sir," one more time.

I said, "I'll find you in a few minutes. How's that?"

He smiled a smile that wasn't quite a waiter's smile.

No matter how the party went—hell, no matter how the whole weekend went—I knew I'd get along with the help.

Unless they made me for a cop.

In recent years, I'd found that rarely ended up being a good thing with the Spanish-speaking help.

The boat was more like a ship, and everyone else at the party apparently had a much better idea about how friggin' hot it was in Miami in April than I did. In terms of style, I was underdressed. My wardrobe not only lacked any benediction to fashion, but it also lacked color. In terms of weight of fabrics, I was overdressed. My crotch and my pits were already moist enough to qualify for federal wetlands protection.

We had begun motoring on a waterway. North. The sun was setting on my left. The city looked nice. Better than nice. Stunning. Miami was like five times bigger than I'd expected.

I found some shade as far as I could get from the three-piece band—I liked the music, it screamed Miami like a good polka announced the upper Midwest. But the beat was too frantic for my mood, and the bass was vibrating the bench on which I was sitting in a manner my bowels found not altogether pleasant. I finished my beer in two long pulls and began contemplating socially acceptable exit strategies.

I recognized that the fact we were on a boat limited my options.

I knew one person at this party—that would be my girlfriend Carmen's daughter. From the moment she and I met, Dulce had made clear that she not only was wary of me but also distrusted my motives regarding her mother. The last time I had seen Dulce, Carmen and I both feared that the young lady was edging close to reaching two conclusions: first, that I was a jerk, and second, that I was people's exhibit five or six in proving the case that her mother had congenitally bad taste in men.

Still, I was looking forward to seeing Dulce's pretty face, congratulating her on her engagement, and continuing my campaign to rehabilitate my image.

In the shorter term, I was intent on locating the genteel waiter whom I planned to beg to bring me más cerveza. Or cerveza más.

I could never remember which was correct.

So far in life, that confusion had not interfered with me getting my next beer.

A woman spoke to me from behind. I hadn't heard her approach or sit down.

"Feeling a little out of place?" she said.

"You, too?" I asked, as I turned toward her. She was sitting so close to me I couldn't make out her features without my Kmart reading glasses, which were tucked away in the bag that had been hijacked by the bearer of chilled towels in the tent on the dock.

The woman had a pleasant voice. Her eyes were blue. The panoply of greens in the dress she was wearing made me think of parrots and jungles.

"No, I'm . . . great. I was being . . . empathetic," she said.

"I'll have to try that strategy with the next person I talk to. Empathy sounds like a potentially winning plan. Yeah," I said, "I am from out of town." I pointed to my name tag. "Samuel Purdy."

She extended her hand. I didn't think she was wearing a name tag, but I would have had to indulge a glance at her chest to confirm my suspicion. Decorum told me to resist that urge.

"Ann Summers Calderón," she said. "Carmen never told me you were a Samuel. I tend to remember such things. I'm good with names. An acquired skill."

Busted, I thought, acknowledging to myself that I could probably have picked a better audience on whom to polish my wiseass routine.

I, too, am good with names. For me, it's a cop skill. I recognized her name, of course, though the fact that she had used all three of them during her introduction felt like the equivalent of slipping me a cheat sheet so I couldn't possibly fail to identify her. On my scorecard that earned her a point for generosity.

"This is your party," I said. "It's . . . a fine . . . fine affair."

She did an affectionate little eye roll. "This is my son Andrew's do, actually. He can be . . . such a girl. I love him dearly, but . . ." She sighed. "This does make his father happy, too. His family is all here from Argentina. And, you must admit, it's a gorgeous night for a sail," she said. "So we're blessed. We are blessed."

"A little warm, maybe," I added.

Ann Summers Calderón sighed another tiny sigh, which I read to be an editorial assessment of my glass-is-half-empty attitude about the weather.

"I was so disappointed to hear about Carmen," she said. "We've only met a couple of times, but I think she is just the nicest person. I was looking forward to getting to know her better this weekend. Now I guess I will—"

"Have to settle for me?" I said.

Carmen Reynosa is not only my girlfriend, but also the soon-to-be mother of my baby. Like me, Carmen is a police detective. Unlike me, Carmen isn't on suspension from the job for professional misconduct.

Unlike her, I'm not on obstetrician-ordered bed rest. Although if I could have traded places with her—I get to spend the long weekend in bed with magazines, a decent satellite package, a remote, and someone to deliver me food; she comes to Miami for her daughter's seventy-two-hour engagement extravaganza with her wealthy future in-laws—I would have gladly done it.

"Andrew is your . . . ?" I asked.

She looked at me sideways. She figured I knew who Andrew was. And she was right. She'd caught me falling into the bad habit I have of conversing like a detective, which means asking questions even if I know the answer. I've learned the hard way that in most social situations people aren't thrilled to be asked questions solely so that the asker—me—can make a determination about the veracity of their replies.

"My son," she said. "The soon-to-be betrothed." She tilted an almost-empty champagne flute at a tall man twenty feet away with perfect teeth and the kind of body I'm accustomed to seeing only in the young and sexually ravenous, and in my firefighting colleagues in Boulder. The low sun reflected off the man's sunglasses. "That is my husband. Ronaldo Angel Calderón."

I loved the way she said "Angel." *ON-hell.*

When Carmen pulled me off the far end of the bench to substitute for her on this trip, she had seen fit to caution me that Dulce's future in-laws had some serious family money. Something about fasteners. I was thinking at the time that she meant screws and nails, but the details of the genesis of their fortune had not exactly piqued my curiosity. Now that I had seen the yacht and begun to guess how serious the money was, I was a little more curious about the hardware. We were talking a lot of screws and nails. Veritable shitloads.

I said, "So this is home? Miami?"

I had just about run through my small-talk repertoire. When that happened, I risked tripping from conversation to interrogation. It's not a welcome transition at most parties. On yachts in Miami, or otherwise.

"Ronnie's home, yes, most of the time." She leaned away from me far enough that I could see her face clearly for the first time. "I spend most of the year in Chapel Hill. Ronnie and I do best when we don't reside simultaneously in the same city. We've made a brief exception in order to cohost Andrew's little *boum* this weekend."

I didn't know what a "boom" was. I let it go. "I'm divorced, too," I said, going with the empathy thing. "I know what that's like."

"Oh, Ronnie and I are not divorced, Sam. We still love each other—Ronnie is a sweet, sweet man with a generous heart as well as . . . some character . . . flaws no woman should have to tolerate. He and his family are way too Catholic for us to ever divorce. And . . . he and I are an incredible dance pair and we are—flat-out—the best cave-diving couple in Florida. We can't just toss all that away, can we? We have come to an . . . arrangement about our marriage that works for us." She winked at me. "We know when to be together and we know when to be apart. The custody issues have all been worked out."

"Us, too. Me and Sherry. We have a son. Simon. He's with his mom this weekend, but he's with me most of the time. During school, anyway. Sherry's gone back to college."

Ann touched me on the arm. Her fingertips were cool from the champagne glass. "Our kids are both grown. I'm talking about the money. The Calderón money. We have joint custody of *it*." She waited for me to figure out a response. When I failed, she said, "Come on, now. You can't be planning to spend the whole weekend sitting by yourself drinking warm beer."

I was tempted to reveal that I had spent more than a few weekends in my adult life doing just that. And that I was much more comfortable with it than she might imagine. But I could tell she wanted none of it.

"I'll introduce you to some people. Oh, good, good. There's the rest of your golf foursome tomorrow. You'll love Franklin. Though I hear he cheats. Keep an eye on him in the rough."

Rough? Carmen didn't say anything to me about golf. I definitely would have remembered that.

I allowed Ann Summers Calderón to pull me to my feet. I meet a lot of people, from many walks of life, but I was having trouble finding a compartment in which to place Ms. Summers Calderón. She was unlike anyone I'd ever come across.

She stopped and stood maybe ten inches from me. Ann had no trouble with close. She said, "Are you trustworthy, Sam Purdy? Carmen is trustworthy, I could tell right away the first time I met her in California."

My hostess seemed to want an answer. "Your instincts are good about Carmen. She is a rock," I replied. "Me? I have my faults, but I do consider myself a trustworthy man." I thought that what Ann was asking was whether I was at any risk of embarrassing her by fooling around with her female friends or, god forbid, relatives while my pregnant girlfriend's feet were propped up on pillows three thousand miles away.

"I thought so. Good," she said. I watched her facial expressions reveal mild concern, then resignation, and then return rapidly to perfect-
hostess pleasant-tude. I didn't know what the progression meant. She
said, "My original plan was to run this by Carmen but . . ." She waggled her head from side to side.

Indecision, I guessed.

She said, "Read this, please. Then find me later on. Tell me what
you think. It's the most perplexing thing." She raised herself on her
toes and leaned in so that her lips were inches from my ear. "This is
just between us." She lifted the lapel on my sport coat and slipped
something into the inside pocket.

Carmen had picked out the jacket for me at Macy's, on sale. It had
been advertised as a "three-season" fabric. Later that night, when we
talked, I planned to let her know that none of the three seasons was
springtime in Miami.

Then she and I would talk about golf.

Yes, we would.

One of the golf partners Ann introduced me to was a guy named Rick Lovett, who was a hardware buyer for Lowe's. I assumed that Rick's ticket to the soiree was that he purchased a lot of Mr. Calderón's fasteners for his employer. It became clear to me after a couple of minutes of chitchat that Rick was almost as out of his element on the sunset cruise as I was.

The segregation of crowds at bashes like the welcoming event occurs naturally. The young couple's contemporaries—fashion-forward, ostentatious, fit, tan, and handsome all—mingled together on the deck above the band at the stern. They didn't mind the late day sun. Guests the age of the couple's parents clustered together in the shade on the deck we were sharing with the musicians.

Rick was an in-betweener. I pegged him as mid-thirties. I could tell his id was urging him to hang with the cool, attractive kids and hope some girl got really, really drunk and he got really, really lucky. But his long-term life goals for a swelling wallet anchored him to the likes of me. He asked me twice what I did for a living. I was evasive both times. He asked me twice if I knew if the yacht we were on belonged to the Calderóns or was a charter. I told him twice that I didn't know.

Rick let it slip that his handicap was thirteen. My ignorance of all things golf other than the existence on the planet of Tiger Woods meant that I didn't know whether his thirteen was something he was proud of or something he was apologizing for. Rick asked me about my game.

I told him that I held my own with a putter.

I didn't tell him that I knew that only because my son and I liked to play miniature golf. Simon liked the golf. I liked being with my kid as dusk fell in the shadows of the Rockies.

I could have also explained to Rick that I was almost always around par, but I was brought up not to boast so I kept that fact to myself.

He nodded knowingly at my comment about putting. "My short game saves my ass, that's for sure."

I said, "Amen to that."

I was having serious doubts that I could keep up my act for a long weekend.

After doing about as much meaningless chatter with strangers as I'm genetically capable of enduring in one stint, I wandered around inside the ship—I'd discovered that the thing had its own fleet of lifeboats, so I was done calling it a boat—until I found an empty room that had a big flat screen TV and some cushy sofas. More to the point, the place was air-conditioned to a temperature that would keep my beer from boiling. I guessed that the room was called a "salon." If I had a big yacht, I'd call this space the family room or the den. I figured that the Calderóns of the world would prefer "salon." I fished around with the remote until I found a Stanley Cup play-off game on the satellite receiver.

I slipped off my Macy's jacket and settled in. The piece of paper Ann had stuck in my coat pocket was a note. The sheet had been folded into quarter size. The note was printed on standard office paper. It looked like generic Helvetica to me. Something close to twelve point.

She had described it as "perplexing." I didn't disagree.

The note was vaguely threatening. Maybe more like ominous.

I was tempted to do exactly what the note warned not to do—discount the thing. Write it off as a provocation, or a prank.

I wondered if Ann Summers Calderón had been smart enough to photocopy the original or if she had received the exact copy I was holding in my hands.

I assumed she'd been careless with it because civilians usually are. Suspension or not, I treated it like I was a detective—I was cautious as I held it.

I read the half page again.

"Are you Canadian, Sam?" Ann said from the open door to the salon.

The woman moved with the stealth of a Boulder mountain lion.

"Minnesota," I said. I allowed the "oh" sound to fill some extra space as I spoke the word. The exaggerated accent gave me unmistakable Iron Range cred. It also helped explain my obvious affection for hockey.

"What do you think of the missive?" she asked.

I looked directly at her for about ten seconds before I replied. She revealed nothing during the interlude.

"If you're taking this seriously, I think you're displaying some cojones by showing it to me."

She grinned, just a little, at my description of her behavior. I noted the lack of offense. "Should I take it seriously?" she asked.

"Do you?"

"It concerns me. Obviously."

"Who else has seen it?"

"No one."

"Your husband?"

She shook her head. "Ronnie's most definitely someone. Don't underestimate him because he's handsome and gracious and Latin. If he read that note, he'd be itching for a fight. He'd get his people on it. Make noise. In life's arena, Ronnie is usually either the matador or the bull. Neither seemed helpful here. It didn't feel prudent to me to have him dashing his red cape or going wild attempting to gore someone. By nature, I'm lighter on my feet. If it becomes necessary, I will tell Ronnie about this, but in my own way."

She closed the door behind her before she kicked off her heels with an unaffected grace. I wondered if she'd once been a dancer.

She took the chair across from me. Ann Summers Calderón sat with her knees well over a foot apart, allowing her parrot green dress to drape modestly between her spread legs. My ex-wife had insisted that it was nothing more than typical male misjudgment on my part, but I always considered that particular posture in a woman to be a sign of confidence.

Sherry's alternate interpretation had more to do with the offending woman's bad breeding.

"Why is that? Why wouldn't that be prudent?" I asked. I could guess the answer, but my guessing the answer wouldn't tell me anything about the confident woman across from me.

"It was in my purse, Sam. Sitting on top, in plain sight. I found it when I was in North Carolina, not here. At work. Three days ago. The note wasn't left for Ronnie. It was left for me."

"What do you make of that?"

"That it isn't about money."

"Leaving it there, in your purse? Someone found you, got close to you," I said, stating the obvious.

"Yes," she said. "They did."

My comment hadn't upset her balance. Ann had some steel reinforcement in her. Emotional rebar. I said, "If it's not about money, what is it about?"

"I don't know. Some threat . . . to me. Mine."

"What threat?"

She shrugged.

Not good enough. "Guess," I said.

She was way ahead of me, of course. "If it's not money, it's family," she replied. "That's where we're vulnerable. All of us."

She was right. "Anything like this ever happened before?"

"No."

"No blackmail? Extortion?"

"No."

I believed her.

"I thought I spotted a couple of guys on board who might be . . . muscle."

"More than a couple. Ronnie employs security, of course, as a precaution. Here, for us, and for his family in Buenos Aires."

"You guys have secrets? You and your husband?" I asked.

"Of course we have secrets. Don't you?"

I thought about it. I had one doozy. The rest? Merely embarrassing or borderline humiliating. I said, "Fewer and fewer as I get older, but yeah, sure. What's your thing, Ann? What do you do?"

"I'm a proud, proud mother, Sam. A good daughter. A middling wife. Professionally, I'm a geophysicist, doing mostly research, but

I love to teach. Top of my field? No, but I don't embarrass myself, either. I take my work seriously. I am teaching one class this semester in North Carolina. I have grad students."

I allowed my eyebrows to float. "Geophysics? Translation?"

"Earth science. Think geology and physics. The intersection."

I was hoping that she didn't feel compelled to give me a longer explanation. "If the note isn't about money, you got anything the sender might want? Monet? Van Gogh? Honus Wagner baseball card? Kickass comic book collection?"

She smiled. "Ronnie's tastes run more toward de Kooning and Rothko." She shrugged, shook her head. "We have nothing the man who wrote the note couldn't buy from someone else if he had enough of our money." For a moment, the wrinkles around her eyes took on definition and she appeared to be her true age, not ten years younger. The image was fleeting.

"Business secrets?"

"Us? Only of interest to a competitor. If this were about business, they would approach Ronnie, not me. Screws are screws, Sam. We're where we are today because Ronnie had vision. Years ago he was the first manufacturer to recognize the advantages of producing product in Asia, one of the first to see the coming dominance of nail guns. His head start has given him significant strategic advantages in this hemisphere. Our competitors are still playing catch-up." She paused. Her eyes descended to the note I held. "I don't have any choices yet, do I? I just wait for the next shoe to drop? Am I right?"

"That's the way I read it. The only option you have is to give this to the cops," I said.

"Didn't I just do that?"

"It may turn out to be fortunate for you, but no, you didn't. I'm on suspension from the Boulder Police Department. Long story. I'll tell it if you want to hear it." I waited for an indication she wanted me to tell the story. Nothing. If she was curious about my abundant free time, I figured she had already learned the broad outlines of my transgressions—they involved a woman, a sexual indiscretion, and a subsequent serious sin of omission—from my significant other. "Officially, I'm not a cop at this moment. If you decide to show this to Carmen—who despite her current horizontal posture *is* a cop—she may feel a need to show it to someone else. Kick it upstairs. Her bosses. Then they might kick it upstairs to their bosses. And so on. Pretty soon, the fact that it's no longer a secret isn't a secret. If you know what I mean." I poked at the page. "Here in the middle of the note, it says pretty clearly that wouldn't be a good thing. Showing it around."

"Even to you," Ann said. "That's why the are-you-trustworthy part is so important to me."

"Showing it to me was risky, Ann. You don't know me well. Is that evidence of those cojones I referred to earlier?"

I allowed her a moment to comment. She demurred.

I moved my index finger close to the note. "Any thoughts about the blue/orange thing. What that means? Have any personal significance to you?"

She said, "Nothing, Sam." Then she asked, "What would a real cop do with this? If I walked into my local police department and showed it to someone."

I could tell she wasn't being demeaning to me with the "real cop" comment. I felt no inclination to be defensive back with her. I said, "Probably nothing. The note is too vague. Being ominous isn't a crime. They would tell you to get back to them if something developed."

"That's what I thought, too. The person who wrote this gave the words and the tone a lot of consideration. He draws lines. Doesn't cross them. That part worries me almost as much as the content."

Smart. "You have no way to contact him?" I asked.

"There was a Post-it on the letter. It had an Internet address on it. A website. In Africa. Dot-n-a. Namibia."

"Namibia? I assume you went to that website."

"Under construction," she said. "I've been praying this might be nothing more than some kind of Internet scam."

"Christ," I said. I caught myself. I added, "Sorry."

"It's okay. Watch it around Ronnie, though. He doesn't approve of taking the Lord's name in vain."

I'm a Christian man, but one who believes the Lord is pretty thick-skinned. I don't see Him starting the next ice age because His feelings are hurt. "I will try to respect that. Tell me about your family, Ann," I said.

The crowd in Detroit erupted before she could respond.

I looked at the screen and said, "Damn." The Red Wings had scored a shorthanded goal. I hate the damn Red Wings. I flicked off the TV before I was forced to watch someone dressed in red toss an octopus over the glass onto the ice.

"Sorry," I said again.

"Ronnie and I have been married for twenty-four years. We have two children. This is Andrew's weekend first, Ronnie's second. Andrew is head over heels for Dulce, who I think is as sweet as her name. But you know all that. After they graduate from Santa Cruz, they're going to live in San Francisco while they—hopefully—grow up a little bit and learn a little something about the world. Andrew will be working for Wells Fargo. Dulce is in Teach For America—she'll be at a school in Oakland. Wedding won't be until summer next year at the earliest. Longer if Andrew's mother has anything to say about it."

"Off the record?" I said. "You have an ally in Carmen on the waiting-for-the-wedding part."

Ann smiled. "I guessed that. She and I had a long lunch together in California. But it's nice to have it confirmed. Jane? My daughter is a year younger than my son. Twice as mature. She's in school in Connecticut. She's smarter and tougher than her brother. You'll meet her tomorrow." Ann smiled a momma's smile. "My Jane."

"She golfs? Hurrying home for the tournament?"

Ann laughed. "No. She has a . . . thing she does on Thursday nights and Sunday nights at school that she can't miss. She promised her brother she'd get down here in between to help him celebrate. She'll fly in midday tomorrow, be here for the dinner with the families. She'll head north again on Sunday."

"I look forward to meeting her."

"She's terrific." Ann did a little dance move with her upper body, unable to contain her motherly pride. Then she stood, retrieved her shoes, and slipped them back on her feet, balancing easily on one leg at a time. She straightened her dress. "I need to get back to my other guests," she said.

"I understand. Is this a copy?" I said, raising the note.

"The original is in a Mylar sleeve, in my jewelry safe at home. It has a few of my fingerprints on it, but after I recognized what it was, I was pretty careful with it. I'm a scientist, Sam."

"Good."

She opened the door. Before she left, she turned back to me. "Do you think the last line is true, Sam? That he's a reasonable man?"

I reread the last line. "Probably thinks he is. My experience is that when people say things like that, though, they're usually anticipating being unreasonable."

"Yes," she said. "That's what I thought, too."

Dee and Poe

"Jerry doesn't get you, you know. That's why this"—Deirdre rapped her knuckles on the scratched mahogany surface that started where the bulge of red vinyl stopped—"would drive him crazy."

What she left unsaid was *If Jerry knew we were here.*

Jerry was CIA, too. Like his wife. Jerry analyzed intelligence. He didn't generate it. In the world of good guys and bad guys, as in the world of unfaithful wives, it is an important distinction.

It meant that unless someone reported the fact of his wife's out-of-town indiscretion, Jerry likely wouldn't have an inkling that she was having a couple of drinks with an FBI agent in a dive bar on the edge of downtown Philadelphia.

That's the knowledge that Jerry's wife thought would drive him crazy. Given that Jerry didn't get Poe.

Since they had originally met in Oklahoma City in 1995, Deirdre and the FBI guy in question—his Bureau ID read Christopher L. Poe; the L was for Lance—had played out some version of the present conversation in at least a half dozen other dive bars across America. Dee and Poe had discovered a few days after their introduction that they shared a penchant for taverns with long histories and infrequent renovations. Deirdre was especially drawn to watering holes with neon martini glasses adorning their signage, while Poe gravitated toward bars with the words "highballs" or "mixed drinks" in their names.

That night in Philly they'd settled on Bob & Barbara's Lounge on South Street. The house boilermaker was Pabst Blue Ribbon and Jim

Beam. To Poe, that was an indication of modest inn-keeping intentions, always an auspicious sign.

He didn't mind listening to Deirdre talk about her husband.

He loved to hear her voice—on rare, peaceful nights he even heard it in his dreams. To Poe's ears, Dee spoke the way great singers sing, with nuance and passion and melody, and truth. For him, her tone carried the chords of memory the way that wind makes aromas fly. He'd long before succumbed to the realization that he would never get enough tracks of her voice down in his head. She could be describing the intimate contours of husband Jerry's privates and the most loving details of what she'd done to him with her mouth and hands on their wedding night and it would not have upset Poe, even a little.

Poe and Jerry—the occasional cuckolder and the occasional cuckold—had met once. It was at a picnic, of all things, in Virginia—a Company/Bureau healing event that some out-of-touch geniuses had thought might be a great way to scab over interagency wounds, build interagency bridges, and simultaneously celebrate the tragically conflicted holidays of 2001. Poe recognized within seconds of being introduced to Jerry that the man was too inconsequential a human being to generate any antipathy from him. By the end of the first minute Poe knew that he would never have to invest any spare hate in Jerry.

That was a relief.

Hate was a commodity that Poe husbanded like a survivalist hoarded his last few bottles of water, or his final few rounds of ammunition.

Abhorring Jerry would be like despising garbanzo beans. Who cares if they're in your damn salad?

Just push 'em aside, was Poe's rule.

For Poe, Jerry was most definitely a garbanzo bean in the salad of life.

The specific reply that Poe made to Deirdre at the bar in Philly was a version of the same response he'd used with her other times they'd spoken their lines, during prior rendezvous. His only disappointment over the necessity to repeat the dialogue again—his disenchantment had almost always proven manageable—was that the repetition increased the likelihood that Dee would get ambushed by her guilt at what they were doing.

When her guilt popped up, Poe felt he had to be ready to take it down. Surgically. Like a sniper.

Shortly after the curtain dropped at the conclusion of an unexpected but amusing drag show at Bob & Barbara's Lounge, Poe spotted Dee's guilt lurking in the shadows. A mugger biding his time. Poe took aim. Steadied. He squeezed off a single round that was intended to do the job at hand, nothing more.

Poe's one shot was "Dee, what Jerry doesn't get is you."

She scoffed. "You just don't like him, Poe."

Her heart wasn't in the argument. He knew it. She knew it. Satisfied that he'd done what he needed to do, Poe packed up his weaponry and deliberately swallowed his next line.

It would have been *Actually, you're the one who doesn't like him, Dee.*

Poe had once committed the sin of uttering that thought aloud.

He'd learned his lesson.

He and Deirdre had met up that time at an almost seedy motel not too far from the Inner Harbor in Baltimore in 1999. He'd whispered the offending words into her hair while they were slow dancing to fast music in a smoky roadhouse a few blocks down the street. A band of aging bikers was pounding out a half-decent cover of Springsteen's "Pink Cadillac."

There's always somebody tempting / Somebody into doing something they know is wrong

In the far corner, near the hallway that led to the bathrooms, three biker-chick band groupies were drinking Natty Bohs, singing along enthusiastically, backing up the song's chorus, swaying their ample hips, clapping their hands.

Poe's open palms were planted on the cheeks of Deirdre's compact ass. Until he spoke those fateful words, she had been doing all the actual dancing, rocking her fine butt from side to side, riding up on her toes, lifting her shoulders one at a time. He had been monitoring Dee's moves by Braille. His eyes were closed and his nose was buried in her hair. To him the aroma in her hair after a couple of hours in a smoky saloon was a blend of his father's Chesterfields and his mother's Chanel.

There was comfort there.

His specific words to her that night—the ones that caused so much offense—were "You don't even really like him, baby."

Deirdre was stunned by Poe's assertion, or maybe by the fact that Poe would break their unspoken rules and assert it. She pushed him away. Her mouth fell open in vague disbelief. Or maybe disappointment—Poe wasn't sure. She blinked her eyes twice and shook her head, staring at Poe as though he had just grown fangs.

He said, "Baby, baby. It's okay."

Dee took half a step back before she wound up and slapped him hard across the cheekbone. Then she marched to their table, grabbed her purse and her jacket, and stormed out of the bar while the trio of biker chicks belted out Bruce's refrain.

And have a party in your pink Cadillac

Poe had mistaken Dee's assault on him for passion.

He knew damn well that Deirdre could have leveled him with a left cross or done some serious organ damage with a side-kick. She had the training—Dee had completed the Company's CT program before choosing to go the analyst's route—and that night in Baltimore, Poe's guard had been about as far down as it could be. The slap said everything Deirdre wanted it to say without needlessly altering Poe's structural integrity.

He finished his cocktail. Poe drank draft beer or boilermakers when he was out drinking alone; he often enjoyed an old-fashioned when he was with Dee, who had a way of putting him in a mixed-drink kind of mood.

He made the short stroll to the motel in an insistent, cold, ambivalent drizzle that was falling as slushy rain but clearly wanted to be sleet when it grew up. The icy droplets pummeled his skin like chilled needles. He rehearsed an apology for his sin the whole way back. He told himself that the mini-dart assault was his penance.

When he got to their room, Dee was already gone.

A cab, the woman at the desk said, had come and gone in the storm.

The handprint on his face from her slap didn't disappear for six days. He began to miss it the moment he realized it was fading away.

He didn't get to talk to Deirdre again for twenty-nine months after he spoke those words to her.

The twenty-nine months came to an end on the morning of September 11, 2001.

His mobile phone rang. He was in an extended-stay motel in San Antonio, Texas. Dee sobbed, "Poe, did you see—"

"I did, baby," he said. "I did."

With the exception of the two lonely Aprils that fell during the shadows of those twenty-nine months, he and Deirdre had talked either in person or by phone every April since McVeigh had committed his atrocity. One way or another, Poe and Deirdre almost always remembered Oklahoma City together.

A few times they forgot Oklahoma City together.

The only interludes during which he was ever able to totally obliterate the memories of that day in April 1995 were on those infrequent nights when Poe was blessed with dreamless sleep, or on those even more infrequent nights in some year's April when he was in bed with Dee and their lust temporarily transcended his pain.

Otherwise, he remembered Oklahoma City constantly and all too well. He remembered every detail. The commotion and the dust. The dark that seemed to last forever and ever.

The desperation that preceded the recognition.

The agony that wouldn't stop.

The hatred that wouldn't go away.

Christopher Poe had been one of the many federal employees trapped inside the Murrah Federal Building.

Deirdre had been part of the first wave of counterterrorism analysts to hit the red Oklahoma dirt later that evening. Her job was to
make sense of what had happened that day.

She was still doing that job.

"This isn't fair to Jerry," she said to Poe in the funky bar in Philly.
"What we're doing."

Dee's words froze Poe. His drink hovered halfway between the bar
top and his mouth. He waited for her to continue.

"I felt so guilty last month. When you were in the District. We
shouldn't have . . ."

She tilted her tumbler high, finishing her drink. Deirdre drank her
scotch from the well. She couldn't have picked out the finest single
malt in a blind tasting any more than she could have selected the best
potential husband out of a lineup of available men.

Deirdre's wounds weren't as visible as Poe's, but she had not arrived in his life without scars.

Poe could have chosen to be argumentative with Dee about whether
or not they were being fair to Jerry. Or he could have been coy with
her. But Poe didn't possess the necessary will, not with Dee. He tried
to save his manipulative talents—they were not unsubstantial—for
the job. In his heart, he knew that the two precious late afternoon
hours they'd stolen together in the hotel on Connecticut Avenue the
previous month had changed nothing, one way or another.

"Probably not," he admitted, granting Dee the point about ultimate fairness to Jerry. "But for us it's usually only once a year, baby,
if we're lucky."

Poe had always been prone to rationalization. He was honest with
himself about most things; if pressed, he would have included the ra-
tionalizing tendency on an inventory of his personal flaws.

He didn't have to remind Dee that he wished they could be together more often than once a year, or that he hoped the recent tryst
in D.C. was portent, not anomaly. She knew all that.

But Dee refused to believe that Poe's professed relationship desire
was anything more than a pipe dream. She armored herself with that

diminution. She'd written in the journal she kept hidden from all that Poe's affection for her was "Tinkerbell love."

Someplace buried deep inside she suspected how he felt about her. When her guard sank low and she got in touch with that place—it was middle-of-the-night territory—she felt more conflicting loyalties than a tribal chieftain on the Pakistan/Afghanistan border.

"Well," Deirdre said, "I'm not going to sleep with you tonight. Not this whole weekend, Poe."

She seemed oblivious to how epic her pronouncement was. She spoke as though she was telling him she had decided not to have pickles on her burger.

The monumentality was not lost on Poe. He actually gasped at her words. He checked the reflection of her face in the mirror behind the bar to see if she was sincere. He had to tilt his head a little to see her expression between the neck of the bottle of Johnnie Walker Red and the neck of the bottle of Johnnie Walker Black. He thought she looked resolute. "You're not kidding, are you? Dee?"

"No, sir, I'm not."

Poe thought the words sounded, well, determined. He had always counted on Dee's determination melting around him. The "sir" completely threw him. He didn't know what to do with that.

He tasted the leading edge of the incipient panic that presaged impending loss.

"You can't—Jesus— Deirdre? Yeah? Really?"

You think I traveled halfway across this country to attend an interagency counterterrorism confab in Philadelphia because I liked the programming?

"It's not right, Poe. It's not right. What we're doing. What we've been doing all these years. You know it's not right, you do. We can't keep on doing this. We can't just . . . If things were the other way around, if it had been—"

He held up his open palm.

He held it out in front of him, not toward her.

No! Not there. Not there, baby. Do not go—

He wasn't trying to be intimidating. His intent with the raised hand was to stop the world, not only Dee's current participation in it.

The panic that was exploding within him with the force of a geyser was about survival, not about sex. She had to know that.

Poe felt the OKC fright rise into his marrow. He felt it as though acid were being injected into the soft hollow of his longest bones. He had to stem it, arrest the corrosion.

He bargained. "How about this? Sleep with me tonight. Let me hold you. All night. All night. I—"

"Poe, sweet man, I understand. But I have to respect—"

Respect? Respect? "Deirdre? Listen to me, listen." She looked at him. "All night. I need that. I need . . . *that.*" He got up from his stool, took two steps away. Spun. Came back. Sat down. Stood up. Two steps away. Two steps back. Sat down again. "No sex? Is that it? I can do that. Yes, yes, I can. That's a promise. No sex, Dee. But sleep with me tonight please? All night?"

"Poe, did you just say 'no sex'?"

"Yes."

"Poe, did you just say 'please'?"

"I did."

"Holy," she said. "Holy."

Sam

My first full day in Florida started out at the driving range.

I was stumped trying to come up with a decent hockey analogy—my preferred metaphorical bias regarding most things in life—for assessing my accomplishments at the day's scheduled activity, so I decided to use baseball as my model.

After a couple of dozen swings with the driver—it had the biggest business end so I figured it should be the easiest to use—I had managed to hit the ball off the practice tee exactly seven times.

I whiffed on the rest.

Truth is I made respectable contact on all seven balls that I actually hit. Five of the seven were hard grounders that no infielder without a Gold Glove could have grabbed. One was a line drive that would have decapitated the first-base coach. The last was a fly ball that might have cleared the fence if it stayed fair.

But it wouldn't have stayed fair. The thing was like a slider, the way it hooked left.

I knew enough about golf to realize that the goal of the game was not just to hit the ball, but also to hit it up the middle in the direction of second base, ideally with some elevation. Still, by my personal baseball-centric accounting, I was hitting just under .300. Not too bad for a rookie.

My assigned starting time in the celebratory tournament was 8:25. By eight o'clock I was beginning to entertain some doubts about my ability to learn the nuances of the game in the remaining twenty-five minutes of practice time. My hands were starting to feel a little spongy in places, which wasn't a good sign. I was no longer even confident I could go eighteen without bodily injury, which felt kind of wussy of me, especially since I wasn't even expected to walk the course. I had my own cart.

I certainly didn't want to leave all my game, however limited that was, on the driving range, so I grabbed the bag I'd been given for the day—why I needed so many clubs wasn't clear to me yet—and joined some of my fellow golfers over at the practice putting green.

There I was more in my element. Putting actually seemed a little easier without all the moving parts and speed bumps and windmills and tunnels and things. Though it became clear that the fact that nothing was precisely flat was going to take some adjustment on my part.

I felt more presentable than I had during the previous evening's sunset cruise. I was wearing my best khakis and a knit polo shirt that read "Boulder Bolder Security" over my left man boob. I considered it serendipity that my "Samuel Purdy" name tag covered the advertisement as though it had been designed for just that task. My sneakers were reasonably new, with unbroken laces that were more white than gray.

I was styling.

The bad news was that I'd been out of the shower for less than an hour and I was already so slick from sweat and sunscreen that I felt like the equatorial gods were marinating me to be the entrée at some luncheon cookout.

Ann Summers Calderón reached around me with both arms and placed her hands on my clammy wrists as I prepared to knock down a twenty-foot putt. The twenty-foot putt was what was left after my initial forty-foot putt. I had not heard Ann approach. She moved as silently as my son did when he was scooping my loose change off the table by the door.

"Fine form," she said. "I may take some lessons from you."

"You should see me on the driving range."

"Sadly for you, I already did. Got a second for me?" she whispered.

I lowered my voice to library standards. "Get me out of this and I got all morning for you."

She took me by the hand. I flipped my putter toward the golf bag, thinking, *And there are people who say there is no God.*

*   *   *

A breakfast buffet was arranged in a handsome room in the clubhouse that had been reserved for the Calderón family celebration. I grabbed a bagel and some juice—orange mixed with the nectar of some other fruit that turned the beverage the hues of a smoggy sunset over the Front Range—and joined Ann at a table on a veranda that enjoyed a fine view of a water hazard. I'd already surmised that is what golfers call ponds. This being Florida, I was keeping one eye peeled for alligators and giant pythons. Ann was dressed as though the winner of the day's tournament would be the player judged to have the outfit containing the most colors of sherbet.

On her, the look worked. I didn't think I could get away with it.

"You are a most lovely hostess," I said. I was committed to being on my best behavior.

"Jane didn't call this morning," she said.

I allowed her eyes to find mine, and to settle. My cop voice, a voice I have fine-tuned over the years, has a couple of dominant notes. One note I can play for authority, one note I can play for calm. I plucked the calm chord. I said, "You know your daughter, Ann. I don't. This conversation will go better if I don't have to guess what things mean."

"Got you. I'm anxious. Sorry."

"Don't be sorry. You didn't ask for any of this."

Ann sighed a restrained sigh. "We're close, Jane and I. She calls me about everything. 'I wish I could tell you about last night, Mom, but I can't.' 'There's this guy in my Modern China lecture that is soooo cute, Mom.' 'I'm at IKEA and I don't know which of these two lamps to get, Mom.' 'I kissed a girl last night, Mom.' 'I'm on the way to the airport, Mom.' Like that.

"She should have left for Hartford—for the airport—almost three hours ago. She should have called me from the shuttle. She always does. Her flight is scheduled to take off right about now."

I kissed a girl last night, Mom. It took some discipline—not my strong suit in matters of prurience in recent years—to let that one go by without a follow-up query.

I said, "And when you called her?"

"Her phone is not in service. Went straight to voice mail. I tried text. Nothing. No reply." She laced her fingers together in front of her and squeezed her hands into a ball. She released the pressure. "If she's busy, she texts me back, 'n-n.' Not now. Do you text your son, Sam?"

"I'm getting there. For me, it's like he's learned a foreign language and the only way I can keep an eye on him is to learn it too."

Ann smiled a smile that was thirty degrees more sincere than her hostess's smile. She wrinkled her nose, too. "One parent to another? It's worth the effort. And the older they get, the more it approximates English." She pursed her lips before she said, "But Jane didn't text me back." She allowed a sigh to evolve into something more. I recognized the exercise from any number of women I knew in Boulder. It was a cleansing breath. She asked, "Is this the other shoe, Sam? From the note? Is this . . . when I become desperate to reach him?"

"Ann? Honestly? There's a ninety-nine percent chance the note is nothing, and the fact that Jane didn't call this morning is nothing. But the note is . . . bizarre enough that some concern is warranted. So I'm with you. I'm still not convinced that I'm your best potential asset, but I'm with you. A hundred percent."

"Thank you, Sam."

"If that note means something serious? I mean, as goofy as it looks—"

Ann interrupted. " 'Goofy'?"

"Minnesota word. Think strange."

She nodded.

"Then I'm not the best person for this. You need to know that. I'm a small town cop on suspension visiting a state where I have no resources."

She stared at me in a way that pinned me to my chair. "I'm not connected to people in . . . law enforcement. It's not my world. So I have no one else I can turn to right now, Sam. This morning, this minute, do I wish that you were some hotshot FBI cowboy who jousted with monsters every day of his life? Of course. But my heart says you are a man with good instincts—that assessment was originally Carmen's, by the way—and as I sit here I am deeply grateful for any help you will give me. My heart also says to trust you. That instinct has served me well in life. I am not going to stop listening to it now."

I'd heard enough. I stood up. "Let's start being discreet then. I'm

going back inside. I'm going to find an empty room back there somewhere." I gestured toward the far end of the clubhouse. "You should
wait a few minutes, talk to some people, be charming, and then come
find me. I'll leave the door open an inch or two."

Ann did what she was told. Five minutes passed before she closed the
door behind her and settled across from me at a fancy conference table.

She set a cup of coffee in front of me. "Café Cubano," she said.

I took a sip and already knew I wanted another. Along with whatever kind of morning treat the Cubans baked to go with it. "Does Jane
have roommates?" I asked.

"One. Penelope's family is in New York this weekend. She left campus yesterday to join her parents in the city. I spoke with Jane after
that. I doubt Penny will be of any help on this."

"Simplest explanation that fits the facts?" I paused to allow Ann to
catch up with me. "Your daughter lost her phone."

Ann shook her head. "You don't know Jane. First, she doesn't lose
things. She's not that kid. If her phone died, or was stolen, she'd borrow
one from one of the other students on the shuttle. Jane's gregarious. Not
life-of-the-party gregarious. But she's the type of person who will introduce
herself to you and will learn your social history particulars within minutes
of making your acquaintance. She's the girl you're glad you were seated
next to at a dinner party. The one you're delighted ended up next to you on
that interminable flight to London or L.A. Jane would have no trouble bor-
rowing a phone, especially on an airport shuttle full of other students."

"Kind of like her mother in demeanor?"

"If that's a compliment, then yes, kind of like her mother."

"It was a compliment."

She mouthed, *Thank you.*

"Jane overslept," I said.

Ann's eyes moistened over. "I wish," she said. "My daughter is a
bit OCD. Again, like her mother."

"Tell me something. Pretend you never got the note. Knowing what
you know about Jane not calling this morning, how are you feeling
right now?"

"Honestly? I'd be starting to panic a little—that's how out of character this is for Jane—but I'd keep it to myself. I wouldn't have pulled you off the golf course."

I said, "One of my concerns is that the more I help you, the more you will convince yourself this is real."

"You mentioned a child? Is that right, Sam?"

"Yes. Simon."

"You and Simon are on the curb. He has to get to the other side of the street. Let's say that there's a one percent chance that he'll get hit by a car if he crosses. With me so far?"

"I'm with you."

"Do you let him go? Knowing that there's one chance in a hundred he won't make it across that street?"

She was acknowledging the odds were long that her daughter was truly in trouble. She was also assigning a value to the jeopardy she felt, even with the long odds.

I said, "I get it."

She said, "This may be the longest of long shots, but I can't take the risk of ignoring it. The consequences are . . . not imaginable."

"I'm in. Here's what I need," I said. "I want the—"

Ann reached into the satchel she was carrying. Maybe it was just a purse, but it was big enough to schlep an entire goalie's kit back and forth to the rink. She handed me an orange file folder containing a few sheets of paper pinched together with a pink paper clip. She did like her colors. "The airport shuttle service information, including today's schedule. The one she should have been on is circled. Jane's flight information from Hartford to Miami. Reservation number. Frequent flyer info. Contact numbers for the airline. Her phone numbers and email addresses. A copy of last month's cell phone bill. Her last few days of emails and texts to me. Her class schedule. Everything I could think of."

"Thank you," I said. "I can make inquiries to the shuttle company and the airlines, but I shouldn't be using my phone to contact her cell. If this is . . . real, the sudden appearance of a new phone number on her phone might tip them off that you have—"

"Failed to follow their instructions. Thank you for that. I will get you a phone. A family phone. Wait right here."

Ann returned in about three minutes and handed me an iPhone. "It's Andrew's," she said. "Using it won't raise any suspicion. He calls his sister all the time."

"What did you tell Andrew?"

"I didn't tell him anything. I took it from his golf bag. When he realizes it's missing, I'll figure something out. He has other things on his mind. Everyone he might want to talk to is at the party."

"I will need to do the computer work from your home."

"Why?"

"We don't know the level of sophistication we're dealing with. At this stage, it would be reckless to underestimate . . . him." Ann's eyes narrowed a little at my choice of pronouns. I added, "Or her. Ann, you may catch me being non-inclusive with my pronouns, but you will not find me being non-inclusive regarding the gender of my suspects. I am equal opportunity in terms of suspicion."

"Thank you, Sam."

"To complete my point—if I make an inquiry that this guy is able to track electronically . . . I want him to track it back to your ISP, and to your specific computer. With me?"

"I understand."

"I'm going to go make some apologies to the rest of my golf party, tell them I'm not feeling well. I will take a cab back to the hotel. Please have someone meet me there who can take me to your house."

"Done. Keep an eye out for a white Suburban with tinted windows. The driver's name is Julio. He will have my computer set up for you. I can't be there. I have responsibilities here. Were I to forsake them it would draw attention, and I can't afford to . . ."

"I understand. Will I need your password, Ann?"

Without a moment's hesitation, she said, "Andrewjane, all lower case. And Sam?"

"Yes?"

"The name tag? It should go."

"Got a second?"

"Maybe five." The shift supervisor looks up from his desk at the Yale University Police headquarters on Ashmun Street. He nods at the uniformed officer standing in front of him. "Kevin, what's up?"

"Just got a call from the master at Trumbull. Some concern about a junior missing a meeting this morning. Turns out his parents are looking for him, there's been a death in the family. His friends don't know where he is. Didn't sleep in the college last night."

"That's it?"

"You said last week that you want to know when we hear from any of the masters."

"You're right. I said that. Is the Trumbull master worried about this?"

"No, I think it was more a heads-up kind of thing, in case the student's parents contact us directly. The master and the dean seem to have the situation under control. They've sent a few of his friends into Sterling and Bass to see if he's studying out of cell range. Tough situation—the death was sudden, a sibling. Sister, I think. Traffic accident, auto-pedestrian? Something. Little town in Western Mass. Family is distraught. But . . . last night was Thursday. So, you know what that means. We intervened in more than a little craziness on campus. If he was involved in any of that? He could be asleep in one of the tombs or on some stranger's floor right now. Kid will show."

The supervisor raises his eyebrows at the reference to Thursday evenings on campus in April. "Was the student tapped? You know that for sure?"

"No, no. I don't know one way or another, but I got the impression from the master that he's that kind of kid. You know. Prominent family, high profile on campus. It's a possibility, something to consider."

"You're right, it is."

"Hey, if it was our job to track down every student who didn't sleep in his room and missed a meeting, we'd do nothing else with our time."

"That's a fact. Where did you leave it with the master?"

"I said we'd coordinate an attempt to locate with the New Haven Police. But that's it for now. He recognizes the limits of what we can do."

"Sounds good. Get the kid's description out, run the ATL. Get Yale Security up to speed, too. You have contact information for the kid? Parents? Family?"

"Yes."

"Girlfriend? Boyfriend?"

"Should have thought of that. I'll check."

"Roommate?"

The officer shakes his head. "Got all his suitemates' cell numbers. Five of them. But he lives in a single." He pauses. "We don't get lists, do we? I mean unofficially. Of the taps?"

"From the societies? Hell, no. We don't." The supervisor grins as he adds, "And that's probably a good thing. Keep me posted. But I think the kid will surface as soon as he wakes up."

The officer turns to leave.

"Wait. See if the kid has a car registered on campus. Check the lot where he's supposed to park, see if the car is there. If we can show he's gone off somewhere, that should end all this. And what the hell, get one of our patrols to eyeball the tombs. See if there's anything unusual going on."

"Boss?"

"Yeah?"

"How could you tell?"

The shift supervisor chuckles at the question.

He doesn't know it will be the last laugh he will enjoy for a long time.

Dee and Poe

"Huh," Deirdre said. She was sitting up in the hotel bed, her Black-Berry in her hands.

They'd made it till morning. They'd each kept their promise.

She'd slept with him. He hadn't touched her sexually.

"What?" Poe asked. He had curled his body close to hers when she sat up, so he could imprint a fresh variation of her scent in some primitive structure in his brain. A sweet and savory aroma from above her left hipbone was his current fascination. He was torn about lifting his eyelids. He wasn't eager to acknowledge the beginning of the day, but he was considering the possibility that if he opened his eyes right then he might be looking up at the sublime line that her jawbone made as it became her chin.

The light filtering through her morning hair going every which way would be a most welcome bonus.

That he had something worth waking up for didn't happen often for Poe.

He stole a glance at the clock. 9:16. He'd woken after 9:02. For Poe, since 1995, that unremarkable occurrence happened only when he was sharing a bed with Dee.

"The secretary of the army's kid is missing," Deirdre said.

Poe wasn't really interested. But he liked hearing her talk. A little Debussy in the morning. "How long?" he asked absently.

"Just overnight, they think. They expected to hear from him this morning, but he didn't show, or call, I guess. No cell contact. Nothing."

"I hear it happens in the best families," Poe said, hoping they could talk about something else entirely. Or nothing at all.

She flicked his temple with her index finger. Hard. "This isn't a joke, Poe."

"Ouch. How old is he?"

"College. Twenty-one."

He made a face that she couldn't see. "He's an adult. So . . . What? Why are— What are— Why the hell are you getting an email about this?"

She leaned across his body, forcing him onto his back. Her breasts were resting on his abdomen. "You think . . . that maybe it's because we're involved in two wars and it's the secretary of the army's kid?"

He was hoping the question was rhetorical. He was sufficiently distracted by Dee's boobs on his belly that he wasn't sure he could come up with a satisfactory answer.

They'd argued only once about the nature of the current Iraq war—the night of that debate they had been perched on stools in Ernie K-Doe's Mother-in-Law Lounge in New Orleans during the last April before Katrina and Rita. Dee and Poe didn't begin bickering about Iraq that evening until after they had resolved a dispute about whether or not the presence of washers and dryers in the back room enhanced or diminished Checkpoint Charlie's—that was the previous night's aging saloon—credentials as a dive bar. The consensus they reached was that the presence of laundry facilities was no more a dive-bar disqualifier than a beat-up shuffleboard table would be.

The Iraq war debate was not so easily settled. Their gradual inebriation, inevitable in the circumstances, didn't help the process.

They agreed to let it go.

About the war, Dee had been pro. Poe had been con.

Poe stated what to him was obvious. "Your missing kid? He's twenty-one. He's in college. Jesus." He closed his eyes and pulled her all the way onto him, maximizing the contact between his skin and hers. He inhaled more of Dee's musk. He was determined to restart his day a little later. And maybe even better.

He had begun to allow himself a glimmer of hope that Dee would yield on her no-sex pledge. He was certain that after a few more seconds of intimate contact the most prominent indicator of the state of his autonomic nervous system was going to cast its vote in an indubitable fashion.

"Huh," she said, as her BlackBerry vibrated once more.

She sat up, again. Grabbed it.

He leaned into her, again. Inhaled, again.

His hope began fading along with his erection.

They walked to a breakfast-lunch place that was not much wider than the corridor in their hotel. The diner wasn't far from the bar where they'd been drinking the night before. Poe had scoped out the location on the walk back to their room.

The bald guy at the griddle and the two waitresses had probably worked there since the waning days of Vietnam. The storefront had a ten-seat counter, a couple of booths, and five tables—two four-tops and three deuces. Four burners and a wide griddle. An old Bunn coffeemaker. A three-tap soda fountain. It was an eggs and toast, pancakes kind of place. A breakfast-always-served kind of place. A definite no-latte zone. At lunch, it'd be burgers and french dips and turkey sandwiches. Disappointing cheesesteaks. Grilled cheese, tuna salad, iceberg lettuce.

The fryer was dead. A penciled, thumbtacked sign on the wall behind the defunct machine read, "R.I.P., Halloween 1995." That meant well over a decade of chips, not fries, with the burgers.

The establishment was the kind of endangered species that was disappearing from urban habitats. There was no public clamor for federal protection programs for either diners or greasy spoons. Poe considered that a crime.

They grabbed the only open deuce and ordered without menus. Deirdre ordered scrambled eggs—three whites, one yolk—dry, and wheat toast, dry. And tea. Poe ordered three eggs up and runny, hash browns, and all the varieties of processed pig the short order guy could fit on a single plate. With two english muffins. And a short stack. Extra butter. Coffee. OJ.

The waitress turned her head toward the griddle and monotoned, "Three beat, dry, hold two eyes. One triple triple suicide, sunny and runny, with a short stack."

Poe and Deirdre had each missed a morning meeting at the Counterterrorism Coordination Conference they were attending at the downtown Federal Building. But they were scheduled to attend different early sessions, so she hoped none of their colleagues would notice their mutual absence and connect the dots.

Poe didn't care if anyone noticed. He had grown indifferent to dot-connecting when it didn't involve his job responsibilities. Since he had no personal responsibilities, and his professional responsibilities were circumscribed, he didn't spend a lot of time looking over his shoulder for the presence of people who might be predisposed to gossip.

"Huh," she said. She was focused on her BlackBerry once again.

He was reading the sports page of *The Philadelphia Inquirer* while trying to keep his fingertips out of a syrup spill that had drenched the lower edge of the page during an earlier reader's interlude with the paper. The 76ers were showing some end-of-season life. Who knew? He felt like talking sports, but it wasn't one of Dee's things. He respected that.

"Army kid showed up?" he guessed.

"No. Another kid's gone missing. Same college. Same time frame."

He lowered the *Inquirer*. With some tease in his voice, he said, "You're in the loop for some amazing trivia, little lady, aren't you? Do you get stuff like this all day long? You do, don't you? I knew it. Do they cover, like, all colleges, or do they only send you stuff from the best schools? Part of me is thinking, *I'm so sorry.* Part of me is thinking, *Damn, you have become somebody—they even send you all the gossipy shit.*"

She liked that he'd noticed.

Deirdre was a near star in the Agency, one of the rising counter-intelligence thinkers of the day, or at least of the moment. Shortly after 9/11 she wrote some provocative assessments of the global terrorism big picture, of the resiliency and patience of the Islamic extremist mind, of the reality that Muslims, like Christians, are defined more by their differences with each other than by their similarities. She continued to generate ideas important people remained interested in hearing. She was one of the analysts who got routine summonses to cross the threshold inside Langley to brief the DDIs. Her actual words found their way into the PDB and into the NIE.

Dee's career had upside.

Poe sipped his coffee. The coffee was bad, only a smidge shy of foul. It was thin and bitter. But it was hot. He sipped some more. With his voice full of affection, he said, "And the Company cares about any of this . . . why? If it's anything, it's grunt work. Don't you guys have like an entire planet to worry about?"

Dee wrinkled her nose at him instead of answering. Poe lifted the paper again. He moved on to a story about what spring training injuries had done to the depth in the Phillies' bullpen. Poe didn't even like the Phillies.

She leaned forward. Lowered her voice to a whisper. She said, "It's Priscilla Post's son."

If Poe ignored the lyrics and focused only on the melody, the sounds he heard were like the first notes of a ballad to him. He looked over the top of the page at Dee. "The new justice nominee? Yes?"

"One and the same. The new nominee for the Supreme Court."

He allowed himself a barely restrained self-congratulatory fist pump for his current-events acumen.

She didn't share his oversized sense of accomplishment. She opened her eyes wide and held up one index finger.

Poe thought she was pointing at the ceiling. He looked up.

It turned out she had been counting, not pointing. She said, "One, secretary of the army's kid." She extended her middle finger as well. "Two, United States Supreme Court nominee's kid." She raised her eyebrows in punctuation.

Poe was starting to find all the facial expression kind of hot.

"Huh," he said, considering the actual news value of what she reported. *Coincidence? Probably,* he thought, *but . . .* He sat up straighter, pulled out his BlackBerry. Powered it up. The first thing he did was check the time. 11:52. His message screen came alive. He started thumbing buttons, nodding his head in an exaggerated bobble-head motion as he scrolled down, hoping to hear her laugh.

She didn't laugh. "You got it, too?" she said.

"I did indeed. What are the odds of that? You and I on the same intel list? And . . . it appears my humble little Bureau email is, well, better . . . than your fancy Company email. Mine says there's a possible third kid involved. Parents need to reach him, can't. The college master, whatever the hell that is, has been looking for him, too. They all want to tell him that his sister . . . or his grandfather? . . . has died. That's an important distinction, you would think the family would have pinned that fact down a little better before raising all this commotion." He finished the last gulp of coffee in his mug. "All in all, many more details than my brain can deal with right at this moment. Maybe later on, after I take a run and clear my head, this will seem more coherent. And maybe even . . . I don't know . . . important."

He smiled at her because he wanted her to know he was happy to be having breakfast with her.

"Is the kid's family connected? The third kid? Like the other two?" Dee asked. She was doing what came naturally to her, trying to draw a straight line through all the data, including Poe's latest itinerant ramblings.

He shook his head. "Got nothing on that, Barbara Lou. But I will keep you posted." He didn't call her Barbara Lou often—it was a made-up name that had originally belonged to his momma's best friend during the few years his family had spent in Oxford, Mississippi—but when he did call her Barbara Lou, he could usually count on a smile in return. Not that time, though. Dee was being serious.

He put his BlackBerry facedown on the table.

Their food arrived. The waitress—the one of the two who were wearing wigs; the thing was cockeyed a few degrees—splashed more bitter coffee into his mug.

"Anything else, hon?" she asked Poe.

Poe winked at her, shook his head.

Poe was enough of a player in the Bureau to be included in the occasional tangential email loop, but he knew that the presence of his name on whatever distribution list it was on existed solely so that the people who controlled access to the raw data could use him for stain-resistant fabric to cover their asses, should the need arise.

Or when the need arose.

Despite the fact that someone in the FBI had thought to alert him about the overnight news from New Haven, Poe remained disinclined to give the situation of the three barely missing kids much thought.

His initial assessment was that it was way too concrete a set of facts that involved much too high-profile people, a combination that placed it, by definition, far outside his investigatory purview. At the end of almost all days that was a state of affairs that was just fine with him. Poe had long before stopped seeking to impress.

Early in his career he had earned a faster-than-usual climb up the Bureau's hierarchical career ladder. That climb had just begun to accelerate in 1995 when it had been almost fatally interrupted by Tim McVeigh and Terry Nichols in Oklahoma City. Whatever might have been left of Poe's ascent had ground to a screeching halt six years later, the day he had accepted an invitation to head the elite—*ha!*—counterterrorism unit that he had been shepherding since months after 9/11.

Special Agent Christopher Lance Poe was the first and thus far only leader of a Special Investigations unit that had been foisted on an incredibly stressed and most reluctant FBI by the micromanaging United States Congress in the go-get-'em days after the Twin Towers fell. The role of the unit that Congress legislated into existence—initially robust in size and budget, it had shrunk to the point that it included only Poe; his partner and friend, Special Agent Kelli Moon, who was currently on a maternity leave from which Poe didn't expect her to return; and one admin aide back in headquarters in the District—was to examine and investigate low-probability, high-risk terror scenarios that had been brought to the attention of the Bureau by various sources, but usually by citizens.

Average Joes.

Basically, Poe's unit was charged with ferreting out truth from fiction in regard to far-fetched plots that had potentially mind-boggling consequences.

Congress was determined that Poe's squad should investigate the types of things that the FBI had proven unfortunately culpable of ignoring in the recent past.

Like the Saudi man who wanted to learn how to fly jetliners but seemed uninterested in learning how to land them.

That, of course, was prior to September 11.

Since? Like the guy with the Geiger counter who was certain his next-door neighbor was building a thermonuclear device in his three-car garage.

It turned out that one involved improperly stored medical waste.

Like the levee inspector who thought that someone was drilling a tunnel through a dike so that he could empty Lake Pontchartrain into New Orleans.

Poe discovered the suspect indeed had nefarious intent, but alas, no engineering skill. That one was pre-Katrina, pre-Rita.

Like the spelunker who'd discovered a new cave route that ran perilously close to the back side of the air force installation inside Cheyenne Mountain. The caver had also discovered a blasting cap and some dynamite on the route in.

Poe never figured out an answer to that riddle.

And there was the guy overheard bragging at his next-door neighbor's barbecue about an idea to send hundreds of weather balloons aloft ferrying incendiary devices into the tinder-dry forests of the interior mountain west.

Poe and Kelli had spent five weeks in Boise, Idaho, examining the plausibility of that risk. The loudmouthed guy who really liked spareribs and talked way too much when he was drinking was just completing the first third of a decade-long holiday at taxpayer expense in a federal prison in the great state of Kansas.

Friends of Poe's in the Bureau—a club of manageable size—called Poe's little unit the "Bogeyman Squad."

Others, greater in number and less fond of Poe, called the unit more uncharitable things.

The reality was that Poe chased a lot of ghosts. Poe never denied it. A microscopic percentage of his cases proved to have any merit.

Dee was occasionally guilty of teasing Poe about his job. She'd been known to call him the "prince of catastrophe." Her teasing was always friendly. Philosophically, Deirdre was in Poe's camp—she was one of the most vocal advocates in the counterintelligence community for investing resources not in preventing repetitions of the most recent assaults, but instead in what she called the "evolution of terror."

She had coined the phrase in a counterterrorism resources strategy paper she had written in 2002, and if there was one thing the intelligence bureaucracy admired it was the author of an enduring sound bite that they might be able to use to increase their annual budget.

The fact that Dee's prescription was also sensible and was proving to be prescient sometimes seemed to be of secondary importance to the suits higher up the Company food chain.

Poe had managed to hold on to his position in charge of the almost mythical FBI bogeyman squad because he was, by nature, publicity averse and because he was adept at keeping the unit's work below the bureaucracy's fine-tuned radar. In addition, the special agent in charge to whom he reported had confidence that Poe was one FBI agent who would not be forever bitching to his superiors about his unit's dwindling resources and ever-increasingly diverted budget.

Poe wouldn't bitch not only because he knew it wouldn't make any difference, but also because he knew that without his current job and the freedom it provided him he wouldn't last three months inside the Bureau. He couldn't imagine himself living in a one-bedroom apartment in the District, trying to survive the bullshit in the Hoover

Building, or even worse assigned to some FBI Field Office outpost in Atlanta or Portland or Missoula or Anchorage.

Poe also knew that without his current job he wouldn't have anywhere at all to steer his hate.

That scared him as much as anything.

That Friday morning in Philadelphia, he found his spirits buoyed by the fact that he had an immense breakfast to devour and a fine woman to savor.

Dee, however, seemed intent on destroying the mood. "What do you think it means? If it turns out that these kids are all connected?" she asked. Domestic puzzles were Poe's business, not hers. Although the CIA could ponder the risks of onshore terrorism, if anyone was looking over the Company's broad shoulders, its agents could only investigate events leading back offshore.

Unless they decided to ignore the law, which happened.

Poe respected Dee's work and her brain. It comforted him that Dee wanted his opinion about the three college kids who had neglected to call their parents. But the comfort he took from her metaphorical caress was a conversation for their next night hip to hip on bar stools.

He said, "Three college kids missing for a few hours? Dee? Come on. Means nothing. Zilch."

She scooped some pale eggs with a triangle of dry toast. "You come on. You can do better than that."

He chomped a sausage in half, recalling with a twinge of melancholy that she'd said those same exact words to him once they'd decoupled after sex during their spring visit in 2003. *You can do better than that,* she'd said. She'd been right. Their lovemaking that night had been oddly pedestrian. Poe remembered that April night in St. Paul well—he had been visited by unwelcome OKC ghosts and had allowed the visitors to distract him during the deed.

He said, "Top of my head? The part of my gray matter that is hovering magically above my hangover? Worst case? The three kids are all friends and they . . . let's say, rolled their car somewhere and nobody's come across the crash site. One's dead, two will survive their injuries. Two Flight for Life choppers, one regional burn unit." Dee flattened her lips and raised her eyebrows. Poe went on. "Best case, best case? They're sleeping off some serious debauchery in Atlantic City. No, these kids sound rich. Maybe Macau. They're in Macau and their cell phones don't work over there."

She shook her head. "The State Department and DHS would know if they used their passports."

DHS was the Department of Homeland Security. In Poe's personal, ironic, competing-agency lexicon, HS was the Hot Shits. Less ironically, and much less reverentially, HS was sometimes Holy Shit!—as in "Holy Shit, the Hot Shits are frisking Grandma again."

Poe said, "Point. We'll make it Las Vegas then. Not as interesting a story, I'm afraid." He changed his tone to adopt the faux seriousness of a documentary voice-over. "An all-too-common tale of hookers, drugs, alcohol, and a poker game with ringers. Fine young men. Bad choices." He tsked. "Kids today."

She shook her head at him in exasperation. But she finally grinned, just a little.

Poe felt triumphant.

They ate. Poe stole glances at Dee from above his paper.

He even liked watching her chew.

His BlackBerry started to vibrate on the scratched laminate tabletop. He put his hand on it to keep it still.

They were both done eating. Dee hadn't touched much of her breakfast. She threw her napkin onto the remains of the eggs and toast. Poe stacked his empty plates to make things easier for the wigged waitress.

He was becoming concerned that she had breast cancer.

Deirdre's BlackBerry sang a quick little two-note melody that sounded like "Hel-lo."

Poe despised the perkiness of the tone she'd chosen for her phone. He got distracted for a moment trying to think of another thing he despised about her. Failed.

He smiled. Not even Jerry. Poe knew that if Jerry were a better man, Dee wouldn't be in that Philadelphia diner with him throwing away most of her breakfast.

Before either of them could look at their devices, Poe reached over and took Deirdre's hand. He squeezed it. He glanced up at her for a second, but wasn't able to look in her eyes the whole time he said, "I want to thank you, Dee. I mean really, truly, thank you. For being with me last night. If you had gone ahead and . . . If you did what you . . . If you didn't sleep with me . . . I mean sleep, sleep . . . If I hadn't had a chance to hold you, touch you, be with you, I was afraid I was going to die."

His vulnerability shook her. She reached across the table, careful to keep the sleeve of her shirt out of the streaks his egg yolks had left on his plate. She raised his chin with her fingertips until she was able to capture his eyes with her own. She locked on to them while she stared as far into him as she could. She was trying to find his soul, looking for truth.

Dee knew that at times Poe had a tendency to lean into hyperbole the way pedestrians lean into a stiff wind.

She could see that this wasn't one of those times. Poe's words had been as honest as he could make them.

She stood up, hoping he wouldn't notice that her eyes had filled with tears. Before she walked away, she leaned down and kissed him softly on the lips. "I have to get ready for my talk," she said.

"You're doing a talk? Maybe I'll come. On what?"

Deirdre smiled the smile that had first caused Poe to seek solace from her back in the spring of ninety-five. She said, "It's called 'Underestimating the Enemy.' And you know damn well you're not invited."

"Dee?" he called out before she reached the door.

She spun. Her hair continued moving after she completed her turn, framing her face in a way that allowed Poe to believe that she was again young and that life was about opportunity, not survival.

If Dee was young, Poe could be young, too.

That meant hope for Poe. For him, hope was almost always horizon material, suspended beyond his reach.

He did notice the tears in her eyes.

He said, "What enemy is that? That we're underestimating?"

She kept walking.

He threw twenty bucks on the table and chased after her.

He knew what enemy it was.

She was waiting for him outside. "Don't, Poe," she said. "I have an errand to run. I'll catch up with you later."

APRIL 18, FRIDAY MIDDAY
NEW HAVEN

"There's a tarp over the outside stairwell that leads to the basement of Book & Snake. Like there's been a leak or something. Other than that, the tombs are quiet."

"That's it?" asks the patrol supervisor.

"Missing kid's car is in the assigned lot. Doesn't look like it's been driven recently. Windshield is covered with bird crap. The Trumbull master had already checked the student's room. His suitemates said it looks like it always looks. No luck in the libraries—he's not there. One of his friends said he's been hitting on a freshman drama major at TD. The master at Dwight is on that."

TD is Timothy Dwight. Another college.

The patrol supervisor sits back on his chair. He says, "We're looking for a total of three kids now. Not one. Three different colleges. No initial indication that the kids know each other. All failed to show up for something they had scheduled late this morning. No one can reach any of them."

The officer's face reveals his surprise. "I don't get it. Since when is a kid missing a class something we hear about?"

"The two new kids are sons of VIPs."

"That's not good. Any connections? Sports? Activities? Frats?"

"One is a Psi U, the other two no. One's in crew. One's in FOOT. One's YDN. New Haven PD is in the loop, too. Feds have been alerted by the parents of—"

"Feds? Why?"

"Supreme Court police, believe it or not. Kid's mother is the new justice nominee. Like I said, VI frigging P."

"Really? Are the feds sending someone here?"

"So far they're just interested. Leaving it to us to do the legwork. Seems to me that everybody's trying to keep everybody else from overreacting."

"One of the suitemates told the master that the Trumbull kid was tapped by Skull & Bones. This is tap week. With VIP kids part of this? That's where I'd start. Maybe they're all still in the tomb sleeping off . . . whatever crazy stuff they did."

"I suppose."

"Do we have a department policy on the tombs? A procedure for . . . checking on them? How do we get inside if we need to?"

The supervisor opens his mouth. Closes it. Opens it again. "All I know is it's complicated. I don't think the secret societies are actually Yale property. The societies own the tombs. The actual real estate."

"The land, too? Really? Some of the buildings are right on campus."

"I don't know, but I think they're private property. We'd probably need to get New Haven PD involved, be my guess." The supervisor shakes his head. "I don't think this has come up recently. Talk to Limerick. He may know something. We may have some agreement in place with the societies for emergency access."

"Who do we contact for permission? Do we have phone numbers? Do we just go knock on the doors?"

"Limerick. If anyone knows, it's him. Is he in today? If not, call him at home."

Jeff Limerick had been on the campus police force since the early seventies. He was the unofficial department historian. If he wasn't at work, he was at home crafting an architectural model of one of Yale's buildings. That was his passion.

The desk clerk interrupts. "You should see this, sir." She walks behind the supervisor's desk and begins moving his mouse. She rotates the monitor to face them.

"*YDN* website," she says.

Yale Daily News. The student-run campus newspaper.

The headline reads, "Tap Gone Bad? Something Wrong at Skull & Bones?"

The paper is reporting rumors of an initiation ceremony that had gone awry at the most prominent of the school's secret societies. It is a "developing story" based on an anonymous tip.

The supervisor turns to the officer. "Get me a list of Skull & Bones members. Current ones and the new taps."

The officer opens both hands, palms up. He says, "How?"

"During pre-tap, lists circulate. Pre-tap was a week ago. The kids always have some idea who will be tapped. Get hold of those lists. This year's and last. The masters may be able to help."

Sam

I had no trouble locating the white Suburban in front of the hotel. The drive to the Calderón compound took twenty minutes.

Julio set me up in front of a large Apple laptop on the second floor in a screened-in room that was the size of a racquetball court. Maybe a couple of racquetball courts. The view was as distracting a thing as I had ever seen in my life. The sky, the water, the skyline of Miami, a pool, a fountain, the boats, the flowers, the bridges.

I thought, *View porn.*

I started my research with Andrew's iPhone. The recent call history seemed unremarkable. No calls to or from his sister's cell phone for over forty-eight hours. Andrew had received a text from Jane Thursday afternoon. Jane had written, "Secrets are so not my thing."

Andrew had replied, "Duh."

"What secrets, Jane?" I asked the empty room. The room ignored me. I began making notes on a yellow legal pad.

I browsed Andrew's email records—the kid had his iPhone set to consolidate half a dozen different addresses—and eyed the last couple of weeks' additions to his photo library. Nothing stood out, other than the fact that the kid was too immature by a factor of four to even consider getting married.

How I handled that news with Carmen was going to be a whole different question.

I moved on to Ann's computer. One of my ex-wife Sherry's ex-boyfriends had bought Simon a Mac laptop for Christmas the previous year so my son could carry it between houses when he switched between his parents' residences. I had toyed with the machine a little bit while Simon was setting up a home network, but that was the totality of what I knew about Macs.

Ann's password let me right in.

Jane emailed and texted her mother regularly.

Thursday afternoon, by text, Jane had written, "Sooo excited wish me luck, lusm."

"lusm"?

Later Thursday, "Almost there, lusm."

Finally, "At Beinecke, so wish I could tell you more, maybe soon, lusm."

I opened a browser and tracked down a Facebook page for each of the kids. Nothing popped that told me anything that I needed to know that morning.

My phone vibrated. I didn't recognize the number on caller ID. "Purdy," I said.

"It's Ann. I called Carmen to get your number. She thinks you're on the golf course. She's stir-crazy and she sends her love. She wants you to call her when you get a second. I didn't tell her about this . . . situation. I hope you understand. You're all set up? Do you have everything you need?"

"I'm good. Great. Nice house."

"Thank you. It's . . . Ronnie's home, mostly. Well, I'm in the car. I need you to know that Ronnie's heading your way—some work emergency. He'll be there in maybe ten minutes. I'm trying to arrive a few minutes ahead of him in case I need to run interference for you. You probably won't see him, but if you do, I—"

"What would you like me to tell him?"

"Julio will be bringing you a bandage. You fell and hurt your wrist. Asked to borrow my computer. Can you do that?"

"Yes."

"You are such a doll. If I ever develop a thing for cops, Sam Purdy, you are going to be at the top of my list."

I didn't know how to respond.

"Don't worry. I told Carmen the same thing. She laughed. We agreed you're pretty cute."

I still didn't know how to respond. "Ann, two quick questions: One, what is 'l-u-s-m'? Jane uses it in her texts to you."

"Love you so much."

"Sweet. Second, what was Jane being so secretive about on Thursday afternoon? She mentioned something about it in her text messages to you and in another one to her brother."

Ann didn't answer right away. "I'm not supposed to say. I'm not even supposed to know."

"What? I don't understand. Know what?"

Ann lowered her voice to a range that evoked conspiracy. "Jane was tapped, Sam. She's in a secret society at school. Like . . . a special club. Private. Invitation only. Very secret. All hush-hush."

"But she told you about it?"

Ann sighed. It was an of-course-she-did-I'm-her-mother sigh. "A while ago she heard that she would probably get tapped. Last week, there was this thing on campus called 'pre-tap' and she found out she was almost certain to get tapped. During tap week there are these lists that get emailed around. Her name was on some of the lists for one of the societies. She sent me a picture of the building where the society meets, but didn't tell me the name of it. I don't know many details. She thought she might be able to tell me more this weekend, after their meeting. She thought it would be like an initiation, but she doesn't really know the rules—what she can do. Say."

"That's the meeting that was Thursday night? The one that caused her to miss the party on the yacht?"

"Yes. And then there's another meeting thing on Sunday. That's the usual schedule, she says. Thursday, Sunday. That's why she has to be back at school." Ann waited for me to say something. When I didn't, she said, "The note I got doesn't have anything to do with Jane getting tapped, Sam. I'm sure."

"Explain 'tapped.' What does that mean?"

"Chosen. Selected."

"How can you be so sure this is all unrelated to the note?"

"I don't know exactly, but . . . Because the fact that she's been tapped is supposed to be secret. How would the person who wrote the note know about it?"

I saw the logic, but wasn't convinced by it. Too much temporal coincidence to ignore. "You said Jane kind of knew she would be tapped beforehand, right? During, what did you call it, pre-tap? If she knew, if there were lists, then other people could know. Are you confident that the damn note you got wasn't part of the initiation?"

"Is the cursing necessary, Sam? And no, I don't think it was part of the initiation."

"Excuse me. Where was this Thursday night meeting?"

"In the tomb, I guess. But I don't know which one."

"Tomb?"

Ann sighed. She sighed a lot, at least with me.

I said, "Ann, remember what I said earlier about how things will go better if I don't have to guess what things mean? It's true now, too. I don't have a context for all this. I went to St. Cloud State in Minnesota. The only thing secret was how we got our fake IDs."

"There are these buildings. . . ." She sighed. "Have you ever been to Yale, Sam?" she asked.

Before I had a chance to tell her that I had never been to Yale, or even to Connecticut, she said, "I'm pulling up the driveway now. See you in two minutes. I will explain."

Ann breezed into the sunroom as though she hadn't a care in the world.

She dropped the air of invulnerability the moment she saw that I was alone. "I beat Ronnie home, thank goodness. But I'm sure he's right behind me. Did Julio—" She glanced at my wrapped wrist. "I see he did. Good."

"Ann, in case the guy who wrote the note has some way to monitor you this weekend—"

Her cell phone intruded by playing the opening few bars of "Nine to Five."

She held up a finger toward me.

I was about to make an argument to her that if she didn't hear from her daughter very soon, I thought it would be better if I worked from the hotel, not her house. We shouldn't make it easy for anyone to connect the two of us.

"One second," she said. "Every time it rings, I'm hoping it's Jane." She checked the screen. "Says, 'Out of Area.' Maybe she did borrow someone's phone. Right?"

I watched hope invade before her eyes closed softly, as though in prayer.

She opened her eyes, mouthed, *Be Jane,* pressed a spot on the phone's screen, raised the phone to her ear, and said, "Hello."

The patrol supervisor at the Yale University Police is beginning to get aggravated.

The only common ground among the three missing kids is that they each have at least one friend who says they were tapped the night before. Two were tapped for Book & Snake. One for Skull & Bones.

The patrol officer who has been running down information on the secret societies walks back into the building.

He says, "I have tap lists for Skull & Bones and Book & Snake for this year and last. Nothing official. I even have a couple for Scroll & Key. For last year, we're good, the lists are pretty consistent with each other. For this year, one doesn't agree with the next—they're close, but not the same.

"Limerick says the tombs are privately owned, even the ones with real estate on campus." The officer starts reading from notes. "Ownership is obscure. Difficult to track. Shell corporations. Trusts, like that. Jurisdiction is 'complicated.' His word. He thinks getting permission to enter any of them will be a 'nightmare.' Again, Limerick's word. He's sure we'll end up needing a warrant and 'probable cause squared.' He said to remind you that there are very powerful people all over the country who will absolutely not want us to see what goes on inside those buildings. He stressed the 'very powerful' part. Reputations are at stake. He expects that they will use all their influence to 'thwart us.' His words."

The shift supervisor mouths, *Fuck me.* Out loud, he says, "My words."

"Officer Cirillo went to both tombs. Nobody answered. No big surprise. It's Friday afternoon. As far as we know, no one lives in either building. The tap festivities should have ended by the time he got there. The societies keep a pretty firm Thursday and Sunday night schedule."

"Phone numbers?"

"We got numbers from the university. I called. Left messages for someone to call me ASAP. I'm not holding my breath."

"Emergency contacts?"

"The most recent ones the university has are from 1999. I left messages."

"I know—you're not holding your breath."

The officer shrugs. "We don't have grounds for a warrant. Not even close."

"I'll call New Haven PD and alert Yale Security. Put a patrol outside both tombs. To observe. If someone goes in or comes out, I want to know."

"*YDN?* Any updates?"

"Just that rumor of a tap injury. We're monitoring the website. DUH hasn't heard anything about any injured students. Neither has Yale Hospital, or New Haven PD."

Dee and Poe

Poe was watching Deirdre pack her suitcase. The counterterrorism coordination conference was over. The country was safer. Had to be. It was time for Dee to go back to Virginia. To G.B. Jerry.

She had tuned the television to Fox News. Considering the previous day's developments on campus in New Haven, the situation in Connecticut was the story of the day. From all appearances, the only story of the day.

"Where are you heading next, Poe?" she asked.

They'd skipped their dive bar ritual the night before. Dee had wanted to go to a movie. While they walked the quiet streets afterward, he had told her that prior to the meeting in Philly he had been in Savannah, Georgia, for a couple of weeks. Before that, Sante Fe, New Mexico. During their time together he had mentioned ports a couple of times. If she were forced to guess, she would have guessed he was heading next to some harbor for some soon-to-be-fruitless investigation. Norfolk, San Diego. Seattle.

Ports.

She didn't know how Poe did what he did. Alone on the road all the time. She also didn't know if he would ever heal enough to get it together to do anything else.

She busied herself folding her underwear into neat little triangles.

Poe was dividing his attention between the television and Dee's deliberate packing. He was growing bored by the same static shot of nothing happening at the front of the Greek temple building at Yale and was perversely fascinated by the precision with which Dee folded her panties and bras.

Even though their network's cameras were pointed at the Book & Snake tomb, the studio anchors were entertaining their viewers, or at least themselves, with stories from movies they had seen that featured Skull & Bones, the most prominent secret society at Yale. One of the studio personalities made a less-than-sincere attempt at keeping the whole thing honest by reminding viewers that the stories they were telling might not be true, seeing as they came from the movies.

Not one of the three people chatting away, however, seemed to be at all disconcerted that the stories they were telling were, even if true, not in the least relevant, since the tomb that was the focus of all the current news attention was Book & Snake, not Skull & Bones.

Poe was more amused than appalled by their act. He thought it was the journalistic equivalent of pointing out locations on a map of New Hampshire because you didn't happen to have one of Connecticut.

Three times in one minute one of the anchors repeated the apparent scoop that Bob Woodward has been a member of Book & Snake. They had a call in to Mr. Woodward, they asserted, seeking confirmation and a comment.

Poe said, "They're reading Wikipedia."

Dee, who Poe knew could get defensive about Fox News, said, "How do you know that, Poe?"

He displayed his BlackBerry. "Because I'm reading Wikipedia. Same stuff."

She made a face at him and returned her attention to her underwear.

The weekend anchors seemed genuinely perplexed about why Bob hadn't called them back live. The whole concept behind a "secret society"—especially the "secret" part—seemed to be eluding them.

A blond woman who Poe had already decided spent more time applying makeup than she did reading current events added, "And now Garry Trudeau, too." She nodded knowingly.

Poe raised his BlackBerry again. He said, "Want to bet it's more Wikipedia? I'll check."

Dee growled.

The anchor chose that moment to go all editorial. "I mean . . . really. That tells you something, doesn't it? Garry Trudeau? If it's true, right? And we have no reason to doubt our sources. What are we talking about exactly? You know? Well, I repeat . . . We have learned—we do understand—that it's also possible that Garry Trudeau; yes, the *Doonesbury* Garry Trudeau, one and the same, was also a member of Book & Snake. Maybe even *is* a member of Book & Snake."

Under his breath Poe grumbled, "Looks like it's actually Scroll & Key. It's also possible that Garry Trudeau's a member of the Masons. Or the astronaut corps. Maybe he's even a Pussycat Doll."

Dee heard the part about the Pussycat Doll. She said, "What?"

Poe said, "Nothing, baby." He leaned back onto an elbow and smiled at her. He'd concluded that the triangulation of Dee's panties was much more interesting than what was currently on television.

Dee said, "Apparently, my old boss is a member."

"What? Who?"

"Porter Goss. I just got an email. Apparently, he's a member of Book & Snake, too."

Poe didn't get that email. He was guessing it was from G.B. Jerry. "Really? Director of the CIA? That is interesting. Maybe you should call Fox and let them know. They can call him for a comment."

Dee widened her eyes and flared her nostrils in consternation at Poe.

Poe memorized the expression for later playback. He was about to ask Dee, *Why on earth did you bring so much underwear?* when sudden motion on the screen caught his eye. "There's a kid," he said. "Out front. Look." He raised his chin toward the television.

"Well," Dee said. She stopped what she was doing. "I guess that means those kids are really in there." She scrambled down to the end of the bed, closer to the screen, an unfolded purple lace bra dangling from her left hand.

Poe didn't remember seeing that bra. On her. Or coming off her.

They watched the young man try to gain his bearings outside the Greek building in New Haven. Dee put on her Company hat. She said, "He's been in the dark. Maybe even hooded. Look at his eyes. Look at him blinking. He's trying to adjust to the light." She paused. "Or it could just be dark in there. There aren't any windows. Is the power off? Do you know?"

"His wrists are red, too," Poe said. "See the bands? He's been restrained. Shackled, maybe. Not," he paused, "good signs."

"Shut the hell up," she said.

Dee wasn't shushing Poe—she was talking to the network anchors who had accelerated their mindless patter.

The young man's clear words broke through.

". . . I am a bomb. Stay where you are."

That shut the anchors up. Below the image of the terrorized young man the crawl on the screen read, "*Doonesbury* creator in Book & Snake?"

"Shit." Poe no longer cared a whit about Garry Trudeau. He scampered down the length of the mattress to sit beside Dee at the foot of the bed. She took his hand, placed it on her knee, and put her hand on top of his.

The kid lifted his shirt, displaying a rectangular pack that was taped around his waist. The camera briefly zoomed in on some comic book lettering on the tape.

BOMB

Dee said, "That's not real."

Poe said, "It's real." His tone was not at all contrary.

"How can you be so sure?" Dee asked.

He wasn't sure how he could be so sure. He could, literally, smell it. He was self-aware enough to recognize that his sudden olfactory prowess wasn't a good thing. He touched her lips with two fingers without taking his eyes from the screen.

Poe said, "This is not good. So not good."

The hostage began to speak. Although they could hear some of what he was saying, it was difficult for them to make out all of his words. The network microphones weren't picking up the comments from the hostage negotiator at all.

"Cell towers . . . cameras . . ." Poe whispered along as the kid's voice broke through in fits and starts. When the young man said, "You have five minutes," Poe pressed the button on his wrist that launched the stopwatch.

"What, Poe? What?" Dee asked.

He touched her lips again.

The negotiator was speaking, but they couldn't hear her.

Suddenly, the woman's voice jumped into the mix. It was a clear sound, a compassionate voice.

She invited the hostage taker to come outside.

She waited only briefly for a reply before she inquired whether anyone inside was injured. She offered medical help.

"She's going by the book," Poe said, shaking his head. "He's not. Can she really not know that?"

"Who's not?" Dee asked.

"The unsub."

The unknown subject. The guy inside. The "he."

The young man started speaking once more. His words were halting. It took him almost thirty seconds to say "He is not here to negotiate about anything. Anything."

Dee and Poe were riveted as the negotiator responded.

They each held their breath as the kid said he would die in three minutes.

The young man blinked twice. Dee said, "Was that important? Those blinks?"

Poe shook his head. The kid shifted his weight from his left foot to his right foot, and then back. Poe said, "I can't tell."

The negotiator asked the hostage his name.

She asked how many other hostages were inside.

Then she asked, "Is it only one man in there?"

The silence felt cruel. Seconds were becoming minutes. Too fast.

Poe could tell that the negotiator was moving from bullet point to bullet point. He was thinking, *You're not seeing what's happening. The protocols are for shit. You need to come back to this stuff later. Give him what he wants. Now.*

The young man blinked two more times.

Poe said, "He did it again. Dee? Any idea what that means?"

Dee shook her head. "Don't know, baby." Her voice was hollow.

The negotiator asked, "What does he want? The man . . . inside?"

Poe said, "Good question."

"Two minutes," said the young man.

"Did you see that? His fingers?" Dee said.

"I missed it. What?" Poe asked.

"He extended an index finger on each hand. One plus one? Is that it? For two minutes?"

Poe pressed his body closer to Dee. He required the contact. They sat silently, transfixed. The kid bowed his head. Frustration? Resignation? Neither of them was sure.

Poe jumped forward suddenly, his eyes within a foot of the screen. He pointed directly at the screen, his finger an inch from the glass. "Look at the kid's left ear. He's wearing a piece. A good one. See it, Dee? It's almost invisible. The kid is being told what to say. In real time. Whoa."

Dee said, "Bluetooth? Impressive." Her voice was an amalgam of sarcasm and irony, any admiration she was feeling for the unsub's tech skills solidly in check.

When the kid said, "I will die in one minute," Dee turned away from the screen.

Poe glanced down at his watch. He thought, *Yes, one minute*.

He felt disembodied.

Poe had started floating. He was able to look down and see himself sitting beside Dee on the bed. It was as though he was watching them from a little blimp.

He knew it was a bad, bad sign.

Dee resumed watching the hostage's torment. Her anxiety was cresting. She said, "Can they get this done in time? Get the cell towers back up? Do you know anything about this stuff, Poe? How long does it take to get a tower running after it's down? Is one minute enough?"

"It doesn't matter," Poe said. He was tempted to ask Dee to grab his feet and tug him back down to the floor. He didn't ask. He knew it would freak her out.

Dee was offended. "What do you mean it doesn't matter? What if that bomb is real?"

"The bomb is real. But it doesn't matter what they do about the cell towers. This isn't a demand to do something. It's just a lesson. The unsub is teaching us who he is."

Deirdre's big-picture training was failing her in the microcosm that was the building in New Haven and the kid and the bomb and the unsub. She said, "What do you mean, 'a lesson'? The cell tower thing is the only demand, right? How can it not matter?"

"Because that—whether or not the cell tower becomes active in time—would involve a degree of chance. Something that is beyond the control of the unsub. Unless I'm seriously misreading him, this unsub isn't about to leave anything to chance.

"This is his first contact with us, with the world, in what . . . two days? Think about it as his introduction. He's been in there with those kids since Thursday night. He's had plenty of time to plan this, to get it exactly the way he wants it. He's spelling out who he is. How he works. How he thinks. How this is going to come down.

"Mostly, though, he's telling us who is in charge."

Dee was having trouble keeping distance from what she was seeing. One moment, she was a woman trying to mend parallel rips in her heart. A woman folding her underwear, preparing to leave her lover for another year, preparing to return to her husband for another year. The next moment she was an international terrorism expert trying to make sense of the most spare information. She knew from experience that the solid transformation back to intelligence analyst would come more naturally in the hours after she parted with Poe.

Many years of Aprils leaving Poe behind had convinced her that she was a better counterterrorism analyst around Jerry. A better woman around Poe.

"Come on, Poe. Look at that . . . Listen to what he said about—"

"This isn't a kidnapping, baby." He reached out to her, comforted that she was actually there. He put his arm around her waist, pulled her tight to him. She curled into him willingly. "This isn't some . . .

crazy college hostage situation. Check the calendar. This is April . . .
April. Again."

She visualized the roster in her head.

Waco. Oklahoma City. Columbine. Virginia Tech.

She knew what month it was.

"Oh my God. Oh, Poe. Holy . . . ," she said. "Holy . . ."

Before this trip Poe had never heard Dee use the word "holy" that
way. It was something new, something he didn't understand about her.
The previous day, he'd asked her about it once, after the movie. She
just shook her head.

He planned to ask her about it again.

The screen shot divided in two. One half of the split screen was the
same shot of the kid in front of the building.

Poe thought he saw something in the kid's eyes that made it clear
he already knew his future. Poe's brain registered an important fact:
The bomb on the hostage's waist wasn't bound with shrapnel. The
bomb had only one intended victim.

Why?

The other half of the screen was a long shot of commotion, people
scrambling, officers waving, pushing.

People were running, but they didn't know why. Someone yelled,
"Bomb! Run!"

Poe looked at his watch.

4:54.
4:55.
4:56.

The explosion caused the screen to flash white and the sound to
roar into static before it went quiet.

Poe's first reaction was unfiltered PTSD. Reflexes on overdrive. A molten hammer whacked at supersonic speed onto the tendon on the front of his knee.

He jumped to his left, covering Dee with his body. Together they crashed to the floor. He shrouded her face with his head and his hands, waiting for the ceiling to fall, for the walls to tip. For gravity to enforce its domain.

For the fabric of the universe to rip.

Poe's five senses collapsed onto one another in a vortex of stimuli overload. His brain tried to filter through the chaos and cacophony of quadraphonic Oklahoma City immersion.

Drowning, suffocating, gasping.

BP rocketing. Pulse rocketing. Palms sweaty. Vomit in his mouth. Instincts in rapid waves.

He had to get to the stairs. Had to. Not a plan, *an imperative.* Stairs. He had to get down. Fast as he could. Had to get to four.

Had to get to—

With Dee.

With Dee?

He caught himself. *Breathe, breathe.*

Dee?

He recognized the anomaly.

Dee.

He fought the panic. Corralled the instinct.

Tried to move. He could. *Huh?*

He breathed. Exhaled before he inhaled.

Tasted the air for smoke.

Instead of fumes he tasted Dee's hair directly below him. He inhaled the aroma. He knew that smell. He loved that smell.

It calmed him as though she had shampooed it in Xanax.

*   *   *

Dee was under him, his full weight almost crushing her slight body. She didn't fight to push him off. She held him tightly, her arms crossed behind his back. She was desperate to keep him from falling through her into some abyss in the earth.

Finally, he rolled off of her onto the carpet, onto his back, his arms splayed to the sides.

She straddled him. "Poe? Poe?" she cried. When he blinked a few times and she could feel his chest rising below her, she leaned down into him, her arms around his neck. Her voice became a whisper. She said, "Oh, baby baby. It's okay. Everything . . . is . . ."

"The kid is dead?" Poe asked.

"Yes, yes," she said.

"What day is it, Dee? Is it Saturday?"

"It's Saturday."

"What happened on Friday? All day Friday?"

"Bad things in New Haven, baby. But we were together, baby. We were together. Remember?"

"No, inside that building. What happened in there all day Friday?"

Sam

Ann didn't have to say a word.

I've been a cop for a long time. The transformation I saw in her face as she processed the first sounds in her ear from the call she'd received on her cell is a thing I've seen on a dozen or so other faces over the years. In the fleeting moment that it takes for life's routine to be replaced by the disarray of despair and for hope to be swapped with horror, the eyes seem to learn the news before the rest of the face suspects a thing.

It's a cascade of anguish as the rumor spreads. The eyes go wide before the brows rise in protest. The corners of the mouth flatten before the cheekbones drop even a millimeter. Tears form before the skin closest to the lips begins to quiver.

At some point there is an audible gasp, then a catch as the lungs revolt at air that is beginning to feel toxic. For that moment, oxygen stops flowing in, carbon dioxide stops flowing out. Moments later, when the respiratory system kicks into gear with its determined preference for toxic air over no air at all, some people exhale before they risk another inhale. Some suck a packet of air in a quick little rush before their lungs begin to constrict and collapse all over again from the weight of what they've just learned.

I'm accustomed to being the bearer of bad tidings. I will introduce myself, usually at the front door. In the reception office at their job. I'm a police detective, I say.

Sometimes it's in the ER. Worst option is on the phone.

But that's all prelude.

"There's been an accident," I might say next. "There was a shooting," I might say instead.

"I'm so sorry for your loss," I always, always say at some point before I'm done.

On those days, I hate my job.

Ann placed the phone on the table in front of her. When she looked back up at me, I saw sparks of fear and an inclination to cower spilling from her eyes like slag leaching from steel. What was left in her eyes was rage and determination.

I have a friend in the town of Loveland, back in Colorado. He's an ex-cop who walked away from the job the day before his seventeenth anniversary. He apprenticed to become a blacksmith, laboring primarily for the many sculptors who have transformed Loveland's cultural landscape from Valentine's Day cutesy-pie to serious art. I love to hang with him while he works, watch him in his foundry. He loves to explain how the steel he pounds gets stronger the more he stresses it. As he fires and hammers and works the raw metal, as he heats it, pounds it, heats it, shapes it, pounds it more, he slowly squeezes the impurities from the steel.

That's the slag.

Ann was getting worked like my friend's steel. And like his steel, she was getting stronger.

She extended her left index finger and touched the screen on her phone. A voice came alive for me to hear.

She pulled her hands back toward her chest, away from the phone, as though another touch might cause it to ignite, or to explode.

". . . wondering, this call means exactly what you think it means." A pause—three seconds, four—was intended to allow Ann to digest the first reality. "You have ten seconds to move to a place you can listen without interruption."

Ann said, "I can talk right now. Is she okay? Is my daughter all right?" At that point her composure cracked. "Oh God. Dear Lord. Is she okay?"

Ann, I recognized, didn't realize she was listening to a recording. Not to a live person.

I didn't interrupt to tell her. That could wait. I was holding my breath while my brain arranged the data. It was a male voice. Accent? I wasn't sure. But . . . maybe. Tone? Authoritative without being overtly threatening.

Did I hear fatigue? I thought yes. I knew it might be wishful thinking on my part.

The message was generic, not specific to Jane. If other kids were involved, their parents would listen to this same recording.

Ann? Surprisingly composed.

"The next time you hear from me, you will be prepared to discuss what you have to offer. The value of your offer must be commensurate with what is at risk. We both know what is at risk."

Commensurate? Well, I thought.

"I don't understand. Tell me what you want," Ann pleaded.

The man spoke over her words. "This is not about money. I am uninterested in your riches."

Ann jumped in. "I don't want to guess. A clue, please. Some guidance. Please! Whatever you want."

"A reminder: Tell nobody. You do not want to disappoint me."

That was how the phone call ended.

My heart was thumping.

Ann's mouth hung open. Her eyes were wide and wet. Lingering in the background, above the horizon of her corneas, I was relieved to see the continued glint of steel.

From behind us, from the direction of the door that led back to the house, a full tenor chimed in, startling me. "Tell no one what? Bunny? What is it? Is there another surprise? How could this get any better? My parents? They couldn't be more proud."

Ann looked at me. Without missing a beat, she said, "Sam Purdy? You remember my husband, Ronaldo? The proud father of the groom-to-be."

"Samuel, Samuel, of course," he said. "Dios mío. What on earth did you do to your wrist?"

I slid Andrew's phone into my pocket as I stood up to shake Ronaldo Angel Calderón's hand. "I am missing a chance for one of the best golf experiences of my life, unfortunately. Your kind wife has been generous enough to set me up so I can catch up on some work. A small consolation. I've never felt so well taken care of in my life."

He smiled graciously. "We are honored at your company. Anything you need. Our house is yours."

"And now," Ann said, "I do have to get back to my other guests. Ronnie, will you be long here?"

He made a dismissive gesture with his right hand. "A couple of calls. I may need to stop by the office. I will be back at the club before the first group finishes the front nine. Any word from my Jane? Her grandmother is so eager to see her."

Ann smiled at her husband with a degree of warmth that confounded me. "Not yet. I'll let you know the moment I hear from her. You go, take care of business. I'll see you at the club."

She still had the rebar.

The New Haven police lieutenant—Haden Moody—summons Christine Carmody to the Mobile Command vehicle that is parked on Grove Street across from the law school. Joey Blanks delivers the message to her.

She is reluctant to leave her post. She feels cemented to the spot where she was standing before the explosion, before she took cover behind the cruiser. She fears that walking away before the last drop of blood had been photographed or the last speck of Jonathan's tissue has been identified and retrieved would be an act of disrespect.

Evidence markers form a rough semicircle in front of the tomb. The cones and tents identify the locations where human remains and explosive debris have been discovered. The coroner is directing collection of the remains. Forensic detectives are cataloguing each precise spot where nonhuman debris is located.

Every spare officer is helping to set up portable screens to block the view of the death scene from the eyes and long lenses of the curious crowds. Onlookers have been pushed back to a more distant perimeter. The cemetery has been cleared of everyone who is not already buried.

Joey Blanks waits a respectful interval before he repeats the lieutenant's order to Carmody. She closes her eyes, hoping to find some composure. Finally she acknowledges Joey and begins the march toward the big vehicle.

Someone hands her a bottle of cold water the moment she gets in the door. She sets the bottle down two seconds later.

"Tough start," says the lieutenant, noting her entrance. "Nobody could have seen that coming."

She counts seven people in the bus. She knows all but one. She thinks she smells fed. She eyes the stranger until the woman looks away.

I saw it coming, Carmody is thinking. *Maybe not the speed that it happened, but I felt it going south, saw the bad outcome.*

"Yeah," she says. She's tempted to wonder aloud, in front of the witnesses inside the command center, who the hell had ordered the cell towers to be turned off in the first place. She resists. That would be her rage talking. There would be time for that later.

Lieutenant Haden Moody turns away from the computer monitor. On the screen is a shot of the front of the building. He could see the same thing by looking out the window.

Carmody literally bites her tongue.

A forensic detective enters the vehicle. "Sir?" He's holding a digital camera. "You should see this."

Moody nods at the image on the camera's screen. "Is that what I think it is?"

Carmody can tell that Moody has no idea what he's seeing.

The forensic specialist saves him. "It's part of an earpiece. The curved part there fits over the ear. The rest is . . . We haven't found it yet. It's a good one, maybe Bluetooth. It was located sixty-three feet from the blast site. On the edge of the sidewalk. Right there." He changes the image on the screen and then uses the tip of a pencil to focus the commander's attention on a detail in the new photograph. "We think that smudge on it is blood. The victim's. We think the kid was wearing the earpiece when he . . . died."

"Which means what?"

Carmody waits two seconds for someone to walk her boss through the evidence. No one volunteers. She is far from surprised. She says, "It means those weren't his words he was speaking to me. He was being fed."

"The guy in the tomb?" the lieutenant says.

In his long history on the force, Haden Moody has never been the guy with the quickest answer. But he's rarely been the guy with the wrong answer. That's why he's the one driving this bus this day. He's the tortoise. All the hares came up lame at least once along the way.

Moody's reputation as a detective was that he was a successful plodder. Since his promotion to lieutenant, though, almost all the troops think he was a better detective than he is a boss.

Moody rubs his forehead with the heels of both hands. The three people inside the vehicle who know him best recognize the warning sign, and take involuntary steps back. He barks, "Give us a moment. Everybody."

Almost everyone starts to exit. Moody says, "Wait."

They all stop.

"The earpiece you found? That news doesn't leave this command center. Are you clear on that?" He directs his next comment to the forensic detective. "Make sure your guys keep this quiet."

"Sir."

"Go on. Get out of here." Everyone but Jack Lobatini moves to the door.

Moody says, "Jack?" Everyone stops again. Statues. It's beginning to feel like an absurd version of Simon Says. "Everybody is everybody. You, too, Jack. Watch the tomb for Christine. Couple of minutes."

Lobatini is surprised. He's not accustomed to being excluded from Moody's orbit. But he nods and follows his colleagues. He pauses one more time before he pulls the door closed behind him.

When Moody looks up at Carmody, his eyes are fire. "What is this, Christine? We go five minutes into this mess and we have a dead kid? Live fucking cable. What the hell we got on our hands here? What the fuck in hell do we got on our hands here?"

His fury is on the loose. She catches her own retaliatory rage as it rears up trying to escape its quarantine. She wrestles it silently until she subdues it. Even if her boss's anger won't wait, hers must. "I don't know, sir. I've never seen one start this way."

"Ever heard about one starting this way?"

"Never," she says.

"What's he want? Now that the cell towers are up maybe we'll get some demands from him? You think? Is that the way this goes down?"

"Sure," she says. The prediction makes perfect sense to her, but something tells her that a fresh demand isn't what is coming next. In Carmody's current universe "perfect sense" has exploded along with Jonathan Simmons.

Moody knows Carmody well. He can sense her reluctance. "You're not buying it, Christine. How come?"

"Contain is now a major problem, sir. The guy even thinks we cut off his cell access? He kills a kid. So how do we manage contain going forward? What if we shut down his access for real? God knows what he does. He'll kill another kid."

Moody stares at her. He didn't call Carmody in so she could enlist him to deal with *her* problems. He called her in so she would deal with *his* problems.

She tightens her lips, drawing them inward for a second or two before she releases them. She says, "He could have had that young man—Jonathan Simmons—make a demand, ask us for something, anything, a gazillion dollars, a tricked-out seven-forty-seven, a magic carpet, a harem, world peace, anything. He could have used the kid to start negotiations with us. Right then, right there.

"He had our attention, that's for sure. We've been waiting to hear from him, right? But he sends the kid out to tell us to flip a switch and, what, that he wants the cameras to stay? That's it. He doesn't tell us what he really wants. He wasn't starting negotiations with us. I'm not convinced he's ready to start negotiations. He sent Jonathan Simmons out only to give us a warning."

"What? Don't mess with my cell phone?"

"No, sir. The message was 'Don't fuck with me.'"

Moody whips his arm forward, hurling a Sharpie against the wall. He pops to his feet. "God in heaven. He blew that kid away to say 'Don't fuck with me'? The fuck. I'll fucking find a way to fuck right back with him." The lieutenant kicks a plastic trash can against a desk before he sits back down. He slumps in the chair. He runs four fingers through his hair.

Hade Moody is more than a little vain. He straightens his tie. Lifts his chin. Checks his chin with his palm for stray spittle.

Moody lowers his voice. "What then? What's our next step? We wait? Is that it? What are our options? We wait? Do we have any fucking choices here?"

Carmody answers as though the question isn't rhetorical. "Tactically, sir, our hands are tied. At least for the moment. We don't have reliable intelligence. We don't know the number of hostages in that building. We don't know their condition. We don't know how they're being held, what rooms. Together? Separate? We don't know the number of hostage takers. We don't know what we're facing in terms of weaponry."

He glares at her. "We know they have fucking bombs."

"Yes, sir. We do know that. Now. Despite all we don't know, there are a number of safe assumptions we can make about our subject. We have an organized subject, sir. This is not an impulsive or opportunistic hostage taking. He is demonstrating effective control of the circumstances and of his hostages. We have a sophisticated subject, sir. He was using wireless electronics to communicate with us through the young man. We have a subject with knowledge of explosives. We have a subject with access to explosives. We have a ruthless subject. He killed an innocent young man for no apparent reason other than to show us he could, and that he would."

"What's your next move, Christine?"

Fuck you, Hade, she thinks. But out loud, she says, "I heard the feds are on the way. Is that true?"

Moody mouths the word *fuck*. He didn't want to be the one to tell her the FBI is coming to town. "Whether we want them or not, yeah, they are. Supreme Court justice's kid? Secretary of the army's kid? Chief fought to keep them away—but he was overruled. We'll see them soon. Jack probably has their ETA."

"We're history the moment they get here," Christine says.

Moody nods. "They're sending HRT," Moody says. "The whole shebang."

Christine has colleagues in other departments who have dealt with the Hostage Rescue Team, but she has never seen them in action.

Moody's voice is beginning to lose its thrust. "When they're here, they're here. If we're history in an hour, so be it. But for now? What are our choices?"

The Siege · 91

She decides not to assume he understands the situation. "We're new to this event. The subject is not. We've been set up here for what? A few hours? Watching the building for less than a day? He's not new to this. He's been planning this for God-knows-how-long, and he's been holding those kids—however many there are—for almost forty hours, since Thursday evening. During that time he hasn't made a single demand. Not a peep. We have nothing concrete to link him to what happened yesterday on campus. Up until a few minutes ago, he's said not one word to us. Or to anyone else."

"He's fucking talking now," Moody says.

Christine is determined not to be distracted by Moody's too-predictable show. "Actually, he's not. Talking. Communicating through his hostages puts us at a distinct disadvantage." She waits for Moody to nod an acknowledgment. "So far, he's not going public either—there's nothing online from him that we can find. There's no propaganda being broadcast. Nothing. He's been the church mouse. Until he sent Jonathan Simmons out that door, I will admit to you, sir, that I wasn't even completely convinced we had a hostage situation inside that building. Up until I saw that young man at the top of the stairs, I would have bet my own money that the damn secret society was up to something they'd end up being sorry about."

Moody has started glaring at her. It's one of his leadership things. When he's stumped, he glares. It drives everybody in his command batshit. Even Jack.

She looks down, away. She knows he won't stop glaring until she averts her eyes. The lieutenant is a large guy. Not for the first time, Carmody finds herself amazed at how big his feet are.

Moody says, "Tell me what you think it means that he's so quiet?"

She pulls her eyes from his feet. "With all due respect, what does any of it mean? Where does any of this fit? Hostage situations fall into only a few categories. Some criminal activity has gone bad—a bank robbery or a burglary is interrupted before the getaway—and the bad guy takes hostages to try to gain control over a rapidly deteriorating situation. Is that what we have here? Doesn't look desperate to me.

We don't have reports of any criminal activity in the tomb prior to this event. Do we?"

Her question is a challenge. She is asking if he is being straight with her.

Moody swats away her not-so-subtle indictment. He says, "We don't know about that stuff yesterday. But it was far away from Book & Snake."

Christine continues. "More typical for us? For our team? A domestic situation goes sour. One family member holds another family member. A knife, a gun. We see those. Most of the time cooler heads prevail. That's me, right? I'm the cooler head. I talk the guy down."

"You're good at that, Christine."

She says, "The second this asshole gives me an opening, I can do it here. But that's not this. No so far. My gut says he's not going to give me a chance."

Moody laces his fingers behind his neck. "Don't like this. Don't like this."

"Rarely there's a planned thing—an intentional hostage taking. The subject wants leverage. He takes hostages to trade them for something more valuable. TV time. A cause he wants to spotlight. Politics. A prisoner he wants released. A policy he wants changed. Munich Olympics. Airline hijacking. That school in Chechnya. Like that. I read about those things. I heard about them at Quantico. We've never had one here. You know that."

"Do we have one now? Is that what you're saying, Christine?"

"We don't know. Maybe yes, maybe no. My gut says no."

"Money?"

"In this economy? Of course it could be money. People are desperate. I'm thinking it could be revenge, too. We could be giving the guy too much credit. Might be something petty that's spiraled out of control."

"Revenge for what?"

"Given the building, it could be a student who expected to be tapped, but wasn't. Feels slighted. Or it could be some secret society rivalry. Could be a student who was a previous member and felt mistreated. Somebody with a grudge."

Moody glances at her sideways. "You're thinking some slow-motion Virginia Tech thing? Is he going to slaughter all those kids?"

"I'm thinking. That's all."

"Can't have that here. Can't. These kids' parents?" The lieutenant is still tripping over money as a motive. "Jack said half of them pay the freight to send their kids here. That means there's a fifty-fifty chance the families are well-off. Loaded. Is he doing this for ransom? Is that what this is, Christine? Is he about to ask for a . . . billion dollars?"

The Hade Moody she knows was the detective who never lost track of his case. Investigating a homicide, he always had the best organized book, but never the most interesting one. Moody isn't a strategic thinker. Carmody knows she has to spell it out for him. "It's possible, sir. But if it is about money, where's the demand? What's the endgame? What amount? In what form? Delivered how? A gazillion in cash? Come on. What's he thinking? Electronic funds transfer? That's trackable."

Moody's face betrays his fear that Carmody might expect him to reply.

Christine lets him off the hook. "Has he thought it through? Is he winging it? And how the hell does he expect to get away to spend it? Because the most important thing to a hostage taker—to that guy in that building—is his getaway. The book says the subject is thinking endgame from moment one. Not this guy. Important fact: Moment one was two days ago. And—and—where are the damn demands for transportation? Why aren't we busy pretending to prepare the guy a car, or a plane?"

Moody shrugs. "You tell me."

Christine checks her aggravation level. "We—us, the good guys—the rules say we're supposed to be the ones acting like we have all the time in the world. But he's letting time leak away like he's prepared to spend forever inside that place."

Moody recognizes they've moved on to territory he understands. "He could, couldn't he? Stay in there? Indefinitely?"

"There's a big kitchen in there. Lots of supplies. Food. This isn't one of those times when we're going to sneak a bug in the door in a pizza box."

She points to the computer monitor closest to him. The entire screen is filled with the staid, classical lines of the front of the building. "You don't see any window," she says. "That means no dropping a mini-robot in to find the bad guys, search for hostages. We have exactly two access points into that place. Main doors and a basement door. Basement door stairwell is covered by a damn tarp. Want to guess what's under that tarp?"

Moody says, "Nothing good." With false assurance, he adds, "Booby trap."

Christine says, "We have to snake a camera under it. Take a look."

"Yeah. We'll do that. I'll tell Jack."

This is painful, she thinks. She returns to her earlier point. "You see any soft spots in those walls?"

"They look like big ol' stone blocks to me."

"It's no accident he's in that building, Lieutenant. We're not going to breach those walls without a tank or big-ass explosive charges. This isn't going to be any wait-till-he-falls-asleep and bust-down-the-door midnight rescue. He knows all that. And it's no accident who he has in there with him. These aren't random hostages."

Moody stands again, starts pacing in the narrow space. His broad shoulders seem to almost fill it. "Why did he blow the kid up, damn it? Why? Goddamn it. If he won't tell us what the fuck he fucking wants, what good does any of this do?"

Christine waits to see if Moody's eruption is over. She says, "He must need the cell towers to do whatever he's doing. If he needs the cell towers, we have some leverage. Not much, but some."

Moody runs his fingers through his hair again. "Keep talking."

"He could be in touch with someone outside the building. He may need information from outside. By cutting the feed, we may have cut him off."

Moody says, "We didn't cut the cell feed."

She looks into his eyes to determine if he's lying to her. She can't tell.

He feels the pressure. "You talking a true advantage?" he asks. Moody wants to change the subject and he wants to hear some good news. Even if it's minor good news.

Carmody says, "He could have accomplices outside. He could be making calls or receiving them. Using email or text. A bulletin board. The Web. We don't know. He may be using landlines. He may be wireless. He may be on the campus LAN. We need to get Yale and the wireless providers on board for help. Can you get taps? Warrants?"

The lieutenant nods twice. "Sewall is on that already," he says. Fred Sewall is the intel officer on the team. "But if we just shut everything down, the guy will blow up more kids, right?"

"Probably."

"Maybe the fuck just wanted us to know it was game on."

Carmody is relieved that Moody has finally spotted the starting line. She says, "Maybe that, Lieutenant."

She shifts her attention out the window. Back to the tomb. She is determined not to be ambushed again. "We need someone who can talk to us about that damn building. Every last detail. Floor plans, structure, electrical, plumbing, cable, everything. Fred Sewall needs to track down people who know it inside and out. A super, a member, an ex-member—I don't care. Sewers, too. Are there tunnels? Do we know if there are tunnels down there? We need a rep from the Yale physical plant to do a briefing about the utilities, the sewers, underground access. Everything."

She starts to walk out of the big converted bus. A step before she gets to the door, she detours to the tiny lavatory. The sounds of her retching fill the interior of the vehicle.

She comes out less than a minute later. She uses the sink on the adjacent counter to wash her face. She grabs the water bottle she'd set down earlier and gargles to rinse her mouth.

"I didn't want to do that outside. Damn cameras. We can't disrespect that kid."

"Yeah," Moody says. "I ordered the network cameras down the block a little. Out of bomb range. Hope to God that doesn't get another kid killed." He holds out a sheet of paper. "This came in while you were puking. List of possible hostages is up to nine. Six of them have active ATLs. Four juniors, two seniors. Now that the whole world has seen what just happened to Jonathan Simmons, we'll get more calls, too. There're more kids than that in there. You watch."

She says, "I'm sure you're right."

Moody says, "Send Jack back in here. I'll talk to him about the building."

Before Christine is able to summon Jack, the door opens and Jack rushes in. He stops halfway between the door and his boss. He points at the monitor.

He says, "Another kid just stepped outside."

Dee and Poe

Dee waited until Poe was back in the room. Back in the present.

Back in his body.

She told him she needed a little time alone. She stepped into the bathroom and started to draw a bath.

The distance from her was almost too much for Poe. While she bathed, he stood at the door so he could hear the sounds of her ablutions. As his terror subsided to pianissimo, he told her what he had decided to do next.

Dee cried silently before she returned to him.

Poe thought she looked wan. He blamed it on watching the kid die. And he blamed it on himself. Poe was hyperaware that once again she'd had to peel him off the floor. He knew he couldn't keep asking her to do that.

She stopped just outside the bathroom door with her hands on her hips. She said, "Can I talk you out of this, Poe? What you're thinking about doing?"

He forced a smile while he thought about her implied warning. He'd already decided to mount the pretense that he was more stable than he was feeling.

He was rolling a pair of pants into a fat trouser cigar. Years on the road had convinced Poe of the advantages of rolling over folding. "You know, I don't think so, Dee. Got a feeling about this one." He pounded the center of his chest twice with the thumb side of his closed fist.

She found his gesture amusing. Under her breath she sang, "Macho, macho man."

He was gratified that his clowning had earned a chuckle. He filed the memory. He knew it was a keeper.

"You okay, baby?" he said.

"Yeah," she lied. "I'm good." But she wasn't trying to disguise her concern about him. "You really think this is . . . your kind of thing? What's going on in New Haven? It doesn't fit your . . . usual parameters very well."

Dee didn't use words like "parameters" often with Poe. It got his attention. Nor did Dee make a habit of editorializing on the idiosyncrasies of Poe's work. She'd been a witness to the damage, physical and emotional, that he had suffered in OKC. The personal and professional recovery he had managed after that April had left him alone on the most distant frontiers of the domestic counterterrorism world. She knew that if he was going to exist successfully anywhere in the U.S. government, it would be safely out on some frontier.

She was reminding him that his portfolio was a specific subset of domestic counterterrorism, and that his responsibilities—such as they were—did not include either hostage rescue or high-profile threats. The government had special units—the Joint Terrorism Task Force, SWAT, and the Hostage Rescue Team among them—to deal with what seemed to be happening in New Haven. Poe wasn't part of the FBI's elite squads. Whatever team player skills he possessed—Dee had come to doubt that they were ever particularly well developed—had vaporized in the rubble of the Murrah Building in Oklahoma City.

"I'm not sure what's going on there yet, Dee. At Yale. But it's not a garden-variety hostage situation. I don't like that we lost Friday. That means something. I want to go learn exactly what it means. That's my goal. May turn out to be nothing of mine." He paused to ply her with another smile. "But you know I have a thing for wild geese."

She was immune. His attempt at charm flew past her like a gnat on a summer evening. "Nobody lost Friday, Poe. We saw the stuff that was happening on campus yesterday. It looked awful. So you don't have all the specifics about what was going on inside that building? Soon you will. Soon we'll know what happened in there on Friday. And it will make sense. Your colleagues are on this. They are. A full intel squad is already mobilized. They'll hit the ground in New Haven anytime."

Without any deliberation, Poe began to argue his case. "But why so little carnage from the bomb on that kid? Why no shrapnel? Tell me that."

Dee said, "Maybe he only wanted to kill the kid, not the bystanders."

"Why? That's not current terrorist thinking, Dee. The mantra is 'maximize casualties.' Nine/eleven. Bali. Madrid. London. Mumbai."

She said, "He's not as smart as we think."

He stared at her, wondered why she was being disingenuous with him. "That building? Those kids? That's not it, Dee. You know that better than anyone."

"Poe, the Bureau is treating this as a high-profile hostage situation whether you consider it to be one or not. HRT is mobilizing. They may already be in the air. They'll get there before you do. You'll be superfluous."

"That's nothing new," he said. "For me. I've been superfluous for—"

She said, "No! Having compassion for you, for what you've suffered, is something my heart does every day, Poe. Unbidden. Don't start pitying yourself. I find it singularly unattractive."

She could see in his eyes that she'd wounded him with her words, that her verbal slap would leave a pattern of fresh petechiae on his soul.

She didn't hurt him often. When she did hurt him, she usually did it to create distance. Near the end of one of their weekends.

They were near the end of one of their weekends.

She didn't know what to say next.

Poe pretended the blow hadn't happened. He said, "HRT will be there soon, but HRT's a weapon, not a strategy. If the commanders run out of options and need to breach that fortress, the HRT operators are the best people to do it. I don't have a problem with that. But I guarantee you that it's the negotiators that will call the shots at first and they are a long way from making a decision to breach. Days away. Even weeks. I will have some time to figure this out. If I'm wrong, I'm wrong. I've wasted a trip to Connecticut. That's all."

Dee growled at him. Poe didn't dig his heels in often, but when he did he set them in concrete. She said, "Let the intel teams do their jobs. They'll find out about Friday. They have resources you won't have."

He shook his head. "The problem is that they believe it, Dee. That the bad guys aren't as smart as us. It's why I have to go. What if this one, this one bad guy, what if he's as smart as us? Huh? What then?"

She feared it as much as Poe did.

He scratched his head. He said, "Jesus. What if he's as smart as *you*, Deirdre? My God. What if he's that smart?"

Dee knew she wasn't going to sway him. "You'll never get reimbursed for the charter. It's going to cost you a fortune to fly up there." She paused. "You know I'm right, baby."

They had never talked about money. She assumed he lived on his agent's salary. He had never given her a reason to think otherwise.

"I can afford it. I'm a frugal guy," he said. It was true, he was. Other than spending a couple of nights a week drinking alone in dive bars, he had no indulgences. Even fewer vices.

Unless you counted his days and nights with Dee in April. Some might consider that a vice. Others might consider it an indulgence.

Poe considered it oxygen.

Anyway, he was thinking, *if my hunch about all this turns out right, they'll reimburse me.*

He was almost done stuffing the last of his clothing into his duffel. Deirdre had started flicking dust off the shoulders of his dark suit with her fingernail. Satisfied, she straightened the coat on its hanger and zipped it into the cheap vinyl thing that Poe called his garment bag.

It gave Poe goose bumps that she was helping him pack. It felt like the most generous thing for a woman to do.

He didn't tell her that. He knew it would make her cry.

They had muted the sound to the TV. It was still tuned to Fox News. Since the kid's explosive death, cable news had gone into all-New Haven-all-the-time mode. It was early in the crisis—Fox was still at the stage in their coverage where they felt compelled to replay the video of a pixilated Jonathan Simmons exploding at least twice a minute.

They had two angles recorded. The network alternated between them as though they were waiting for the replay officials to make a ruling on a disputed call.

Poe found the footage more appalling each time they ran it. They were using human tragedy as video wallpaper. *Naked people aren't pornographic,* he thought, *this is pornographic.*

He kept hoping that a grown-up would show up at the network and take over the programming. That it was daytime on a weekend was no longer a sufficient excuse for the repetitive display of carnage.

The text at the bottom of the screen indicated the anchors were doing phone interviews with people whom they had designated as "experts," hoping that the public might confuse these people with professionals who were actual experts on the blowing up of college students held hostage inside impenetrable buildings owned by secret societies.

Each expert noted it was too early to know who was responsible. Then each one named a fresh possible suspect. Domestic. Foreign. Religious. Agnostic.

The anchors interviewed a cop who had been at Virginia Tech. Then the father of a kid who died at Columbine.

Poe couldn't figure out the point.

He stared at the screen. He said, "Killing the kid like that? Blowing him up. The unsub plans to die in that tomb."

Dee knew that. "I've been thinking the same thing. This is a . . . stop-action suicide bombing."

"From a hostage negotiation perspective, it changes everything. Do they know that? In New Haven? That the unsub is already dead?"

Dee had more faith in the Homeland Security apparatus than Poe did. "Yes, baby. They know that."

"I hope so," he said. He stood up. "I should wash my face."

"Where do you go to catch it?" Dee asked Poe when he returned from the bathroom.

He recognized her question as conversation. That meant she knew the end was near. He felt it, too. His core felt hollow, as though all of his organs had been replaced by inert gas. "Pier Thirty-six. I have no idea where that is. I should probably get going."

He smiled at her with a softness that almost paralyzed her. The grin he deployed was the one that he hoped would liquefy all of Dee's anxiety. She'd succumbed to that smile once or twice before. She called it his "Botox grin."

She tried to smile back. Her mouth did its part. Her eyes failed miserably.

He caught her gaze. "You saved my life this weekend, Dee. You know that, don't you?"

"Poe," she whispered. "Don't."

He slid his hands into the back pockets of his jeans. He took a half step toward her. "I get to where I'm barely hanging on sometimes. You're my lifeboat. You're always my lifeboat. You've kept me from drowning ten times since Oklahoma City."

She loved hearing it and didn't want it to be true. She said, "You're fine without me, Poe."

He shook his head. "Some days I don't exist without you, baby. You know what I do? I store memories of you in my brain. Sounds. Smells. The dimples above the hipbones on your back. The way you taste on my tongue. The way your hand feels when we weave our fingers together. What I do all the time we're apart is that I play them back, a little at a time. I ration them . . . stretch them out and get them to last me for the whole year." He bit his lower lip. "But sometimes I get greedy. Before this weekend, I swear I was almost out."

She turned her back to him and wrapped her arms around herself. "I can't stand this," she said. "I can't stand to watch you go."

"It'll be okay," he said. "It will." He knew his words were unconvincing. He wasn't sure how convincing he was trying to be.

Dee said, "You shouldn't go to Connecticut, Poe. The unsub is using bombs, baby. *Bombs.*" She sounded like the concerned mother of an eight-year-old child with food allergies warning her son that the birthday party he was desperate to attend would have cookies and cakes with nuts in them.

Poe spun her back around so that she was facing him. He unpeeled her arms and replaced them with his. After a long, strong embrace—her head beneath his chin—they kissed like it was their first, and then like it was their last.

Dee ran back into the bathroom. She couldn't say good-bye to him.

The helicopter trip to New Haven from Philadelphia lasted over an hour. Poe's administrative assistant in D.C. finagled emergency landing permission at the Yale New Haven Hospital heliport.

Poe's assistant had chosen a hotel on Chapel Street. The Study at Yale. He had instructed her to pick a place where his colleagues were unlikely to stay. The name gave Poe pause. He wasn't sure he could handle a surfeit of tweed and corduroy. Poe asked the taxi driver to wait while he dropped off his bags. The cab carried Poe the few additional blocks across town to the corner of York and Elm.

The GPS in his BlackBerry let him know he was close. He walked from the corner, eventually coming up near the location of the tomb from the rear.

If he had rented a car and fought the incessant traffic out of Philly, he would probably barely have cleared New York City by the time he was stepping into position behind the tomb. And he knew that if he'd driven to New Haven he'd be in a bad mood. I-95 always put him in a bad mood.

I-95 was not a road designed to lift anyone's spirits.

Crime scene tape was strung the length of the block adjacent to the sidewalk. Two campus police sentries were patrolling the perimeter of the adjacent plaza. Poe didn't know the landmarks, didn't know what building was what. He asked a Chinese woman for help. She had a plastic vinyl Hello Kitty bag slung over one shoulder. Poe got temporarily distracted wondering why a Chinese woman in America would be carrying a bag emblazoned with a Japanese cultural icon. Cradled in the woman's other arm were two mathematics texts. The titles were in English. Poe couldn't decipher either of them. He wasn't even sure what branch of mathematics she was studying, only that it was one in which he was not conversant.

He forced himself to focus. He told her he had heard there was a problem, and asked her where everything was happening. She nodded across the adjacent plaza in the direction of the blank back wall of a building on the opposite corner of the wide plaza. She said something in Chinese, caught herself, and said, "Over there. That one, the building with the plain wall." Her English was heavily accented. She provided the directions without pointing.

Poe spotted a cluster of special unit officers congregating near the building with the blank wall. The cops were local SWAT. City or county, he couldn't tell, but they were prepped for action. Despite their obvious weaponry and their helmets and body armor, the Chinese student had not mentioned their presence. She had not said, "That building there, near those police." She was either accustomed to this kind of authoritarian posturing, or just uninterested.

Poe added China to the roster of places he wanted to go someday with Dee.

He decided to walk the long way around the block until he got to a checkpoint. At that point, he would come up with a plan. The plan might be to flash his FBI credentials to the local cops and hope that things went smoothly.

More likely it would be something else.

That's the point in his preparation when he saw the SWAT officers start running.

The two sentries closest to Poe reacted to the sudden commotion behind them. They stepped away from the tape.

Poe saw opportunity. At the first sound of trouble, the sentries should have redoubled their vigilance on the perimeter, anticipating a breach. Instead, their insufficient training caused them to turn to the noise.

Poe stepped under the yellow tape and walked between two buildings. The one to his right was an elegant, small stone building adorned with ornate Oriental flourishes. While he walked, he hung his FBI credentials around his neck.

One downside of his new position was that he could no longer see what had happened with the SWAT team behind Book & Snake.

He was about to try to find a way to sneak into the plaza in front of him when a woman barked, "Stop."

He raised his hands. He stopped walking. In a conversational tone, he said, "I'm FBI."

Poe recognized that he had apparently spotted only two of the three sentries on the plaza. He promised himself he would be more careful in the future.

The woman was a uniformed campus cop. She moved slowly in front of him, keeping a distance of ten feet. Her weapon was pointed at his chest.

"I'm FBI," he repeated. "My ID, my badge." He gestured with his chin.

The campus cop—a black woman with dark, sparkling eyes and cheekbones other women would kill for—was much more terrified than Poe.

Guns didn't scare him much.

Deirdre? Dee scared him. God, Dee scared him.

Bombs, too. Bombs scared him. Dying didn't scare him, but bombs did.

Poe heard SWAT members yelling, "Clear!" "Clear!" "Clear!"

He wondered if they had the unsub. He resisted an impulse to turn his head.

"You with HRT?" the cop asked him.

Poe exhaled. "Thank God. Where are they? That's who I'm looking for."

It wasn't exactly untrue.

She lowered her weapon.

He kept his hands up. "Which way?" he said.

"They just got here. They're setting up a whole tent city over on the Green. The guys with the black suits and automatic weapons are staging on the other side of Woolsey. I heard they're getting ready to move into Commons, take it over."

Poe said, "They're the ones I want. The assault teams—the guys in the black suits. May I lower my hands?" She nodded. "Thank you. I'm from headquarters. In Virginia?" She nodded again. "Commons? Where is that?"

"This big building? That side is Commons. This side here is Woolsey." With her non-gun hand, she gestured at the largest building on the plaza, an ornate Harry Potter–ish thing that towered above them. The Woolsey/Commons combination formed an L-shaped structure that consumed a huge section of the block.

To Poe the building appeared to have been built during the Middle Ages, by serfs. More important to him, Commons seemed to be the nearest structure to the building where the hostages were being held.

"Best way for me to meet up with HRT?"

"Go back outside the tape. Walk past Woolsey to the corner. You'll find your FBI friends."

"Thanks," he said.

He retraced his steps to the sidewalk. He paused there, waiting until the young cop turned her attention away from him. Instead of going left to make it around Woolsey, Poe turned right to go around the block the other way.

He stuffed his ID back into his pocket.

Poe didn't want to find his FBI friends.

If the first act was played out in front of a full audience, this act is going forward on a closed set.

The crowds have grown much larger, but the swelling throngs are restrained beyond more distant perimeters. Police video cameras are mounted on tripods directly across Grove Street from the tomb. News cameras that had been set up on the sidewalk across the street from Book & Snake are farther down the block.

Reporters and producers are bitching about access. Hade Moody has already told Jack Lobatini that it didn't matter who in the media was asking, that he didn't care about their problems. But Jack knows his boss well enough to know that if Brian Williams or Katie Couric is on the line, Hade Moody will want to take the call.

The cemetery is locked off to the public, providing a wide buffer between the tomb and the surrounding community. Cops on horses are patrolling the graveyard's many acres.

Hade Moody stares at the latest hostage on the computer monitor for ten seconds before he looks at Christine. "You got a plan to handle this second kid?"

She hears the implied criticism: *Better than you handled the first kid.*

She says, "I always have a plan."

He says, "What about contain? We continue to allow him cell access?"

She knows that decision is his, not hers. "You want to bet another kid's life on that one, Lieutenant?"

"Just tell me you got a plan that will work."

"I'm open to suggestions, sir. Always grateful for your counsel."
She gives him a few seconds squirming time. After he straightens his
tie, she says, "You coming out, or are you staying in here?"

"Here for now. Jack's still your second. He'll liaise." Moody has
long had a thing for the sound of that peculiar soft verb. His love for
the word is almost a fetish. He sometimes mangles simple sentences in
order to find a way to insert it. He turns back to the monitor. "Jack,
you have the log? Time from the . . . explosion until now?"

Jack lifts his clipboard, looks at his watch. He says, "One hour,
fifty-four minutes."

Carmody has no idea why the timing matters.

"Feds?" Moody asks.

Jack knows his role. He says, "Full response is on the way."

"But not here?" Moody is thinking out loud. Stringing together
small facts, his favorite kind.

Jack checks his watch again, as though he has forgotten the time.
"No. ETA is . . . twenty, twenty-two minutes into Tweed. Another
thirty or so here. Then some time to orient and get set up. I've never
seen them deploy, don't know how efficient they are." He looks at
Carmody, then at Moody. "Either of you know how long it takes for
Hostage Rescue to get up to speed?"

Carmody wants to scream. She ignores his question. "This is ours
for now and we have work to do. The asshole could kill half the junior
class before the FBI gets in position." She turns to leave the vehicle.
She stops. "Any surprises still waiting for me, Lieutenant? Anything
I don't know as I go out there and say howdy to that kid? You know,
like maybe . . . that the cell phone towers are turned off again? You
have people I don't know about who have maybe started screwing
with the plumbing or the electrical? Anything I'm going to get ambushed by this time?"

She knows she has let the rage escape, just a little leakage under
the door.

Hade Moody stands, steps forward. He dwarfs her. His voice is measured. "We didn't do anything to the cell towers, Christine. The providers can't explain what happened to the signal. But it wasn't us."

"Coincidence?" she asks. She knows her sarcasm has squeezed under the same door that allowed her rage out. She also knows that her sarcasm can be toxic enough to require hazmat response. She has to watch it.

Moody turns his back on her. "Do your job, Christine. You don't have to worry about me doing mine."

As she moves past Jack toward the door, he holds up a body armor vest for her. "Your size," he says.

She shakes her head and pushes open the door.

When Christine Carmody marches out of the Mobile Command vehicle she deliberately returns to the precise position she vacated in the middle of the street. She is on the tomb side of the car that caught the remains of Jonathan Simmons's left hand.

Between her post and the stairs that lead up to Book & Snake are dozens of tiny, numbered evidence markers.

One tent, number forty-three, rests on the hood of the car behind her. It marks the spot where Jonathan's thumb fell from the sky.

The thumb has been collected.

In case someone inside the building is looking for a target, Christine is happy to appear to be a good one. She doesn't feel vulnerable. Although she knows nothing about the subject's plans, she is confident that, thus far at least, his strategy involves wasting college kids, not cops. She also knows that could change.

We didn't do anything to the cell towers, Christine. She allows herself to consider the possibility that Moody was telling her the truth. And what that might tell her about the guy inside the tomb.

One of them, either the man inside the tomb or Hade Moody, hasn't lied to her yet.

She isn't sure which one.

She lets her eyes settle at the top of the steps. She softens her focus. *See, don't look,* she reminds herself.

The second young man to emerge from the building has his hands in the air. They are empty, the fingers extended. He is wearing baggy chinos and a navy Yale zip-up hoodie. He is barefoot. He hasn't shaved for a few days. His wrists are red.

She has the sense he has been waiting for her to get into position because his instructions are to wait until she gets into position.

Christine goes through the motions of introducing herself and seeking the young man's cooperation.

He doesn't speak to her when she speaks to him. He doesn't lift his sweatshirt when she asks him to do so. He doesn't kneel when she tells him to kneel.

He looks down in the direction of his feet the entire time. She's thinking that if he looked up he might freak out at the two dozen weapons pointed at his body.

Carmody has decided to wait, at least for a while, to give the young man a chance to begin to speak on his own. Or, more likely, to speak at the direction of the unseen man inside the tomb.

Joey Blanks marches up behind her. He hands her a sheet of paper. His whisper is so resonant it sounds like he's speaking from inside a bass drum. "We have a tentative ID on this one. His name is Michael Smith the third. He's on the ATL list—he's one of the kids we've been suspecting might be inside. But the report that he's missing came from his roommate at Saybrooke. His parents haven't contacted us, have not returned calls. That's the bio we have so far. The photo is from his student ID."

"I don't want to take my eyes off him. Tell me what it says, Joey. Keep your voice down. You know, as much as you can."

"It says . . . he's a junior out of Houston. Saybrooke College. Major is HPE, whatever the hell that is. Linebacker on the football team. My partner—you know Andy Gomez?—was at the Harvard game last year. He just told me this kid was the best player on the field. Hard-hitter. Well-liked apparently. Average student. Sings a cappella. He's a tenor. I can relate to the average student and the singing part, at least." He pauses for a moment. "Got into a fight freshman year outside G-Heav with a bunch of other players. Disorderly. Charges were dropped."

"Family? Is there a government connection?"

"No. Family is Lutrex Oil. Refining, offshore pipelines, terminals. Gulf of Mexico mostly. That's what it says."

"That's it?"

"That's it."

"Get more. Find Fred Sewall. Get him to Google the family, every member individually. Do LexisNexis. Fred can grab a student volunteer to help search Facebook and MySpace and YouTube and Twitter and all the clones. And get our photographer to zoom in on his ears right now. I want to know if they can see an earpiece."

Michael Smith's hair is cropped short. With her naked eyes, Carmody can't see any evidence of plastic or wire on either of his ears.

Joey Blanks returns to confirm the news half a minute later. "No earpiece," he says.

The second he finishes speaking, a single sharp *craaack* pierces the air.

Michael Smith makes a short high-pitched sound that comes from deep in his throat. He falls to one knee.

Half the cops go down into protective postures.

Carmody doesn't move anything but her eyelids. *Discipline,* she tells herself. Her pulse explodes. *See, don't look.*

Although her fear is screaming *gunshot,* her brain decides that the noise was someone hitting the inside of the front doors with something hard. It was, she suspects, a signal to Michael Smith III.

A blatantly low-tech signal.

She wonders about the change from high-tech to low. A message? She doesn't know. The list of what she doesn't know is way too long.

If the noise was a signal, a signal to do what?

She doesn't know that either. She will wait. Time is supposed to be her friend.

The young man gets back on his feet. He regains his balance. Finally, five seconds after the loud crack, he lifts his head, looks directly at Carmody, and says, "I'm coming down."

"No," she says. "Not yet." *Goddamn.* She goes back to the beginning. "My name is Christine Carmody. I'm a negotiator with the New Haven Police. We'll get you to safety as soon as we can. Okay? But we have to do this . . . right. So that everyone can be safe. Do you understand? First, lift your shirt, front and back. Then turn around, a full three-sixty."

Michael, his arms still above his head, takes a step forward. It is clear that the step is reluctant. This is a kid who would rather do what he is told.

But he has two masters.

"Do . . . not . . . move . . . forward," Carmody says. "Please. Stay exactly where you are. I need to determine that you are safe. We can't allow you to—"

Michael takes another step toward the stairs.

Carmody senses what is happening. The kid is on autopilot. He has been instructed to carry out a specific choreography regardless of what she might do or say.

He has, she assumes, been threatened with unimaginable consequences if he disobeys.

What consequences? She guesses that if Michael disobeys, the subject will kill one of his friends inside the tomb.

She has decisions to make. She has no time to make them.

What if Michael Smith is a bomb?

What if she lets him approach and a hidden device explodes, killing her and a few other cops?

And what if Michael Smith is not a bomb?

What if she stops his approach—with lethal force, if necessary—and it turns out that he is completely unarmed?

Smith takes the first step down the stairs. He pauses.

She raises her left hand, extends her index finger. Joey Blanks steps forward. She feathers the fingers of her right hand in front of her mouth before she speaks to him. "I need volunteers to take him down when he gets to the bottom of the stairs."

"Shoot him? Ma'am," Joey asks, disbelieving.

Michael moves down one additional step.

"Tackle and restrain until we can assess his risk. The kid is big. Strong. He could be wired to explode. I need volunteers. Now."

"We could Tase him, try nonlethal force."

"Too unreliable. He's a friendly—a victim—until proven otherwise."

Christine and Joey both know that "until proven otherwise" might mean the death of anyone in the young man's vicinity.

Michael's descent is deliberate. Christine recognizes that the hostage taker is giving her time to react. She doesn't know why. Michael takes another step down.

With urgency frosting her voice, she says, "Volunteers, Joey. Now."

Jack Lobatini is two steps away, liasing. He is relaying by radio all of what he can hear to his boss in the Mobile Command vehicle.

Carmody knows that Hade Moody should be outside, coordinating the troops behind her. Managing the scene is not her job. Her boss is keeping his hands clean. She wonders what he knows that he hasn't told her.

Michael's steps continue. They remain measured. Step. Pause.

What if he starts to run? she worries. *God.*

Michael is two strides from the sidewalk when Joey returns to Carmody's side. "Three volunteers, Sarge."

She glances at the three. She nods. She recognizes that two of them are National Guard Iraq War veterans. Both back from combat for less than a year. The word that comes to her mind for them is "valiant." The third cop is Joey Blanks. She hopes that her nod begins to express the depth of her admiration and appreciation. She says, "Get in place on each side of the gate. On my order, the moment he steps through. Everyone else takes cover now."

She turns her attention behind her. "I want a shitload of guns aimed at those doors no matter what happens with this kid. Do not get distracted from those doors."

The young man is one step away from the bottom of the stairs.

"Michael, stop right there." It's Carmody's most authoritative voice. But she knows that her protest is only an exercise. If Michael Smith has any intention to stop, he would have already stopped.

Michael reaches the area between the stairs and the iron fence. He is as tall as the fence. He is an even larger man than she thought.

She's ready for him to open the gate.

He approaches it.

Okay, she urges him silently. *Go ahead, open the gate. Let's do this.*

He stops.

His hands remain in the air. His eyes stay focused toward his feet.

Jack Lobatini takes up position at Carmody's shoulder. He says, "HRT is here."

"What?" she says.

"FBI Hostage Rescue. They arrived . . . early."

"I'm a little busy," Carmody replies under her breath. "Jack, go take care of welcoming the feds." She doesn't have the authority to tell Jack to do anything. She intentionally spoke loudly enough that any defiance on his part would be public.

She's still waiting for Michael Smith III to open the gate. She gets ready to give the order to take him down. To give an order that might kill brave cops.

That's when Michael Smith III pivots and turns right.

No, she thinks. *No.*

He takes two steps and stops. Then he spins one hundred and eighty degrees.

At that point his hesitation is gone. He darts up the gentle slope of a dirt berm and makes a ninety-degree left turn. He sprints into the narrow side yard between the Book & Snake tomb and the sidewalk on High Street. He is separated from the sidewalk by a tall iron fence that has posts that look like snakes and pickets topped with spears.

Carmody calls out, "Shit. Joey, tell me we have contain over there."

She is jogging toward the corner so she can visually follow Michael Smith's route.

Joey Blanks is right behind her. "The tomb's fenced in on that side. I don't know where he's going."

"What about the other side of the fence?"

"The whole perimeter is ours. High Street's closed. There's a library, the law school. Some stairs down to the plaza."

"The plaza's secure?"

"That's where SWAT is mobilized."

They both watch the kid vault over the tall fence with the spiked pickets as though he's been practicing the move. He races down High Street for a few long strides before turning down the stairs toward Beinecke Plaza.

"I hope SWAT's ready," Carmody says. "'Cause here he comes."

Sam

Ann stayed with me at the house until the plane that was supposed to be carrying Jane from Hartford landed in Miami. Ann had dispatched Julio to meet the flight. He reported back by phone that Jane wasn't on board.

I watched Ann as she killed the call from Julio. She looked over at me with eyes full of poisoned wonder. "This is real, Sam. I can't believe that this is real."

I said, "I'm so sorry."

"Thanks for being here. Helping me."

I could have gone macho and mounted my white horse, but I didn't. I said, "I'm so far out of my comfort zone right now that I can't . . ." I didn't know how to finish the sentence. I said, "I'm afraid I'm not the right person to be helping you."

She adopted a tone of voice that I remember hearing from my dad when he was bucking me up after I got advanced an age group in pee-wee hockey and was getting my butt kicked on a regular basis by the older kids. She said, "Last night on the yacht? When I decided to show you that note, I was telling myself that there was a one percent chance that it was really something to worry about. Now I'm telling myself that there's only a one percent chance that it's not really something to worry about. The truth? I'm not sure I would take the same risk with you again, Sam Purdy."

She had my attention. I thought she was waiting for me to react to her criticism. I didn't. Mostly I welcomed it. It reflected reality. I liked that she could spot reality from where she was standing. I waited to see where she was going next.

"But something in here"—she spread her hand over her chest—"told me to trust you then. So I'm going to trust you now. Don't you even think about going invertebrate on me, mister."

"I'm a small-town cop. I need you to know who you picked for your team, Ann."

"I'm fine with my team."

Did Ann have a choice any longer? Not really. She was, in Stephen Stills's words, loving the one she was with.

That would be me. I said, "Okay then. Do you know any other kids who are in this club? The Thursday and Sunday night club?"

"No," she said, swallowing some exasperation at my ignorance. "It's . . . secret. A *secret* society. She's a new member. Brand-new. A . . . tap. I don't have the list. She knows very little. I know less than that."

"How many members?"

"Once, when she was wondering if she'd get tapped, she mentioned fifteen or sixteen. That the societies mostly have fifteen or sixteen members. I don't recall if that was new members—taps—or total members, including the seniors. They're small clubs. It's exclusive. It was an honor for her to be chosen."

I wondered how many of the kids were missing. How I might be able to find out. If all fifteen or sixteen—or thirty or thirty-two—sets of parents had received the same note Ann had received.

"Earlier, you were going to tell me about the tomb," I said.

Ann sighed before she began. "These secret societies go way back. The oldest societies constructed their own buildings, meetinghouses, well over a hundred years ago. Some of the buildings are prominent structures on campus. Others are off campus."

"Why are they called tombs?"

"I don't know. Maybe it's because that's what they look like," she said. "Some of them don't have any windows." She started touching the screen on her phone. Touching, flicking, touching again. She handed me the phone. "Jane sent me pictures of a few of the society buildings before she was tapped. This isn't a great picture; she took it with her cell. After pre-tap, she kind of described her society's building. I think this is her tomb."

Her choice of words—the last sentence—made Ann gasp. Her hand flew to her mouth. "I can't believe I said that."

I have a good friend named Alan who is a psychologist in Boulder. He would have gotten distracted right there, would've invested a whole mess of energy and way too much time into trying to un-ring the bell that Ann had just rung. That was Alan.

That wasn't me. I focused on the photograph. I thought the building looked like a simplified version of the U.S. Supreme Court Building. As advertised, it appeared to have no windows. Fancy thing. Marble. Columns. This secret society wasn't meeting in some clubhouse built out of scrap lumber in an oak tree in the woods.

"Does the place have a name?" I asked.

"Jane didn't tell me. But I looked up the photo online. This building is the tomb for the society called Book & Snake," she said.

"Book & Snake," I repeated. I was about to ask why it was called Book & Snake, but knew it made no difference. "The text you got from her on Thursday afternoon? There was a copy on your computer. I saw it. Was she going here? This building?"

She took the phone, found the text on her phone, showed it to me. "This one?"

It read **At Beinecke, so wish I could tell you more, maybe soon, lusm.**

"That one," I said.

"Yes. It was more like Thursday evening. Jane had been told to dress up in some costume—no, I don't know what kind of costume— and wait in a specific location on campus. She thought someone would find her and escort her to Book & Snake."

"What's that word? 'Beinecke'?"

"It's the rare book library on campus. It's right behind Book & Snake. Both buildings are on Beinecke Plaza."

"St. Cloud State didn't have any of that. No rare book libraries. No secret society tombs. No fancy plazas."

She exhaled audibly. She stepped close enough to put a hand on each of my clavicles. "My father was a butcher who ended up running his own neighborhood grocery store, Sam. My mother never finished high school. I went to Florida State on a private scholarship that is specifically reserved for left-handed girls—originally left-handed white girls—from the Confederate South," she said. "Now? Things are different. Ronaldo and I are wealthy. We own a yacht. Jane goes to Yale. Get over it."

She was telling me not to get distracted by the Ivy League glitz or the Calderón money. It was excellent advice.

"That's the last time you heard from her?" I asked. "This text?"

"It was," she said. "There will be a next time, Sam. But for now, that's the . . . most recent time."

I'd been with crime victims before. The longer they could find reason to hope, the better. Ann still had a firm grip on hope.

I feared, of course, that the rope she was gripping was made of smoke.

"Okay," I said. "That's something. We know where she was then. Now we have to figure out where she is right now."

"The tomb," Ann said. "She has to be in there."

I didn't share her confidence, but I nodded. "Good place to start," I said. I narrowed my eyes and told her I had one more question.

"Yes?"

"You're not left-handed, are you?"

"No, Sam. I am not."

In retrospect, what happened in the next few minutes shouldn't have done as much damage to my equilibrium as it did.

Ann started the ball rolling with a simple question, one that I probably should have seen coming. She said, "Will you go to New Haven, Sam? Today? Now? Be my eyes and ears? I know it's a lot to ask. Please. I can't leave. Everyone would wonder. I wouldn't be able to keep the secret. And . . ."

She didn't have to finish that sentence, not for me.

Ann went on. "If Jane is inside that . . . tomb, that building, I have to be close to her. You can do that for me."

I didn't respond right away. I was trying to come up with a rational reason to refuse. Why it shouldn't be me, why it was wrong that it be me. I couldn't.

It would have been better, I was thinking, if Ann's son had fallen in love with a girl whose pregnant cop mother had a boyfriend who was more like James Bond or at least like some character that Denzel Washington would play in the movies. But Ann's son didn't fall in love with that girl.

Second best would have to do. And second best was that Ann's son had fallen in love with a girl whose pregnant cop mother had a suspended cop boyfriend with time on his hands and a stubborn sense of obligation to do what was right.

That was me. Other than the suspended part, it was a rare day that I wasn't okay in those shoes.

Ronaldo Calderón's fastener company had a plane. I wasn't surprised by that news. Ann said, "I'll get the jet fueled and the crew ready." She started touching the front of her phone to connect the call.

I put the brakes on her impressive efficiency.

"Ann, that won't work," I said. I told her that she couldn't risk sending the company plane, that it would be too easy for someone to track an aircraft to New Haven. I told her that I'd fly commercial.

"That's too slow and too unreliable. We'll arrange a charter," she said. She began to make a fresh call with her mobile phone. She was a person who had an airplane charter company in her cell's contact list.

I was a person who didn't. I stopped her again.

I held out my cell. "Use my phone to make the call, Ann. Again, just in case this guy is plugged in. And . . . I don't know how these things work, but can you delay the billing, or have a friend arrange this in her name? I don't want it to show up on your credit card . . . or your account for a few days. Is that possible?"

"Thank you, Sam. Of course." She took my phone, made a call, and took care of business.

Once she completed the call, I said I needed to go back to the hotel and get my things.

She said, "Time is precious. Money, for me, is abundant. Buy what you need for tonight once you get there. Julio will FedEx your things to the hotel in New Haven."

Yeah? That's how this works for rich people?

Within minutes—five, six—I was in the front seat of the Suburban with Julio. We were on our way to Kendall-Tamiami Airport.

I was flying to Tweed New Haven Airport in Connecticut to be Ann's eyes and ears.

I called Carmen. I'd already decided that I wasn't going to worry her about the change in my itinerary. She laughed at the story of me playing golf.

After the call to Carmen, I took the Ace bandage off my wrist.

Julio noticed. He said, "I am glad your arm is feeling better, señor."

A swarm of New Haven PD SWAT officers takes Michael Smith III down as soon as he reaches the hard stone of Beinecke Plaza.

He is hit at the chest and at the knees by two different cops, then gang tackled by four more. He doesn't struggle.

The book says he has to be restrained and searched.

So Michael Smith's wrists are shackled for the second time in his life.

Carmody almost decides to abandon her post. She's tempted to follow her impulse to chase with other officers after Michael Smith. Instead she returns to her position on Grove Street.

Because she doesn't yield to that reflex, she is still in position when the front door of Book & Snake opens yet again. A young woman walks out. The door closes behind her. She hesitates for a split second before she continues forward until she is roughly in line with the row of pillars. She stops and immediately turns her back to Christine and to the other cops gathered out front. Unlike Michael Smith III, her arms are not up in the air.

It's unclear whether she notices all the weapons pointed in her direction.

Carmody is contemplating her first move with this young woman. She suspects that the choreography is just beginning.

Seconds later the door opens again. A young man backs out. He is carrying something. He is slightly bent at the waist and his shoulders are rounded forward from the physical effort.

A second later another young man appears in the doorway.

Carmody feels some restrained joy. *Is this over?* she wonders. *Is he letting them all go?*

The second young man is facing forward. He, too, is carrying something heavy. He, too, is bent at the waist, stooped over. Because of the columns and the shadows and because the position of the young woman is impeding her view, Carmody can't see what the two men are carrying.

Her spirit deflates as she guesses.

The door closes.

That's not all of them, Carmody reminds herself. *There are more kids inside.*

The two men place whatever they are carrying on the stone right in front of the doors. They are gentle. Not just careful, but gentle.

The tenderness they display extinguishes any embers of hope for Carmody.

The two men step forward, one on each side of the young woman. She turns around. The three of them nearly fill the space between the two pillars closest to the doors.

Whatever they were carrying is hidden from Carmody's view from the street. She is sure that is intentional. *We are supposed to know, but we're not supposed to see.*

Carmody clears her throat. She says, "Stay right where you are, please. Stop." Her voice is loud enough for them to hear, but it is not demanding.

The young woman reaches out on each side of her, grabbing a hand of each of the men. Her lips move.

Carmody thinks the girl said, "Okay." She imagines the word in her head and decides that the girl didn't mean "okay" as in "good." She meant "okay" as in "now."

The trio begins to move forward, descending the steps in unison at a measured pace, as though they're making an entrance at a cotillion. Their heads are up, their eyes straight ahead.

Carmody confirms with Joey Blanks that his volunteers remain ready.

She calls out to the hostages on the steps. She says, "For everyone's safety, please stop right now. Please." She knows enough already to be certain that they won't stop, unless that is what they've been told to do by the unseen man in the tomb.

She has to go through the motions.

Without turning her head, Carmody orders everyone behind her to take cover one more time. Almost everyone already has.

As the three young people make it to the first landing on the stairs, Christine can see what the boys left outside the doors. It's a body.

The kids continue their peculiar march until they reach the bottom of the stairs. They pause there. Christine notices that the girl squeezes the hand of each of the boys. They start again, continuing together toward the gate without hesitation. The young man on the left opens the gate. The two men step back, allowing the young woman to pass through first. The men follow her.

"Ready?" Carmody asks Joey one more time.

"That's a yes, Sarge."

"On my order."

As the young woman reaches the sidewalk in front of the tomb, she drops suddenly to her knees and then lowers herself to a prone position. She stretches her arms at her sides.

One at a time the men take the same position on each side of her. Less than a foot separates one of them from the next.

Carmody says to the officers behind her, "Everyone keep your positions. I'm going forward."

Jack Lobatini attempts to block her path. His tone is crisp. He says, "Christine, the bomb squad should do this. Any of them could be wired."

She walks through him, almost knocking him down. She doesn't believe the three kids are walking bombs. If these kids are wired with explosives, she has already concluded, having them lie down makes no sense. The ground would absorb the charge.

Then again, she admits, *it could be a trap to lure me into the blast zone.*

She stops her march one step away from the three hostages. In a conversational tone, she says, "I'm Christine Carmody. I'm a negotiator with the New Haven Police. I need to search you. Once I do that, we will take you to safety. Do you understand?"

None of them replies.

She starts with the young man nearest to her. As she pats him down and lifts his shirt to check his waist for explosives she can hear the young woman whimpering. Christine lowers her head. Her hair hangs down, providing a screen around her face and mouth. She whispers to the man she is searching, "Slowly close your hand into a fist if the person you carried outside is already dead."

The young man hesitates. After three seconds, he begins to close his hand.

"Keep it closed if the body is booby-trapped."

He slowly opens his hand.

Christine is thorough. It takes her about a minute and a half to search all three students. She does the girl last. She is confident they are not armed or wired.

Carmody remains in a crouch, her hand resting on the girl's back. In a voice loud enough that all three students can hear her, she apologizes but explains that each of them is going to have to be restrained before they are escorted to safety.

Then she turns toward Joey Blanks and the other two volunteer cops. She says, "All clear here. Joey, make sure the snipers cover me and cover that door. Hold your positions until I'm done checking the . . ." *Body? Door?* She doesn't know how to finish the sentence.

"If they run?" Joey asks.

"Restrain them. When I signal, remove the hostages and send the bomb squad."

She stands and walks through the gate. She begins to ascend the stairs of Book & Snake for the first time. She is aware that behind the doors, the hostage taker—the murderer of Jonathan Simmons—is likely watching her through a peephole.

She knows she shouldn't be getting too close to that door, especially alone. Becoming a hostage herself would be a major fuckup.

She is in no hurry to look at the body in front of the doors.

She keeps her eyes up until she is between the pillars. She exhales slowly to rein in her anxiety. She prepares herself for the worst.

As she lowers her eyes, she recognizes that she was not sufficiently imaginative.

The amount of blood on the body shocks her. It shocks her until she sees the blue tint to the girl's skin and then the inch-wide, inch-deep gash carved in the young woman's throat.

With that big a hole, she thinks, *there has to be a lot of blood.*

She raises her hand above her head, extends one finger, and makes a small circle in the air. "Let's get going," she is saying.

After Michael Smith III is searched, a quick medical check determines that he has suffered nothing worse than bruises during the SWAT takedown. The young man is taken to the dining hall in Commons to be debriefed about his captivity. That's where FBI intel agents are waiting for him.

The three kids who came out next are separated from each other to be interviewed individually.

Jurisdiction concerns are being sorted out inside the Mobile Command Center between Lieutenant Haden Moody of the New Haven PD, the special agent in charge of the FBI Hostage Rescue Team, and representatives of the Yale Police and the Connecticut State Police.

Christine Carmody is not invited.

The jurisdictional negotiations are protocol. The result isn't in doubt. The FBI is taking over. After that fact is made clear to all, the special agent in charge announces that the New Haven PD Mobile Command vehicle will function as the FBI's temporary Tactical Operations Center. FBI operations personnel have already begun creating the necessary communication and computer links.

An HRT mobile village is being erected on the nearby New Haven Green. HRT will stage out of sight inside Commons and Woolsey. Discussions have started about the best location to rehearse a potential assault on Book & Snake.

The early favorite is another tomb—the one diagonally across Beinecke Plaza: Scroll & Key.

The FBI HRT special agent in charge steps outside his new Tactical Operations Center. He introduces himself to Christine Carmody on the street in front of the tomb. He is six-three, two-ten, and looks to her like he sleeps in a bronze casting of Atlas. He is the star high school quarterback gone good.

She greets her new Bureau colleague with as much grace as she can muster. After half a minute he introduces her to the lead HRT hostage negotiator, the man who will replace her in front of the tomb.

Christine is pleased that the hostage negotiator isn't the physical specimen that his boss is. Once the SAC steps away, Christine briefs her successor succinctly. She is done in less than five minutes. The man makes an obvious effort to swallow his there's-a-new-sheriff-in-town attitude. She gives him points for trying. He is not as much of a jerk as she expected him to be.

His only specific question to Christine is about the blue tarp at the rear of the building. She explains that New Haven PD is preparing to snake a camera into the space for an initial look.

"We're on that," he says politely. "Notify your people. They can stand down."

She thinks, *I don't have people. I have The Sun and The Moon.* She requests permission to observe the interviews of the kids inside Commons. He says he'll check.

Christine takes the first reluctant step away from her post. She begins to walk down Grove Street toward the entrance to Commons. Joey Blanks, the uniformed officer who had been assisting her outside the tomb, touches her shoulder. "Sergeant?"

"Joey? Yes?" She doesn't turn her head. "Thanks for your help earlier. Appreciated. I mean it. More than I can say."

"Not a problem. Wanted you to know we finally got a wit."

When Joey has news to share, his resonant voice makes it sound like a shout-out from God. She turns her head. Stops walking. She asks, "Besides the kids who were just released?"

"Yeah."

"Tell me."

"A student who works at Beinecke—that's the library behind the tomb—was on the plaza taking a smoke break Thursday, early afternoon. Said she saw caterers going into Book & Snake, setting up for something. She thinks there were four, maybe five people. A big white van on High Street. Lot of supplies and equipment. Mostly into the basement. Some around front. They were using carts and dollies. The stuff looked heavy to her. She was thinking she'd love to be invited to the party."

"Any descriptions?"

"It was raining Thursday, if you remember. She said that they all had hoods on, were covering their stuff with plastic. She thinks maybe one was a woman, only because of her size. She was small."

"Anything distinctive about the van?"

"She thinks it was unmarked. Doesn't recall seeing any lettering. Says she wasn't really paying attention. Oh, almost forgot—she did say there was a dress bag, the clear plastic kind like my daughter had to carry her wedding dress in. She said the one she thought was a girl carried the dress into the tomb on a hanger."

"A wedding gown?"

"That's the story."

"Are there any surveillance cameras that might have picked up any of this?"

"Detectives are checking. Appears negative. Feds have the wit now. I wanted you to know the latest."

"Joey," she says. "Thank you."

"What happened out there . . . I like what you did, how you handled it, Sarge. And I'm not alone. There's no way any of what went wrong earlier is on you. The guy inside, he was gonna do what he was gonna do. Right from moment one. Cell phone stuff was bullshit."

Christine nods. She resumes her march toward Commons. Joey stays half a step behind her.

He says, "Can I ask a question, Sarge? The orange? Is it a club thing? A club color or something? From the secret society? Like a uniform? None of us, well, we don't know much about that stuff."

Carmody is perplexed. She stops, faces him. "What? Is what—"

"The orange? The two kids who were killed were both wearing something orange. The four kids who walked away—they aren't. Are all the kids members of that place? Or were some like . . . guests? Pledges? Is it like a fraternity? How does it work? We're all trying to figure out how he's choosing who . . . dies."

APRIL 18, FRIDAY AFTERNOON

Sam

The cab from the airport had dropped me at the Omni Hotel. Ann's idea. Place was way out of my budget. But then Tom Bodett's guest room was way out of my budget. Ann had called me while my private little Maverick Jet was just beginning to taxi on the New Haven airport runway, marking the end of my own once-in-a-lifetime *Top Gun* moment. Ann let me know that nothing was new on her end, and that I had a reservation at the hotel under my own name. I should take a cab to town and use my personal credit card—she hoped that was okay. She would reimburse me later.

Using my personal credit card was a potential hitch. My extended suspension from the Boulder Police Department had nearly run its course. So, unfortunately, had my financial resources. First I had plodded through my not-too-substantial savings. When that cushion was gone, I started living on plastic. My Visa had butted up against its credit limit about three weeks before my trip to Florida, and my Discover was perilously close to the same fate. The trip east subbing for Carmen at the Calderóns' engagement extravaganza hadn't helped my budget. Did I have enough left under the limit on my Discover to cover the Omni for a night?

I was about to find out.

I asked for a room with a view of campus. When questioned about luggage, I explained that the airline had lost my bag. The desk clerk wasn't the least bit surprised. I held my breath as she swiped my card.

It cleared. I exhaled, but I didn't feel any richer. With tax, I felt two hundred and fifty bucks poorer. I'd already felt broke. I was broke minus two-fifty.

Once I received my key card, I stepped down one desk and asked a young African-American woman for directions to campus, specifically the location of Beinecke. "The library? Stunning building," the concierge told me. "One of my absolute favorites." She circled its location on a giveaway campus map. "Take a tour if you get a chance," she advised. "The treasures in there? You won't believe it, will not. Takes your breath away. Ever seen a Gutenberg Bible? You will in there. My momma cried like a baby. I took her in, she stood in front of that Bible staring for a full minute. Then she got down on her knees and she just cried, cried, cried."

I almost asked her to circle the location of the nearby secret society tombs on the map. But my question would have told her more than her answer would have told me. I'd have to figure out the location of the tombs myself.

It didn't turn out to be much of a challenge. The ones I knew about were all marked on the map. Before I'd walked a block from the hotel, I'd checked off the locations of Book & Snake and another secret society–sounding place called Scroll & Key. They were both on the perimeter of Beinecke Plaza. The much more legendary Skull & Bones was a few blocks farther away from Book & Snake on High Street.

I started walking toward Beinecke Plaza and Book & Snake. After a short stroll from the hotel, I found myself adjacent to Woolsey Hall at the corner of College and Grove.

What I had no way to know until that moment was that the local authorities didn't seem to have any better understanding of what was going on than I did.

I had been assuming that Jane Calderón was one potential hostage of many. I was also guessing that although the authorities were aware they had a situation of some gravity developing inside Book & Snake, they were ignorant that the problem included Jane Calderón.

Given those assumptions, I thought I'd see evidence of a police presence down the block. I expected to find some indication—a barri-caded road, some emergency vehicles, something—that the local cops recognized that they might have a hostage crisis on their hands inside the Book & Snake tomb.

The first thing I noted as I turned the corner was that most of the Beinecke Plaza side of Grove Street was a continuation of the Wool-sey Hall building. The map identified the new section as Commons. I paused on the sidewalk, playing tourist, using the map as a prop while I peered farther down Grove Street. I couldn't see the Book & Snake tomb, but the map indicated that it was just beyond Commons on the next corner.

Directly across the street was a large cemetery surrounded by a substantial stone-and-iron fence. Halfway down the block, a solitary Campus Police cruiser was parked alongside the curb. I couldn't be sure from where I was standing, but I thought there was an officer sitting in the driver's seat.

That's it? I thought in wonder. *A solo campus cop parked across the street from the tomb?*

The restrained police response caused me to begin to consider the possibility that maybe it wasn't the rest of the army that was march-ing out of step, but that it was Ann and I who had everything wrong. Maybe Jane Calderón had simply done what almost every college kid does at some point in her life—she acted out of character and did something her parents weren't expecting. Maybe Jane's temporary si-lence with her family had nothing to do with the ominous note her mother had received.

I began allowing for a couple of new possibilities. One—Ann had pegged it at a one percent likelihood—was that Jane wasn't missing and that there really wasn't something sinister going on inside Book & Snake. The other was that this situation involved only Jane, and the local authorities were unaware that she was missing.

I continued down Grove Street until I was steps away from the front of the tomb.

I immediately recognized it from Ann's cell phone photo. The col-onnade side of the secret society building looked down on the cemetery. The wall on the side that was exposed to Commons was nothing but an uninterrupted plane of stone. The only surprise was that the tomb was much bigger than I had imagined. The photograph had left me with the impression that the building was clubhouse-sized.

It wasn't. It was mansion-sized. The interior could be three stories, or four. It might even have an elevator.

If there were hostages inside the tomb, the large scale would complicate everything from a law enforcement perspective. More square feet to account for, more rooms to search. More stairs to climb. Closets to open.

I continued walking, turning the corner at High Street. The exposed wall on that side of the Book & Snake tomb was another fortress wall. Solid stone, forty feet high or more. *What do these people have against windows?* At the back corner, a blue plastic tarp was stretched tight from the ground up about three feet. I thought it might be covering access to a basement door. A basement would mean additional square feet to worry about.

Across High Street from the tomb was a block-long structure that—were I guessing on a midterm—I would have labeled as Gothic in design. A quick glance at the map told me I was looking at part of the Yale Law School. A few more steps down High allowed me to look back at a row of evergreens and, above them, most of the blank back wall of Book & Snake. That side of the tomb faced a modern building—the Beinecke Rare Book and Manuscript Library, the place where I'd been told I'd find a Gutenberg Bible. Between the two buildings, stairs led from the High Street sidewalk down to a plaza that consumed the center of the block.

After trying to digest the neoclassical splendor of Woolsey and Commons, the classic Greek design of Book & Snake, and the Gothic flourishes of the law school, I was stopped in my tracks by the contrast posed by the Beinecke Library. My brain said it didn't fit. The rare book library was a large modern geometrical form—the sides were long rectangular planes composed of dozens of concrete-framed shimmering squares of stone. Marble? Granite? I didn't know. Stone.

I like architecture, took a class in college, but my taste runs toward

Arts and Crafts. Still, my gut said Beinecke was a wonderful building. Goofy, sure, but wonderful.

I climbed down the stairs that separated the back of the tomb from the library. The Beinecke Library offered a wall of stone to match the back wall of Book & Snake. No windows interrupted the opposing vertical faces of either structure.

What was I thinking after checking out all four sides of the Book & Snake tomb? I was thinking that if Jane Calderón was being held inside that building against her will, it was unlikely that it was a location of convenience.

Someone had chosen it. And chosen it well.

The building is Masada is what I was thinking. *It's the damn Alamo.*

I wondered how I would do it. Breach the place. I couldn't figure out an ideal way. The only apparent vulnerabilities I could see were the front entrance doors and maybe that rear basement door. If someone inside was determined to keep authorities outside, the two access points—both on lower levels—wouldn't be impossible to defend. A rescue assault might work—hell, with enough armor, horsepower, and firepower, it would ultimately work—but good people, hostages or law enforcement, could certainly die during a breach through only one or two lower portals.

I retraced my steps as casually as I could, heading back around the tomb onto Grove Street. The solo campus police cruiser had cleaved—I saw one campus cruiser and one New Haven Police cruiser. A total of three cops. One of the two city cops was standing at the driver's door talking to the Yale campus cop. I kept walking, pretending not to pay attention. I sensed no particular urgency from my cousins in blue.

I turned the corner, walking past Woolsey. I reentered Beinecke Plaza on the opposite corner from Book & Snake. My map said I was between the Scroll & Key tomb and a building called Woodbridge Hall. Diagonally across the plaza I could see the back corner of Book & Snake framed by the much larger and taller walls of Commons and of the Beinecke Library.

I focused my attention on the Scroll & Key tomb. Scroll & Key had some narrow openings in its walls, though I wouldn't exactly call them windows. It was much more whimsical than Book & Snake, in a mythical-palaces-of-Baghdad kind of way. The exterior reminded me of the *Ali Baba and the Forty Thieves* set creations of movies from the early days of Hollywood. During one memorable finals week in college, I'd watched a marathon of them on late-night TV.

Most important? No patrol car was parked in front of Scroll & Key. Whatever the cops suspected was going on around the corner at Book & Snake, they did not suspect the same thing was going on inside Scroll & Key.

As I walked away, I continued to ponder the Book & Snake hostage rescue dilemma. If I had to get into that tomb to try to retrieve a kid, or ten kids, how would I improve my odds during a breach of the building?

The roof? Maybe. A well-equipped SWAT team could use explosive breaching charges to blow down the front doors and maybe that basement door. A simultaneous assault could be set up to breach the roof and drop in from above. Top down. Bottom up.

Could work.

Could be a bloodbath, too.

I asked a student who was passing by where I could find the campus bookstore. He took the map from my hand and drew a line down Wall Street toward Broadway, then across a plaza. That's where he put an *X*.

I intended to read everything I could find about secret societies, Book & Snake, and Yale architecture. In a perfect world, I'd stumble onto a dirt cheap used copy of something like *An Architectural Guide to the Secrets of the Book & Snake Tomb*.

I took a detour first. I headed down High Street past a few residence halls—the map called them "colleges" for some reason that I didn't understand. I kept walking until I got to the vicinity of the Skull & Bones tomb.

A campus patrol car was parked at the curb about fifty feet away, almost directly across from a tall stone tower. An officer sat at the wheel.

The tomb the cop was monitoring was another damn fortress. Squat, blunt, brown, and, although I wouldn't have considered it possible, even more unwelcoming in design than Book & Snake. I thought Skull & Bones looked more like an abandoned Civil War armory than any kind of fancy-pants secret society meeting hall.

Like Book & Snake, the Skull & Bones tomb was a building that had apparently been designed to appear smaller than it really was. Unlike Book & Snake, the Skull & Bones tomb had at least two windows fronting the street—though the openings were such narrow slits that their only worthwhile use would be as archer ports.

The law enforcement arithmetic was simple enough—cops were posted in front of both Skull & Bones and Book & Snake, but there was slightly more police interest at Book & Snake than there was at Skull & Bones.

What did that mean? Something, presumably.

I wandered through an iron gate into a large grassy area on the block across the street from the tomb. My map identified the expanse as Old Campus. It took me a while to find a bench that provided a decent view of Skull & Bones. I sat there for almost twenty minutes, alternately studying my map and glancing at the tomb. The building—the place looked not only neglected but also deserted—provided no clue of its interior life. No one went in. No one came out. No lights came on. No lights went off. I was thinking that a cop could continue a stakeout of the place for a day, maybe an entire week, and never see an indication that anything at all was going on inside.

I reminded myself that the fortresses at Masada and the Alamo had eventually fallen to invading forces, although the sieges had proven to be long and the number of casualties high.

Were the police to attempt a classic breach in either of these tombs—Skull & Bones or Book & Snake—anyone holding hostages inside would be able to use the time it took for the rescuers to breach the exterior to execute hostages.

Maybe all of their hostages.

The invading armies didn't have hostages to worry about at Masada or at the Alamo. They only had to worry about the invincibility of the fortresses.

Thousands of years of military history had proven the hard lesson that no fortress wall was invincible.

But history also proved that many people could lose their lives during a forceful breach. Waco and Ruby Ridge were recent cases in point for law enforcement. It sometimes took a long time to pierce defenses, but fortresses fall. Eventually.

I began to worry about what I was going to tell Ann. I started to pull my phone from my pocket.

The sound of a gunshot—crisp, loud, definitive—froze me.

The clap was followed instantly by the distinctive *ping* of ricochet, then by the insistent replay of echoes off stone.

My ears read the initial retort as rifle fire.

Carmody changes her mind about watching the debriefing of the hostages. After Joey Blanks's comment about the orange clothing on the dead students' bodies, she decides to detour back to the command vehicle to review the video footage of each of the students who had exited the tomb.

With HRT in charge, she recognizes an immediate change in tenor inside the vehicle. At the top of the big white board someone has written "TACTICAL OPERATIONS CENTER (TOC)" in six-inch block letters. FBI personnel are manning the computer and communications gear.

Hade Moody is engaged in hushed conversation with one of the feds. Carmody thinks Moody is acting like a rabid fan who has just scored a pass to visit some rock 'n' roll legend's bus. He doesn't acknowledge Christine as she enters. To him, she is no longer a player.

She sits down at a spare monitor and locates the video of Jonathan Simmons exiting the tomb. She pauses it the moment Jonathan lifts his shirt to expose the bomb. Simmons was wearing a faded orange T-shirt beneath the striped shirt that was covering the bomb.

She searches another video file until she finds the footage of the body of the girl with the slit throat. Carmody has indelible visual images of the blood and the wide gash and gray skin and the red hair and the blue eyes. But that's all. She doesn't recall any orange.

It's immediately apparent to Christine that the department videographer who was handling the camera experienced difficulty managing the shadows. During the initial few seconds of the footage he was trying to nail down the right exposure. The second he found it, the girl's body popped vividly onto the screen.

The appearance of the body shocks Carmody all over again—the dead hostage is wearing her own blood as a full body apron.

She is also wearing orange socks.

That's two for two for orange apparel on dead hostages.

Christine checks the video of Michael Smith III and of the three kids who walked through the gate after him.

No orange clothing.

If it's a pattern, Christine wonders, what does it mean? Clue? Message? Coincidence?

Christine approaches Hade Moody as though all is forgiven. She wants to ask him for more details about the wedding dress the witness saw on Thursday, but assumes she is not supposed to know those facts. Instead she says, "I'd love to see the dead girl's family information the second you have it. The others, too. The four survivors."

"Yeah," he says without looking at her. "Jack'll liaise."

She swallows a string of profanities as she heads toward the debriefing.

The dining hall in Commons is cavernous and ornate. It smells like fifty thousand uninteresting lunches. Michael Smith III is at an oak table in one corner, opposite a man in a suit and tie. An FBI special agent. Carmody takes a chair five feet from him. She is diagonally across from Michael.

Below Michael's striped button-up shirt is a blue T-shirt. Not orange.

She recalls that Smith was barefoot. That means no orange socks.

The FBI guy glares at her. "Yeah?"

"Sergeant Carmody, New Haven Police. I was . . . I am the hostage negotiator. Your SAC authorized me to observe the interview."

To Christine, Michael Smith III looks as defeated sitting in the fancy dining hall as he had looked standing at the top of the stairs of Book & Snake with his hands in the air. His shoulders are slumped forward. His eyes are down. His fingertips are tracing the pattern of the rifts of the grain in the oak tabletop.

A sports drink bottle in front of the kid is half-empty. A bottle of water is unopened. A tray of food—fruit, energy bars, cookies—sits untouched a few feet away.

Michael isn't talking. All the special agent's questions are met with silence.

Michael's only movement is his fingertips combing the rifts.

"Tell me what it's like in there."

"How did it all come down? Thursday night? Right?"

"How many people are involved? Bad guys?"

"Any of your friends hurt?"

"Are you all being held together in one room?"

"Your wrists are red. Were you restrained? How?"

"Were you threatened if you spoke to us?"

Michael Smith responds to each inquiry with silence.

After ten minutes, the FBI interrogator stands and takes a couple of steps away from the table. He turns to Carmody. "You got a question?"

She's ready. "Michael," she says. He doesn't look at her. "Are you wearing your own clothing?"

His fingers stop moving for two seconds before they resume running the rifts.

"Carmichael?" the FBI guy says. "Come with me."

"It's Carmody," she says. But he's already too far away to hear her. She stands and follows him to the other end of the huge room.

She waits for him to speak. The man turns his back to the room and rubs his eyes. "'Is that your own clothing?' You kidding me?"

"We have our own styles."

"Fucking kid," he says. "We don't have time for his games."

She almost wants to thank him. Until she met him, all the FBI personnel on the scene had been professional and gracious. This guy was enough of an asshole to remind her to keep her guard up.

She wants to tell him to give the kid a break, to remind him that Smith had been a hostage for almost two days, and that he had been blindfolded and shackled and almost certainly been threatened. She doesn't say any of it.

After ten seconds, he says, "I asked you for your opinion."

"I don't think you did. You called the released hostage a 'fucking kid' and said you didn't have time for his games. I think that's about all you said to me. On the way in here I received word that there's a witness from Thursday afternoon. A student saw four or five caterers enter the tomb. They were moving a lot of equipment."

"Go on."

"Your intel colleagues have the wit now. We don't know if we are dealing with one subject or five, or more. For all we know there may be ten. He—or they—is acting in a way that contradicts our usual assumptions. He won't talk with us directly. He is making no demands. He is coercing his hostages not to communicate with us. He is acting as though time is his advantage, not ours."

"That's it? I've been briefed already."

"That's not *it*. The building they're in is a fortress. It has two-foot-thick stone walls. No windows. Two doorways—one on the main level, one to the basement. We have no knowledge where inside that structure he has the hostages, or how he is maintaining control of them.

"The subject is sophisticated with explosives and comfortable with electronics. He is likely armed. If we interfere with his communications, he has already demonstrated he will retaliate lethally. We must assume that he is prepared to kill all the remaining hostages if he suspects an attempted breach."

"I said I've been briefed."

Christine ignores his impudence. "I do not expect your witness to talk. I suspect that Michael Smith is convinced that the consequences of talking to us are much worse than the consequences of maintaining his silence."

The agent sneers. "You were out there. Why did he run at the end?"

Christine wants to slap him. "He ran at the end because he was told to run at the end. My guess is that the hostage taker was probing SWAT, and clearing the area in front of the building so the other three could exit without incident.

"I also suspect that Michael Smith the third, and all the others, witnessed the execution of the girl whose body was just left outside the door. They have already seen the very real consequences of not doing what they are told. They aren't going to talk until this ends. Maybe not even then."

Christine is thinking this may be her last chance to say her piece. She fills her lungs and continues, "The hostage taker killed Jonathan Simmons, the first hostage out the door, so we would know that he was capable of that. He has now released four other kids, and sent out one more dead body. We have to recognize those are messages as well. He is making it crystal clear that he is capable of those things, too."

"Of releasing his hostages?"

"Yes. He is capable of releasing his hostages. And he is capable of executing his hostages. The girl with the slit throat reminds us that he is not done killing."

The agent's face is impassive. "I should get back to the debriefing."

Christine no longer wants to slap him. She wants to kick him.

As he turns away she says, "One observation from our uniformed officers may be of interest. It could be coincidence, but all four kids who were released were wearing blue shirts. Michael's shirt is blue stripes. The two kids who were killed were both wearing an item of orange clothing. I just confirmed it on the video."

The special agent is staring back over his shoulder at Carmody as though she just broke into a tap routine.

She goes on, "Let me explain. You're from out of town. Blue is a Yale color. A lot of kids wear it here. Orange isn't. It's the color of a rival. Princeton."

The agent asks, "Why would he be letting us know in advance which kids he is letting go, and which he plans to kill? That doesn't make any sense."

Another special agent marches up to the interrogator. Carmody waits.

The agent says, "Two things. One, the girl with the slit throat . . . We have a tentative ID. She is Emily Lanthrop, a junior. She's a co-coordinator of something called Dwight Hall. Her family is from suburban Chicago.

"Second, an AP guy got a shot of her body with a long lens before the area was draped. The photo is out, the media's running with it. A couple of possible names are circulating, including the one we think is correct. Some people who are afraid they are the victim's parents just called the Chicago Field Office. Apparently they got some kind of note. After that, a phone call. We have an agent on the way to interview them."

"Do we have the note?"

"Within minutes."

"Keep me posted. What else?"

"Whiskey, X-ray, Yankee, and Zulu sniper teams are now in place. We have secured the perimeter and have full-time surveillance of the target."

Poe

Poe wasn't in a good position to watch the three hostages emerge from the door of the tomb. High Street, like Grove, was blocked off by barricades. The crescent park near the cemetery was packed with gawkers. He'd had to circle around the law school, cross Grove, and climb up on a sign that identified the campus power facility.

He was too far away from the action. Tree limbs intruded into his line of sight. Once he recognized there was some new activity outside the tomb, he thought he was able to make out three kids—he pegged it as two guys and a girl—finishing their climb down the stone steps. They filed one by one through a gate. Each in turn dropped out of his line of sight. A solitary cop in plainclothes approached them before she, too, dropped out of sight.

A few minutes later, the same cop continued up the stairs, before again disappearing from Poe's view. Poe could tell she was not HRT, not FBI. He didn't know what it meant that HRT was on-site but not in command of hostage negotiations.

The three released hostages were led individually toward Commons.

Poe knew the protocol. The trio was about to be debriefed. The FBI intel squad attached to HRT would do the interviews.

Poe had to find a better vantage. The release of the kids didn't make sense to him.

He texted Dee: **Where r u d?**

PHL

Dee was at the airport, about to get on a plane to go back home to Jerry.

At a tv?

Near one.

What do you see?

Three more kids came out. One dead body.

Body?

The three kids left it outside the door.

Is it another kid?

Bad angle. Can't tell yet.

Definitely dead?

I can't confirm that. No TV sound where I'm standing.

Thanks for helping me.

Dee said, For you, anything. You solo?

It's my nature. HRT is here. I'm keeping my distance. Any intel from Langley?

No, but one hostage is son of one of us.

Company?

No, DIA.

Poe thumbed, **These kids aren't hostages.**

What are they?

Poe had to think before he came up with the right word. When he hit on it, he knew that it fit.

He thumbed, **Ammunition.**

He waited almost a minute for a reply. It was a solitary word: **Holy.**

Poe typed, **God I miss you.**

Dee replied, **Ditto.**

Poe read the text and smiled. He typed, **God I miss you more,** but he didn't hit SEND.

He hopped down from his perch and backtracked along his original route. When he got all the way to Wall Street, he saw that a sedge of five mobile cranes was staging on the other side of the law school, out of sight of Book & Snake.

What HRT was doing was prudent—they were getting assets deployed and ready. Any assault on the Book & Snake tomb had to include the roof. Since the building had no windows, HRT could safely bring the cranes up from behind without being spotted from inside. A risky helicopter drop wouldn't be necessary.

Wall Street remained open to traffic, but the section of sidewalk closest to Beinecke Library was blockaded off. Poe crossed the street to get past the library.

His BlackBerry vibrated as he stepped off the curb.

Dee. **What am I doing, Poe?**

He thought of five ways to interpret her question. He picked the one that caused his gut to seize, figuring that was the most likely.

He thought, but didn't type *You're going back to Virginia, Dee. To Jerry.*

He allowed himself to splurge on some memories the way an alcoholic might sneak a few extra sips from the last bottle in his stash. He remembered how soft the skin felt on the back of her neck just above her spine and what her hair smelled like after a couple of hours in the bar. That she had a rough spot on her left heel and a quarter moon–shaped scar on her right knee. How her armpits felt right after she shaved. That the nail on the pinky on her right foot was missing just a tiny fleck of polish.

That she ate the crust of her toast first.

That she always moaned when he put pressure on a certain spot on her hip.

He knew right then that he didn't have a prayer of titrating the memories of their few days together so that the ration would last him an entire year. At his current consumption, the inventory of memories of Deirdre might not even last Poe a month.

What am I doing, Poe?

He typed, **Don't know, baby, don't know.**

He stared at his screen for a full minute awaiting her reply. But nothing more came back from Dee. He resumed his walk, his BlackBerry in his palm. He stopped abruptly when he was halfway across Wall Street.

He pretended he had changed his mind and spun on his heels, retreating to the sidewalk. He continued in the direction of College Street. He crossed at the corner and walked another ten yards before he looked back.

The BlackBerry buzzed. Another text from Dee.

Torn torn torn.

Poe had suddenly changed his plans because he had spotted a man standing in the precise spot that was his destination—the narrow strip of sidewalk on Wall Street that afforded a view past Woodbridge Hall toward the rear wall of Book & Snake.

The man hogging Poe's desired spot was a white, forty-plus guy with a big head and a body that was solidly in the no-man's-land between husky and overweight. He was dressed like a tourist—chinos and a polo shirt—but early forties or so made him almost too young to be a Yale parent or even a prospective Yale parent. He had no kid in tow. *An alum, maybe?* Poe's gut said not. Instinct said that the man he was watching hadn't attended Yale. Tourist? Possible but not likely. Local? Not a chance.

Poe's BlackBerry vibrated one more time. Dee's text read, **Ammunition??? Holy.**

The arms and shoulders of the man Poe was watching were strong. They didn't quite lie flat against his sides when he was at rest. His eyes were vigilant. Although he was focused on the narrow sliver of view he had across Beinecke Plaza, he also checked every few seconds to see what was on his periphery.

Poe was close to reaching a conclusion about the man but wasn't completely sure until the guy squeezed his left triceps against the big muscle below his left armpit. Poe thought the muscles that wrapped around the sides from the back were the lats, but he was a cardio guy, not a lifting guy. Poe liked long solitary runs. And he worked his abs. Crunches. Hundreds each week.

His mind wandered to Dee. When the light hit him just so and he held his breath and focused all his energy on tightening his abdominal muscles, Poe could convince Dee he had a six-pack. He couldn't hold the definition for more than a few seconds—which was usually just long enough to make her laugh. He would do a thousand crunches a day to hear that.

Poe shook off the memory. He refocused on the man who was fixated on Book & Snake.

The squeeze Poe had just observed—that quick compression of the triceps against the lats—told Poe that the man across the street was unconsciously checking his weapon. When the man was on the job, he was a shoulder-holster guy. The squeeze was a force of habit, something he likely did all day when he was on shift. Second nature.

Cop, military, or private security? Poe added some information to the "very likely" category: The man's not private—if he had a carry permit he'd be wearing his weapon. He didn't look military. And the man wasn't a local cop. If he were local, the gun he had just felt for would not be imaginary; it would be in place tucked below his shoulder, disguised by a light jacket or a sport coat.

Poe's own service weapon was on his belt at the small of his back. A one-size-too-big Chicago Cubs sweatshirt nicely covered the bulk.

Poe thought, *This guy's an out-of-town cop.* The other information Poe added to the "very likely" category was that the man was a detective. A patrol cop would brush his hip to find his gun. But detectives have carry options—if a detective is wearing a shoulder holster, the easiest way for him to check his weapon is to press his arm against his side. It's a totally different tell from that of a patrol cop.

He's an out-of-town detective with a reason not to be carrying. He is standing precisely where I want to be standing—in the best vantage left available to the public to view any activity on the rear side of Book & Snake.

Why? What the hell are you doing here, guy? What do you know?

APRIL 19, SATURDAY AFTERNOON
NEW HAVEN

The HRT special agent in charge finishes watching some video on a laptop in the Tactical Operations Center. He turns to Haden Moody and says, "Lieutenant? I think you might want to see this. It's clear we're dealing with someone familiar with how we work."

Moody jumps from his chair. He says, "Sure. Absolutely. What do you got?"

Moody's not an idiot. He knows he's appearing too eager.

The SAC says, "A few minutes ago we snaked a flexible camera under the blue tarp in back—the one that's covering the stairs that lead to the basement door at the rear of the building. This is the video. It's short. A little more than a minute."

Moody says, "I'm with you."

The SAC briefly turns to the information technology officer. "Put it on the big monitor, please, Adam," he says. "I'll give you the voice-over version. What you're seeing right now is a continuous loop of a couple of hundred feet of coiled, ultrasharp concertina wire spread out so that it completely fills that little stairwell. The razor wire extends a good two feet above the door. The wire is attached to the staircase, to the stairs, and to the stone walls in at least a dozen locations with fasteners shot into the concrete. Simple, but effective. Apparently, the unsub doesn't want us in that stairwell.

"At the bottom of the stairs—there—are two paired wires, purple and green. See them? The wires appear to be connected directly to each end of the concertina cable before they disappear below the basement door. With me?"

Moody doesn't know what it all means. He says, "Yes."

"Our camera is now focused on the exterior of the door—it's a steel door, by the way—that leads into the basement, where we find this photograph conveniently posted for our inspection." He turns to the IT officer. "Pause please. We think this photograph is a rear view of a hooded hostage bound in a large chair. Below the chair you can see a package almost identical to the one that exploded on the waist of the first hostage. We assume this package, like that one, contains a detonator as well as an explosive. You can also see another paired purple and green wire entering the package after leaving a twelve-volt battery on the floor to the left of the chair."

Moody says, "How do you add it up?"

"It could mean that the razor wire in the stairwell is charged so that our agents will suffer shocks during a breach. But our explosives people don't think so. They think that if we attempt to cut the concertina wire to gain access to the door, the detonator will be triggered, the bomb will explode, and the hostage in the chair will die."

Moody spreads his feet, lifts his chin twice in quick succession. He feels a need to add something. For some reason he decides to go all Pollyanna-ish. "So we know this kid's in the basement? That's something, right? We didn't have that before."

The SAC says, "Actually, no. We don't know that. The backdrop to the photo is a white sheet. This hostage could be anyplace in the building. Basement? Top floor? We don't know. Advance the video, please. Okay . . . Now we're looking at the corner of the outside stairwell, near the concrete floor. That . . . there . . . is a remotely operated video camera. To keep an eye on us, I guess. Stop it again at the second photo."

The video advances. Pauses.

"Finally, here is a second photograph that the unsub left for us. This one is attached to the wall opposite the door in the stairwell. We are told by a former member of Book & Snake that this picture is an inside view of the basement door, which is hinged to swing in. Note a few salient details. The edges of the door, all four sides, have been reinforced with three-inch-wide, quarter-inch-thick steel bars that are set in a thick construction adhesive of some kind. Liquid Nails or something like it. We think he did that to keep us from trying to insert . . . anything through gaps around the door. Next, if you look carefully you will see extremely small-gauge copper filament strung through tiny eye fasteners that are screwed to the casing. See it? The filament runs in a continuous loop, back and forth across the door every few inches. It zigzags all the way from the top of the frame to the threshold."

Moody says, "I do."

"Each end of the filament is connected to a separate lead on the purple and green paired wire right . . . there, at the bottom of the door. What does it mean? We think the entire doorway is wired to be a trigger for the explosives. If we open that door, we break the filament. If we breach that door with force, we break the filament. If we break that filament, the detonator below that chair gets juice."

The video ends.

"With enough time we're confident we could get past all of it. Could we do it without being seen? No. Our conclusion is that if we breach at this location, we have a high probability of being detected. In fact, it's possible that our camera was already detected by the unsub's camera. Any attempt at forceful breach through this door will most likely result in the sacrifice of at least one hostage, possibly more. We will have to account for that as we go forward."

Moody says, "Jesus."

The SAC says, "What we're gaming right now is an alternative breach. If we get orders to send in our assault teams, our primary ingress will be the front door right after he opens it to release a hostage. We'll probably simultaneously pierce the roof and drop in from above. If we extrapolate from the defenses he installed in the exterior stairwell, we can expect to find razor wire blocking the interior staircases and some doorways wired to act as triggers. We are staging heavy equipment to help us with the roof drop. We will rehearse the assault inside Scroll & Key."

Moody nods, relieved he at least knows what Scroll & Key is—it's another tomb diagonally across Beinecke Plaza. He says, "Good choice."

"We're not there yet—ready to breach—but I wanted you to know what we're up against."

"Gotcha," says Moody.

Sam

I popped up at the sound of the gunshot, looking for cover.

I backed up against the nearest building, hugging its side as I walked toward the grassy area in the center of Old Campus. A few kids were running toward buildings for cover. Others were standing, looking around, frozen, unable to process the meaning of the ominous *craaack* and the extended *ping* and echo of the ricochet.

A kid called out to a friend who was stuck in place in the middle of the lawn, "I think it was a gunshot, man. Get out of here. Run, man, run. That was a fucking rifle."

I wanted to know what the cop in the cruiser thought. He was out of his car, crouched behind his vehicle, his handgun in his left hand. He was scanning the landscape, unsure where the rifle retort had originated. When he saw me, he said, "Take cover, sir. We have a situation here. Find a building. Away from Old Campus. Now!"

I heard sirens nearby and knew things were about to get complicated, especially for someone like me determined to keep a low profile.

I said, "Thank you, Officer," and began following at least a dozen students who were running toward an arched gate on the Elm Street side of Old Campus. I detoured to encourage a couple of girls who were crouched behind a big bronze statue to come with me to get out of the open. They ran toward the arched gate at full speed.

A second shot rang out. Another ricochet. More echoes.

I broke into a jog, urging the girls not to slow.

Someone yelled, "Harkness! It came from Harkness!"

The gate turned out to be an arched tunnel that ran through a building from the open area I had just crossed, toward Elm Street. I joined about thirty students inside the tunnel. "What's Harkness?" I asked the kid standing closest to me.

"The tower," he said, pointing toward the residence hall that was adjacent to Skull & Bones. My trusty map assigned Harkness Tower to Branford College. I had to figure out this college thing. I thought Yale was the college. What the hell were all these other colleges I'd never heard of?

For many years, I'd made my living as a city cop in the university town of Boulder, Colorado. Until Columbine and Virginia Tech changed the rules of academic tragedy forever, few things put more fear into the town/gown law enforcement community than the possibility of a repetition of the horrors of the University of Texas tower shootings.

Even weighed against modern high-bar carnage and inhumanity scales, the UT sniper had left a horrendous legacy on academic law enforcement. I'd been part of two training exercises with the University of Colorado campus police to coordinate resources in the event we ever had the misfortune to be faced with a campus sniper.

"Is anyone hurt?" I asked loudly.

"There was somebody down in front of Dwight," one girl said. "I don't know, though. I don't know. Oh God."

Dwight, I remembered, was a building on Old Campus. "Which one's Dwight?"

Most of the students around me were already on their cell phones. Three girls were hugging each other. A couple of kids pointed at a building across the wide lawn.

The law enforcement response was picking up steam. Officers—campus and city—began appearing from all sides of Old Campus. Body armor was on. Weapons were drawn. Students were being escorted from hiding places into buildings. The boy who was down in front of Dwight was half-carried into the building. I didn't see any blood on him.

A bullhorn bounced the soprano voice of a female cop off the stone faces of the old buildings. "Students, stay away from windows! Go into your center halls."

Behind me, a New Haven cop's voice—this one male—echoed like a clap of thunder. "Police. Clear out this tunnel. This way now! That's an order. To your right! Right! Elm to College. Get away from Old Campus. Go. Go."

The cop was a black man about thirty-five. His voice carried authority the way Ben & Jerry's carries calories. I'm an expert on both.

Before I'd taken the steps I'd need to clear the tunnel, he blew past me into the open area. The way he moved, I was sure he was ex-military. He ran low and fast in a manner that only looks natural after some serious training. He looked natural.

A young man—hell, a kid, he didn't look old enough to be attending college—was crouched down behind a tree about thirty yards from the tunnel. "I dropped my card," he yelled. "I can't get into the entryway."

A third shot pierced the chaos. This one was different. Echoes, but no ricochet.

I kept my eye on the cop and the kid. The cop joined the kid in the shadow of the tree. He put his gloved hands on the sides of the kid's face and he told the kid what was going to happen next. I heard him say, "You got that?"

"Yes, sir," the kid said.

"We go on my three. One, two . . ." Another shot. The cop didn't hesitate. He did not want to get pinned down by the sniper. The duo stayed low while they ran to the tunnel.

To me, he said, "Get this kid someplace safe. The Green. Off campus. You, too."

"My pleasure, Officer."

"Durfee's?" the kid asked me. "Can I go to Durfee's?"

I didn't want Ann to hear about the sniper on the news. After I escorted the student to safety, I found her number, hit SEND. When she answered, I said, "It's Sam."

"Hello, hello. One moment, please," she said in the same pleasant voice she'd used to introduce herself to me on the yacht. I heard her make an excuse to someone about needing to take the call. The golf tournament was over by then. I hadn't memorized the rest of Friday's party schedule, so I didn't know what her hostess responsibilities were for the remainder of the day.

Fifteen seconds later, she said, "I'm here, Sam."

"First," I said. "Do you have any news? Have you heard from Jane? Any new contact from . . . ?"

"No."

"Okay. Next, there's a sniper in New Haven," I said.

"At Yale? Oh my God. Where?"

"Harkness ring a bell?"

"Of course it does. Jane's in Jonathan Edwards. Oh my God!"

I pulled out my map. Jonathan Edwards was the college between Harkness Tower and Skull & Bones. *Perfect.* I was temporarily suspending my belief in the possibility of coincidence in the universe. If a lightning bolt struck me down right then, I planned to blame it on the guy who wrote the note to Ann Calderón.

"Just happened," I said. "Last five minutes. Three shots so far. I haven't seen any casualties. Right now I'm on the edge of Old Campus, across the street from the New Haven Green. You know where that is?"

"Sure. You're near Phelps Gate. Are you safe?"

I didn't know from Phelps Gate. Back to the map. "Reasonably. I've walked around campus some, figured out where things are. Before the sniper started, there were two patrol cars on the street outside Book & Snake, one outside Skull & Bones. Mostly campus police, but some New Haven cops. That's all I saw. That means a couple of things. First, it means that independent of Jane, the police have reason to be concerned. Two, they aren't fully mobilized—they're not convinced, for instance, that any students are being held against their will. There would be a much more visible response if they suspected a hostage situation."

Ann said, "It also means they're slightly more worried about Book

& Snake than they are about Skull & Bones. You saw the Book & Snake tomb?" she asked.

"I did. It appears quiet, but there could be a rock concert and an orgy going on inside that place and I think it would appear quiet. The place is a fortress."

"I never thought I would say this, Sam, but I so wish that Jane was at an orgy . . . at a rock concert. You have a theory? Do you know where the sniper fits?"

My impulse was to make something up. Something that might provide some solace. Instead I said, "No. I'm still in the dark. The sniper could be part of what's going on with Jane. Or it could be unrelated. I'm trying to keep an open mind."

"This will be on the news," Ann said. "I should go find a computer or a TV."

Another shot clapped. This one was more muted. A fat stone building—some chapel that looked older than our republic—was separating me from Harkness Tower.

"I heard that," Ann said.

"That makes four," I said.

Five, six, and seven followed in quick succession.

"I'll call again when I know more, Ann. If you see anything on TV that you think I might not know, give me a holler."

"Of course."

"Ann," I said, "if Jane is inside the tomb, at least she's safe from the sniper."

"Thank you, Sam," Ann said. "You are so much more of an optimist than I gave you credit for."

Ann Calderón called back in ten minutes.

The number of rifle shots was holding steady at seven. I wasn't in position to know what the law enforcement strategy to locate the sniper entailed. At least one helicopter was in the air. Media or law enforcement chopper? I couldn't tell. I would have bet media. They have more resources.

"Have you seen a television?" she asked.

"No, I circled by Book & Snake—right now I'm in front of Commons near the cemetery. Wanted to see if they pulled that patrol car to respond to the sniper. They haven't. That means that the stakeout of the tomb continues to be important to the Yale Police."

Ann said, "Ronnie and I have a suite at the hotel so we don't have to constantly run home. That's where I am. CNN is showing a local feed from one of the New Haven affiliates. I could be seeing things, Sam. It's a long camera shot, but I think there's something orange up there. A knit hat, something. On the ledge at the top of the tower. Near the belfry."

Orange will show my disappointment. God. "Thanks. I'll find a TV."

"I'm thinking I should make an anonymous call to let the New Haven Police know about the color thing. So that they're not completely in the dark. I mean, they may not know that the sniper and whatever is happening in the tombs might be connected."

I went from A to Z in about three seconds.

"Don't do it, Ann. His instructions may be color-coded. If there are other kids involved, the notes he sent to their parents may have used colors other than blue and orange. If the police start making sense of the orange clues he's leaving, he will know it was you who talked to them. It could be a trap to test your cooperation. You can't tell anyone anything that's in that note. Nothing. If you do, he may retaliate against Jane."

I could hear her breath catch in her throat. "I almost called them two minutes before I called you." Her voice cracked. "Sam. I am so grateful for your help."

"Ann, I'm not helping. I'm trying. Those are two different things. Don't act without talking to me, okay?"

"Yes," she said.

She knew it was good advice, but she didn't like that it was good advice. I could tell she was a woman who didn't take orders well. In most circumstances, my kind of gal.

"Ann, are you covering for me with Dulce? If she knows I'm here, Carmen will know I'm here. This sniper story is going to go national. I don't want Carmen worrying."

"I will make sure Dulce doesn't miss you."

I went back down College Street, intending either to find a television or to get as close as I could to the perimeter that had been erected around Old Campus in the vicinity of the sniper. The tunnel that opened onto Elm Street would have been ideal, but Elm had already been blockaded by patrol cars.

I followed an open path down the center of a grand lawn that my map labeled as Cross Campus. From the walkway, I couldn't see Harkness Tower. That meant the sniper in Harkness Tower couldn't see me. Which meant he couldn't shoot me. That was good.

I walked past two more residence halls. The first one was called Calhoun College, and then one called Berkeley College. Yale Security had moved personnel into position at the entrance to each of the colleges. I was beginning to wonder how many freakin' colleges there were at this place. This being Yale, I was also thinking that some more creative energy might have been invested in naming the primary open green spots on campus. "Old Campus" and "Cross Campus" were not the most imaginative of labels.

I had Cross Campus to myself. The student body wanted nothing to do with the sniper. Smart kids.

I cut behind a flat, round, black granite fountain, but I wasn't able to make the left I was hoping to make. A Yale cop with sergeant's stripes appeared out of nowhere. He was a little older than me, about my size and build. He had a good cop aura—his presence on the path was about twice the size of the physical space he consumed. I knew he was having a legendarily bad day. I had no intention of making it any worse.

He raised his right arm and pointed his index finger. He said, "No. Go back the way you came."

His uniform identified him as a campus cop, but his badge said he was with the New Haven PD. I was completely confused. I said, "Yeah, sorry. I'm kind of . . . lost."

His eyes flared. "You can go that way"—he pointed toward Beinecke—"or you can go that way"—he pointed back down Cross Campus the way I had arrived—"but you can't come this way."

As I turned my back to leave, his shoulder-mounted radio rumbled with a call from Dispatch. The report was succinct, and delivered with an admirable lack of inflection, considering the content. The call was: "New report, possible one eighty-seven, male student, Ingalls, seven-three Sachem."

I forced myself to take another step. I really tried to force myself not to turn back around. I failed. I rotated my upper body, holding out the map as a prop. I wanted to see the sergeant's face.

His expression had hardened, his eyes had narrowed. He touched the button on his shoulder-mounted microphone and confirmed the transmission.

I started to say, "Could you show me—"

"Get out of here," he said. "Now." His voice was in full don't-fuck-with-me mode. He had to feel like his peaceful campus world was crumbling at his feet.

In cop radio parlance, a one eighty-seven is a suspected homicide.

The Yale cops were thinking that a male student had been murdered at Ingalls.

That would be my next stop.

Ingalls, it turned out, was already on my must-visit list if I ended up having any free moments during my time in New Haven. I just didn't recognize the formal name of the building. I knew the building only by function, and by nickname.

Ingalls was the Yale hockey rink. Legendarily, the Yale Whale. Among college hockey fans—I'm one of those—the place is a celebrated sheet of ice.

The map revealed that I would find Ingalls on the other side of the cemetery, so I headed in the direction of Beinecke Plaza. The pulsing shrieks of one siren, and then another, were starting to move away from Old Campus, toward Grove Street Cemetery.

Those would be the first responders to the one eighty-seven.

I followed the footpath that led toward Beinecke, pausing for a fire department pumper truck steaming in the direction of Old Campus. The plaza in front of the rare book library was deserted. I climbed the stairs to High Street, passing within feet of the Book & Snake tomb before I crossed over to the cemetery. The earliest headstone I spotted on my way across the graveyard was marked "1806."

A couple of blocks past the rear boundary of the cemetery I eyed the distinctive outline of the Yale Whale—the home of Yale hockey.

I smiled at the form. Despite the circumstances, I couldn't help it. It was an even more joyful building than I had guessed from the pictures I had seen over the years. I thought it was terrific that someone had put so much creative energy into designing a barn for playing hockey.

Three patrol cars—two Yale, one New Haven—were parked in front of the building along with a rescue rig from the New Haven Fire Department. A patrolman was already stringing crime scene tape. He had completed a run of yellow ribbon from one street corner to another. He was busy extending official territory all the way down the sidewalk in front of Ingalls. I could hear more sirens firing in the distance. I couldn't tell whether they were heading toward the hockey rink or toward the sniper on Old Campus.

The local cops were being yanked every which way. I wondered, of course, if that was someone's intent.

The hockey arena was the center of an obvious construction zone. A long wooden barricade blocked the entrance to the building from the sidewalk. Two immense roll-away bins for construction debris were planted along the curb. Pallets of building materials were staged outside the long line of entrance doors. Trailers for the general contractor and the plumbing and electrical subs were on-site, farther down the block.

I asked a passing student if he knew what was going on. I'd startled him. He pulled iPod buds from his ears before he said, "What?"

He was scruffy. Clean, but scruffy. A week's worth of growth on his cheeks, more than that on his chin. Old black jeans, a stretched-out gray sweater over a thrift-store dress shirt. Tails hanging out. Black horn-rimmed glasses. The pièce de résistance of his outfit was a well-worn brown felt fedora. It was a fine fedora—the feather was a little moth-eaten, but it was intact—and the kid wore the topper with aplomb.

I recalled the way my son had recently described a man his mother was dating. Simon had said, "The guy thinks he's a hipster, Dad. But he's just an old poser."

That worked for me. I gestured toward Ingalls and asked the hipster, "Do you know what's going on over there? Ingalls?"

He glanced across the street. His eyebrows came out of hiding from behind his horn-rims. "No," he said. "Cops? Lots of cops. Whoa. No. Sorry."

He apparently hadn't noticed all the hoopla across the street. He apparently also had an antipathy to verbs.

His eyes were puzzled. He looked at me and said, "Biker ninjas? Here? Shit. This time of day? Whew."

Biker ninjas? That was a tempting diversion. Despite my curiosity, I let it go. "The construction?" I asked him. "Do you know what's going on at the rink? Any idea?"

"Rink? I'm really . . . I don't. . . I mean, ice skating, right? Sorry, man."

I found it sad that he didn't know how special the place was, and that he obviously hadn't known that the big, exuberant building with the spine of the roof as lovely as the profile of a whale was just a big old hockey rink.

I thanked him.

"Yeah," he said, sticking the buds back into place, walking away.

The next student to come down the sidewalk was a girl put together like a couple of girls I dated in college. Strong. Solid. Girls I could play touch football with and not be afraid I would break them. Girls who owned hockey skates, not figure skates. Girls who knew how to fish.

Girls who liked to fish. Since I was the odd guy who actually liked to dance, I never thought it was too much to ask to find a girl who liked to fish.

"Excuse me, any idea what's going on over there?" I asked her.

Her hair was dirty blond and kind of stringy. Her eyes were the blue of the pottery my mom liked to collect. Unlike the fedora-ed one, she had already noticed the police activity across the street. "I do not know," she said definitively. "I can tell you they weren't there when I went to class an hour ago. Whatever it is going on, it's new." She raised her phone. "I just got an emergency text to stay away from Old Campus. Maybe it has something to do with that." She shrugged.

A whole paragraph full of complete sentences. I felt renewed optimism for her generation. But I also felt concern that she seemed less than alarmed by the warning she had received.

I recognized her accent. She was from Wisconsin. There was a time in my life when the nuances of her spoken words would have allowed me to pinpoint the cluster of counties near the town where she had grown up. My ears no longer had the required fine-tuning, but I would have bet my last few bucks that she'd spent a few hundred predawns hooking cows up to machines in her family farm's milking parlor.

"I was hoping to see the rink. It's under construction?"

She was carrying a hefty microbiology text. She moved it from her right hand to her left. "For a while, yeah. Major renovation, been going on for a while. They're making space for the women's team. Title Nine, ADA stuff. New locker rooms. The place is old—it needed some help. One of my friends is a center—second line. I think they're almost done with the work. Sorry, though, about your visit." She smiled. "Maybe you can catch a game in the fall. You're from up north?"

It wasn't really a question. To a practiced ear my northern Minnesota accent provided a whole lot of demographic information.

"Minnesota," I said. "Iron Range. Not far from Hibbing."

"You play?"

"Did. Defenseman. I mess around a little."

"Cool. My dad's a center. He still plays a couple times a week. Wicked slap shot."

I had to smile again. "Good for him. Hey," I said. "Thanks."

She made me miss Minnesota. I hadn't had that feeling in a while.

Three distinct pops, muted by distance, found my ears. The wind blowing off Long Island Sound was carrying the cracks of the gunfire up the hill from Old Campus.

"Did you hear that?" she asked me.

I nodded. "Apparently there's a sniper," I said. "People are saying he might be in Harkness. That message you got? You should stay away from Old Campus."

"Darn," she said. "I was just starting to convince my mother that New Haven is safe."

I wanted to stick around, strike up a conversation with one of the uniforms in front of Ingalls, maybe try to get one to spill some details about the body that had been discovered inside the Whale. I really would have loved to be free to loiter near the cluster of cops who were waiting for the forensics van and the coroner, to listen in when one of the guys uttered the first inevitable, dark, Jonas-in-the-whale joke.

But I knew I couldn't risk hanging around near a fresh one eighty-seven, especially one that wasn't drawing a crowd. Alert cops notice watchers at crime scenes.

To have any prayer of finding Jane, I had to stay invisible. I turned to head back down the hill toward Beinecke Plaza, giving the Whale one more long admiring glance.

I stopped. I couldn't believe I had almost missed it.

A line of doors runs across the entire street façade to handle the crowds that exit the Ingalls rink after a game. On one of the two doors in the center of the row, directly below the dramatic spine that runs down the building's ambling roof, someone had placed an X on the upper half of a glass pane. The mark was about two feet by two feet.

I crossed the street and walked right up to the crime scene tape. I had to be sure I was seeing what I thought I was seeing.

"That's far enough," a uniformed officer told me.

I made eye contact. I said, "Yes, sir." The X on the door was made of orange reflective tape. The tape was shiny and new. It hadn't been up there long.

Ann's worst fears for her daughter were now, for another family, the stuff of reality.

I walked away. The setting sun and my watch told me it was almost six o'clock.

My stomach told me I hadn't eaten in a week. I persuaded myself to complete an errand before I went in search of food. On the way, I called Carmen, waking her from a nap. I told her I loved her and that she should go back to sleep. I was stepping up to the door of the campus bookstore on Broadway when my phone vibrated. I thought it might be Carmen calling me back. But it was Ann.

I said, "Yeah." Nothing. I said, "It's Sam. You there?"

She managed to say, "I—" before a cough intruded.

I said, "Ann, the sniper seems to have stopped for now. But I need to let you know that the body of a student was discovered in another part of campus. An apparent homicide. It's a male, I think. I'm trying to get information." I hadn't decided whether to tell her about the orange X. About the nature of a certain man's disappointment.

It turned out that for the moment Ann wasn't interested in the dead body in the hockey rink. "I just . . . got . . . another call," she said. She was trying to talk on a halting inhale. The sound kept catching. "It just came . . . in."

"Okay," I said. I could feel bad news looming.

"This time it was Jane's voice. A recording of her voice. A very bad connection. Delays, echoes. It was as though it was routed around the world a couple of times. I'm not sure I caught every word."

I'm no tech genius—in my son's generous appraisal, neither am I a complete tech dweeb—but I had a hunch that the voice recording Ann had received had been sent overseas by the guy inside the tomb as an attachment in an encrypted email, maybe to Namibia. A compatriot there had then routed the recording to Ann in Florida via Internet telephony. VoIP. Skype.

Tracing the calls would be a nightmare, even for an outfit with the toys of NSA.

But the bad news Ann had to share wasn't the crappy connection. The bad news was still to come. I said what was obvious to me, on the off chance that it wasn't obvious to Ann. "That's all good news so far. You heard your daughter's voice. That means she was okay when she made the recording."

I didn't say that in the hostage/kidnapping/ransom business, that's called "proof of life."

Ann said, "Jane gave me instructions on how to leave the information he wants. It involves websites and passwords about our family and downloading encryption software and . . ."

Here it comes. The bad news is . . . right around the bend.

She released an exhale that had all the power of an exclamation. Then she said, "I know what he wants, Sam. I . . . understand now."

I knew then that what he wanted would be the bad news.

"Just a second," she said.

I waited.

My phone to my ear, I walked past the bookstore onto an adjacent plaza. This one was rimmed by more colleges. Stiles. Morse. One was undergoing some major renovation.

These two colleges were a whole different world architecturally. The Middle Ages were gone. So was Georgian Britain. I was betting the 1960s for the birth of these babies. Lots of concrete and stone. Many angles. I said, "Ann, you still there?"

I could hear the background sounds of a yet another gathering. I wasn't sure how she did it. I'd only lasted for half a day and I was partied out. Maybe I wasn't cut out to be rich. I found that kind of reassuring.

The background sounds faded, then stopped. "Sam, you with me so far?"

"Hundred percent, Ann. You okay?"

"Fine, thank you. Let me catch my breath. Okay. Last year I wrote a letter to the *Journal of Geophysical Research*. It was in response to another letter that had just been published about a controversy in the field after some television documentaries."

Huh? I kept my mouth shut.

"Part of my letter was redacted on the advice of the *Journal* editors. They said it was for . . . security reasons. I thought it was silly at the time. The odds of anyone ever being able to use the information are so long that . . . Anyway, I agreed to the editing. Basically, a few facts that were not essential for establishing my point were removed."

I didn't understand. I hoped it would become clear.

"What I wrote was part of a debate among scientists, Sam. That's all. Someone with a political agenda on the periphery of the field had made a point that they weren't really qualified to make. I was correcting the geophysical record. Not a big deal. It's the sort of thing that happens in journals in every scientific discipline."

I was having a hard time seeing a road that ran in the vicinity of the story Ann was telling me that would also end up passing anywhere close to the village of Pertinent. I didn't have to remind myself that the woman was in the middle of a weekend that was so difficult I could hardly imagine. I would grant her all the latitude I had in my heart.

I found a bench. My feet hurt. They'd been carrying my too-fat ass around for too much of a too-long day. I smelled Indian food. It smelled like comfort. "Okay," I said.

"Do you know much about the Canary Islands?" she asked.

Like what body of water they're in? I thought. *No, not really.* I would have put a couple of bucks on the Atlantic Ocean. I said, "That thing I said before about context? Goes for geography, too. Double. Please tell me what you think I need to know."

"The Canary Islands are a Spanish archipelago in the Atlantic, not too far off the coast of Morocco in Northern Africa. The specific island that my letter was about is called La Palma. It's the westernmost of the seven islands in the chain. The scientific controversy involves a well-known, active volcano on La Palma called Cumbre Vieja that last erupted just after World War II."

I'm thinking, *This has to do with Jane, right?*

I don't know much about Indian food other than I like it. The aromas were killing me. I would have gladly traded what was left of my fortune for a plate of basmati rice, some tandoori, and an ice-cold Kingfisher.

"I think the person who has Jane wants the information that the editors redacted from the letter I wrote to *Geophysical Research*."

"That's it?" I said.

"That's it."

"How bad could that be?" I asked.

Ann's answer destroyed my appetite.

Sam

I woke early on Saturday anxious about money. I was oddly grateful for the distraction.

The diversion didn't last long. I soon resumed my rumination that I was missing something crucial about Jane Calderón's situation.

I feared that I wasn't alone in my ignorance. A return stroll past the tombs and the hockey barn just before I went to bed on Friday had revealed that the local police agencies were focusing more of their resources on the sniper and on the murder investigation in Ingalls than they were on the Skull & Bones and Book & Snake tombs. The law enforcement presence outside the secret societies remained cursory.

I remained concerned that the local cops didn't recognize what they were dealing with.

Saturday's breakfast was the three ninety-nine special at the Copper Kitchen, a café just down the street from the hotel. I read the local newspaper, the *New Haven Register,* during breakfast to catch up on the events—the Old Campus sniper and the dead student in the hockey rink—of the previous afternoon.

The *Register* identified the dead student in the hockey rink as a rumored recent Skull & Bones tap. His name and hometown were withheld. He had apparently been strangled, his body left just about where the penalty box would have stood had the arena had a sheet of ice down and the boards and glass up for a game.

Because of the ongoing renovations to the building, there was no ice sheet inside the Whale. No boards. No penalty box. Probably no Zamboni.

Only a dead tap from Skull & Bones.

Why Skull & Bones and not Book & Snake? I couldn't make sense of that.

I had a headache. I asked the waitress at the coffee shop if she had something that might help. She offered a sympathetic smile before she tossed me a sleeve with a couple of Advils. "Here you go, hon," she said. "On me."

She thought I was hungover, bless her heart. The table of fraternity boys slumped forward with their elbows on the table in the back booth? *They* were hungover. They were also covered in paint. I didn't really want to know.

A large color photograph on the front page of the paper showed some of the police activity outside the hockey arena. The paper also provided a nice diagram of the inside of the Whale. A small x marked the spot where the body was discovered.

Even though it was clearly visible in the full-color front-page photograph, the newspaper article made no mention of the other x, the more poignant and terrifying x, the large taped orange X on the entry door to the Whale. Anyone who noted the orange mark probably assumed that the construction crews had put it there for some benign purpose.

I was one of a very small cadre of people who recognized that the orange X was one particular person's way of expressing his displeasure. No. *Disappointment.*

The other big story on the front page of the local paper was the Old Campus sniper, which turned out to have been much more and much less than had met the eye.

The entire crisis had been an elaborate hoax. A sophisticated remote-controlled audio setup carefully hidden in the belfry at the top of Harkness Tower had been rigged to play the sounds of rifle shots echoing off the stone and brick walls of Old Campus.

There had never actually been either a rifle or a sniper in the tower. Only digital electronics and fine speakers. A student prank was suspected. There were reports that a ski hat had been recovered at the scene. Campus police were investigating.

I'd actually learned about the hoax before I made it to breakfast. The bellman in front of the hotel—he's the one who had pointed me toward the Copper Kitchen—volunteered that one of his brother-in-law's poker buddies was a New Haven cop who said that the Yale campus police were thinking that the tower sniper prank had been pulled off by Cantabs. Or by Princeton or MIT students trying to blame it on Cantabs. He wasn't sure which.

I'd said, "Can tabs?" hoping for clarification. I suspected that it was another opaque local colloquialism, like the previous day's "biker ninjas."

"Harvard students," he'd said. "Cantabs."

"Really? They're called can tabs?" I repeated.

"Yes, sir," he said with some exaggerated smugness. "They call themselves Cantabs. What can I say?"

I let it go. I didn't believe him. If it were indeed true, it seemed like the sort of thing I should already know. I'd seen Harvard play hockey. They weren't the Cantabs.

The local paper did note that the hat discovered in the Harkness Tower belfry was orange, not crimson. I'd watched enough college basketball on TV to know that the Ivy League team that used orange as a school color was Princeton, not Harvard. Harvard was crimson. But the Crimson Cantabs? I didn't think so.

Although I was still naïvely holding on to the hope that the rumors about Harvard's—or Princeton's, or even MIT's—responsibility for the sniper hoax were correct, I suspected that they weren't. I was holding tight to my assumption that the hat was orange not because some devious MIT students were trying to lay blame on Harvard by leaving a clue that the hoax had been pulled off by kids from Princeton, but rather because the person who had written the ominous note to Ann Calderón was expressing his continuing disappointment.

I left two bucks on the counter after I scraped my plate and paid my tab. As I stepped out onto the Chapel Street sidewalk, I had exactly twenty-seven dollars and a Discover card that was as close to its limit as a sloppy drunk at last call. I was not even sure I could use the card to swipe for my lunch at a fast-food joint.

I had been dreading this day since the moment I learned I'd been suspended from the Boulder Police Department. Here it was, the day that "broke" became more than theoretical. Damn me. Damn suspension.

Damn economy. Damn credit default swaps. Damn arrogant politicians.

I really never thought I'd see the day that I was watching my middle-class identity disappearing in the rearview mirror. I put my financial future on the list of things I would worry about when I got back to Carmen.

The center of gravity at Yale had shifted overnight.

My after-breakfast reconnaissance revealed that while the solitary patrol car remained parked in front of Skull & Bones, the law enforcement presence outside Book & Snake was growing exponentially. That fact told me that the local cops weren't completely sure where the action was, but they were beginning to lean decidedly in the direction of Book & Snake.

I tried to stay inconspicuous as I watched additional resources get deployed. By mid-morning, perimeter barricades had been erected at the ends of the Book & Snake block on Grove Street. The entrances to Beinecke Plaza were taped off. The gates to the cemetery were closed. I watched an incident command vehicle—basically a fine class A motor home with a couple of bump-outs, the whole thing packed with electronics and communication gear—get driven into place down the block. The New Haven PD probably acquired the big bus with a thick tranche of their post-9/11 antiterror funds. A nearby SWAT vehicle was almost as large as the command bus. An aging New Haven Fire Department pumper truck was a little farther down the street, paired with a brand-new fire/rescue rig. A large hazmat van was behind it.

Hazmat? Probably a precaution. I knew that when law enforcement doesn't know what to expect, we tend to plan for almost everything.

A block farther down the street in the other direction—beyond Commons—four husky microwave trucks had rolled into sight, beaming signals for the network affiliates broadcasting from the scene. The stations' cameras were mounted on tripods on the sidewalk across from Book & Snake, lenses aimed at the front of the tomb.

After the previous day's sniper drama and the discovery of the murdered student at the hockey rink, the local community was rife with rumors that something was going on in the secret society tombs. A crowd of a couple hundred people were gathered behind the barricades at Book & Snake. About half were of student age; the rest were folks from town. The people from town were mostly African-Americans. Young, old, everything in between.

I got the sense from wandering through the crowd that town and gown weren't exactly chummy. Whether or not that meant anything in regard to the current situation, I didn't know. I added it to the list of variables for which I had not yet assigned a value.

Determination earned me sole possession of a narrow stone podium at the base of a section of the cemetery wall. I was on the back side of a tiny park about fifty feet past the cops' command vehicle, not far from Book & Snake. I could see most of the front of the tomb from my perch.

People around me were talking about "hostages." Plural. Local knowledge, or rumor? I didn't know.

I counted twenty-two uniformed cops in the vicinity of the building. Some were campus, some were city, some were county. Most were in riot gear and helmets. Many were carrying weapons. I didn't see any sign of SWAT, but I assumed they were nearby doing their get-ready thing. If hostages were a concern, SWAT would be involved.

I didn't spot a state police presence. I didn't know how things worked in Connecticut, but assumed that if New Haven PD wanted help, the state police would provide it. Nor did I see any feds. If New Haven cops were like Boulder cops, they wouldn't reach out to the feds until the situation was clearly beyond their tactical capabilities. Even then, they would call in the cavalry with great reluctance.

When someone did call in the FBI for support, agents from the local field office could get on-scene quickly. But if the FBI Hostage Rescue Team—HRT—was mobilizing, they would be traveling north from their base in Virginia, probably by air. That would take time.

I figured Saturday morning was still for the local boys and girls in blue.

A solitary woman about my age—black? Latin? I wasn't sure—with a badge hung around her neck was pacing on the sidewalk across from the tomb. She was in plainclothes and wore shoes that told me she was prepared to be on her feet for a while. One moment she would look serene and self-assured. The next time I looked at her she would be on her toes ready to jump right into the game.

I pegged her as the hostage negotiator. Local, probably New Haven PD, probably a sergeant or lieutenant on a designated hostage negotiation team. For now, she was warming up on the sidelines. At some point, when and if contact was made with someone inside Book & Snake, she would be sent into the game to take over the action. She'd be the quarterback. She had to be ready.

The presence of a hostage negotiator on the scene told me that the local cops had reason to believe they had a hostage. Ann had not received a call from anyone in New Haven law enforcement, which meant that the local cops had not yet identified Jane Calderón as a potential hostage. If the New Haven cops weren't aware that Jane was missing, the presence of the hostage negotiator in front of me meant that Jane Calderón was not the only possible hostage inside the Book & Snake tomb.

Ann and I had been working under the assumption that Jane was one of many students being held inside Book & Snake, but I was witnessing the first confirmation that supposition was true. Simple law enforcement calculus also told me that the higher the number of hostages, the greater the likelihood that feds would show up, and that the higher the profile of the suspected hostages, the greater the likelihood that feds would show up.

Thus far, no feds.

The presence of the hostage negotiator also indicated that—if the same MO had been used with the other kid's family as had been used with the Calderóns—some other kid's parents had not been as assiduous as Ann about not sharing the contents of the communications they'd received from the guy in the tomb.

Orange will show my disappointment.

Ann had explained to me that the meeting Jane was planning to attend on Thursday evening could have included fifteen to thirty-two students. That was a lot of potential hostages. I wondered how many of those students were officially unaccounted for, and how many were, like Jane, only missing in the eyes of their families.

What did the local cops really know on Saturday morning? Time would tell.

During my first hour and a half of observation outside the tomb, I called Carmen a couple of times. She was bored. She had gas. She was constipated. She had a hemorrhoid the size of a walnut. Her ankles were fat. She was worried about the baby. He kicked too much. He didn't kick enough.

Mostly she needed to talk. I was grateful I was able to listen.

I watched the hostage negotiator's futile attempts to initiate contact with someone inside the tomb. She tried on three different occasions, about thirty minutes apart. She was proceeding according to the book. She used a bullhorn. She identified herself as a New Haven police officer. She asked the subject to come out the door with his hands in the air, or to contact the New Haven Police by telephone.

Her tone was even. Nonconfrontational. Businesslike. *License and registration, please.* She expressed an eagerness to talk and a willingness to work things out.

The person or persons in the tomb didn't respond to any of her entreaties.

My impression was that she was going through the motions. She wasn't really expecting anyone to respond. I didn't know whether that was because she had some intelligence that I lacked, or because she had a gut feeling no one was inside. I would have loved to know whatever intelligence the New Haven PD had.

I spent most of the morning doing the same thing the local cops were doing—waiting for the person who was holding Jane, and at least one of her friends, to make his next move.

Carmen called me again just before noon. Before I had a chance to get my phone open, the call failed. My strong cell signal had suddenly devolved from five bars to none.

Being a suspicious guy, I wondered if the local cops were up to something.

My feet were growing numb from maintaining my balance on the stone pedestal. I was about to relinquish my coveted high ground when a kid—a tall male—suddenly appeared outside the door of the tomb. I wasn't in position to see the front doors open—the pillars blocked the doors from view—but when the young man stepped forward I could see him clearly.

We have contact, I thought. *Shit. Here we go. Game on.*

Cops began to move toward him from each side of the tomb. He called out, "Don't shoot! Don't fucking shoot!"

The reactive murmurs in the crowd prevented me from hearing the next couple of lines he spoke.

The crowd quieted just in time for me to hear him say that he was a bomb.

A bomb.

The approaching cops stopped. Then the kid showed off the bomb.

It was a small, square pack taped to his body. Despite my dependence on Kmart readers, my distance vision is pretty damn good. The pack, I thought, was conveniently labeled "BOMB" in cartoonish lettering.

I wondered if the marking was a joke, but I was preoccupied by something else. For me, at that moment, the bomb was a secondary development. Primary was that, beneath his wrinkled dress shirt, the young man was wearing an orange T-shirt.

Which either meant the kid liked orange or the man in the tomb was suffering yet another episode of disappointment. I wouldn't have bet the contents of my full bladder on the former conclusion.

I thought of the kid in the Whale, and winced at the indication that more of the unseen man's disappointment was coming.

The bomb is no joke.

The next few minutes passed in a split second that took a year.

Stephen Hawking could have debated it with the ghost of Albert Einstein, the whole thing moderated by Neil deGrasse Tyson.

Then maybe Tyson could explain it to us, in English, on *Nova*.

Yeah, during my suspension I'd been watching a lot of PBS.

As much as the space/time cosmology was throwing me, it wasn't sufficient confusion to prevent me from seeing the near future. I saw the end clearly and kept anticipating that the local cops would see it, too, and act.

But the cops kept not acting. *Can't they see?* I wanted to scream at them to do what they had to do. I knew that if I spoke up—if I intervened—I would cease to be of any use to Ann. Worse, I would put Jane in increased danger.

I clenched my jaw. A piece of my soul died with each tick of the clock. I could feel the decay as the young man counted down the minutes.

"I . . . will die . . . ," he said, "in three minutes."

When he said, "Two minutes," he extended the index finger on each hand for just a moment.

Who counts that way? I thought. *Why not two fingers on one hand?*

The young man in front of the tomb felt the end coming. When he said, "I will die in one minute," he extended those two index fingers one more time. Barely. But he did.

Why? Why not one finger for one minute? I didn't know that.

I did know that he believed that his end was coming.

It was as though those words—*I will die in one minute*—finally flipped a switch for the authorities. Cops started moving. Civilians began running. Emergency personnel raced for cover. The cops were forced to accomplish in one chaotic minute what they could have done in three or four semi-orderly ones.

I stayed where I was. As people sprinted past me, I pushed myself back against the fence so that eighty percent of my body was shaded from the front of the tomb by the thick stone pillar. I comforted myself that the twenty percent of me that was left exposed was mostly fat.

The cops pushed the crowd farther down the street.

My attention was locked on the young man's face. I convinced myself that I saw his eyes soften into bewilderment and his jaw set into iron as he tried to digest the indigestible—the fact that he was about to die.

I watched his lips move but heard no sound come from them.

A burly cop yelled at me to run. He was hustling past me as he communicated his order.

I wasn't going anywhere.

Someone with a bullhorn said, "All personnel, take cover."

I heard the explosion. I was able to keep my eyes open during the aftermath.

It didn't matter. Some events happen so quickly that they are not actually seen in real time. The eyes can't do it. The brain is either unable or unwilling to process all the data.

It was, I knew, just as well. There was nothing that happened that I wanted to remember.

And nothing I'd be able to forget.

Gravity dropped me off the pillar. I walked slowly away from the tomb. I felt heavy and light, a two-ton man floating in one-tenth gravity.

The smoke hadn't cleared.

Sirens shrieked. People were screaming. Running. Cops were shouting orders at the bystanders who had become immobilized—their mouths open, their eyes unblinking—by the insanity that their brains were trying unsuccessfully to comprehend.

The aftermath of the explosion didn't interest me.

I felt my phone in my hand though I didn't remember taking it from my pocket.

I checked the screen. I had four bars.

I would give Ann thirty seconds to call. If she called me first, it would mean she had been watching television and had seen what just happened on Fox or CNN. If she didn't call me, I would phone her and I would tell her to sit down, and then I would tell her what had happened to the young man in front of the Book & Snake tomb.

After I described it, I would try, but fail, to explain it.

I prayed that the young man's parents had not been watching. I prayed that Ann had not been watching. I knew my version of the kid's death would be more palatable than cable's, my rendition would be more compassionate than theirs.

Unlike cable, I wouldn't demand that she watch the replay of the explosion again, and again, and again. I wouldn't show old footage from Lower Manhattan and Virginia Tech and Mumbai, for no other reason than because I had it.

The facts I needed to share with Ann were these: This thing in New Haven was real. The man who was holding her daughter hostage had again revealed his disappointment at the parents of one of Jane Calderón's fellow hostages. As he had the previous day at Ingalls rink, the man had framed his disappointment in orange and expressed it by murdering someone's child.

He'd done it this time with a bomb. He'd done it coldly and cruelly on national television.

The thirty seconds passed. I allowed ten more to float away before I scrolled for Ann's name in my phone and hit SEND.

She answered after half a ring. She didn't bother with a greeting. She didn't wait for me to try to console her. She said, "I am at the hotel. I am walking to the elevator. When I get to the suite, I will go to my computer and I will follow his instructions. I will give that man exactly what he wants. Everything he wants. Anything he wants."

"I'm so sorry," I said.

"I'm making a deal with the devil, Sam. I know that. I wish I didn't have to, but I do. I love my daughter too much . . . to lose her."

"I can't imagine being in your position, Ann. How it must feel, seeing what you just witnessed. I am so sorry."

My words weren't quite true. I could imagine. The previous year I had taken a not-so-innocent life to protect my child when I felt a killer's dark shadow looming over him. I'd had second thoughts about it, and third, before I'd taken that person's life, but I took it.

I hadn't yet lost a night's sleep over what I did. My lack of remorse didn't trouble me.

But there was a crucial difference between the threat that Jane was facing and the one that had faced my son, Simon: I had been able to save Simon that day without putting anyone at risk other than myself and the person who was threatening him.

Ann did not have that luxury. To save Jane, Ann would have to knowingly increase the risk to many, many other parents' children. She would go to bed each night knowing that there was a tiny but real possibility that other parents' children might someday have to pay the price that Ann was unwilling to let her daughter pay.

Perhaps so that I might understand her decision, or maybe so that I might forgive her for making it, Ann said, "I'm sorry. Jane is not a soldier, Sam."

"She is not," I said. "She is an innocent."

"What are the odds that anyone could ever use the information I have?" Ann asked me. "It's absurd. One in ten million? Higher?"

The odds aren't zero, I thought. *We are having this conversation because the odds aren't zero.* I didn't know Ann Calderón well, but I knew her well enough to know that the reason she hadn't followed the man's instructions when she had first received them on Friday was because Ann Calderón knew that the odds of someone using her information, although infinitesimal, were not zero.

But I kept my appraisal to myself. Ann didn't need that reminder.

Ann's words—*Jane is not a soldier, Sam*—underscored the great divide between the parental experience she and I shared, and the parental experience of so many others. But she didn't even begin to cross it.

The bridge between the two camps was crowded with strangers.

Millions, literally millions, of sons and daughters who were Jane's age—some maybe a little younger, some maybe a little older—*were,* in fact, soldiers, or sailors, or airmen, or Marines. They were volunteers in the Armed Forces of the United States of America who had taken oaths to sacrifice—including the real possibility of making the ultimate sacrifice by giving their lives—in order to protect our country.

Jane was not one of those soldiers. She had not volunteered to be among those who would serve and protect. And sacrifice.

Jane was one of the majority. She was one of the protected.

Did that free her from personal responsibility to guard our shores with her life?

I didn't know. I knew that Simon, my son, was—like Jane—not a soldier. Not yet, anyway. As his father I would not, I could not, volunteer to sacrifice him for the greater good.

Was that selfish of me?

Yes. Of course it was.

I added the conundrum to the tally of things I'd ponder some other time, once I was no longer in New Haven.

I said, "Ann, how are you supposed to . . . How do you . . . reply to him? Send the information?"

The line was silent for a few seconds. She said, "Is it crucial that you know, Sam?"

I understood what she was asking me. What she was telling me. "No, it's not. Of course not."

"I trust you, Sam. That's not it."

"No explanation is necessary. The less I know about that the better it is for you. And for Jane."

"Thank you, Sam."

"You know I'm here until she's free. Until she is in your arms."

"I can't ever repay you."

"You don't ever need to."

Poe

Poe watched the guy without the shoulder holster loiter on the edge of Beinecke Plaza for a few minutes before the man stuffed his hands into his pockets and turned up Wall Street in the direction of the law school.

The man's route kept him within a block of Book & Snake at all times. Poe didn't consider that to be a coincidence.

Poe waited thirty seconds before he began walking in the same direction. He was maintaining a good hundred feet of separation between him and his new prey, well aware that it was neither an ideal time nor location to attempt to tail someone, especially solo.

The man slowed. He pulled an iPhone from his pocket.

Poe slowed, too, mirroring his pace to that of his target. He was surprised at the man's choice of electronics—he hadn't made the out-of-town cop as an iPhone kind of guy.

The man stopped. He pulled an old-school flip phone from another pocket.

Poe thought, *He carries two phones. Why?*

The man didn't dial the phone. He opened it and put it to his ear. He was answering a call. Within seconds he was shaking his head, forcefully.

Poe kept walking, closing on him. He got near enough to hear the man say, "Really? Right now?" Seconds later, not as clearly, Poe thought he heard, "Damn. Okay, I'm on my way there."

Poe was only ten feet from the man when the guy took off at twice the earlier pace.

Poe followed him around the law school, past the campus power plant, and then across the street to a small crescent-shaped park that was formed as Grove Street curved away from the cemetery. Poe knew from his earlier reconnaissance that the park and the power facility both offered a vantage from which to see the front of the tomb.

He was working under an assumption that the man had heard something on that phone call that made him determined to be able to see the front of Book & Snake.

Poe edged closer, attaching himself to a trio of students heading in the same direction. Across the street from the little park, he broke away from the group and stopped in the shadow of a tree near the power facility.

Poe texted Dee. **Where r u d?**

Still PHL.

On board?

In line.

Poe knew the favor he wanted to ask of Dee. He thought he knew how she would respond. He figured it was best to ease into it.

He typed, **What happened to those hostages? From earlier?**

The one I thought was dead is dead. Total of four were released.

Four? That's progress, right? This could be over soon.

Don't misread it. I doubt it's a good sign.

Poe wasn't able to see how releasing hostages could be a negative indicator.

He typed, **Why is that not good?**

It means this isn't about carnage, baby.

He typed, **Then maybe he wants out. He's ready to end it?**

Dee replied, **And maybe he's planning something worse than carnage.**

Poe felt a chill on his back. He realized what Dee was telling him.

He typed, **I need your help. Don't go, be my eyes and ears.**

Qué?

He scrolled for her name. Called her.

"Listen to me for a second. Don't say no before you hear me out. I need help. Professional help." Poe laughed. "That didn't come out right. I need your assistance. I need you to sit in front of a television and tell me what's happening in New Haven in real time. Right now, this second. With the perimeters so far back there's no way to get a good view of the building, certainly not within earshot. I'm working blind. Please, Dee. Something important is happening right this second in front of the building. Maybe another kid, I can't see it from here."

"Poe, you're a special agent of the Federal Bureau of Investigation. Check in at the perimeter. They'll let you watch. Professional courtesy."

"I can't, Dee. You know that. The commander on the scene will box me. I'll be anchored to a babysitter or sent packing."

Dee needed Poe to understand she was fencing with her own demons. "Poe, I have to go home. It's . . . time for me to . . . go home."

To Poe's ears that was not a no. He almost said, *Jerry can wait.* He caught himself in time. He pressed her. "Take the next flight, Dee. What? Another hour or two? What's that? I'm tracking an out-of-town cop who's curious in ways he shouldn't be curious. I may be beginning to figure this out. But I can't do it blind."

She asked, "Can't you get CNN or Fox on your BlackBerry?"

"I can't get video to stream. The local networks are swamped. Anyway, I need—"

He stopped himself before he said, *you.*

He said, "—your perspective."

Dee growled at Poe for the second time that day. For her, that didn't even approach a personal record.

From the boarding line where she was standing she could see a concourse monitor playing the CNN news feed. The ongoing New Haven hostage saga was the day's big story. Even thirty feet away from the TV, Dee could tell that another kid was indeed standing at the top of the stairs of the tomb. *Holy,* she thought. *Please don't blow that young man up. Please.* She didn't want to watch that again. Ever. Not for Poe, not for anyone.

She knew what Poe wanted and she knew why he wanted it. "If I step out of this line, Poe, I'm going to regret it, aren't I?"

You are such a doll. "It'll be our first case together. We can save the world."

"No, Poe. I think it'll be our second case together. You and I? We can't save the world. We tried once. How did that work out?"

Poe didn't know how to respond. He considered it to be a perfect topic for them to toss around between cocktails two and three in their next dive bar rendezvous.

She said, "I can see a monitor, Poe. So you know, I'm still in line. It looks like there's another student in front of the tomb. The camera angle is poor, the shot is from far away, and it's partially blocked by a tree. I would say it's a black kid. His arms are in the air. Just like before. He's wearing glasses."

For Poe, the presence of another hostage confirmed his suspicion that the out-of-town cop was getting real-time feeds on his cell phone about the situation at Book & Snake. The question was, from whom?

Inside the tomb? Outside the tomb? And why?

Poe said, "I knew it. What's the kid saying? What's going on? I can't see from here. If I try to get a better vantage, I'll risk losing the guy I'm after."

Dee growled again. She stepped out of the boarding line and walked until she was standing beneath a speaker transmitting the TV sound. "There's no live audio from the scene, Poe. It's just the studio anchors. More pap, like before. Wait—oh my God—CNN says this kid is the secretary of the army's youngest son. The kid we got the email about on Friday morning."

"Damn it," Poe said.

"I have to go, baby. I'm getting back in line. But now I'm going to be at the *back* of the line. If there's no room left for my carry-on, Poe, I'm going to—"

Poe had started walking in a little box pattern on the sidewalk. Two steps, turn. Two steps, turn. Two steps, turn. He tried to stop. He couldn't stop. The pressure was building in his chest. His legs were beginning to smolder.

He smelled smoke that wasn't there. Experience taught him that was never a good sign.

He kept walking the box. The panic inside him was swelling. The acidic sting was budding into his bones. Infiltrating his marrow.

"What about— Can you access the live feed, Dee? There are law enforcement video cameras right across the street from the tomb. I can see them from here. That means there's a feed. Can you get hold of that signal?"

"On an airport television? Have you lost your mind?"

"On your laptop, baby. From Langley? The airport has Wi-Fi. Given the identity of the kids in that building, and what happened yesterday on campus, you know that the Company is getting that video. Can you, I don't know, just tap into the feed somehow?"

"What? Poe, please, I—"

"Deirdre," he said. He rarely called her Deirdre. He knew it would get her attention. "This isn't about us. This isn't about you and Jerry." He gave her a chance to bicker. She didn't. He considered that an omen. "This isn't about the weekend we just had, or about you feeling guilty, and it's not about you needing to get home, or about me not wanting you to go home. This is about—"

"Don't tell me what this is about, Poe. You do not know what I'm dealing—"

"It's about the work we do, Dee. What we believe. This is about what really happened inside that tomb on Friday while the world outside the damn doors was distracted. This is about Nine/eleven and London and Chechnya and Madrid and Bali and Mumbai, and it's about what makes this time different. This is about what is new, and what is next."

She didn't reply right away. She used a knuckle to hijack a tear.

He added, "Dee, this is the evolution of terror. Right now, in New Haven, Connecticut. This is the adaptation you've been predicting. This is the adaptation we've been fearing."

She was silent for at least ten more seconds. Poe found the pause interminable. He covered his mouth with his free hand to enforce his silence. He feared he'd already overstepped, that Deirdre would be livid that he had co-opted her words.

He continued to pace the box, because he couldn't stop. Two steps, turn. Two steps, turn. His femurs were in danger of melting. His brain entertained an image of himself as the Wicked Witch devolving into a mercurial puddle.

Finally, Dee said, "You don't know what you're asking. You don't, Poe. God, I'll call when I know something." She killed the connection.

Aloud he said, "Thank you."

He typed, **I love you.** He didn't hit SEND.

Not on April 19. Maybe he could send that message in May.

It took all his will, but he exited the box.

He just stepped out of it. It felt like a miracle to him, something a superhero might be able to do in the movies.

Poe couldn't see the front of the tomb from where he was standing, but he could still see the man he was following just fine.

The man without the shoulder holster pulled a throwaway map from his pocket and glanced at it for a few seconds. He turned away from the tomb and began marching up the sidewalk that led around to the other side of the cemetery.

Poe surmised that whatever had been going on outside the Book & Snake tomb had concluded, or was on intermission. The out-of-town cop had also inadvertently given Poe some new data: The map the man consulted was bordered with the logo of the Omni Hotel.

Poe allowed himself a tiny fist pump. Even after a decade and a half of mostly futile effort chasing largely invisible and often imaginary foes, Poe continued to adore new intelligence data the way a chef loves seasonal food. For Poe, the feeling of discovery was doubled if the new data was something he had farmed. Data from soil he had tilled always tasted better to him than data that someone else had produced and delivered to his door.

He would put some distance between them by giving the shoulder-holster cop a head start before he followed him around the cemetery.

Poe stepped sideways. Almost incidentally, his eyes settled for a few seconds on a young woman fifteen yards away. She was on the sidewalk adjacent to the pocket park, about halfway between where Poe was standing and the departing back of the out-of-town cop. She was of graduate student age, mid-twenties or so, and dressed like many of the other young women he'd seen near campus since he arrived in New Haven. Jeans, sneaks, a blousy top, shoulder bag. She was on a step, on her toes, and—like half the people in the vicinity—craning to see over the crowd and around the obstacles. Like almost everyone else she was looking in the direction of the Book & Snake tomb, hoping to see something interesting or tragic, or both.

Poe didn't focus his attention on the woman because his secret agent instincts were magical or because his spy craft was particularly well honed. He noticed her because she was built like Dee, and because his instinctive assessment of her looks was that she was slightly on the pretty end of the plain-to-pretty spectrum.

Poe tended not to get too distracted by girls who fell on the gorgeous end of the pretty-to-stunning spectrum. Yes, he would notice, but those women typically failed to hold his interest for a couple of reasons. One was because decades of experience had informed him that those women had never shown a grain of reciprocal curiosity about him. The other reason gorgeous women didn't captivate Poe was because he felt their attractiveness had nowhere to go, no realm in which to develop. On those rare days when Poe admitted to optimism about anything, he acknowledged that one of his favorite things in life was discovering how much more beautiful a woman became as he fell in love.

Deirdre was an attractive CIA analyst on the day she walked into his hospital room to interview him in Oklahoma City in April 1995.

She was damn near dazzling only one April later.

He watched the young woman who had caught his eye as she lifted her right hand to tuck her blond hair behind her ear.

That casual gesture was what caused Poe to freeze.

He froze in place like a day hiker who had just heard a rattle in the nearby grasses. A backcountry skier who had just spotted a fresh fault quake in a massive slab of snow.

The freeze was instinct. Survival.

Poe swallowed. Then he reminded himself to breathe, because he had stopped doing that right in the middle of an inhale. On the deliberate exhale he told himself to concentrate. He had to use all his will not to rotate his head to scan the rest of the crowd to see if the young woman was alone.

He knew she wasn't alone.

In a three-second span his training started to kick in. The practiced response was familiar, an old friend. *Like riding a bike,* he thought. He allowed the focus of his vision to expand from near to far. In the distance, he watched the out-of-town cop disappear behind a curve in the graveyard wall.

Poe knew in his gut that he couldn't follow the cop. Not with his eyes. Not on foot. Not after what he'd just seen the blond girl do.

He brought himself back, permitted his focus to return to near. The blond girl touched her hair again.

She wasn't wearing earrings.

He registered other observations: Her pretty hair fell past her shoulders. Natural color. A little thin. Straight, with bangs. She had wide-set, green-gray eyes. A slightly crooked nose.

Has her nose been broken? Maybe. Huh.

Nothing else struck Poe as remarkable or memorable about her features.

That, he knew, was important.

The specific act she'd performed that had frozen Poe in place was a small thing. Both times she hooked her pretty hair behind her ear, her lips moved almost imperceptibly. She was using the hair-tuck gesture as a way to camouflage the fact that she was speaking a few quick words into the underside of her right wrist. Into the blousy cuff of her trendy, blousy top.

The absent earrings guaranteed that there would be no inadvertent clunking of metal or plastic on the well-concealed microphone.

Poe waited until she made her next move. He tried not to be obvious. He knew that if his suspicion was on the money, he wouldn't have to wait long for her to do something.

If his appraisal about her proved accurate, her next move would not include following the out-of-town cop down the path behind the cemetery. That would be too blatant. That wasn't her role. She was too well trained for that.

She didn't disappoint. Once the out-of-town cop was barely out of her sight, and after she had sent along the verbal confirmation of his progress to her unseen colleagues, she took three quick strides directly into the thickest part of the crowd gathered behind the nearby barricades. In seconds, she disappeared from Poe's view amid a dense forest of shoulders and heads.

Her brief presence in front of Poe had been like the trail of smoke from a cigarette in the wind. Here, then gone.

Poe intuitively understood the choreography. Her pass was complete. She was rotating off the field, heading to the bench. She would get fresh direction, would receive an update on the out-of-town cop's progress from a compatriot. She would prepare to return to the game later, fresh and ready.

The next time she stepped on the field she might be wearing a hat, or sunglasses. A jacket in a neutral color. Her hair might be in a ponytail, or up under the hat.

Poe refocused his attention on the path the out-of-town cop had chosen toward the rear of the cemetery. Poe was determined to locate the receiver who had caught the pass the young blond woman had tossed.

The sidewalk that the out-of-town cop had just been on was empty. No one was following him on foot. Poe saw no activity in the cemetery in that vicinity.

Where, where?

He thought, *Damn.* He knew someone was there. Or had been there. Some other member of the SSG team would have caught the toss— would have picked up the tail of the out-of-town cop after the blond girl had marked him and checked off. Poe moved his eyes between three cars driving past the power plant. *No.* He checked the cars that were parked along the curb. *No. No.*

He was afraid that he had somehow missed it. Missed him. Missed her. Missed them. Missed the receiver.

He scanned more slowly. Once more, twice.

There. There?

A jogger was just beginning to climb the gentle hill in the late-day shadows on the other side of Ashmun Street. A middle-aged guy. Indian or Pakistani ancestry, maybe. A practiced runner. A man with decent form.

To Poe, the man looked like he was faculty, by age probably an associate professor, squeezing in a run before the end of his week. Absent the blonde talking to her wrist a few minutes before, Poe wouldn't have given that particular jogger even a moment's consideration.

But because Poe had spotted the blonde talking to her wrist, Poe also noticed the guy who was jogging into the shadows across the street. Poe noted the direction the man was running—toward the rear of the cemetery, where the out-of-town-cop had been heading—and he noted what the running man was wearing. The outfit was standard jogger's garb: shorts, sneaks, T-shirt.

Poe also catalogued the fact that the jogger did not appear to be at all winded and that his shirt wasn't sweaty. Not in the center of his chest. Not in the pits under his arms. No sweat-matted hair was stuck to his forehead or to his temples. No tendrils were moistened on his neck.

In the New Haven humidity that meant either that the man was a freak of nature, or that he had just started his run.

Without trying to stare, without being obvious, Poe registered every last thing about the guy.

The runner's most obvious tell was that the back of his bone-dry T-shirt read "NYU."

The team has just landed from the City, he thought. *And that jogger is my receiver. He's wearing his New York City tracking clothes— he's so new in town he didn't even have time to switch it out for Yale garb. He's the one who caught the blonde's pass.* Poe thought that the runner's microphone was hidden in the gray headband he was wearing. His earpiece was disguised in his mop of dark hair.

SSG is here, Poe concluded. *Well, damn.*

The FBI had brought their crack surveillance squad—the Special Surveillance Group, SSG—up from New York City. The NY team, the Bureau's most elite, had urban tracking skills that were refined to perfection. On foot, or in vehicles, they were legends. Poe felt like a bird-watcher who had somehow stumbled across the rarest and most elusive of species. He knew he'd been fortunate to spot SSG at all. He felt particularly proud that he had managed to ID two of the surveillance team members while they were actively working a tail.

He knew he had probably missed three or four more that had been part of the intricate choreography. But still, *Damn.*

SSG guys were the superheroes of domestic surveillance. Their powers were their teamwork and their practiced, bland invisibility. They were the ones called on to invisibly track the pro who was certain he was being followed. As individuals, SSG team members were designed to be easy to miss. They blended like blades of grass in a lush lawn, snowflakes in a drift. They were the hay-colored needles in the golden haystack.

Poe thought, *These SSG guys like my out-of-town cop for something.*

Poe knew that with SSG in New Haven he couldn't tail the out-of-town cop any longer. If he made one false move, SSG would sweep him up, too. They wouldn't miss the attention he was paying to their prey.

Poe had to disappear without drawing any additional notice to himself. He chanced one last glance toward the jogger—the man hadn't reappeared around the back of the cemetery—before he marched into the same throng that had swallowed the blond fake grad student.

He made his way through the crowd and exited the throng behind the law school. He cleared his head and spent a moment considering what he knew about the response in New Haven from his colleagues in the FBI.

The Hostage Rescue Team was in New Haven. Poe had seen them.

That meant that HRT commanders had undoubtedly taken over planning and control for rescuing the hostages at Book & Snake. HRT typically traveled with both assault and sniper teams. The sniper teams deployed quickly; Poe felt confident they were already in place. That meant that multiple sniper teams would have set up shop in high-ground positions—in this urban landscape that would mean rooftops or building windows. Poe was certain that the snipers had already begun twenty-four-hour-a-day surveillance of the tomb, their scopes and weapons aimed at preassigned target fields covering a three-hundred-and-sixty-degree view of Book & Snake. The snipers missed nothing. If a fly landed on a doorknob, they would report what direction it was facing.

In a jungle, in a desert, in the mountains, or in this urban miasma, the snipers were masters of camouflage. Poe knew that he could spend all day staring up at the tops of the nearby buildings trying to spot the snipers' lairs and he would not find them. He wouldn't spy the glint of glass on their scopes' lenses. He wouldn't find the hard horizontal lines of their rifles' barrels. He wouldn't see whatever city version of ghillie veils the snipers had constructed to augment their camouflage.

If HRT was in New Haven, then the FBI talkers were surely in New Haven. The talkers were the hostage negotiators. They were the FBI agents whose job it was to make contact with the hostage takers. They were tasked to coax an outcome that would keep the FBI commanders from ever having to give the orders to send in the assault teams.

If the Hostage Rescue assault teams were ordered into Book & Snake, they would not proceed ambivalently. HRT did not stand for "Hesitant, Reluctant, and Tentative." Assault teams went in hot and heavy. Their introduction into the Book & Snake tomb would involve explosives, firearms, and blinding speed. People would certainly die.

The talkers were supposed to prevent that.

Once the assault teams moved in, the talkers' job was done. The second an order was given for an assault team breach was the second after headquarters acknowledged that the negotiators had run out of time. Productive time, tactical time, political time. Whatever.

Poe thought, *Waco. Ruby Ridge.*

If HRT were in New Haven, and the talkers were in New Haven, then the support personnel that fed them, literally and figuratively—minds and bellies—while they were on the road were in town, too. Helicopters, both small and large, were deployed nearby, at the ready. Medics and medical support units were in place. Transport vehicles, armored and not, were at their disposal. Mobile communications were active. Investigative officers were doing intel. A logistics unit was making it all possible.

Although any individual HRT operator could deploy as light as air, HRT en masse did not travel light.

And Poe had discovered that SSG was in town, too.

SSG wasn't attached to HRT. SSG was not comprised of special agents. The FBI's Special Surveillance Group had one job. They tracked people and vehicles. Poe wished he knew if they were in town to stand by to support HRT, if they were in town to go fishing, or if they'd already had targets identified when they arrived.

Was it possible that the out-of-town cop without the shoulder holster—the one that SSG was tailing—was a target of opportunity, someone they'd stumbled across at the perimeter? Could he be an accomplice of the guy inside the tomb?

Poe didn't know whether he would learn more by watching the surveillance team or by looking for the out-of-town cop. Poe knew he wouldn't know the answer to that question until he knew the identity of the out-of-town cop.

Poe considered the roster of fed involvement that went beyond the Bureau. If anyone else in FBI intelligence had come to the same conclusion as Poe—that the events at Book & Snake were a potential terrorist act—then JTTF would be active in the investigation, too. The Joint Terrorism Task Force was a multiagency, multidisciplinary team with responsibility to do local emergency response to perceived terrorist threats. They could be in town already—emergency response is what they were set up to do.

A dozen other counterterrorism agencies could be on the ground, too.

For Poe, it all meant that he had a long list of feds he didn't want to bump into.

Poe texted Dee. **SSG is here.**

Who?

Poe forgot sometimes that Dee worked the other side of the aisle, that she was CIA, not FBI.

Bureau's best trackers, from NYC.

Oh.

He asked, **Did you hear anything from Langley?**

Nothing. It's all ntk.

The cryptic "ntk" didn't compute for a second. Poe finally made the translation: need-to-know. Dee was telling him that she wasn't getting access to whatever raw data Langley was receiving from New Haven.

That posed a problem for Poe. He was counting on her help with the intelligence side. He couldn't risk operating solo and blind. He hoped she could at least let him know what had just happened in front of the tomb.

Poe typed, **What happened to the secretary of the army's kid?**

He read something off a card. I didn't hear it. Then he went back into the tomb.

Is he the first hostage to go back inside?

He is, Poe. He is.

Poe texted his assistant in the District.

FBI regulations prohibited the use of text messaging for official communication—special agents were required to use email for business.

But Poe didn't want to use official channels. The hostage situation did not fit comfortably into his portfolio. The media profile was way too high. The victims were too prominent. The moment his superiors learned he was in New Haven was the moment he would be ordered to abort whatever he was doing. That's why he was texting instead of emailing. In Poe's hierarchy of official sins, use of an unapproved communication method was venial.

He thumbed, **SSG is here. Why?**

His assistant's reply was **On it.**

Poe

After he left SSG behind to complete the tailing of the out-of-town cop, Poe continued to blend in with the crowd. He returned to the backside of Beinecke Plaza, hoping to learn something new, and hoping to get lucky. He tried to become part of the cluster of gawkers that was gathered on the far side of Wall Street. But there wasn't much to gawk at. From that location, the blunt form of the Beinecke Library completely blocked the line of sight to the back of Book & Snake.

Suddenly, the insistent beat of a bass guitar accompanied by enthusiastic drumming engulfed Poe.

The volume started off loud. With each beat it seemed to get louder.

At first it was four notes. Pause. Four notes. Pause. Four notes. Pause.

The stone buildings and the stone plaza provided the necessary ingredients for echoes. The reverberations soon filled the pauses with ever-diminishing beats of bass and percussion.

The volume of the song topped off at eleven on a ten scale. The music seemed to be coming from everywhere at once. Poe spun to find the source of the beat. He completed a three-sixty. The noise—it had gotten too loud to be considered music—seemed to be emanating from everywhere at once.

He saw almost everyone around him doing the same thing he was doing—looking every which way to locate who was playing the music. Where it was coming from.

A kid pointed toward the law school. Poe was baffled. His ears would have guessed one of the colleges on Cross Campus.

A few more seconds and it was clear to Poe that the song was hip-hop. What artist? He knew nothing about hip-hop.

As a male vocalist kicked in with some rap lyrics that Poe couldn't decipher, the volume seemed to increase. He wondered if that was an illusion or if it were possible that his ears could really register anything as louder than the noise he'd already heard. Some of the people gathered closest to Poe started to cover their ears and grimace.

Others began walking or running to get away from the noise.

Poe stayed put. He was determined not to be distracted. He focused his attention on the back of the Book & Snake tomb.

What are you up to?

The tomb gave up no secrets.

The music pounded.

He tried to make a judgment about how the authorities outside the tomb were responding to the noise. He stepped down the sidewalk across from Woolsey, moving closer to the cemetery.

The noise on the backside of Woolsey was even more deafening.

Is this possible?

Poe's BlackBerry vibrated. Deirdre's name lit up the caller ID. He raised the device to his face. "Hey," he said.

"What is that noise?" she said.

Poe couldn't hear her. He said, "Somebody started playing some hip-hop so loud I can't even hear myself think. I'll call you back. I have to think it's the unsub. I don't know what it means."

He killed the call. He was close enough to the corner that he could see the black suits of an HRT assault team congregated out of sight of the front of the tomb. The individual HRT members were looking in different directions. They couldn't locate the source of the music either. He assumed they had all inserted ear protection. They weren't known for their lack of preparation.

After about five minutes the music stopped. At first, the silence seemed as loud as the song had been.

Poe returned to the backside of Beinecke Plaza so he could once again eye the rear corner of the tomb. He couldn't identify any changes.

He returned Dee's call. "You're not on board?"

"I missed that flight. I'm on the next one. Do you know what that noise was?" she said.

Thank you. "Not sure. I'm thinking the unsub just bombed the whole area around the tomb with a hip-hop song at outrageous volume."

"I got that much on CNN. Distraction?"

Poe said, "I guess. The question is for what purpose."

Dee said, "Could be a million things. Anybody puts together that I'm helping you, I'm dead, Poe. You know that?"

"They won't, Dee. But thank you for . . ." Poe didn't know how to end the sentence. "Do you have something for me? I'm hoping, you know . . ."

She went silent for ten seconds. "Yeah, I do. I missed it live the first time—and no, I don't have access to whatever Langley might be learning—but before the music started CNN replayed the footage of the last kid who came out of the tomb. The secretary of the army's son, the one who read something, then went back in.

"He wasn't killed, and he wasn't released. That means that there's no pattern we can rely on, yet. Your unsub has killed a couple of kids he sent out. He let others go. Now he sends one out before he brings him back in. By being unpredictable, he's keeping us guessing. That's probably intentional on his part. We can't be certain what he will do next, how to react to the next kid he pushes out the door. It'll make your cowboys think twice or three times about a breach."

"Yeah. You said the kid read something. Did you get that?"

"There were a few parts to it. I wrote as fast as I could—taking dictation is not my thing. Like I said, this was the secretary of the army's kid. Stoic. Strong. Steel jaw but gorgeous Bambi eyes. Kid was reading from a card, like an index card. I'm quoting him here the best I can. It's probably not exact:

Number one, remove the contact microphones from the outside of the building. Five minutes. Don't replace them.

Number two, remove the cranes and cherry pickers from behind the law school. Don't use them.

Number three, the original hostage negotiator will resume her role.
    She will stay there for the duration.

"Then the kid disappeared back inside. That's it."

"What do you make of it, Dee?"

Dee had given it plenty of thought and had already reached a conclusion. "Your unsub has accomplices outside that he's communicating with. Or . . . he has multiple cameras set up that overlook the
tomb and the surrounding area that he is able to monitor remotely,
maybe online. Or both. Either way, he's watching our every move.
Anticipating our every tactic. The law enforcement response hasn't
surprised him."

Poe knew she was right. Dee's conclusion also explained the presence of the FBI surveillance team. SSG was in town in order to spot
and track potential accomplices. Was the music the work of the accomplices? Was the out-of-town cop part of the unsub's plot? Poe's
gut said no, but he couldn't be sure.

"Damn," he said. "The unsub is good. He's done his prep."

"I'm afraid so."

"If he's watching the law enforcement response—which we have to
assume he is—then he has to know HRT has arrived in New Haven,
but still he prefers the local hostage negotiator over the FBI negotiator.
What's that about?"

Dee said, "Maybe he prefers the lack of experience."

"And maybe he prefers the devil he knows. He's watched her for a
while already. He might have identified a weakness."

"We do," Dee said. "We prefer the terrorists we know. When we
turn over rocks, that's who we're looking for. The ones we know. That's
why we're prone to miss the ones we don't recognize as familiar."

Poe had heard Dee hum that tune many times before. He wanted
to hear her sing the lyrics. He loved to hear her riff. Sometimes she
improvised. "Go on," he said.

"If your instincts are right about this situation—that it's not a hostage thing in any traditional sense—then this could be brand-new,
Poe. New group. New goals. New grievances. New strategy. Most of

all, new tactics. Definitely new tactics. He may not be on our radar at all. Not in our experience model. I don't have a read on this. But it could be fresh. We may not find tracks."

"An evolution," Poe said. The word was his way of acknowledging that he was hearing her loud and clear.

"I'm sorry I can't get more from Langley," Dee said. "I'm still pecking away, looking for an avenue into the data streams so I can see what they've been able to pick up. But all of my traditional routes are dead ends. If I start being any more persistent they'll recognize what I'm up to and shut off my access. Then I'll be useless to you."

"Impossible, baby. Did they get anything from the microphones they attached to the outside of the building?"

"They'd been in place for less than an hour. If anything's been analyzed from them, I wasn't able to see it. I don't have access to any reports or the raw data," Dee said. "Thick stone walls? I would guess they didn't get anything, but that's not a technology I know well . . ." Dee took a long inhale. "Other than your gut, you still haven't explained why you think this is yours, Poe. What makes you so certain this a counterterrorism problem?"

Dee wanted to hear Poe's thinking. He stepped away from the group he was using as camouflage. He checked to make sure he could not be overheard. "The key is the kids, Dee. Can you see what he's got in there? Yale's the cream of the crop academically, right? The kids who apply are from the top ten, maybe top five percent of high school seniors. Yale accepts what—one out of ten of all those applicants? That makes Yale's students the top one percent in the country. That's elite, right?"

"There are a lot of elite schools, Poe. Same thing is true for ten others colleges. Twenty others. Yale's no different."

"Stay with me, Dee. All together, these secret societies like Book & Snake take what—two, three percent of current students? That makes the kids locked inside that building the elite of the elite. John Kerry was in Skull & Bones. So was George W. Bush."

"Go on," she said. "I'm not sure what argument you're making with your examples, but go on."

"This is what I'm saying—we can assume that the hostages in the

Book & Snake tomb are among the best and the brightest kids this country produces. We already know that some of them are from the best families, right? We can guess that some of them are from uncountable wealth. And if history is a guide, we can assume that some of them have the bluest blood running in their veins. Their parents are running our government. Ruling our industry. Overseeing our banking. Our military. Our judiciary. Everything."

Dee felt a need to bring Poe back down to earth. "Garry Trudeau, Poe?"

Poe didn't want to argue about which secret society counted Garry Trudeau among its members. "Come on, Dee. Supreme Court nominee's kid? Secretary of the army's?"

"Are you thinking ransom, Poe? How much money he could get? What he could fund with it?"

"I wouldn't be in New Haven if I thought the unsub wanted money. No, he wants something else."

"Yes?"

"I don't know what."

"Earlier? Before you left for New Haven?" Dee said. "You said that the mysterious thing was what was going on inside the building all day Friday."

"That's the part that worries me most. Friday. Why nothing from inside the tomb on Friday?"

"What about the murder at the hockey rink? The sniper scare in the tower? All of that? That was all Friday."

"Definitely related. But it all happened outside the building. Had all the local cops running every which way. The murdered kid in the hockey rink was from a completely different secret society. The sniper fiasco was on the other side of campus. I think it was all intended to ensure that the unsub has had all the time he needed for whatever the hell he was doing inside that building since he took control on Thursday."

"Misdirection?"

"Has to be. Like the music he just played. He was up to something during that noise. The question is, did he get away with it? Damn. There's so much I don't know."

"What can I do, Poe? Realistically, how much help can I be? I'm in an airport departure lounge watching television."

His tone suddenly changed, his voice more subdued. "What I could use most is whatever the Company has put together about the kids. The ones who have already come out of that tomb. Alive or dead. And about the kids who might still be inside. Parents, grandparents, family connections. The more detail the better. I . . ."

Poe went quiet while he fought off sudden intrusive images. He was remembering things he'd been trying to forget.

Dee said, "You still there? Did I lose you?"

His voice changed again. It was hovering in a range that was barely above melancholy. Unbidden memories oozed into his consciousness. He couldn't plug the cracks fast enough. He tried to cover. He said, "I'm here, baby. You can't lose me. Don't even think about trying."

She recognized the unmistakable timbre of old pain in his voice. His vulnerability was a magnet for her. Always had been. "Where are you staying?" she asked. She made the nimble transformation from analyst to woman. She needed to know if he was okay, if he had a nice bed. Something to eat.

"Don't know. My out-of-town cop is at the Omni. May end up there. I have to keep an eye . . . You heading out soon?" Poe was fighting the dangerous draw of the undertow, trying to allow simple conversation to anchor him to current reality.

"I'm on the next flight to Dulles, Poe. I have to get home. For real this time—boarding starts in a couple of minutes. I'll let you know when I'm on the ground in Virginia. I'll text or call. I will . . . do what I can to help you, but you need to be prepared that it may turn out not to be much. This stuff is locked down tight."

Poe's voice continued the gravitational slide. All he managed to say was "Thank you, Dee. For . . . everything. I mean . . . everything. My breath."

"No. No," Dee replied in staccato. She tried to catch herself. She was determined not to succumb. "No you don't. Stop it, now! Don't you go sentimental on me, Poe. Not when I'm in public. You know how much I hate to cry in public. You behave yourself right now."

Her voice was cracking. Her eyes were wet. She'd lost whatever composure she had.

Poe had started walking, moving away from the pain. His pain and her pain. He'd turned the corner onto College Street. He was across the street from the big lawn that was the New Haven Green. His back was turned to Beinecke Plaza. He was creating distance between himself and Book & Snake. Away from the unsub. Away from SSG and HRT. Away from the noise.

From Dee? He hoped not. But he knew that everything would change when she got on that plane.

He was allowing himself the luxury of getting lost in the melody of her words, until Dee said, "Oh no, Poe. Poe? There's another kid outside the tomb. He just moved out near the steps. He's carrying a box."

Poe stopped walking. He focused. His voice became a version of ordinary. "I'm over two blocks away from the building. I can't see anything, Dee. You're my eyes. Tell me."

"It's a cardboard box, like you would get at the grocery store. The bottom half of a produce box. He's just standing there. He's a . . . you know, college kid, um, student, five-ten, Asian . . . Japanese. Japanese-American. One-seventy? Strong. He's blinking. His wrists are red. He's barefoot. He's just standing there with the damn box. Looking around. He's terrified, Poe. Oh Lord."

"Earpiece?" Poe asked.

"His hair covers his ears. Can't tell."

"SWAT? HRT?"

"Offscreen. Can't see what they're up to."

"Shit."

"And . . . wait . . . he just turned the box around. There's some printing on it. It says . . . umm . . . 'YouTube. Breach. Book & Snake.' Hold on. Hold on. I got that. I'm still online. I'm putting you on speaker while I search. Just a second . . . Okay, okay . . . YouTube is up. I'm typing in the key words. And . . . a video comes right up. Right up."

"What? What is it?"

"Just a sec . . . Posted ten minutes ago. It's four minutes and change. Title, *HRT: What Happens if You Breach . . .*"

Poe said, "Oh, shit."

Dee went quiet.

Poe said, "Talk to me, baby. Talk to me."

"I think the video was made inside the tomb, Poe . . . Holy. I wonder if there are any kids in it."

Poe didn't know what to ask first.

Dee said, "The TV screen just split. I'm looking at the CNN feed. They've started the video. And the kid is squatting down. He's tilting the carton he's carrying. He's like . . . pouring it . . . emptying it out on the ground. . . It's a box of . . ."

"What, Dee? What?"

"Holy."

"Pouring, Dee? What do you mean? What's he doing? What's in the box? What— Tell me . . ."

"He's pouring oranges down the steps. Dozens of . . . oranges. They're just rolling down the steps. Onto the grass."

"Oranges?" Poe said. "Fruit?"

Sam

I had circled behind the cemetery, continuing past the Whale on the sidewalk across the street. There was no new activity outside the hockey rink. The yellow police perimeters remained in place. Two campus cops were acting as sentries. They looked bored because they were bored.

They were bored because they didn't know the big picture.

The orange *X* remained taped to the glass.

I kept walking, skirting campus, heading toward downtown. When I was two blocks from the hotel a cacophonous racket of hip-hop music started playing. I stopped in my tracks on the other side of the New Haven Green. The noise was definitely coming from the direction of Beinecke Plaza. The volume was astonishing to me.

I stood still for almost five minutes until the music finally stopped. The noise had meant something. I didn't know what, but I was guessing it had been a diversion. I hoped that I would learn more when I had a chance to get to a TV. I was only a block from the Omni Hotel when my phone buzzed in my pocket.

It was Ann. She said, "Another student just stepped outside the tomb, Sam. A boy. I'm watching it on the news. He's been outside the door for twenty seconds or so. He has a box. That's all so far."

"I'm not close, Ann. I'm blocks away, near the Omni. A box? Take me through what you see. What you've seen. Everything." Even if I were as close to the tomb as the authorities would allow me to get, I knew I still wouldn't be able to see what Ann could see on television.

"Like I said, he's carrying a box. Like a cardboard box. He's so scared, Sam. His eyes. His poor parents. He's moved all the way out front, near the steps. Past those pillars."

"Any . . . orange, Ann? What's he wearing?"

She was fighting to keep the pressure out of her voice. "The box is cardboard. Regular . . . brown cardboard. Not orange. He's barefoot. Jeans. Baggy? Light blue polo shirt over a . . . white T-shirt, I think. Yes. White. No orange I can see. Oh God. Thank God. No orange."

"What about his hair?"

"Wavy."

"Color?" I felt as though I was playing *Password* with my kid while he was distracted thinking about some girl. "He doesn't have red hair, Ann?"

"Oh, oh. God. No. Dark hair. He's . . . Asian. Maybe Japanese."

"Go on."

"He's standing. Looking around. He's so scared. I can tell how frightened he is. He doesn't know what to make of any of it."

"Keep talking, Ann. Everything you see."

"That's it so far. Wait! Now he's . . . he's just turned the box around in his hands so the other side is facing us. It . . . it has printing on it. Big letters. From a computer printer. Like that. It says, wait a second . . . 'YouTube . . . Breach . . . Book & Snake.' All on separate lines."

Keywords? I wondered immediately. "You close to your computer, Ann?"

"I'm ahead of you, Sam. Just a second. It's loading slowly. Damn. Okay, here it comes . . . Those search terms bring up a YouTube video. It's called *HRT: What Happens if You Breach.* It's starting to play. Oh my God. Oh . . . my God. It's from inside the tomb, Sam. Inside! Where's my baby? Where is she? Jane? Jane? Baby . . ."

I had to draw Ann back to the young man with the box at the top of the stairs. "What's the kid doing, Ann? Right now?"

"He's . . . um . . . he just crouched down. He's in the same place, but he's squatting. He still has the box in his hands."

Five seconds passed. Then ten.

"Oh my Lord! Sam, the box is full of . . . He's tilting it down, toward the camera. Oh no, no, no. Noooooo. No, no, no, no . . ."

"What, Ann? What?"

She was whimpering. "He's pouring oranges down the stairs. Dozens and dozens of . . . oranges. They're going to kill him, Sam, aren't they? They're going to kill this boy. . . ."

I made my voice as soft as I could. I found every bit of tenderness I'd ever felt while being my son's father and I packed it tight around the next words I said to Ann. "You don't have to watch this, Ann. Walk away. Just get out of the room. You don't have to see this. You shouldn't see this. Stand up now. Walk away now. . . . Go. . . . Now. Right now. Listen to me. . . ."

"He just tossed the box aside. He's up again, just standing there. Looking down at his feet, at the steps. No, no, no, no."

Soft hadn't worked. I put an edge on my tone. "Get out of that room, Ann. Now. Do what I say. Turn your head. Walk away. Now!"

"Okay, okay. I'm going."

I felt the concussion. I heard the explosion. In the void right after my body shook I thought I could hear the whole country gasp, too, but I wasn't completely sure about that.

Or about anything.

 **APRIL 19, SATURDAY EARLY EVENING**

Poe and Dee

Dee said, "Baby, he tossed the box off to the side. Now he's just standing there. His hands are empty."

Poe saw the frame in his head. He could feel the progression of the scene as though he had already witnessed it. He whispered, "Oh God."

Dee felt Poe's apprehension as clearly as if his quivering hand were resting on her flesh. Their many years together had convinced her that Poe had radar for calamity.

"What, Poe? What does it mean?"

"Turn away, baby," he said. "Cover your—"

Dee screamed.

Poe's brain registered a scream.

He didn't know at the time if it was Dee's current scream pummeling his ears or if the scream he heard was a replay of one of the chorus of screams that were indelibly imprinted in his brain from that distant April in Oklahoma City.

His bones felt the shock waves of the concussion before his ears registered the roar from the blast.

His body began reacting to the reality long before his mind could begin to process the tidal wave of information flooding into him through his senses.

Imagination and reality were indistinguishable.

He dropped his phone before he heard Dee's distant, plaintive "No! Oh no, no, no! Poe, Poe."

Poe was on the ground facedown, his arms covering his head. He didn't know how he got there, but he knew he had to prepare himself for the coming cascade of horror, the one that would bury him in debris. He had to steel himself for the onslaught of blackness, for the tornado of dust. For the almost certain suffocation. For the certain pain, for the take-it-to-the-bank sense of loss.

For the despair. For the eternity. He held his breath, his lungs full as he waited for the world to fall on him.

The world didn't collapse.

For a flash of an instant, Poe was disappointed.

The transient disappointment cut through all the chaos.

Furiously, he began to dig.

Seconds later, or maybe minutes—Poe didn't know—he crawled off the sidewalk toward a building. He was on a patch of grass. He reached for his BlackBerry two feet away on the lawn. Dee's voice drew him to it.

The sound of her voice confused him.

His hands were black with mud. Grass and dirt were packed beneath his fingernails. He'd been digging down through the rubble.

Dee? Dee?

She was talking nonstop. "Baby, baby. I'm here. Baby, you're okay. We're okay. I'm here, I'm here. Poe? Poe? Talk to me, baby. Talk to me. It's Dee. I'm here, right here with you . . ."

"Dee?" he said.

"Poe! Baby! You're all right. You understand? You're all right. I'm here. I'm here, baby."

"They killed that boy?" Poe said.

"They did," Dee said.

"It was an IED," Poe said.

Dee made the connections. She said, "Holy."

Poe sat cross-legged on the grass as they talked. Dee was desperate for assurance that Poe was connected to the present. That one more bomb hadn't been one bomb too many.

Slowly, he convinced her.

Although he didn't know how long they talked, he knew he needed to move on.

"You go get your plane, Dee. You go home. This only makes me more determined. I need to go find my out-of-town cop before SSG realizes what they have and hide him from me."

"Are you sure, sure, sure you're okay?"

"When I'm talking to you, I'm fine. I know you don't like to hear that. But that's just the way it is, Dee. The rest of the time, I just am. Maybe if I help stop this guy, you know? Maybe then, maybe then I'll be . . . you know, free."

Dee said, "You're a wounded man, Christopher Poe."

She'd had the thought a thousand times before, but that was the first time she had ever said it aloud.

He didn't have to consider her appraisal. His wounds weren't news to Poe. "I suppose I am."

"You take care, Poe. No, wait—there's something else I want to tell . . . I need to . . . I . . ."

The breathiness in her voice betrayed her. Poe felt something monumental coming. He gave her three seconds before the urgency overcame him. He said, "What? You want to tell me what, Dee? What do you need to . . . ?"

It took her a few seconds to reply. She said, "I have to go, too. Last call for boarding."

"I love you, too, Dee," he said aloud.

She had already killed the call. Poe knew that.

Maybe in May. No, not maybe. Definitely in May, he thought. *I'll tell you for real in May.*

Dee said a silent prayer before she stepped out of the boarding line. She twirled her carry-on around and started walking in the direction of baggage claim.

She stopped suddenly halfway down the concourse. She held her hair back with one hand, leaned forward, and vomited into a big gray Rubbermaid rolling dustbin that was being pushed along by a custodian who was in no particular hurry.

"I'm so sorry," she said when she was done. She grabbed a tissue to cover her mouth. "That was awful of me. I'm . . . so sorry. I didn't feel . . . I didn't know that was . . . coming."

The janitor's face was impassive. His eyes were soft. "No, ma'am. Not t'all. Bett'n on da flo'," he said. "Much bett'n dat."

Christine Carmody tries three times in quick succession to get the attention of the young man who had just exited the tomb carrying the cardboard carton. She introduces herself. She asks him his name. She asks him to lower the box to the ground. She asks him to stop.

He ignores all her entreaties.

She asks him twice what he has in the box. He doesn't even look at her.

When he finally spins the box to reveal the printed message—

YouTube
Breach
Book & Snake

—she turns her head from him long enough to say, "Look that up, somebody. Joey?"

Behind her she hears an order for everyone to take cover.

Christine doesn't leave her post.

Joey Blanks takes his familiar position just behind her shoulder. He says, "Got somebody checking those words. You recognize this hostage, Sarge?"

Christine says, "No," without turning her head. "Should I?"

"This is one of the VIP kids. That new Supreme Court nominee's kid. His name is Reginald Oshiro. Mother and father have different last names. Let me know if you want more details. And, Sarge? His parents have been in touch with us from early on."

"Voluntarily? Oh God." Christine winces. She says, "I do not want to know that."

Christine recognizes that the fact the kid is a VIP and the fact that his parents have already reached out to the authorities increases this young man's vulnerability.

The kid lowers himself to a squat.

When the oranges begin to spill down the steps, Christine has to keep herself from gasping.

The SAC doesn't see the oranges tumbling down the stairs. He is at an intel meeting inside Woolsey Hall called to review a just-received technical assessment that the morning cell tower failure had been caused by a portable signal jamming device, likely operated from inside the tomb.

The purpose of the meeting is to assess why the unsub had intentionally precipitated his own communication crisis.

Haden Moody wasn't invited to the Woolsey confab. He remains inside the Tactical Operations Center cursing at the initial playing of the YouTube video, *HRT: What Happens if You Breach*.

He is so angry that his face looks sunburned.

The HRT hostage negotiator is accustomed to being outside the intel loop. He is more even-tempered as he watches the video over Moody's shoulder. He says, "I guess we go to plan B."

Moody says, "What the hell is plan B?"

The negotiator says, "The Army Research Laboratory is sending a team up from Maryland with some . . . technology that can detect activity right through the walls of that tomb. If it's practical, we'll deploy it as soon as it's here."

Hade Moody says, "Fuck my uncle. The army has shit that can see through stone walls?"

"It's a new radar that ARL's been developing. It's called STTW. Sense-Through-The-Wall radar. They started using it experimentally in Iraq. Against al Qaeda. Before they had it, the Predator drones could visually track al Qaeda operatives into a specific building. Then they'd lose them. With the penetrating radar, they can pinpoint the specific location where an individual has moved inside. They can identify potential civilian casualties. Minimize collateral damage. It's been a major advantage."

Moody raises his chin. "Good for us," he says. "Good for the good guys."

The FBI negotiator regrets revealing the technological option to Moody. He chooses his next words with care, hoping to undo any damage. "Deploying the hardware here may not work. After the commander sees what's in this video, he may decide it's too risky."

"Of course. Sure," Moody replies. When he's out of his comfort zone, he goes vague and conciliatory until he can spot clues that will allow him to disguise his ignorance.

"And these marble walls may be too thick," the negotiator says.

"Exactly what I was thinking," says Moody.

Neither man notices what is happening with the hostage. They don't see the young man tilt the box, or the oranges begin to bounce down the steps in front of Book & Snake.

The negotiator says, "The army guys think they might have better luck through the roof, in the attic space. At least we'd be able to tell exactly where people are up there. Who's moving, who's not. That's something. That way, we'd know—"

The harsh, crisp clap of an explosion stops him in mid-sentence.

The concussion rocks the big vehicle. Shrapnel peppers the aluminum skin and shatters the two small windows facing the tomb.

A bomb has exploded outside Book & Snake.

Two young officers working in the TOC instinctively drop for cover. Both did multiple tours in Iraq.

One looks at the other. They are both waiting for a second blast.

After ten seconds, the younger one, a woman, says, "I-fucking-E-D."

Sam

After Ann convinced me that her husband, Ronnie, was at her side, I half-walked, half-jogged to the Omni. A few dozen people were clustered in front of the hotel, staring in the direction of the slowly diffusing cloud of smoke and dust that had risen above Beinecke Plaza. I threaded through the throng into the lobby. Once inside I tracked down the hotel business center and plopped down in front of a computer. It took me five tries to get the new YouTube video playing.

A whole mess of people were apparently trying to see it.

I didn't recognize the voice doing the narration on the YouTube clip. I was ninety percent certain it was not the same voice I'd heard on the recorded threat that Ann had received the day before. I thought the person doing the video voice-over had an almost imperceptible British tint to his tone. Like a fine English actor doing an almost spot-on generic American accent.

The first section of the video involved a series of close-up shots of the interior of the front doors of Book & Snake. The camera's focus was narrow, highlighting an array of alarm sensors that had been attached to the doors and adjacent walls. As the camera angle changed, the narrator described each security feature. There were four different magnetic sensors set to trip if the doors opened or closed, or if there was any other change—something more forceful—that affected the doors' plane. Basically, if a door opened, the sensors would fire. If the door blew off, the sensors would fire.

A few feet inside the doors, a half-dozen motion detectors were mounted on the walls. The beams of the detectors crisscrossed the area directly behind the doors. Should the magnetic sensors fail, the motion detectors would sense the body heat of anyone who ventured beyond the doorway.

The narrator spent some extra time describing the purpose of the multiple glass-break sensors that were attached to two-foot-by-four-foot panels of clear, thin glass. The glass panels were clipped to the backs of the doors, exterior and interior, with plastic brackets. If any of the glass panels suffered damage, the sensors would record it.

The narrator described the fail-safe setup in a matter-of-fact tone. "All the components of this alarm system are powered by batteries. If the doors are opened or knocked down, the magnetic sensors will record the breach. If anyone passes into the room behind the doors, the motion detectors will record the breach. If any attempt is made to overwhelm the other sensors, the glass on the back of the doors will shatter and the glass-break sensors will record that breach. If any of the batteries fail, the system will record a breach.

"Any single identified breach will instantly trigger a series of explosive charges in the areas of the building where the hostages are being detained."

The narrator paused. He then said, "Are there any questions?" One, two, three. "Good. Let's move on."

The second part of the video showed a similar alarm setup in the attic of the tomb, but the focus of the defenses arranged in that space was on a complex pattern of motion detectors, and on eight different glass panels and the breakage sensors affixed to them.

The narrator stressed that hostages were being detained in the attic space and explosives were wired in that area.

If any sensor in the building identified a breach or an attempted breach, all the explosives in the vicinity of any hostage would detonate.

Carmen called. I paused the video and took a deep breath. I tried to find a tone of voice that sounded normal. She wanted to talk about the unremitting tragedy in New Haven. "It's on all the channels," she said. "I can't get away from it."

"I know exactly what you mean," I said. "Turn off the television. You don't need this right now."

It took me another minute of cajoling to get her to agree to rest.

A few seconds after I restarted the video, the screen went dark. For an instant, I thought the killer's message was over. Then a single sheet of paper came slowly into focus. In the middle of the page, in a font I didn't recognize, were three simple words.

I am America

The overt message of the YouTube video was a simple one that was intended for HRT and for SWAT. It was: If you breach this space, the hostages will die.

The fact that the message was posted on YouTube was, in itself, a significant subtext: The world now knows what will occur if you attempt to breach this tomb.

The public posting of the video was also a taunt to the authorities: *I dare you.*

The final three words were, to me, a complete cipher.

Was "I am America" intended for general consumption? For the parents of the hostages? For the FBI? I didn't know.

I wondered if Ann Calderón knew something she hadn't told me.

In the hallway outside the business center, I heard someone yell, "What does that mean? 'I am America'? What does that mean? Does anyone know?"

Yeah, I was thinking, *does anyone know?*

Poe

He knows. The out-of-town cop knows what's been going on in the tomb. He has to. Poe didn't know how the cop knew. Or what the cop knew. He only knew that the cop knew.

If Poe's FBI partner, Kelli Moon, were at his side, she would have chided him right then about his mid-investigation tendency toward magical thinking. But Kelli was with her newborn baby in that cramped little apartment of hers in Adams Morgan. Dee was on a plane waiting to take off from Philadelphia. Poe had no one around to caution him about his always short-lived, almost always unwarranted, and otherwise uncharacteristic optimism.

The most recent explosion had left Poe's nerves raw. Exposed.

He kept his eyes ahead of him. He commanded his legs to take measured steps even though they were screaming a desire to break into a sprint. He continued walking until he arrived at the downtown hotel where he'd dropped his things earlier that day. He traded the doorman ten bucks for his bags before he hiked two and a half blocks across New Haven with his duffel strap slung over his shoulder and his garment bag hooked on the middle joint of his fingers.

His plan was to check into the Omni.

The front desk clerk informed him that the hotel was full. "Sorry. This . . . problem on campus," he explained. "The bomb that just went off? Can you believe what's happening? Media has shown up from . . . everywhere. I am so sorry. Usually, we'd be able to do something for you."

Poe's attention was distracted. He was using a mirror on the wall behind the clerk to survey the large lobby for members of SSG who might already be in position in the hotel. He watched a businessman heading out the revolving door. A couple—she was African-American, he was Asian—was waiting for an elevator. They were either in love, or they were damn good actors. A middle-aged woman was sitting on a sofa reading *In Style* magazine. She had those eyeglasses that turned dark outside. She hadn't been inside long—the glass had not yet returned to clear. Her big designer knockoff purse was beside her.

She could be a guest. Or not. Poe memorized her face. He thought she possessed a bland, out-of-town aunt, perfect SSG kind of face.

"I'm sorry," Poe said, as though he hadn't heard the clerk.

The clerk repeated that there were no rooms available.

Poe tapped the counter to draw the man's attention downward. He flashed his FBI ID, displaying it only long enough for the clerk to recognize what he was seeing. The credentials had the desired effect. The clerk was suddenly motivated to look a little harder for an available room.

Poe slid a twenty to the man to acknowledge his additional effort. "To help you forget where I work. Understand?"

The desk clerk smiled discreetly and said, "I don't think you ever said where you work. Many of our guests are here for something to do with the college. You, too?"

"Me, too." Poe gave him another twenty.

While he crossed the lobby toward the elevators, Poe made sure to scan the sidewalk in front of the building for loiterers. A taxi driver was standing in front of his cab waiting for a fare. Across the street Poe counted at least half a dozen pedestrians. People were still clustering together to try to make sense of the explosion across campus.

SSG? Poe knew he was out of his league with SSG. He had been lucky to spot them earlier. He wasn't likely to get lucky again.

The elevator arrived. Poe checked the lobby one last time. The couple in love had departed. The woman reading *In Style* was gone.

He found his room on the corner of the sixth floor. The room the hotel had been saving for some desperate VIP was small but well appointed.

How many hotel and motel rooms since OKC? Five hundred? A thousand? Poe knew it was a lot. Moving in to each fine hotel and each cheap motel involved the exact same set of moves by Poe.

He tossed his duffel onto the chair. He hung his garment bag on the rod in the closet. He removed his shaving kit and tossed it onto the counter in the bathroom. He splashed cold water on his face and dried it with a fluffy white towel.

Poe had moved in.

He stood at the window. From the vantage provided by the Omni, Yale was a Hollywood vision of college. It evoked the melodies and twang of Cole Porter songs. Students wearing tweed suits. Fall Saturdays watching the home team on the gridiron. A cappella choirs. Girls in Mary Janes and pleated skirts and ponytails. Brightly colored leaves falling from big oak trees in the quad.

Unsubs in the tomb, and IEDs on the plaza. What the hell is next?

The hotel room overlooked HRT's tent city on the New Haven Green. Beyond the Green, Poe could see the very top of Harkness Tower. He tried but he couldn't see Beinecke. He thought he could make out the rooftops of Commons and Woolsey, but he couldn't find the blunt form of Skull & Bones, or the gable of Book & Snake.

The smoke and dust from the explosion lingered in the still air hundreds of feet above Beinecke Plaza.

Poe knew that the siege at Book & Snake had developed into a federal law enforcement resource black hole. Its gravity would prove so immutable that it would attract and absorb any national resources that weren't committed to fighting wars.

It was Waco. It was Ruby Ridge. It was 9/11, on 9/12.

Poe suspected that an important war was already lost. The decisive battle had been fought on Friday, when none of the good guys had even showed up on the right battlefield. His current plan was to do an autopsy on that battle—to discover the nature of the ammunition that had been captured, and where it had been moved—and to do everything possible to save the kids remaining inside Book & Snake.

He texted his assistant. **Anything?**

Seconds later he read his assistant's reply, **SSG is fishing. No target identified.**

But they had a nibble, Poe thought. *And now we're after the same fish.*

Keep me posted on all hostage and family data please.

Will do. Also, DHS has identified 161 potential Persons of Interest leaving the US by plane or vehicle since Thursday.

Poe typed, **Let me know when they've narrowed it to ten. Have we located the white van?**

Negative.

Poe didn't know how he was going to find the out-of-town cop without SSG recognizing his interest in the man. He only knew he had to do it.

He turned on the television and began flicking the remote. Fox came up before CNN. He would toggle back and forth between them hoping to find an occasional kernel that resembled truth.

Fox was replaying the YouTube video. Poe hadn't seen it. He watched it all the way through, narrowing his eyes and tightening his jaw at the final words.

I am America

He wanted a drink. He grabbed the key to the minibar and went in search of a beer.

Juice and pop and water. No alcohol.

He called downstairs, figuring the previous guests had asked that the alcohol be removed from the room's fridge. But he was wrong; alcohol-free minibars were hotel policy. The front desk clerk spelled out Poe's options: There was a bar on the top floor of the hotel. Or room service could bring him a bottle.

Poe figured the room service beer would cost him ten bucks and take half an hour. He had the ten bucks. The half hour? In circumstances like he was facing in New Haven, Poe didn't take time for granted. He rode the elevator to the bar.

The view from the nineteenth-floor lounge included a lovely set piece of

the sun disappearing behind rolling Connecticut hills, late-day lights dancing on the waters of Long Island Sound, and shadows engulfing the wide
expanse of the Yale campus. Poe admired the view while he pondered his
options. Drink at the bar or carry his beer back down to the room?

Holy, he thought. He quickly added, *shit.*

The out-of-town cop was sitting on a stool at the end of the bar,
with his hands cradled around a bottle of Miller Lite.

Poe tried his best to act nonplussed. The out-of-town cop couldn't
see him without turning around. Poe settled at a cocktail table to make
an assessment of the surveillance situation in the lounge.

Poe wanted a boilermaker. He also recognized that he was perilously close to needing a boilermaker. Or two. When the waitress came
over, he ordered just a beer.

Poe counted eleven people in the room including the bartender, the
cocktail waitress, and the out-of-town cop. An adjoining restaurant
was about a third full with the early dining crowd.

If SSG had sent a team to the bar to tail the out-of-town cop, Poe
was realistic enough about his own capabilities to acknowledge that
he would probably not be able to spot any of them until someone—
the out-of-town-cop in particular—went on the move.

The Special Surveillance Group was comprised of ghosts. They
were either already in the lounge of the Omni Hotel and he was in-
capable of spotting them, or they weren't in the bar and he was inca-
pable of recognizing their absence.

SSG either had reason to continue to track the cop or they didn't.

He considered the possibility that he had misread the earlier clues
about the cop, and he revisited the possibility that the man wasn't an
out-of-town cop at all.

Poe decided he could live with the consequences of those mistakes.
He'd made worse.

Dee's text riff from earlier in the day kept running through Poe's
brain like a song that wouldn't go away. *And maybe he's planning
something worse than carnage.* If Dee was right—and she was right a
hell of a lot more often than she was wrong—Poe knew he could not
live with the consequences of ignoring her caution.

This out-of-town-cop might be the key to understanding why the unsub wasn't killing all the hostages. Why some were being released. What else he had planned.

In Poe's mind's eye, he was looking out his office window. He was seeing a Ryder truck parked at the curb.

He tried to shake the image away. It didn't work.

The waitress brought him his beer. Poe carried it to the bar. He slid onto the stool next to the out-of-town cop, intentionally sitting so close that he couldn't be ignored.

APRIL 19, SATURDAY EVENING
NEW HAVEN

Seventeen minutes after the explosion of the IED in front of the tomb, the FBI HRT Zulu sniper checks in with command. Each façade of the building is being monitored twenty-four hours a day by rotating members of separate sniper teams; Zulu sniper has responsibility for the surveillance of the rear wall of Book & Snake. He notes a visible change in the small triangular attic vent at the top of the shallow gable near the roof—one of the vent louvers has been adjusted a couple of centimeters.

His communication is received at the Tactical Operations Center.

Six minutes later he reports that two of the louver panels appear to be in the process of being adjusted.

Seven more minutes pass. He sends word that the two louvers have been removed. The opening created at the top of the vent is approximately seven inches in height and fifteen inches at the hypotenuse. The sniper notes that the gap is too small for a body to pass through. He confirms that infrared is revealing overlapping heat signatures in the attic space.

Unsubs or hostages? He is unsure. He has no visuals. Attempted escape in progress? He can't confirm. Weapons present? Rifle barrel? Scope? None identified.

The sniper's well-disguised aerie is atop Beinecke Library, high ground that provides him with an unobstructed view of the backside of the nearby tomb. If circumstances develop that require the sniper to take a shot, the distance to target is twenty yards. Wind is out of the south at less than five miles per hour. For someone with an HRT sniper's training and skill with weapons, the conditions are nearly perfect. The range is virtually point-blank.

The sniper's shot would be equivalent to an extra point try for a Pro Bowl placekicker. In a dome.

In the cavity of the building below the sniper's belly is one of the world's most valuable collections of rare books and priceless manuscripts.

Christine is not informed about the activity in the attic of the tomb, or about what the sniper is seeing from the rooftop of Beinecke Library. Her job remains circumscribed. Neither HRT nor Hade Moody is willing to risk the possibility that she might inadvertently reveal intelligence to the unsub.

The HRT SAC is waiting for an update on an attempt to get a microphone and camera inside Book & Snake via the sewer lines, and ultimately through a toilet.

He's also waiting to hear from intel with theories about the meaning of the final message on the YouTube video.

Sam

Here's something I hate.

I'm sitting someplace where I'm determined to mind my own business—I'm in my dentist's waiting room, or I'm having a couple of eggs over easy at the end of the counter at Dot's or the Village Cafe in Boulder, or I'm enjoying the first sip of a cold beer on my favorite stool at the West End on Pearl at the conclusion of a trying day—when somebody walks in and decides the best place to sit in the almost empty room is the spot right friggin' next to me. The idiot doesn't take the empty chair on the other side of the room or the stool at the other end of the bar. The fool sits right in my damn lap.

That's something I hate.

That Saturday night in New Haven I was contemplating my impotence and my rage while I lubricated the process with a much needed beer in the Omni's top-floor lounge. I'm not a hotel bar kind of guy, but it was the only place I knew where I could sign for a brew and not use real money. This guy comes up from behind me carrying his bottle of beer and proceeds to plop down on the stool right next to me. There were at least five other open stools at the bar, all farther away from me, including the one beside him on the other side, but he chose the seat that was two inches from my damn elbow.

I glanced over at him for half a second with my best get-the-fuck-out-of-my-face face. The asshole was ready, waiting for me to look his way. He smiled back at me.

Does he actually want to friggin' chat?

His reaction left me wondering if I was really that far off my game. When I want to, I'm usually pretty successful at emitting unmistakable not-sociable vibes.

"Hello there," he said.

"Yeah," I replied. I was about to pick up my beer and go find a table. One that had only one chair. But I liked my current stool, and the day's events had left me in the kind of mood that doesn't predispose me to voluntarily yield territory. I kept my voice even as I added, "You mind maybe moving over a stool or two, or even three? I could use some breathing room. Thanks."

He didn't move. Ten seconds passed. He was looking straight ahead, not at me, when he spoke again. He said, "I know what you're up to. I just don't know why you're up to it."

I wasn't sure what I was expecting from him, but that wasn't it. I gave his response a few seconds of focused cogitation before I concluded that the odor I was detecting was the scent of a reporter possessed with an irritating dramatic flair. Guy was probably working for some second-tier local paper and was maybe hoping to turn this tragedy into a screenplay or a novel on the side. The movie would never be made, the book would never be published. How he'd stumbled onto me I had no idea, but I already didn't care too much.

Failing to come up with any alternatives, I decided he'd made a lucky guess. On a day when innocent college kids were being slaughtered like quail on a caged hunt, I had no patience to spare for the man.

Even "no comment" would have been telling him altogether too much. I said, "I got nothing to say to you."

He responded by sighing like my mother used to when she was disappointed with me. That pissed me off. My mother could get away with it. I'd even let my ex-wife get away with it for a while.

That was the end of the list of the people from whom I had ever tolerated it.

I had watched a kid get blown up earlier that day. I'd heard another explosion kill another kid less than an hour earlier. I didn't feel like I had to make any excuses about what would soon become clear was my complete lack of manners with this stranger. In my most sarcastic tone, I said, "Nice talking to you." I scooped up my beer and began to stand up.

He grabbed my wrist.

Once again it was not at all what I expected.

I'm not the kind of guy who gets his wrist grabbed by strangers. I tend to send off the kind of signals that are successful in keeping even complete knaves with self-destructive tendencies from even thinking about grabbing any of my body parts.

I'd had enough. I switched from my not-sociable voice to my cop voice. "What the fu—"

"Sit back down," the intruder said in a low, serious tone. He released my arm. "Now."

Turned out that the guy had a cop voice, too. I began to adjust all my prior calculations.

The new equation revealed that any advantage I thought I had was an illusion.

He was holding his FBI creds just below the edge of the bar. He held them in a way that I couldn't miss them, but that no one else could see that he was displaying them. I wasn't wearing my reading glasses so I didn't know anything more than that the man was a fed. Given the circumstances, that was a lot to know.

It explained some things. But not others.

My first thought about the new developments? So much for my low profile in New Haven.

I paused to consider my options with the special agent. With the cards I had in my hand—I was holding less than nothing, and the fed whom I had been treating as though he didn't even deserve a seat at the table was suddenly showing a full house—my choices were limited to either bluff or hold.

"Sit down," he suggested, again.

I sat. His eyes were still straight ahead. He wasn't looking at me.

He said, "I showed you mine. Now show me yours."

I thought his voice was tired. Not long-day tired. Long-life tired. I was thinking he was mid-forties.

If he were a used car, he'd be one to be wary of. Body looked okay. But the frame was probably bent. Sheet metal was covered with putty. Seals leaked. Needed rings. Bottom line? He had way more mileage than the odometer revealed.

"Don't know what you're talking about," I said without a whole mess of reflection coming first about whether it was a prudent thing to say.

From my short list of options—bluff or hold—I'd apparently chosen bluff.

He sucked some air between his front teeth. "Neither of us has time for an extended courtship," he said. His tone was low, conspiratorial. "The asshole in that tomb could be killing another kid while we sit here and finish our beers. You going to talk to me, or am I going to make you wish you never came to New Haven? Your fucking choice. Just don't waste time that I don't have."

My new drinking buddy didn't talk like a fed. He didn't dress like a fed. But he had that my-way-or-the-highway manner that was certainly fed reminiscent.

I didn't trust him, of course. Why? Well, he was a fed. That alone was sufficient cause for distrust. Why else? I knew he wasn't interested in helping me out of my predicament, whatever my true predicament turned out to be. And he certainly wasn't interested in helping Jane or Ann Calderón.

"Great talking to you," I said. For the second time I made it all the way to standing.

He said, "I have enough to detain you."

"Then detain me," I said. Once again I had omitted the contemplate-my-options phase of deliberation. I'd spoken on pure instinct.

Probably not good instinct. Pure instinct.

That instinct, apparently, was that I should go all-in. Since the reality was that I couldn't even rub two damn deuces together, it would have been a wise moment to consider the consequences—at least for a second or two—that a federal arrest might have on my commitment to help Ann and Jane, and on my plans to effect a positive outcome of my suspension from the Boulder Police Department.

He zipped open his sweatshirt with his left hand.

It turned out that move was a distraction. I fell for the misdirection like a drunk conventioneer at a Vegas magic show.

The very next thing I felt was the cold steel of handcuffs closing around my wrist.

My new fed friend had a little David Blaine in him.

"Give me the other one," he said. Noting my hesitation, he added, "I suggest playing along. In case you haven't noticed all the activity, I'm not in town by myself. You know enough about us to know we tend to travel in posses."

At that point I considered my bluff called. I was of no use to Ann or Jane in federal detention.

"My name is Sam Purdy," I said, offering neither my other wrist nor any additional information.

"You're a cop. A detective. Who you with, Sam Purdy?"

What? I wondered how he knew that much. And if he knew that much, what else did he know? I had to be careful about the lies I might choose to tell. I said, "What are you talking about?"

He grimaced. More disappointment with me. I really didn't want to hear another sigh. He said, "Don't chew on my hemorrhoids, Sam. Makes me grumpy. You don't want me grumpy. We both know you're on the job. Who you with?"

The cuffs continued to hang from my left wrist. I kept my arm still to keep them from jangling. I said, "Turns out that is kind of complicated."

He sipped from his beer. "I'd like to tell you we have time for a leisurely back-and-forth about the complexities of your employment situation. Well, we don't. Either you get helpful fast or I move on. What happens if I move on without you? I pass you on to my colleagues in intel. I will let them know exactly how you spent your day. I suspect you won't enjoy what happens after that."

I looked at him. He had a pleasant face and wounded eyes. I needed more information to read him. His use of the word "courtship" was bouncing in my brain. Was he a potential ally?

He held up his beer. He said, "I think I'm going to have one more. You want to join me?"

"You buying?"

He laughed. He thought I was trying to be funny, which meant he didn't know enough about me to know that I was merely broke.

I sat back down. What a friggin' mess I was in.

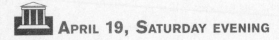

Poe

Cuffing the out-of-town cop was a risky move. Poe knew that. Soon enough, he'd know whether it was the right move. Poe needed to get the guy's attention, but he didn't want to frighten him into clamming up. He needed to learn what the man knew.

If anyone from SSG was in the room, the tracker would not have failed to recognize the telltale clack of closing cuffs. No one from the surveillance team would move in. Instead, the point tracker would invisibly signal for help from the special agent cavalry. Maybe call for an entire HRT posse.

Poe kept one eye on the mirror behind the bar that reflected the entrance to the room. He saw no one exiting, or entering.

That fact told him nothing more than that no one was being careless.

He made a circular motion to the bartender with his index finger. He then waved the finger between himself and Purdy.

Sam Purdy's purportedly complicated story—he was a detective on suspension from the Boulder, Colorado, police department—didn't take that long to tell and, because it betrayed human weakness, rang true enough to Poe's ear.

"So what brought you here, Sam?"

Sam's answer was "How'd you make me?"

"Were you actually trying not to be made?" Poe asked, a little incredulous at the cop's question.

"Not really," Purdy said. "I didn't think anyone would be paying that much attention. I'm not that distinctive."

"We're paying attention to everything that moves. Why are you here?"

Purdy hesitated. Poe tasted the interval of the delay for the presence of precious metal. His assay said: gold.

Poe said, "So you know where we stand—if the next words out of your mouth have even a passing resemblance to a mistruth, we're done. At that moment your life changes forever, and not in a good way. Your career? Such as it is? History. I am not playing games with you."

"What's your name?" Purdy asked.

The beers arrived. Poe waited for the bartender to retreat before he said, "Special Agent Christopher Poe. Now answer my damn question."

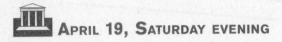

Sam

To stay out of custody I needed to be of some peculiar value to Special
Agent Christopher Poe.

I didn't have a good lie ready so I teased him with a few morsels
of the truth.

"I'm helping . . . the family of one of the students who is inside
Book & Snake." I remembered Ann's phrase. "I am here strictly as a
volunteer. I am not here in any official capacity. I am their eyes and
ears. That's all."

"Which student?" Poe asked me.

Without any hesitation I said, "I'm not ready to tell you that."

I thought my reply might cause Poe to close the cuffs on my right
wrist and march me away. But that didn't happen. Poe seemed con-
templative. He narrowed his eyes.

The man had more gray hair in his eyebrows than he did in his
stubble.

I knew I had to figure out quickly what it meant that Poe hadn't
ended the conversation right then and there. In his shoes, I would
have.

Apparently I'd made a decent move. A buy-some-time kind of
move. The fact didn't tell me much because I didn't know the game we
were playing and I didn't know the rules I was expected to follow. But
somehow I'd stumbled onto something. My confidence barely afloat,
I took another shot. "What field office you with?"

"Not currently attached. Special investigations." Pause. "I'm
thinking this mess qualifies." Pause. "If I demand to know the kid's

name, what do you do next? Just curious how far you've thought this through. Whether you think this match is checkers or chess."

I haven't thought this through as far as you, I'm afraid is what I thought, but didn't say. I was already confident that I didn't want to get into a chess match with the guy. I was pegging him as the kind of reckless player who would dangle his queen after half a dozen moves.

And then somehow get away with it.

I was assuming that Poe was pondering the nature of my relationship with the student's family.

I was also wondering what kind of special investigations Poe did.

He took a slow pull from his beer. "Kid's name? If I insist?"

I held out my right wrist.

In a tone that teachers reserve for instructions to the slow student, he said, "I'll get a subpoena for your cell phone. Saw you using it today. That will tell me everything I need. Is that where we're heading?"

I rotated my wrist so my hand was palm-up, exposing the vulnerability of the veins and arteries for his appraisal. I could feel my pulse accelerating. *You take my phone,* I thought, *Jane is dead. Orange dead.*

Time stopped, yet the echo of his words wouldn't stop reverberating in my head.

He'd said, "tell me everything I need," not "tell us everything we need." My experience was that FBI special agents played team sports. I recognized I was engaging in wishful thinking—I knew I wanted to believe that the use of the personal pronoun revealed something that I wanted to be true about Christopher Poe.

Specifically that he wasn't a team guy.

I caught him looking in the mirror behind the bar. I said, "My phone won't tell you anything that might actually help you. And it will put someone's child at . . . immediate risk. I would argue that's not necessary. And more importantly, it's not going to give you what you really need."

"So you know what I really need?"

I'd walked right into that one. I didn't have a quick reply ready.

Poe took two long pulls from the bottle of beer, waiting. Finally, he said, "What if I agree not to demand to know the kid's name? Not right away. Then what? Think we have a future? You and me?"

I wondered if it was possible that Poe had the hostage taker's rules figured out. Had the FBI talked to another hostage family already? The family of one of the dead kids maybe? Yeah, probably. If that was true, this offer to play along cost him nothing.

"I'm thinking," I said.

"While you're thinking, tell me something. You got to New Haven when, Sam Purdy?"

The question was a trap. If I didn't answer quickly, he'd know I was screwing with him. If I lied, he might already know enough about what I'd been doing to recognize that I was pumping my answers from a septic tank full of bullshit.

"Yesterday," I said. I thought my delay was within margins. Two or three seconds.

"Time?" he asked.

"Early afternoon. Before the sniper scare and before the body was discovered in the hockey rink."

"Early *Friday* afternoon? Huh? How long was your trip here? I'm not asking you where you started, I'm just trying to get some sense of how early the student's family knew to be concerned."

The agent had put special emphasis on the word "Friday." I filed it.

I wasn't going to mention Miami or the length of my private jet flight. "The family was initially concerned sometime . . . Thursday evening. By Friday morning, they were worried. Their kid is a kid who stays in touch with family. The silence screamed at them."

Poe said, "So it's a girl." He said it with a little wonder in his voice.

"Think what you want."

"If it was a boy, you'd have said, 'His silence screamed at them.' You should have just lied, Sam. Would have been better. I wouldn't have known the difference." He shook his head. "Almost every cop I know would have lied right then. Which means you're not every cop I know. You're either stupid, or honest, or, God help me, both."

I said, "Fifty-fifty chance you're right."

"Binary," he said. "The way life has gone? I'll take those odds."

I didn't know what he meant. But I had a hunch about how to be useful to him. Since it was all I had, Jane's life might depend on the quality of my hunch.

I said, "Friday is the key to all this, Poe. The quiet time in the tomb on Friday."

He blinked twice, fast, but otherwise he didn't react.

My phone rang. Seconds later, Poe's BlackBerry vibrated.

"Can I get this?" I asked.

"Yeah. Stay right here."

He glanced at the cuffs and smiled.

I looked at the screen of my phone. Ann. I said, "It's me." I listened. I said, "Just now? This minute?" I was editing my responses to try to ensure that Poe couldn't discern anything important from my words. I asked, "That was first? That order? Then the jersey? I got that right?" I listened to her reply. "Yes, yes. I'm sorry. You got it, not a great time. I'll get back to you."

Ann closed the call with "I'm sorry, too, Sam."

I didn't know what the hell that meant.

Poe had turned his BlackBerry screen so I couldn't read it. I saw the screen just long enough to recognize that his message was a text, not an email.

If it was official government business, it wouldn't be a text message.

He read it. Then he looked at me. He offered a melodramatic "Well?"

I said, "Another kid is outside the tomb. Solo, shackled, blindfolded."

I could tell from Poe's eyes that what I was telling him wasn't news.

He learned about it via text message.

Huh.

APRIL 19, SATURDAY EVENING
NEW HAVEN

Christine Carmody knows little more than what she can see in front of her.

Earlier that afternoon, after the tall black student read the unsub's demands before retreating back inside the tomb, her HRT counterpart had summoned her inside the command vehicle. He told her the mobile cranes and cherry pickers were being driven away from the staging area behind the law school, and the contact microphones had been removed from the stone walls on the sides of the tomb. Finally, he instructed her to resume her role as lead hostage negotiator.

Unclear what it all meant—other than that the cranes weren't going far, that assault helicopters remained on standby, and that the FBI undoubtedly had an alternative plan for getting an audio bug into the building—Carmody took her post again. She was back where she had spent much of the day, out in front of the tomb.

That's where she was standing when the young man stepped outside the tomb with the cardboard box in his hands. That's where she was standing when he squatted and poured the oranges down the stairs. That's where she was standing when the IED that was buried in front of the tomb exploded.

The blast killed the young man.

The IED explosion left Christine with six stitches above her left eye and a sliver of shrapnel embedded in her right calf. She insisted on being treated where she was wounded—at her post, in the middle of Grove Street. A local EMT—he'd done two tours as a medic in

Iraq—cut her trousers and dressed her wound, but didn't go after the shrapnel. He'd leave that to a surgeon. He told her that the IED that had been buried in front of the tomb had been a shaped charge. Its force had been directed toward the building.

As he poked a tetanus booster into her upper arm, he let her know that if the charge hadn't been shaped, she might have been killed.

That's when she decided to accept a flak jacket.

As the cold white illumination at the crime scene supplants the last useful daylight, Christine stands in front of the tomb on Grove Street, waiting. The HRT hostage negotiator, the man who originally replaced her—but who she has now replaced—hovers nearby. Earlier, Moody exited the command vehicle long enough to make clear to Christine that her counterpart in the FBI remained available for consultation about the "unsub" when he was not inside the "Tactical Operations Center."

She should, he said, "continue to liaise liberally."

So far, her FBI counterpart is spending more time inside the TOC than out. His frustration at his secondary role is palpable. But he's handling the demotion like a pro, she thinks.

Christine is aware that this unsub has received everything he's asked for. She is curious how long the official magnanimity will last. She can sense that patience is running low.

She paces to keep her leg from stiffening up. She is literally waiting for the next surprise, unsure whether it will come from the man in the tomb, from Hade Moody, or from one of the guys from the FBI Hostage Rescue Team.

Christine's husband, Ray, is a foreman at the nearby shipyard. Christine and Ray have almost nothing in common. She is a vegan. Ray is no more a vegan than he is a woman, an African-American, or a Puerto Rican–American. He's a white kid from suburban Chicago whose idea of supper starts and stops with the well-cooked flesh of creatures that had mothers. Alongside some form of pale starch.

On paper, they make no sense as a couple. But Christine adores the guy. Ray adores her right back.

On his way to his late shift, Ray detours by the crime scene to deliver Christine a new pair of pants and a cold supper he fixed for her that's heavy on soy and nuts and leafy greens. He fusses over her injuries a little bit during his visit, but not enough to embarrass her. He was following events on television and knew that his wife would need extra protein for the endurance trial she was facing. He threw in a couple of bananas so she'd be sure to get enough potassium to stay sharp.

After Ray leaves to head to the shipyard, Carmody eats her dinner. She saves a banana for later. She resumes pacing the street in front of the tomb. Her steps have taken on a pronounced limp. The flak jacket she's wearing feels wrong.

She is tossing shelled pistachios and almonds into her mouth like popcorn.

At precisely seven-thirty, a young man wearing a Tampa Bay Buccaneers jersey appears out in front of Book & Snake. The door closes behind him.

The football jersey is tangerine orange.

All activity outside the tomb stops as though a switch has been thrown. The sudden quiet feels surreal. The roaring whine of a motorcycle revving on the other side of the cemetery intrudes like a profanity.

Christine recognizes that this young man is about to die. She doesn't know how.

Worse, she doesn't know why.

She is acutely aware that she can do nothing to betray to the man in the tomb the fact that she—and the rest of the authorities on the scene—knows about the code.

That orange means death.

She suspects that the unsub already knows that the authorities know. And that he wants the cops to know.

But that he wants the pretense of ignorance to continue.

She stuffs the bag of nuts into her back pocket and returns to her spot. She faces the young man.

This new kid standing at the top of the Book & Snake stairs is shackled. His wrists are bound in front of him with plastic cuffs. His legs are hobbled loosely at the ankles with a leather belt wrapped in a figure eight.

He is blindfolded.

Since he can't see her, Carmody steps halfway across Grove Street to get closer to him. She wants him to hear her clearly.

Joey Blanks whispers to Christine that the HRT hostage negotiator has exited the command vehicle. Her counterpart strolls into position ten feet behind Carmody. Christine can feel his presence. She wonders if he is preparing to intervene.

Carmody introduces herself to the latest hostage. To no one's surprise, the kid doesn't respond. She asks him to raise his shirt. He doesn't. She asks him to drop to the ground. He doesn't.

He swallows. Licks his lips.

Christine waits.

His voice swollen with fear, he finally says, "Don't come near me. I will die."

She knows what he is saying is true. She wonders if he knows how true it is. She wonders if this young man knows that even if she doesn't approach him, he will die.

The air in her lungs gets heavy, as though it has mass. Her heart sinks in her chest. She waits for most of a minute to pass before she asks the young man if he has anything else to say. He doesn't reply.

Joey Blanks steps to within a foot of Christine. He whispers, "His name is Gregory Tantalus, he's twenty-one, from St. Louis. I have complete background on him and his family whenever you want it, Sarge."

Without turning her head to face him, she says, "That jersey is orange, Joey. Is this kid already dead?"

Joey's words sound especially profound, like documentary narration by James Earl Jones. He says, "He is one of the kids with an ATL. Parents have been in contact. None of that's good. Whenever you want more information about him, you let me know." Joey steps back two paces.

They stand in silence.

A while later Carmody asks, "Joey, how long has the kid been outside now?"

Joey checks his watch. "Eight minutes and change."

Ten feet behind Carmody, the HRT hostage negotiator touches his earpiece with his left hand. He mutters a reply into a hidden microphone before he hustles back toward the TOC.

"Something's going on," she says, stealing a quick glance toward the command vehicle. "Whatever it is, the feds don't want to tell me. Any ideas?"

"My patrol partner, Alfred, he heard that the feds disabled two webcams that were focused on the tomb from outside. One was over in Swing Space. Another at the top of Berkeley. Guy inside's been monitoring us in real time, online."

"I bet he has more than those two," Christine says. "He's still watching us. I can feel his eyes. But that's not what's going on right now. I got a bad feeling, Joey."

"I feel something, too," Joey Blanks says. "I do."

Sam

The bar in the Omni was growing more crowded.

Poe kept his voice low as he spoke to me. "In case you're tempted, you can't go back over there to watch this hostage, Sam Purdy. Sorry."

"That's bullshit," I said. Despite my compromised circumstances, I felt like arguing.

Poe lowered his chin toward his chest and momentarily closed his eyes. He exhaled loudly. "You're under surveillance. The moment you leave this building they will be on you like syrup on pancakes."

He'd said "they," not "we." I said, "Then I'll lose them."

Poe's voice was tired. "With all due respect, no, you won't. You know anything about the Special Surveillance Group? SSG?" He didn't wait for a reply. "You won't even be able to find them. They're that good. We've both been over there, you know you can't see anything from the perimeter at the tomb anyway."

"TV?" I suggested.

He thought about it for a few seconds. He slapped a pen onto the bar. "Write your room number and your cell number on the napkin. I'll follow you in a few minutes. We'll talk some more."

I said, "You're trusting me?"

"Sam? With all due respect, you're dead in the water without me. Miles from shore. My initial appraisal of you is that you're smart enough to realize that."

I wrote down my room number. I made up a cell phone number.

Poe released the cuffs.

*   *   *

My room was on the eighth floor. I didn't close the door all the way.
Poe waltzed in about three minutes later. After he hung the "Do Not
Disturb" sign outside, he closed the door all the way. He turned the
dead bolt, hung the chain.

He wasn't locking anyone out. He was locking us in.

He took the room's only soft chair. I sat on the end of the bed. I
flicked on the TV, began searching for cable news. I said, "I'd offer
you a beer, but the damn minibar was stocked by Mormons."

"Mine, too," Poe said.

CNN came up first. The shot was grainy and indistinct, but Poe
was right, it was a better view than I would have gotten from the perimeter established around the tomb.

As Ann had described to me on the phone, a solitary male hostage—
shackled and blindfolded—was standing between the pillars at the top
of the stairs. The network apparently had no audio. The time stamp
on the corner of the screen read, "7:47 ET."

The hostage—the crawl identified him as Greg Tantalus—was
wearing the tangerine-colored jersey of the Tampa Bay Buccaneers.

Ann had already warned me about his clothing. But seeing the orange, my heart sunk to my toes. I wondered how he would die. I wondered if I should tell Poe that the young man was about to die.

"Can I see your ID again?" I said to Poe.

He didn't hesitate. He pulled it from his pocket and tossed it to me.
I examined it. It was real. I tossed it back. He caught it with the casual
confidence of a goalie guarding his glove side.

"You're not with the local field office?"

"I already said I wasn't."

"You're not with hostage rescue?"

He shook his head. He found the idea of being attached to HRT
amusing.

"Not with SS—whatever—your super-duper surveillance guys?"

"Nope. I work a small special investigations unit formed after
Nine/eleven."

"Counterterrorism?"

"You could say that."

"Okay, I'll say that. If I talk to you tonight, where does it go?"

"If? Don't kid yourself. Right now? It goes nowhere. Later? Depends what you tell me. I'm not going to ignore viable intelligence. I don't do this for amusement."

I knew I wasn't going to get any more assurance than that. My suspicion was growing that Poe was some kind of anomaly in the FBI culture. I also knew that my time in New Haven as a free agent for the Calderóns was over. If I was going to be of any continued use to them, the time had come for me to take a calculated risk.

Poe said, "I think you know why some of those kids are being released and some are being killed. If the asshole was just massacring kids, that'd be one thing. We understand that kind of terror. If he was bartering his hostages for ransom, or tactical advantage, that'd be something else. We understand those situations, too. As far as I can tell, he's not doing either. I want to know what you know about that."

I couldn't decide how much to reveal. I gestured toward the television. "This boy is about to be killed," I said.

Poe eyed me for a good five seconds before he said, dismissively, "What, you got a hunch?"

Poe really didn't know. He wasn't aware of the color code.

"No hunch. I know for a fact that this young man will be killed. Any minute. On national TV."

Poe sat forward, his elbows on his knees. "Go on."

"I'm not ready to tell you how I know, but the families of the kids have been given a way to identify the . . . mood of the hostage taker. I can recognize that he—the hostage taker—is disappointed right now. So far, each time he's disappointed he has killed someone's child. The families knew yesterday that the guy in the tomb was responsible for the sniper scare, and for the dead kid in the hockey rink."

"The families were notified about all this when? Even before the first kid died?"

The fact that Poe asked that question told me how little he knew. I wasn't ready to give up my knowledge without getting something in return. I said, "I don't know when the first kid died, Poe. Do you? Was it the kid in the hockey rink? Was it the girl with her throat cut whose body was left outside the door? Which kid died first?"

"I don't know that," he said.

I said, "The families were initially given an oblique . . . warning about coming events. It was cryptic. That was a few days ago. Earlier in the week."

"What form? Phone? Email?"

"A note, delivered in person. Left anonymously."

"Really?" Poe said.

He had some digesting to do.

I heard a sudden pop from the TV audio. I focused my attention on the screen.

Greg Tantalus pitched forward like a gymnast trying not to take a big step on his dismount. His face revealed surprise. I realized that he hadn't really believed he was going to die.

He managed to catch himself for a split second before his shackled ankles failed him. He pitched forward a second time. I saw flashes in the shadows behind him. The shots were coming through holes in the doors I didn't even know were there. I heard more pops. *Two? Three?* Dark dots appeared on the chest of the orange football jersey he was wearing.

I counted four dark dots.

Greg Tantalus's knees collapsed as he neared the top step. He fell to his side. He fell hard, and fast. His body teetered there for almost ten seconds before it began to roll, awkwardly, down the stone stairs. His head and shoulders were slightly ahead of his feet. Each movement of his body, each rotation, was torturous to watch.

I wanted to close my eyes. I couldn't close my eyes.

He came to rest on the landing midway down the steps, on his side, one knee slightly up in a runner's posture. The left side of his face had been crushed by the hard stone. His right eye was open wide. If that eye could still see, it was seeing the expanse of the Grove Street Cemetery.

I glanced at Poe. He looked like he'd just watched a loved one murdered. I saw horror and rage in his eyes. His breathing was shallow. Beads of sweat dotted his forehead. The muscles in his forearms were as taut as cables.

I could count his heart rate by watching the pulse of the vein in his temple.

I gave him some time, waiting until the inevitable moment when CNN decided they had to replay the tragedy. The network might have felt compelled to replay it, but I didn't feel compelled to re-watch it. I turned away from the TV. I said to Poe, "The parents I'm helping don't want to watch their child die like that."

Poe said, "I understand."

"I can't put their child at risk."

"I said I understand."

I heard a sharp edge in his tone. I said, "I would like to help you. I think that I am able to help you. But I won't reveal anything that will increase the risk to their child. I can't do that. I'm sorry."

"Then help me. You know there's more coming. Help me save a kid or two. Help me figure out who this guy is, what he wants."

"I know what he wants," I said.

"What?" Poe said.

I looked at him. His eyes were locked on mine. The passion in the man's gaze was almost frightening.

"This is a big step for me, Poe."

"Something I learned the hard way? That's the only kind that matters," he said.

"He wants ammunition," I said.

Poe nodded. In a tone that was almost matter-of-fact, he said, "That's what I've been thinking, too. But . . . the kids aren't the ammunition. The kids are the keys to the armory. I don't know what is in the armory."

The hotel room felt suddenly smaller.

Poe, I thought, knew more than he was letting on. I had to be even more careful with him. My phone buzzed. I welcomed the interruption. I glanced at the screen. It was Carmen. I sent it to voice mail. "Personal," I said.

Poe said, "When you said 'ammunition'? Just to be clear—you're not talking about bullets?"

"I'm extrapolating. I could be wrong, Poe. I know only what happened between the guy in that tomb and one family. It could be completely different with the other kids. The other parents."

"Okay. Tell me about the ammunition."

I walked to the window. "I can't believe he just shot that kid. I knew it was coming and I still can't believe it."

"I might be ignorant about some important things, Sam. But hostage rescue knows whatever you know about the signs of disappointment, or whatever it is. They knew the kid was a dead man the moment he walked out the door. I can't tell whether the local hostage negotiator knows. But HRT knows."

"I can't believe this," I repeated.

Poe moved up behind me. He was close enough that I could hear him breathe. "Want to know something else? HRT knew those holes had been drilled in the door. The ones those shots were fired through. They had a pretty good idea what was coming. Did you notice that one of the HRT suits backed away just before the first shots were fired?"

I shook my head. I turned to face him. "You know that for sure? They knew the holes were there? How could they—"

"HRT sniper teams are monitoring every square inch of that building, round the clock. With high-power scopes. If bird shit lands anywhere on that stone, the snipers know the moisture content of the crap. No way they missed those fire holes in the door. Maybe he drilled them while the music was playing. To disguise the sound. Maybe they've been there all along and he just had to remove plugs. Either way, they knew."

"Shit."

"What could they have done? What would you have wanted them to do differently? Warn the kid? Reveal their level of surveillance?"

"I don't know," I said. "Save the kid."

"You didn't save that kid," Poe said. "You knew he was about to die."

"Don't remind me."

"HRT didn't act for the same reason you didn't. If they save this one, the unsub kills two more in retaliation. You want the FBI to start playing God with these kids' lives? I have a pretty high opinion of myself, Sam. But I don't have the credentials for that. I promise you."

I walked away from Poe, went to the chair. Poe sat down on the bed. I started talking without looking his way. I said, "The guy behind all this? He thinks big. He's not interested in massacring those college kids. This isn't Virginia Tech or Northern Illinois."

Poe said, "Bigger? Nine/eleven? Mumbai?"

I shook my head. "No, this is different." I needed to change the way Poe was thinking. "This isn't like Nine/eleven or the London Tube thing or the massacre in India. He doesn't want to blow up a building, or a train. Or crash a plane. Or sink a ship. Or knock down a bridge. He's not content to slaughter a few hundred innocents."

"I'm not convinced. There seems to be plenty of slaughtering going on," Poe said.

I wasn't sold on trying to convince him. But I was sold on not doing anything to alienate him. "Trust me, he's not trying to wound us or shock us. He's looking for ways to bring us down. Cripple us. Bleed us to death. Starve us of oxygen. That's the kind of ammunition he wants."

"Us?"

"America," I said. "Us. U.S. us."

Poe rubbed his eyes. He said, "He's an asshole who kills innocent kids. That doesn't look like evidence of some grand strategy to me."

"Then he's managed to distract you with the blood. If we get distracted, ultimately he'll win."

"Who is 'he,' Sam? Who is doing this?"

"I don't know," I said.

"Extremist?" he asked. "Like McVeigh?"

"Don't think so."

"Nut?" he asked. "Like Virginia Tech?"

"No."

Poe got up. Almost immediately, he started walking a little box. Two steps, turn. Two steps, turn. Two steps, turn.

"A zealot?" he asked. "Like bin Laden?"

"He may be a zealot. But not like bin Laden."

I watched Poe's confined march for a while, wondering what prison cell he was pacing.

He said, "You saw that video on YouTube? What did he mean at the end? 'I am America.'"

"I don't know, Poe. I don't know."

"Few years ago," Poe said, in a once-upon-a-time voice, "a state patrol officer in Illinois spotted a guy taking photographs of an industrial building. The patrolman kept his distance—to this day, he probably can't tell you why he kept looking—and he watched as the guy got back in his truck and then proceeded to set up his camera three more times from different angles. The whole time, all he's interested in is this one building. Cop writes it up, files a report with a description of the guy and the pickup. License plate. That's it.

"A few higher-ups see his report. It gets pushed around. It goes where it goes. Channels. Couple days later, someone makes sure it ends up on my desk."

Poe paused his rectangular march momentarily to look at me with his tired eyes. "My desk has a lot of shit on it, Sam. Not 'lots of shit.' I'm talking a lot of *shit*. Every last suspicious piece-of-crap thing that looks a little wacky to some citizen or semiparanoid local cop anywhere in this country, or anything that anyone in the Bureau or anyone with an imagination at HS—fortunately or unfortunately that's not too many of them—can't fit into some neat compartment, well, it eventually ends up on my desk.

"Any half-laughable, far-fetched thing that anybody out there wants to be able to tell some congressional committee that he or she took seriously—sir or ma'am—they eventually send my way. Why? Because that's my job. Reading their crap reports. Running around the country. Staying in cheap motels. Covering their asses."

Poe started walking again. Two steps, turn. Two steps, turn.

"What does that make me? That makes me the man in the FBI who's supposed to follow up on the story of a guy in a pickup taking pictures of some factory in the Midwest because some state cop can't figure out why the hell the guy's so interested. Then what? A few hours or days or weeks later, I'm the special agent man who's supposed to finish his investigation, close the file, and make everybody feel better by saying 'All clear. Not to worry.'

"Well, that was the year that Chiron—they're the big pharma company in Britain that makes about half the flu vaccine for the Western world—had to shut down production at its biggest plant in the UK because of contamination. Remember that? The shortage of vaccine worldwide that year? Made the news, not the biggest story. Not as big as Britney or Paris, but it was out there for a while. If you read past the headline, the articles made it seem like the contamination in the plant in Britain was accidental.

"Well, it wasn't accidental, Sam. It was sabotage. Very clever sabotage. We managed to keep that part kind of quiet."

"I remember," I said. "There was a bit of a panic at first that there wouldn't be enough vaccine for all the old folks in Florida."

Poe nodded his agreement. "This industrial plant? The one the guy was taking photographs of in Illinois? Turns out it was making an additional forty percent of the U.S. flu vaccine supply. Add it together with what Chiron was supposed to produce—and then take them both off-line during the buildup to the same flu season—and the U.S. is suddenly ninety percent short of its annual flu vaccine needs.

"I had the Center for Disease Control run simulations of the ramifications of that potential shortage. The epidemiologists argued about it for a full week or so. In a normal year, the flu kills thirty to fifty thousand Americans. That's a lot, and that's with vaccine readily available.

"What if there's almost no vaccine available? Turns out there are lots of variables to consider. How well the evidence matches the virus. Strain virulence—that's a big one. Prevalance, incidence, rates of contagion. Available hospital beds. Ability to immunize health care workers. Effectiveness of splitting doses. Need to protect the military. Public panic. Efficacy of antivirals. Availability of antivirals. Distribution of antivirals. Impact of air travel. Impact of international air travel. A long, long list of variables.

"Bottom line? If that had turned out to be an average-to-bad flu year and there was only ten percent of the normal amount of vaccine available for distribution to the entire U.S. population? CDC said one to three million people might have died in this country alone. Hundreds of thousands more in Canada and Western Europe. Many, most, would have been elderly, infirm, or very young.

"And if it turned out it was a bad year? A particularly virulent strain of flu? A strain for which the population hasn't developed antibodies? They said that if that happened, ten million people might've died. And that twenty million wasn't outside the realm of possibility."

"Wow," I said.

"It actually happened, back in 1918. The worst flu pandemic on record killed twenty to forty million people around the world. And that was before air travel. That's more people than died during the Black Death, Sam. More than all the casualties of the two World Wars. Just from the damn flu.

"World Trade Center collapse took two thousand, six hundred seventy-two lives. The Pentagon? One hundred and seventy-nine. United Ninety-three? Forty more."

I didn't know what it meant that Poe had those numbers at the tip of his tongue. But it meant something.

Poe went on. "But imagine a different world. A world of *evolved* terror. Imagine we're confronting terrorists who are using their brains instead of looking at recipes on the Internet and building fertilizer bombs. Imagine we're confronting a guy who's as smart as the brightest one of us. Imagine this new evolved terrorist wants to be as good at wounding America as Google is at search, as Amazon is at online retail. Imagine that this new terrorist has destructive, horrendous dreams that are as grand as our grandest dreams for our children."

I said, "That's what I've been imagining since Friday afternoon, Poe, when I got here. It's so hard for me to—"

"Yeah. Well, welcome to my world. I've been imagining that terrorist since a few weeks after Nine/eleven. I go to bed at night wondering what our world will be like if the next angry man *isn't* using all his energy trying to figure out how to get a shoe bomb onto a plane. *Isn't* spending all his resources trying to choreograph a way to get shampoo bombs onto ten different planes. I stay up at night petrified that the next angry man will be focused and determined. Innovative and imaginative.

"What if the next angry man is brilliant? An entrepreneur? An innovator? What if he's thought up a way to hurt us that we haven't even begun to imagine?"

I didn't know what to say. I did know that my feet had stopped screaming for the first time in hours. That told me something.

"If that state trooper hadn't spotted that pickup truck and hadn't wondered about the guy with that camera, then one small group of terrorists—there were four of them, Sam, that's all—might have succeeded in sabotaging two highly vulnerable industrial buildings at just the right point in time. If they had managed to contaminate that vaccine lab, and if the right flu virus had popped up that year, that handful of angry men—inventive, angry men—could've killed five hundred times, even a thousand times as many people as died on Nine/eleven."

I said, "Until this week, I had no idea that sort of thing was possible."

Poe said, "Is the guy in that tomb the same guy who was in that pickup truck in Illinois? Is he the next terrorist entrepreneur?"

I saw where he was going. I asked, "Is that what you think he meant? When he said 'I am America'?"

Poe's next words surprised me. He said, "The best of us and the worst of us?"

My reply might have been "maybe." Before I could say it, though, I saw that a hooded, shackled young man had just stumbled outside the doors of Book & Snake. This kid wasn't blindfolded.

I gestured at the muted TV. Poe flicked on the sound.

I hesitated before I commented to Poe about the hostage's fate. I wanted to be certain that there wasn't something orange below the hood he was wearing.

After a few moments the young man removed the hood. No orange. I gestured at the television screen. "Poe," I said, "this kid will be released or pulled back in. He is not going to be killed."

"You know that?"

"Yes."

"How?"

I shook my head. "Not yet."

Poe didn't argue or threaten. He said, "What do you make of it?"

"Optimistically? His parents cooperated. They had something the guy wanted. They gave it to him. The guy kept his word."

"Pessimistically?"

"Your entrepreneur has even more ammunition," I said.

Poe fumbled with the remote to mute the sound on the television. He kept his eyes on mine the whole time.

We were two middle-aged cops who barely knew each other, sitting hip to hip on the end of a queen bed in an upscale hotel room in New Haven, Connecticut.

Poe seemed not at all discomfited by either the circumstances or the proximity.

He said, "Ammunition? We were talking about ammunition? So there's no confusion, the unsub is trading each kid he releases for information from the parents. The information is the ammunition, right?"

I couldn't share space with him any longer. I got up and moved across the room, twirling the desk chair so I could straddle it before I sat back down. I said, "Yeah. That's what I said. That's what I meant."

He fell back onto the bed. His feet remained on the floor. He was looking up at the ceiling. After a brief pause, he said, "With this particular group of parents, that could be something. Jesus. Jesus. Jesus. What if . . . You know, if . . . With the right . . ."

I didn't think he was eager for me to interject my thoughts. He was having this portion of the conversation with himself. I was content to allow him to catch up with me. If he filled in the blanks on his own, it would teach me something important about him.

He said, "This all happened on Friday? The individual negotiations with the parents? That's why Friday was so quiet inside the tomb? That's why he set up the distractions outside? The hockey murder? The sniper? He was in the middle of all these negotiations?"

Poe seemed to want an acknowledgment. I said, "There were two reasons for what happened outside the tomb on campus on Friday. Distraction was one of them."

"What was the other?"

"He wanted to ratchet up the pressure, to demonstrate to the parents how easy it is to kill a kid on a college campus, and he wanted the parents to see how willing he was to murder their children if they didn't give him what he wanted. He was making the previous threats real—making it clear that they had no chance to bargain, and they had no time to decide."

"Okay," Poe said. He sat up. "The negotiations with the parents? The threats he made? Determining exactly what information they would give in exchange for their kid's life? That's all Friday?"

I turned to the television.

The young man was standing at attention outside the tomb. His gaze was down, toward his feet. He wasn't speaking.

"Pretty much," I said to Poe. "He'd done his homework. He didn't go into the negotiations blind. He had some idea what kids would be tapped by Book & Snake. He had background information on the kids' families. He knew their parents' work histories, had done research on what important information they might know, what broad categories of secrets they might have access to. Especially what might be valuable to him.

"He used phone calls—VoIP, all Skype is what I'm thinking—texts, links to obscure websites, PGP encryption, passwords that only family members would know. He used recordings of the kids' voices. Parents were led to one website, then were expected to post the encrypted information on another. As soon as they did, the website would go down. With the one situation I'm familiar with, he didn't pressure the parents individually. He allowed the kids he killed to provide the pressure."

Poe digested for a moment. He said, "We're talking national security, right? That kind of information, right? Not financial information?"

"Yes. National security. He explicitly declined seeking money."

Poe said, "And even though he made the parents jump through all the hoops—Internet, Skype, encryption, yada yada—he has to know we'll eventually track all that down. Right? Everything he's doing is starting with a solitary machine or two in that one building. He knows NSA will be able to follow his trail. He probably knows that NSA is already on his trail. He has to know that."

"He doesn't care," I said. "He never said a word about his own safety. I'm thinking he knows he won't survive this siege. His solitary goal is to get the information to the next station. Whatever that is. Whoever that is. He had all day Friday to accomplish that."

Poe nodded. "Unlike money, information is easy to move and difficult to track. Once he gets it offshore electronically, it'll be hard for us to know where it's gone next."

I said, "Impossible. Once it's offline? Impossible."

Poe opened his eyes as wide as he could. "I think I got it. He threatens the parents that if they don't pony up something valuable, he'll kill their kid. He gives the parents a way to know when another parent doesn't cooperate. He then kills that kid in a way that all the other parents recognize? I got that right?"

"Pretty much. You left one part out. If anyone talks to the authorities, he kills their kid."

Poe looked over at me. Held the glare for a good ten seconds. "Your kid? Is she still alive?"

"As far as I know the kid is still alive."

"The parents cooperated?"

"I'm not going there," I said. "It got to the stage where he made it clear what he wanted. I won't tell you how the parents responded."

"What did he want?"

"Something big, Poe. Leave it there."

"No," he said. "I won't leave it there."

"Sorry," I said. I meant it. I was exhausted.

I checked the screen. The kid hadn't moved.

Poe exhaled in a way that caused his cheeks to balloon with exasperation. Then he said, "Those two vaccine labs? If they were both contaminated during a bad flu season? Remember what I said? Three million people could have died. So I know all about ammunition, Sam. Is what you're talking about worse than that? Is this guy going to be able to top three million casualties with the information he wants from the parents you know personally, the ones you're working for?"

Poe said it to me the way a confident champion poker player lays down three queens across from an upstart challenger.

I said, "I'm no expert on the subject, Poe. But the person who is an expert in this particular field tells me the answer is yes. The potential casualties do top three million."

"Yeah?" Poe said, obviously surprised. "I'm talking six zeroes here."

I took a deep breath. I said, "Up the casualties by a factor of ten."

Poe didn't blink. "Physical damage?"

I said, "Catastrophic."

"New Orleans? Katrina? That kind of catastrophic?"

I didn't want to think about it. I said, "A hundred times worse."

Poe didn't challenge me. He leaned forward. He asked, "Could the information your client provided on Friday be useful already? Is the risk clear and present?"

As fast as I could I said, "No."

"How doable is it? Exploiting the information?"

"Here's what I was told: Not very. The threat is theoretical. Is it practical? In this one expert's opinion, it's real. Others might disagree. Apparently there continues to be a scientific debate about whether or not it's actually possible to use the information . . . that way. To . . . weaponize it, I guess. And even if it is possible, the logistics of exploiting the information as a military threat or terrorist threat is daunting. Doing it is . . . complex. It would require major strategic resources."

"Could we do it? The U.S.?"

"To ourselves?" I thought about Ann's scenario. "Yes. To someone else? No."

Poe said, "I don't understand."

"The weapon is aimed at us. At the U.S. That doesn't change. That cannot change."

"I still don't get it."

"Sorry."

Poe stood up. He took a step. I knew what was coming. He pivoted ninety degrees. He took another step. He was back in the damn box.

"Could Israel exploit it?"

His question surprised me. After I considered it for a moment, I thought I recognized what he was trying to do with the question. "Yes," I said. "Probably."

"Iran?" Step.

"Maybe." Step.

"Al Qaeda?" Step.

"I don't know." Step.

Poe paced off his box while he thought about my answers to his questions for another half minute. He said, "There's no location a terrorist could set off a small nuke in the United States that would kill thirty million people, Sam. Believe me, I know. I've talked to experts about it. I've seen the maps, the casualty projections. Contamination zones. Long-term radiation illness rates. Can't be done. Not even close to a number like that."

I thought about denying the nuclear part of his argument, but quickly convinced myself that there was no way Poe could use that information to get from New Haven to a volcano on the Canary Islands and then back to the Calderóns. I said, "The nuke in question wouldn't be set off on U.S. soil."

Poe thought through the new piece of the puzzle for another thirty seconds. He expanded the box to two steps in each direction. The confines of the room wouldn't permit him to annex any more territory. Finally, he said, "I seriously don't get it. How does an offshore nuke kill thirty million Americans?"

I didn't reply. We were both temporarily fixated on the television as the young man not wearing orange stripped down to his underwear. I didn't know whether he had been ordered to undress by his captor or by the hostage negotiator.

He was wearing white briefs. He was not carrying any explosives or any weapons.

Suddenly, he spoke.

"Don't interrupt me" was how he started. The young man waited until all was quiet.

"His strategic interests supersede all other interests. All others."

The hostage paused long enough at that point that I thought he was done.

But he continued. "Prior to launching this mission, other factors were considered, including the likelihood of civilian casualties. A determination was made that some civilian casualties were acceptable in order to achieve the strategic objectives."

He marched down the steps. He stepped out the gate. He turned and assumed the position. Hands on the fence. Feet spread.

Poe said, "What the fuck was that?"

"Rationalization," I said.

"No . . . No. What the—"

"Poe," I said. "This hostage is free. That shows me there's still a chance that the kid I'm here to help could be let go." I shook my head. "I can't put that at risk. I'm sorry."

"But other people's kids?" he asked. "That's okay with you?"

His words pierced me like a sharp knife.

I watched cops hustle the latest hostage away from the tomb.

Poe said, "Have you noticed that none of the families of the kids who have been killed are grieving publicly? Have you seen even one interview with an irate or despondent mother? Have you watched one eloquent uncle step outside and offer any words on behalf of the family?

"The networks have reporters and cameras parked outside their houses. But the families aren't talking."

I said, "I noticed that, Poe. The parents know that one misspoken word might kill another parent's child. The guy in the tomb? He has his fist"—I growled the word as I tightened my fist in front of my face—"clenched around those parents' hearts, Poe. He's squeezing life from what is most precious to them. I'm not happy to admit this, but in their shoes, the parents' shoes, hell, any of those parents' shoes—these same circumstances—I would give the guy what he asked for. Everything he asked for. As callous as that sounds. I wouldn't sacrifice my kid that way. I couldn't. Could you?"

"Moot," Poe said. "Don't have a kid."

Poe suddenly stopped his confined march. He said, "I need some sleep, but first I need to make sure they're not going in tonight."

"You mean the Hostage Rescue Team?" I asked. "You know something? I've been thinking about it since I saw that building for the first time. He chose that place because it's a fortress. A breach of that tomb could end up being a bloodbath. Now with those sensors he has in place everywhere? Jesus. All the kids will die."

Poe winced. At first I thought I'd said something so stupid that it caused him physical pain. But I quickly recognized that it was the kind of wince that acknowledges the accumulation of a day's strain, nothing more specific than that.

He shook his head, disregarding my entire line of thinking. He said, "During a crisis like this, with innocents being held, deciding to breach isn't a rational act. You want it to be, in a perfect world it is, but in the end, it's not. You never know when patience is going to run out during a hostage event. Could be a day, could be a couple of months. But at some unpredictable point, someone high up the chain will succumb to pressure—personal, political, lunar, whatever—and decide it's time to stop talking and send in assault teams. I can almost guarantee you that looking back on it, the decision won't seem logical. History never makes it seem like it was an imperative."

Even before he finished speaking, Poe had started pecking away at his BlackBerry. I thought he sent out three different texts. I looked out the window. In the distance, the sky above Beinecke Plaza was lit bright.

I counted three texts coming back to Poe in the next few minutes.

After he read the final message, he said, "Doesn't look like HRT is planning a breach overnight. There are high-value kids still inside." He got to his feet and took a step toward the door before he stopped and pivoted to face me. "I'll be here to get you tomorrow morning at six. You'll be here. We'll plan our day. Together."

It wasn't an invitation. I nodded. I said, "You know, they're all high-value kids to somebody."

He glared at me. "Yeah. Thanks for the reminder. Write this down. It's my cell." I picked up the pen from the desk. He dictated a number. "You hear from that family, I want to know. And give me your real phone number." He stared me down. I blinked. "Don't fuck with me again, Purdy. I'll run over you and I will treasure the tire marks I leave on your neck."

He spoke the threat without a detectible alteration in inflection. Destroying me would be all in a day's work.

I gave him my cell number. "Why are you doing this?" I asked.

"This being what? Threatening you? Tormenting you? Protecting you?" He offered a spare grin. "My intelligence colleagues in the Bureau already know everything I just learned from you. I'm sure they got it, and more, from the families of the kids who were killed yesterday and today. All that would happen if I told them what you revealed to me is that I'd waste you as a source and I'd put your girl at risk. I don't see how it helps anyone to do either of those things. For now, I'm willing to string you along and hope it pays off. Your job is to make it pay off. Hey, hope keeps us alive, right?"

I couldn't tell if he was indulging in irony. I said, "Your bottom line? You want to know what all the parents gave up and where the information is going?"

"More likely where it's already gone. Yeah, that'd be nice. I'd also like to know who the hell the unsub is and why the hell he's doing what he's doing. Once he moves the information out of that tomb, we're never going to get it back. If we figure out who he is and why he wants it, we might be able to mitigate some of the damage."

"Your colleagues have the same agenda?"

"Not exactly. I have no doubt that the Hostage Rescue Team negotiators are trying to persuade the parents to come clean about their dealing with the unsub and, of course, to encourage them not to provide any more information. But the parents are watching TV, too. They can see how impotent the FBI is so far. I suspect there's a stalemate going on out there that I don't want to replicate in here." He waved a finger between us. "With you and me. I want your help. I want you to trust I'll do anything I can to spare your kid."

I believed him. "So we're clear, Poe? You and me? I want the kid alive. Unhurt."

"That'd be nice, too, Sam. So we're clear, you and me? It's not the highest priority on my list. But you can rest easy tonight that it's in my top three or four."

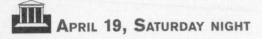

Poe and Dee

The first thing Poe saw when he opened his hotel room door a couple of minutes later was a purple lace bra that had been carefully tossed carelessly on the floor.

The damn thing brought tears to his eyes.

Rudy's was a cultures-collide dive bar.

Since it was in a student neighborhood, some of the variance was seasonal. There were nights Rudy's was the most déclassé of New Haven's student bars. Some nights it took on the harder edge of a biker bar. Other nights it had the affectionately neglected vibe of a mutt neighborhood watering hole. Some nights, when the stars lined up just so, Rudy's had to manage to be everything to everybody, and the disparate clientele had to find a way to coexist through the natural tension.

Dee had been to Rudy's once before, without Poe, to interview a Yale professor about some worrisome military developments in China. The guy was in his late fifties but rode a Harley whenever the weather allowed. He chose Rudy's for the consultation, thinking the biker aura might gain him some advantage with Dee, either consultative or predatory. Dee left the meeting hoping the guy's judgment about China's infantry was superior to his judgment about women.

Returning to the tavern with Poe was Dee's idea—she was the sole official who made the call that the pub met their dive bar standards. Poe was so happy to see her he would have been thrilled to be drinking at a T.G.I. Friday's.

They took the last two seats at the bar. Dee had to bribe a couple of gruff old boys wearing black leather vests with one of her sweet smiles and a free round to cajole them to scoot their asses over a stool so that she and Poe could sit side by side. She chose the stool with the seat that was already warm from one boy's wide butt.

Poe said, "I hoped you'd come."

"No, you didn't, Poe. Never crossed your mind that I'd come." She said it with affection.

"True. But if it had crossed my mind, I'd have hoped you'd come."

Dee ordered a scotch neat and a ginger ale back, no ice. Poe, a Pabst. No whiskey shot. He was working.

He had never seen her order scotch neat before. The ginger ale? Maybe once. "Neat?" he said.

"My stomach . . . ," she said. "Today? I'm not accustomed to watching . . . I don't know how—"

Poe put his hand on hers. "I know. You look tired."

She shook her head. "Compared to these families? What they're going through?"

"You fly here from Philly?" he asked her.

"Amtrak. Missed the connection in the City, had a long layover at Penn Station. At least it gave me time to run to Duane Reade and . . ." She put a hand on her gut. She left the sentence unfinished.

"Had I known you were coming, I would've sent my chopper."

Dee smiled at him. "Cute. For some reason I have trouble visualizing you and The Donald comparing helicopter woes." She leaned over and gave him a soft kiss. "I have some new information, theories about the unsub, background about the families of the kids in the tomb. Interesting pattern. Not surprising, but interesting."

"How?"

"Can't say."

Poe knew that "can't say" meant G.B. Jerry.

Poe's beer bottle arrived already sweating like Shaq's cranium in the final minute of OT. The barkeep snapped a rocks glass down in front of Dee and free-poured her scotch with a steady hand. The ginger ale came last. It wasn't from the beverage gun. It was a cute little bottle of Canada Dry.

Old school.

It had a screw top. Almost old school.

Poe said, "I'm listening, my lady." Poe wanted to hear Dee's impressions before he told her what he learned from his out-of-town cop.

She exhaled audibly. She dipped her chin and allowed the gravity of the day to subdue her tone until it was a gravelly whisper scented with wafts of whiskey and promises of intimacy. "There's a lot of attention being paid to the usual suspects. Al Qaeda, Hezbollah, Hamas, splinter groups from Sudan or Yemen or Indonesia, even Morocco or Tunisia, exports from the likes of Lashkar-e-Taiba, even some possible minor players from Morocco and Tunisia. Government sponsorship from Iran or Syria. Or it could be a new threat from South America. Rebels from Venezuela, Peru. The list goes on. We know nothing about the guy, so we can't rule anyone out. No surprises. You know everyone on our list, Poe."

"I admit I do have the Death to America roster memorized. But you're not convinced it's even the right list, Dee. I can tell."

She pushed her hair back and tucked it behind her ear. "The prevailing analysis links this straight to Iraq. So far today we've had a suicide bomber, a slit throat with a body left 'on the street,' a sniper victim, an IED casualty. Each victim, each method is a clear echo of some phase of the Iraq War. Many of my colleagues think it's an Iraqi national in there. Maybe an ex-prisoner from Abu Ghraib. More likely a Sunni than a Shia. Others think it may be a U.S. vet. A disturbed vet. One of us. Playing out some vision of hell he knows all too well."

Poe sipped some beer. "You buying any of it?" He knew she wasn't.

"The analyses are defendable."

That, Poe knew, was an ambivalent wife's weak endorsement of her husband's current analytical prowess. He said, "You're damning with faint praise. Which means you're not convinced. What does 'I am America' mean? What was that about?"

"I've heard a half dozen theories."

"I only need to hear one, baby. Sing me the song that gives you chills."

"Look at me. See yourself."

Poe turned his head, looked at Dee. He didn't see himself. She laughed at the confused expression in his eyes.

"That's what 'I am America' means, Poe. He's telling us he's not different from us. That he is like us. He is us. What he's doing is what we're doing."

"Slaughtering innocents? Come on."

"Step back from your anger. Step back from your fatigue. You can't know the enemy if you won't plant your feet where his are and see what the world looks like from where he stands."

Poe gave it some thought. "That's a scary one, babe," he said. "Shit. I think I'm too tired to guess where you're going." He pushed the outside of his thigh against hers. "What on earth are you thinking?"

"You saw the final speech tonight? The one the kid in his underwear gave before he was released?"

"I saw it."

"That was your unsub's explanation for 'I am America.' That little speech? It's a version of what we said when our bombs went slightly off target in Baghdad during Shock and Awe. It's what we say each time one of the missiles we fire from our Predators accidentally kills civilians in Pakistan. It's what Israel said a few months ago in Gaza during the New Year's invasion, to criticism they were using phosphorus around civilian populations."

Poe held his beer bottle like a TV reporter would hold a microphone. He said, "I am here with Deirdre Drake from the Central Intelligence Agency." He tilted the bottle closer to Dee. In his best network correspondent impersonation, he said, "Ms. Drake, who is it? Tell the American people—who is in that tomb?"

Dee pushed the bottle away. She said, "I don't know, Poe. I don't know who is in there. I do know this isn't about trading hostages. Not in a traditional sense. He's letting too many of his hostages go. And I know it's not about revenge. Same reason. Pure retribution would mean pure slaughter. Without more evidence, we're left with a frustrating conundrum."

"Which is?"

"The list of people that America has pissed off recently is too long.

It would be easier for me to tell you who is not inside that tomb than to tell you who is."

Poe put the bottle on the bar. He said, "We're on the same page. You and me."

Dee said, "Unfortunately, the page I'm looking at is mostly blank. Now you tell me something—what does HRT do now? Do they attempt a breach despite the defenses the unsub has in place? How do you read it? What options are available? Which ones are viable?"

"No breach tonight, apparently. The government has more toys at its disposal," Poe said. "I gare-an-tee"—Poe inflected the word like a Cajun might because he still wanted to hear Dee laugh, but she wasn't amused by his accent—"that they are still trying to see inside those walls. There could be some specially equipped Predator circling over us right now. I'm not in the loop on the latest and greatest technology, but the army has developed all kinds of new shit to peer into stone houses in Iraq and Afghanistan so they can track whoever it is they're tracking over there. Secretary of the army's kid is still inside that tomb. You can bet that any of the new whiz-bang army toys are potentially in play on this.

"And I doubt they've ruled out using paralyzing agents. Something that would put everybody down, unsubs and hostages alike. If they do that, they'd have to instantly initiate a highly destructive breach on part of the building that isn't wired—which basically means putting a tank through the wall and praying the place doesn't collapse. Then they rush the medics in and hope they're fast enough with triage to save the kids. Using sedatives and paralytics is high-risk stuff, but you never know, at some point it may look better than the alternatives. The bureaucratic tolerance has to be diminishing for watching kids get marched outside those doors and murdered."

"For the drugs? How?" Dee asked. "How do they get the drugs in? No windows. Roof's protected."

"Getting gas into the tomb is doable. They could feed it in through the roof vents—though the unsub might detect any activity up there—but more likely they'd go in through the sewers. They'd snake a tube in through the waste lines and then into the bathrooms or kitchens through the toilets or sink drains. They can get microphones and cameras in that way. Those could already be in place. That's pretty standard, straightforward stuff for HRT. They call them 'crap cams.'"

She lifted the scotch, touched the glass to her lips. "You didn't hear this from me, okay?"

"Of course."

"Crap cam's been tried and failed. They have no video inside that building. No viable audio. Virtually no intel. He's been prepared for everything they've tried."

"That complicates things."

"The released hostages aren't talking. Nothing."

Poe said, "I'm not surprised by that. Their friends have been threatened."

Poe wondered which betrayal was harder for Dee. Was it pretending she was his wife and bribing a housekeeper so that she could drop her purple bra on the floor of his hotel room? Or was it passing along intelligence that her husband had shared with her as part of the daily currency of their faux marital intimacy?

Poe asked, "Before you tell me what you learned about the families of the kids in the tomb, can I guess how you got it?" He wasn't trying to be a smart-ass. He was trying to minimize Dee's sense of betrayal. If he could frame the data she got from Jerry so that it seemed less valuable than it was, she might feel less guilty about sharing it with him.

It was partially a selfish quest. Life always seemed better for Poe when Dee was less tormented about Jerry.

She lowered the scotch, took a sip of the ginger ale. "Sure, go for it."

Poe said, "Parents of the kids who walked out alive know something . . . that was valuable to the unsub. They gave up what they know. He released their kids. And they're not talking to the sheriff because it's been made clear to them that the threat to their children does not expire."

Other than the anguish etched in her eyes, Dee's face remained without expression.

Poe went on. "But the parents of the kids who were murdered

broke one of the unsub's rules. They either went ahead and talked to the sheriff. Or they didn't give the unsub what he wants."

"Close," she said.

"Close? What am I missing?"

"At least two of the dead kids' parents kept all the unsub's rules, but their children were killed anyway."

Poe turned his head toward her. Thought about it for a moment. He said, "I don't get it."

Her voice was low. "This is me, okay? Just me."

She wanted a reply. Poe said, "Yeah. You." *Not Jerry.*

"I have to conclude the parents didn't have anything valuable to trade. That they aren't connected. The father of one of the dead kids is a plastic surgeon in LA. Big house in the Palisades—he apparently has SoCal plastic surgery money—but that's it. The other dead kid's mother—he's a financial aid kid, she's a single mom—is a municipal bus driver in Fargo, North Dakota. Waking up Thursday, she knew nothing more than the Fargo bus schedule and that she had a brilliant, charming son she cherished and adored."

"Fargo?" Poe said. "The kid in the hockey rink?"

"That one."

"Shit. The ones who were released? Do we know what they gave up?"

"No, but they had stuff to trade. Partial list? Try this on. One's grandfather owns controlling interest in a company that floats half the barge traffic on the Mississippi River. One's father is COO at Bell South. Another's is a senior officer in the Army Corps of Engineers. One's mother is the top-ranking woman at ConAgra. Another's mother is a researcher in a CDC BSL-four lab in Fort Collins, Colorado."

"BSL?"

"Biosafety level. Four is highest. Think ebola, SARS. Biohazards with a capital *B*."

"What a list. What do you think, Dee? Is this as bad as it looks? What do you think they gave up to save their kids?"

"At this point, we have to use our imaginations. Just with that little group? Maybe . . . a simple but effective way to sabotage the locks and shut down barge traffic on the Mississippi during harvest . . . The soft spots in our nationwide telecommunications architecture . . . The most vulnerable locations in our levee system or the identities of our least secure dams . . . Imaginative ways to contaminate the nation's food supply . . . The soft underbelly of the recent global financing fix. An exploitable weakness in our infectious disease containment architecture."

Poe said, "Ammunition."

Dee said, "Yeah. Good ammunition, baby. But the reality is we're left to guess because none of the families are talking. I'm sure the guy has threatened to go after the kids again if the parents talk to us." She touched Poe on the wrist. "What was up with the secretary of the army's son? He came out and went back in. What did that mean?"

Poe didn't have an answer.

Dee sipped from the bottle again. She changed her tone. "You found your out-of-town cop, Poe. He told you some of what's been going on, right? You didn't cover all this ground on your own."

Deirdre was smart. Poe had had no doubt she would figure that out. He was about to tell her all about Purdy anyway. "Ran into him sitting at the bar in the hotel. Turns out that the parents of one of the hostages sent him here to eyeball things."

"Is he yours? Or did the surveillance team get him first?"

"For now, he's mine. If SSG is still watching him, I'm missing it. That's certainly possible. The cop is sharp and he's . . . honorable. He's not going to reveal anything that puts the kid at risk. He hasn't told me what kid, or what family. But he told me the logistics about how it all came down earlier in the week."

"And you left him alone in the hotel?"

"I put the fear of surveillance in him. He also knows I'll burn him if he doesn't play nice. The screwiest thing? He used the same word I used with you earlier, Dee. He called the kids 'ammunition.'"

She blinked twice. "Really?"

"Really."

"That's scary," she said. "Someone who thinks like you." Then she smiled.

Poe freeze-dried the smile. Stashed it someplace safe in his memory. Thought he'd thaw it out for his birthday.

Dee asked, "Did the parents he's working for cooperate with the unsub?"

"I think they did, but I don't know. Get this: The cop—I had my assistant run him, he's a detective on suspension from the Boulder, Colorado, PD—says the information from the parents he's working for conceivably puts thirty million lives at risk."

"Suspension?" she asked.

"Not important," Poe said.

Dee faced him. "Did you really just say thirty million?"

"I did. It's a long shot—the guy says the parent considers the degree of difficulty to use the information sky-high. He said there's a one in ten million chance of anyone making it work. And he denies imminent danger—says there's no concern it's something that can be thrown together next week or next year. But that potential casualty number is chilling, even to me. It exceeds anything I've run across since I started this job. Hell, Dee, it might exceed the sum of everything I've run across since I started this job."

"Thirty million?" Dee said. Her gaze was straight ahead but it was focused on infinity. "Holy. How do you kill thirty million Americans, Poe? You'd need a multi-warhead ICBM, pinpoint targeting, and perfect winds. Hell, you'd need to hijack a fleet of Tridents."

"I don't know, Dee. Guy hasn't told me yet. My brain can't figure it out. Does he have a way to cause a meltdown in a nuclear reactor? In the right location, would that do it? I don't think it would." He touched her cheek to get her attention. "How about a meteor strike? That could do it. Did somebody figure out a way to steer meteors while I wasn't paying attention? I am praying that the guy's just damn wrong."

Poe hadn't actually prayed to God since April of 1995. His last conscious prayer occurred before his head had cleared that morning, and long before the dust had settled in the Murrah Building.

Poe considered it an unanswered prayer.

He had hoped Dee would say something that would convince him how wrong he was about the thirty million. But she seemed lost in her own dark vision of the future. He couldn't tell whether the view from her stool was as calamitous as the view from his. Poe rarely insisted that Dee share his perch, or his perspective. He didn't insist on much, with Deirdre.

With no warning, he suddenly felt himself begin to slide. Poe could hear his recent words still reverberating in his ears as though he'd spoken them inside a fat pipe.

Dee sensed something, too. She heard him beginning to submerge.

He tried to come back, to crawl out of the tunnel. He said, "When we met—you and me, baby—the nation was feeling that what had just happened in Oklahoma City was the worst thing imaginable. Remember that? What it was like those first few days after the bombing? The magnitude of it all? A hundred and sixty-eight people had died. It was an epic tragedy. It caused us all to take stock. As people. As a country. We were all trying to find some big collective mirror to look into. But somehow . . . before too long Oklahoma City wasn't monumental anymore. By 2001, we looked back, and it was just one hundred and sixty-eight folks who died. That's what, one seven-fifty-seven's worth? Now, fifteen years later, the bombing has become a quaint tragedy."

Dee reached over. She took his hand to steady him, and to steel herself for what she feared might be coming. Poe rarely talked about Oklahoma City. He never talked about the people who died that day.

He never, ever minimized the significance of that grievous loss. Of the endless mourning.

She knew he wasn't done.

"Here it is, all these years later, and you and I are sitting together in a, frankly, very confusing bar in New Haven, Connecticut, trying to figure out how some asshole locked inside a secret society tomb might be planning to kill thirty million Americans.

"What happened to us, Dee? This country. This world. What went wrong? How the fuck did we get here?"

From the moment on Saturday afternoon that the man in the tomb sent the secretary of the army's kid out to direct that she be sent back into the game from the sidelines, Christine Carmody decided that she had no choice but to interpret the instruction about her literally. The words the kid spoke were:

> *. . . the original hostage negotiator will resume her role. She will stay there for the duration.*

Her role is hostage negotiator.
There is Grove Street in front of the tomb.
The duration is until this situation gets resolved.
That's what the man in the tomb wants. That's what he gets.

In the earliest minutes of Sunday, shortly after midnight, Christine begs a cot from one of the fire department rescue crews. She sets it up in the middle of Grove Street, directly in line with the door of the Book & Snake tomb. It's the exact spot where she was standing while she first spoke to Jonathan Simmons on Saturday morning. It's the spot where she was standing when each of the other kids came out the door.

Some of them lived. Some were killed.

Earlier that evening, she was standing on that spot on Grove Street when the IED exploded, killing Reginald Oshiro.

Later, she watched Greg Tantalus shot to death from that spot on Grove Street. And when the next kid was released in his underwear.

Christine could be a little superstitious.

She was telling herself that the spot hadn't been all good luck.

But that it hadn't been all bad.

At twelve minutes past midnight, the Zulu sniper on top of the Beinecke Library calls in a report to the command vehicle. He has detected the reflection of light off a glass surface inside the gable vent. He cannot confirm it was the glint of light off a scope. He is allowing that the brief reflection may have been from eyeglasses.

He also confirms infrared signature in the attic space.

FBI intel immediately begins to assemble a roster of the possible hostages who may be wearing glasses.

An agent is sent to re-interview the solitary witness. *Were any of the caterers wearing glasses?*

Christine has always been an accomplished sleeper. Front seat of a car, middle seat on an airplane, crosstown bus. Movie theater during a bad action flick. Shea Stadium bleachers when the Mets are down seven in the eighth. She's proven she can sleep almost anywhere.

On a hard cot in the middle of a street in front of a serial crime scene with half the world tuned in? For Carmody, it's not a problem. She rests on the cot on her side, her face to the tomb. She manages fifteen minutes of sleep here, ten there. The noise of the police presence behind her doesn't bother her too much. She's raising two teenagers in eleven hundred square feet. She has a Ph.D. in noise.

It is the pain in her calf that keeps jolting her awake.

Hade Moody and Jack Lobatini have gone home to their own beds.

When she is tapped on the shoulder and summoned to the TOC a little after three A.M., it is by one of the FBI comm operators on behalf of the second-shift HRT talker. Christine follows the woman to the command vehicle.

Christine doesn't have a feel for the second-shift FBI hostage negotiator. She grows more wary when he sends a few colleagues outside so he and Christine are alone in the fancy RV.

The place is starting to look like a dorm room after a tough weekend.

He offers her coffee, something to eat. She declines the coffee. She is still hopeful about getting a few more winks in before morning. She's shocked to see a carton of LäraBars among the sugar and white flour crap that is spread on the counter in the galley.

She stuffs three in her pockets.

"Sit," he says. His tone is friendly, which immediately heightens her suspicion. She sits. "Think the unsub's asleep in there?" he asks.

Christine weighs his words for meaning in some alternative universe. She can't spot any nefarious translation. She says, "I'm thinking no. That would be predictable. He's not predictable. I think he can go for a while sleeping in short bursts."

"A catnapper?"

"I guess. I can do it. Sleep in . . . increments." She hates the word "catnap," but that's a quarrel for another day.

"You? How many days could you go? Sleeping like that, a little here, a little there?"

"A few. When both of my kids had croup and my husband was at his parents' in Florida, I did it for three, four days. This guy's only had to do two so far."

"We need intel. We need it badly," he says. "Want you to be aware we've been trying to insert crap cams into the building. You know what those are?"

Christine thinks, *I'm a little tired, but I'm not stupid.* "Yeah. You're trying to get cameras into the building through the sewers. Sinks, toilets." She considers the roof. "Vents, too? I didn't see anyone up there."

"Just the sewers so far. Based on what we heard earlier about what he has in the attic, we have to assume he's monitoring the roof."

"Probably the sewer lines, too. He's thorough."

"Yeah."

Christine impulsively shows a card. "Although I'm always grateful for information and all the up-to-the-minute tactical headlines, do you mind if I ask why you want me to be aware of all this? Usually

I'm kept a little more in the dark." She knows it's far from routine to keep an active hostage negotiator apprised of the behind-the-scenes efforts to free hostages.

He shrugs. She interprets the shrug to mean that he has a reason, but he's not going to tell her what it is. Her suspicion about the nature of his motivation gets jacked up a notch.

Christine asks, "So? How's it going in the sewers? You get video? Audio?"

"Got nothing. That's the point. Toilets? You ready for this? It appears he fucking pulled all the toilets in the building and bolted steel plates over the drains. Have you ever heard of that? I've never heard of it. I been doing this for most of my adult life and I've never seen anything like it. He opened up the p-traps below all the sinks and fitted metal covers over the exposed pipes. Shower and bathtub drains, too. All plugged with something. Rags? Who knows? What it means is we can't get access to the building through any of the usual waste lines.

"Maintenance guy for the tomb says there are a couple of floor drains in the building that the unsub may not know about. He's shown us on the building's plans where they should be, but we haven't been able to locate them with our equipment. We're continuing to look, but we're worried about making noise with the snakes if we fish around too much."

"You don't sound hopeful."

"Not about that. We got our microphones in as far as we could—we're in the walls behind the sinks—but we're getting no useful audio through the plates and pipes and plaster. He's obviously sequestered the hostages far away from the plumbing.

"We even tried to get in using the fresh water lines. All the supply lines in the building—faucets, toilet supplies, showers—are completely closed off, too. He shut the valves. Water meter shows zero use of water inside that building since Thursday. Even though it would have been a much more difficult approach for us no matter what, that means we can't get any access through any of the building's hot or cold water lines."

Christine says, "And that also means he's not using the local water supply for consumption so you can't use the tap water to deliver any . . . let's say, medicine. The bad guys could even be wearing chemical masks. We don't know, do we?"

"That's right. We don't know."

Christine says, "We have to assume that he has his own food and water. I'd like to say I'm surprised. But I'm not. He's been ahead of us from the beginning."

The FBI talker turns his back on her. "Really? That's what you got after two days? That you're not surprised?" His voice is modulated, but she can tell that he's unsheathed his blade.

She's tempted to write off his reflexive strike to frustration, but she's too tired to allow his derision to go unnoted.

She blurts out, "What? Excuse me? You are—I want to make sure I got this right—actually taking offense at that? Kids are walking out the door of that tomb getting slaughtered one after the next—blown up, shot, cut up, blown up again—and you're taking offense that I may have noted that our subject has been a step or two ahead of us?"

Christine watches the man's back expand as his lungs fill. She prepares herself. She wants to be ready to step forward when he turns on her. She wants to be right in his face and bounce his anger back at him so that it packs his airways and he can't breathe.

He says, "Difficult night. Sorry." He continues to look away from her. He asks, "Are you a Pepe's person or a Sally's person?"

Christine, who is never speechless, is speechless.

"Come on? Nobody's neutral in this town. Which is it for you? Pepe's or Sally's?"

Christine considers explaining the restrictions of her vegan diet. Rejects it. She answers based on Ray's well-defined Wooster Street ardor. She says, "Sally's Apizza. It's not a contest."

He makes eye contact with her. He says, "Maybe I'm no expert, but I vote for Pepe's."

She waits until he looks away again before she shakes her head dismissively at the man's obvious lack of judgment about Wooster Street pies.

She's waiting for him to ask her what she thinks of a Wenzel.

He goes back to business instead. He says, "You've been staring at that building longer than any of us. You got any thoughts?"

She's not buying his act. The FBI doesn't do casual calisthenics with local cops. Her suspicion is getting near "MAX" on the dial.

"Thoughts on what? Access?" she asks.

"Sure, on access."

She gets up and walks to a window that faces the illuminated front of the tomb. The two explosions and the subsequent carnage have ravaged the once pristine facade of the building. Her mind wants to be elsewhere. It starts jumping like a stone skipping on a glassy lake.

The tomb. Athens. Rome.

Ruins.

Ray.

Costa Rica. Trees.

Damn. Ray.

She says, "Last month was my twentieth anniversary."

He hesitates. Her segue has him stumped. He makes a guess. "On the job?"

She likes that she has him off balance. *Whatever.* "No, my marriage. My man, Ray, and I have been married '*dos equis,*' that's what Ray says. Double X? Roman numerals? Last month—seems like five years ago to tell you the truth—Ray and I did an anniversary trip to Costa Rica. Best part? Other than Ray, of course? By far? The canopy tour of the rain forest. Ever done anything like that?"

"No. Haven't." The special agent's patience is running thin.

Christine is fine with that. She'll tell him what she thinks. Then she has a cot waiting outside.

"Too bad for you. Canopy tour is something." She pauses long enough that he gets the impression that she's done. The moment his face begins to screw up in consternation, she adds, "I think the same principle would work here. A zip line."

He closes his mouth. His eyes narrow. She sees the faintest hint of a nod.

She says, "We would have to do it at night. Given how sharp this unsub is, it would be risky as hell, but it may be one low-tech thing he hasn't anticipated."

The FBI agent looks at the tomb, then back at Christine. He locks onto her gaze. "Go on."

She walks to the narrow conference table on the side of the vehicle. On it is a big aerial photograph of the Yale campus.

"Come here," she says. She waits for him to move next to her. She points to Book & Snake. "This is us."

He sighs. "I know."

"Since you're from out of town, I'm going to pretend you don't . . . know. Try not to take offense. We have exploitable high ground on each side of the tomb. Commons is on one side"—she uses an unsharpened pencil as a pointer—"this building here is Commons. It's the one where your intelligence friends have set up shop. I assume you've noticed that Commons is taller than Book & Snake. On the other side of the tomb, Payne Whitney—that's the college gymnasium—is over this way, over a block away. Right here." She moves the tip of the pencil to a huge building that fills a large block on the far side of the law school. "Payne Whitney isn't only tall, but it has a tower that's even taller. This part right here is the tower. You with me?"

He nods. Christine isn't looking at him but she feels the nod. It isn't sufficient for her. She wants a verbal acknowledgment. She looks at him. Waits.

He says, "I'm following you."

You are indeed. "What I'm suggesting is that we"—she stresses the inclusive pronoun—"could shoot a zip line from the top of the tower at Payne Whitney all the way to the roof of Commons. That entire run is gravity assisted. We send agents down the zip line from the tower. They'd be able to hover right above the roof of the tomb."

She pokes at the roof of the tomb with the pencil eraser. She can tell that the agent is intrigued by her idea.

She goes on. "The unsub's contact sensors and glass breakage monitors won't be able to detect your agents if they don't actually touch the roof, which they won't because they don't make mistakes like the rest of us humans. His motion detectors don't have the capacity to sense body heat outside the attic space. The attic gables face Beinecke Library and the cemetery. Even if he has a lookout or a camera pointing out those vents, he won't spot an approach from the direction of the Payne Whitney tower. Unlike a helicopter hovering above the building, the zip line will generate no noise that will alert him we're up there. The agents should have no trouble inserting the cameras and cables down into the roof vents. The only possible tell would be any sound the cables might make as they're snaked through the vent pipes. We would have to create a distraction so the sound wouldn't be detected." She thinks about it. "Yeah, I think we'd use a distraction. That'd be the way to go.

"Like I said before, we would have to do the operation at night. If we pulled everything back before dawn—the zip line, everything—the unsub wouldn't even know we'd been there."

"What if he has exterior cameras we haven't found yet?"

"You have twenty-four hours to find them."

The agent ponders her suggestion for a few seconds. He finally turns to face her. "It's smart. I like it. I think it could work." He pauses.

Christine thinks, *Shit, here comes his shiv.*

"Except for one thing."

The asshole, she thinks, *is enjoying this.* He wants her to say *And what is that?* She'd rather not.

He waits her out. Finally, she says, "And what is that? The one thing?"

"The only problem with your plan is the nature of plumbing. If he's blocked the toilets and showers and tubs at their drains and he's blocked the p-traps outside the interior walls, the roof vents don't provide any better access for cameras and microphones than the sewers do. Using your idea, we could get our snakes into the pipes, but we still have the same problem we have coming in from the sewers—we can't get into the rooms. Our access is still blocked."

Christine concludes that he isn't being condescending. She tries to translate what he said. She can't. She doesn't really speak plumbing.

Christine manages a small smile. She's no girl's girl. She can talk offensive line trap blocking with her husband all day Sunday from September until the Super Bowl. But she knows she can't talk p-traps with anyone who understands plumbing.

She says, "Where plumbing is concerned, I'm a bit of a girl. What do I know? Not enough to be of any help. I'd like to go back to my post. Any objections?"

He shakes his head. He's fighting a smile.

She detours to the lavatory. After she pulls the door shut and lowers herself to the toilet seat, she's already looking a few moves down the pike. The FBI hostage negotiator should not have included her in the discussion they just had. To Christine it either means he is careless, which worries her, or that Christine's job is already over and that no one has told her about it.

That leaves open the possibility that she is about to be sacrificed. Or that HRT is about to breach.

The FBI hostage negotiator waits as Christine uses the toilet.

Once she is outside the door of the vehicle, he hits a couple of buttons on his cell. He says, "Sir? Couple of things. Intel just reported that only one known hostage is wearing eyeglasses. That's the secretary of the army's son, sir. The one who came out briefly earlier. He's the only one." The agent listens for a moment. "I agree, sir. I think it is likely that the secretary of the army's son is in the attic, behind that vent . . . Yes, the unsub wants us to know that he's being held there . . . What else? I may have a way to get the penetrating radar in place so it won't be detected by the unsub." He listens to the commander's reply. He says, "No, it would have to be night only, sir. We'll need to bring in some equipment. I'm not confident we could get it in place, train our people, and test it in time to get it done before morning. It will be Sunday night."

He pauses to allow a brief tirade.

He says, "Yes, sir. Do you know what a zip line is?"

April 20, Sunday morning

Poe and Sam

Deirdre had bad dreams almost all night. Still, she managed more sleep than Poe.

Despite the prurient promise of the purple bra, they did not have sex.

He didn't offer; she didn't ask. She didn't offer; he didn't ask.

Poe held her all night. He held on to her even after she kicked him hard, twice. He wasn't sure what to make of her heel cracking against his thigh. Poe thought she was running away from something. He hoped it wasn't him, but he wasn't certain.

Poe usually held Dee because he required the connection with her. That night he held Dee because he sensed she needed the connection with him.

His eyes were open as dawn's light crept around the perimeter of the curtains. He was out the door early to keep his appointment with Sam Purdy.

Purdy was waiting. He'd left the door cracked open. Poe strolled in without knocking. "You've been in town longer than me. Know any place for breakfast? I have to start the day with some food in my stomach. Hot, if at all possible. Wish it wasn't true sometimes, it's not always convenient, but . . ."

Sam noted that Poe had switched hoodies. The new one was a navy blue Yale model.

"You mean outside the hotel?" Sam asked. "What about all the super-surveillance?"

"Word is they're off you." Poe had no fresh information about what SSG was doing or not doing. But he remained determined to find out. If that meant sacrificing Purdy, Poe was willing to take that risk. Purdy was of little further use to Poe if he was being tracked by SSG. "I'll go out first so I can get in position to see if you're followed. One favor? If they do pick you up, please don't mention my name. Small thing."

"Why would I do that for you?"

"Bros? I didn't arrest you. That has to count for something. You owe me, right?"

Poe strolled down Chapel Street until he got to the Copper Kitchen. From outside, he was pleased at Purdy's selection. It was a place he would have chosen himself. But Poe postponed any gratification; he parked his ass at the bus stop across the street. Behind his back the ever-growing twenty-four-hour FBI tent city was humming to morning life on the New Haven Green. Poe used the time waiting for Purdy to catch up on overnight news on his BlackBerry.

The websites loaded slowly. The local cell network was overloaded by the sudden invasion of law enforcement and media. The network was operating like it was 1999.

Poe saw the out-of-town detective turn the corner and stroll down Chapel. He stopped to buy a newspaper from a machine before he disappeared inside the coffee shop. Poe eyed nothing suspicious in Purdy's wake. No SSG watchers trailed after him from the Omni, no one closed in casually from the opposite direction of the restaurant. Poe continued observing everyone in the vicinity of the Copper Kitchen for five more minutes before he shot off a single text message and followed Purdy inside.

Poe hesitated near the door while he absorbed the vibe. The diner wasn't a chatty place. Some aging greasy spoons are. Some aren't.

He also noted that burly New Haven patrol cops occupied the two stools closest to the register. The waitress was treating them like she knew their orders by heart. To Poe, that was a good sign—it minimized the likelihood that their presence at the counter had anything to do with Purdy's presence in the house. Poe spotted the Boulder cop smack in the middle of a bench in a booth in back of the room on the right side. He headed that way. "Nice place," Poe said. "You are a man after my nitrate-loving heart. Switch seats with me. I need to keep an eye on any new arrivals."

"My cousins in blue up front don't worry you?"

"They're regulars. Waitress is treating them like they're her big brothers."

Purdy gave up his seat with some reluctance, and only after he considered the consequences of resisting the request. He slid the coffee cups and water glasses around. "Ordered you some coffee," he said. "It's hot, but it's not Starbucks."

"Hallelujah for that. Thank you."

Purdy remained puzzled about Poe. He asked, "Tell me something. Are you attached to the Joint Terrorism Task Force? Is that what this is all about?"

Poe found the question amusing. He kept his voice low. "You still playing Homeland Security twenty questions? You are persistent, aren't you? Do I look like I'm on the Joint Terrorism Task Force? Hell—more to the point—do I act like I'm on the Joint Terrorism Task Force? Can you imagine me showing up at their next staff meeting?" He shook his head. "I'm suddenly a tad disappointed in you, Sam. I was beginning to think we were distant relatives or something."

Purdy had to admit that Poe didn't look like any FBI agent he'd ever met. He sat back. He said, "You don't have the slightest idea what your Bureau colleagues are up to here, do you?"

Poe was in the midst of a silent inventory of the customers and staff. He hesitated before he said, "And . . . vice versa. That's one of the distinctive parts of my portfolio. A certain ignorance is one of my calling cards. HRT? JTTF? SSG? Fine people, most of them. I mean that. Well schooled, well trained, fine character, by and large. But we rarely work the same side of the street. When we do, I give them wide berth. I try to make sure they don't get distracted by me. Unless they're determined to get in my way, I tend not to get distracted by them.

"The simple reality is that if they succeed in doing their job, there's absolutely no need for me to do mine. It's better for all when they come up winners.

"They're in town in droves working this thing—you can be sure of that. And you can be sure they're beating the bushes to make some sense of that bad boy in the tomb. Can I editorialize for a minute? Of course I can. Shit. What, you're gonna tell me to shut up?" Poe smiled at Sam. "My experience is that sometimes the alphabet boys do great work, and sometimes . . . I don't know . . . their focus gets a little narrow. Are they thorough? Yes, to a fault. Imaginative? Not so much. But then that's just my opinion."

Sam said, "Your focus? Not narrow?"

"Hardly. I'm the FBI's bastard kid Mikey." Poe slurped some coffee. It was hot enough to burn his tongue. "I'll investigate anything."

"The guy taking photographs of a building in an industrial park from his pickup truck?" Sam said.

"You're getting it, Sam. I watched you leave the hotel, walk in here. Two things. First? You didn't choose that granola palace on the corner. Wouldn't have expected that from a Boulder boy. Thanks. I'm not a fruit salad and muesli kind of guy. Second? No one followed you. As far as I can tell, you are truly off SSG radar for the moment."

Purdy recognized that Poe was letting him know that he'd done his homework overnight. He'd learned Purdy's hometown was in Colorado. Purdy wondered what else Poe knew.

Purdy wasn't sure how to process Poe's self-deprecating side. He was also suspicious about the change in Poe's disposition overnight. Sam wasn't ready to believe that all Poe had needed to improve his mood was a night's sleep.

Purdy asked, "Was I ever really on the radar of the surveillance team?"

Poe made a disappointed face. He said, "Trust is so important in a relationship like ours, don't you think?" He gave Purdy a chance to disagree, for amusement's sake as much as anything. Then he said, "Actually you were. That's the only way I knew SSG was in town in the first place. When I was tailing you, I spotted them doing the same thing. They don't exactly send out memos—they're notorious about the whole secrecy thing. Anyway, you must have done something to dissuade them of your strategic importance. Kudos on that. But if they spot you hanging around that tomb again, they'll be back on you like paparazzi on Brad and Angelina, only they'll be the invisible kind of paparazzi. Tell me, anything new overnight from back home?"

"You'll be making a mistake by assuming any of this has anything to do with my home." Purdy stared at Poe.

"Okay," Poe said, feigning capitulation.

Purdy said, "The kid is still inside the tomb. That's all I care about right now."

Poe lifted his mug and puffed away some steam. "Do the parents have a reason to believe their kid should have come out already? Alive?"

Purdy weighed his response. Poe wanted to know if the parents had given up the information the man in the tomb wanted. Purdy wasn't ready to divulge that—he still didn't see an advantage for Jane Calderón. "They're optimistic people," he said to Poe.

Poe toasted Purdy with his coffee mug. "Well played." He lifted his BlackBerry with his other hand. "The *Times* is reporting there're only two girls left inside the tomb. Most of the remaining hostages are male." Poe knew the *Times* report was inaccurate. His assistant had confirmed overnight that HRT was estimating that seven girls remained inside—two juniors and five seniors.

"Saw that on Fox this morning while I was getting dressed," Purdy said. "Mainstream media, what do they know?"

Poe said, "You're right, the *Times* makes mistakes. That's not news. But you're saying Fox screws up, too? Really?" He paused, hoping for a reaction. When he didn't get one, he added, "I have the two girls' names." Poe actually didn't.

Purdy shrugged. "What do you want from me, Poe? Like you said last night, I'm sure the FBI has already heard a version or two of everything I know from the parents of the kids who were killed. So let me do what I came here to do. If I learn something, I'll share what I can with you. What do you say?"

Poe squinted. He asked, "You like Fox, Sam? I mean, CNN's no prize. Some nights, if I thought I could get away with it, I would superglue Wolf Blitzer's beard to Anderson Cooper's ass. And don't even get me started on Lou Dobbs. But you . . . you actually like Fox, don't you?"

Before Sam could defend his cable news preference, Poe stood. Purdy feared his personal cable bias might have been enough of an irritant to cause Poe to start walking that weird little box of his again. But Poe stayed anchored in place once he was on his feet. No marching formation. His eyes brightened. A soft smile began to grace his face. He said, "Good morning, sunshine. This is Sam. Sam, this is my friend."

Deirdre slid into Poe's side of the booth before Sam had a chance to jump to his chivalrous feet. She kept her modest bag on her lap. It wasn't zipped.

"Nice hoodie," she said to Poe. "Brings out your eyes. You almost look like you belong."

"Here? Yale?" Poe turned to Purdy. "Some reality? I could never have gotten into this school. The sweatshirt is as close as I get."

"That's God's truth," the woman said.

Purdy thought she looked more like a federal agent than Poe did. But then Purdy thought his pubescent kid looked more like a fed than Poe did. At least on Sunday morning when he was dressed up for church.

The woman greeted Purdy with a tight smile and a fixed gaze. She said, "Good morning. I've heard a little about you. I'd like to know about the messages the family received from the subject. Right from the beginning. The tone. The language. Everything you know. Everything you think. All details are helpful. Don't edit, please."

Although Purdy was resigned to cooperating in a way that reflected his true disadvantage, he said, "You are . . . ?"

Without any attitude discernible Dee said, "Think of me as an interested party."

Purdy said, "Federal-payroll interested party?"

Poe chimed in, "Don't bother asking. She won't tell you. And she's smarter than both of us put together." He sipped from his mug. "For the record? She could've gotten into school here."

Purdy waited to see the woman's reaction to Poe. She didn't reveal a thing.

Purdy was close to concluding that the woman had at least one foot in the formal counterterrorism world that Poe seemed so determined to keep at arm's length. He looked her in the eye and said, "I saw the initial note, the one that was on paper. It was a simple Word document. Helvetica. Half-page, double-spaced. Well written. Ominous, but not threatening. Not overtly. It's the one where he intimated what was coming, told the families how to recognize his displeasure. Excuse me, he used the word 'disappointment.' A web address was written on a yellow stickie that was attached to the note. Site was under construction then. It was an African domain. Third world country. At the very end of the note he professed to being a reasonable man."

"Those words?"

"Yes." Sam silently reviewed what else he might share. He said, "I got most of the rest of my information secondhand, from the parents. I only heard one of the phone messages that followed."

"You heard one of the messages?" Dee rested her upper teeth on her bottom lip as she stole a fast glance at Poe. Poe hadn't told her that his cop had heard a phone message. The sheepish look on Poe's face revealed to Dee that he hadn't known that, either.

Sam watched their interaction—he concluded that they knew each other well, and not only professionally. He was seeing the residue of history between them, but he didn't know what kind. Ex-partners? Ex-lovers? Same class at some academy?

It was clear to Purdy that she illuminated a life force in Poe that had been dark before she slid into the booth. Purdy also concluded that it was her presence that was responsible for the general improvement in his mood.

"Go on," the woman said.

"The message I heard was prerecorded. He placed the phone call to the parents, then he played the recording without saying anything else. I suspect all the families heard the same one. It was first person— 'I want this' kind of thing. His voice? That's beyond my ability, I'm afraid. My first thought was that the guy had an accent. He started off by giving the person who was listening ten seconds to get somewhere they could listen undisturbed. I thought that was interesting. At the end of the message—it was no more than a minute in total—I wasn't so sure about the accent. Was it real? Was he pretending? I don't know.

"The content was generic, something that applied to all the families. It came after the parents might've guessed something was wrong, after they had a chance to suspect that something might have happened to their kid. Part of the tone was the same cooperate-or-you-won't-like-the-consequences thing he spelled out in the note. He specifically stressed that he did not want money. He urged the parents to consider how else they could be useful to him. Reminded them they already knew what the price would be if they failed to cooperate."

"Their kids?" Dee asked.

"Yeah. Didn't come out and say it, but yeah."

"Go on," she said. "You mentioned an accent."

The waitress came by. They ordered breakfast. Purdy, who had a prodigious appetite, marveled at the size of Poe's order. Neither Poe's friend nor the waitress was similarly awed.

Purdy was guessing that Poe and his friend had breakfasted together before.

He noted her modest wedding band. Poe wasn't wearing a match.

Sam picked up the earlier question. "Mediterranean, maybe. Accents aren't my thing, unless you're talking the upper Midwest. Remember, at the end of the taped spiel I wasn't even sure he was foreign. Guy is educated. That was clear. Nuanced with language. Comfortable with English. Big vocabulary. He's not new to Western culture. Not disdainful, you know. I would guess he's lived here."

"Here, New Haven?"

"Here, the West. Maybe the U.S. Maybe Europe." Purdy considered the issue for another moment. "Here, the U.S."

"Age?"

Sam shrugged.

"Guess," Dee said. She wanted his impression.

"Near thirty. No more than forty."

"Affect? Was he angry?"

"I'd say determined. Calculating. Businesslike. Not urgent. More like he knew he had a winning hand. Was happy to let the game play out. Remember, he had the kids by then. His plan was working."

She asked, "You saw the YouTube video? Same voice? Different?"

"Different," Sam said. "Similar, but different."

Dee said, "Sam? May I call you Sam?"

Purdy nodded.

She leaned forward and lowered her voice. "All I'm doing is listening to your impressions of what happened, using them to create a portrait. Like a sketch artist. That's all. Okay? Tell me if you disagree with what I'm hearing. What do I get from you so far? Poe's unsub is a thirty-ish man who speaks English well, but probably as a second language. He was born abroad. Educated in the West, perhaps from an early age, maybe only secondary school and college. Most probably in the United States. Comes from significant family wealth. He's comfortable in our culture, not dismissive or repulsed by it. He is likely not a radical Islamist. This isn't holy war. Quite the opposite—for him, what he's doing in that tomb has a strong personal component."

Purdy took a big gulp of coffee. "That's even clearer than what I had in my head. But what about the Mediterranean part?"

"Some people who have mastered a second language are better at disguising a residual accent after they get a rhythm developed in their speech. That might explain why you thought you heard an accent at the beginning of the recording, and why it might have disappeared by the time he was done talking. Mediterranean? It's probably just what you think it is. He could be from coastal Southern Europe or even Turkey or Northern Africa—Tunisia, Libya. Or maybe Egypt. If I put some headphones on you and played tapes of a variety of non-native speakers of English, you could probably narrow it down for me even further. To some ears, well-educated English-as-foreign-language speakers from certain Middle Eastern and Northern African countries, even some people that are native to the parts of Asia nearest the Indian Ocean—Iran, Afghanistan, sections of Pakistan—can translate as generic 'Mediterranean.'"

"You're including Israel and Palestine?"

"Yes. And their neighbors."

"How does any of that help? Doesn't narrow down the list of possible suspects much."

"I'm a data slut," Dee said. "Every bit, literally, helps. Let's say that based on your impressions of the accent we decide we can rule out native-born suspects. I'm talking our own native-born citizens. That's huge. And based on your description, we can tentatively eliminate the Latin-speaking population of North and South America, right? And non-Mediterranean Africa. Not to mention a chunk of the immense population of the Indian subcontinent, and the largely Muslim populations of island Asia. China, too. That's billions, literally. We've eliminated a lot of people."

"And the Canadians," Poe said. "Don't forget them. Seems they're always a problem in my line of work."

Poe's humor was so dry that for a moment Purdy thought he was serious with his comment about the northern neighbors.

Deirdre suddenly stood. "Excuse me," she said. "Ladies' room."

As Sam watched her head toward the back of the restaurant, he finally got Poe's joke and smiled.

"You know your friend is pregnant?" Sam said a moment later.

"What?" Poe said.

"My girlfriend—back . . . where I've been living—she's pregnant right now. Third trimester. She's on doctor-ordered bed rest. Her best girlfriend is pregnant, too. She's a few months behind. See, I'm surrounded by all things prenatal. It's been like a cloud around me. It's gotten so I can smell it. Pregnancy. The hormones, whatever it is. We go to a movie or walk into Wal-Mart or Trader Joe's or In-N-Out, I can point out the pregnant women with my eyes closed. Seriously. I just feel it. It's like I got baby-dar. You know, like gay-dar."

Poe said, "Interesting skill. But you're wrong. Maybe your skill doesn't travel."

Poe could have told Sam the story Dee had shared with him in April 2004 while they were sitting at the end of the bar at Don's Mixed

Drinks in Denver. The barkeep at Don's kept free-pouring Dee scotches. The abundant whiskey provided her with the courage she needed to tell Poe a story she really needed to tell.

Storytelling wasn't Deirdre's thing—especially personal story-telling—but once she crossed the inebriation threshold with Poe that night in Denver, she found the resolve to tell him about Valentine's Day.

Deirdre had picked the previous Christmas Eve—that was December 24, 2003—to reveal to Jerry the monumental news that she was finally ready to start a family. Jerry reacted by getting up from the holiday dinner table and walking away from her. He switched out CDs, changing the music from Christmas carols, Dee's choice, to Toby Keith, his choice. He circled back to the table. He sat down. He said, "Let me tell you what I'm thinking."

It took him a while to get there, but he finally got around to saying that he preferred to wait another year, or two, to have kids. It was mostly about money, he explained.

Dee had heard it all before. It was the exact same excuse Jerry had used the last time they'd discussed starting a family. That was in the summer of 2000. Since then they had both gotten raises. They had tripled their savings, reduced their debt to nothing more than a mortgage and a car loan that was almost paid off.

Dee didn't see a point in arguing. She had no illusion that Jerry's extended procrastination was due to a financial planning oversight. The joyous holiday that Dee had been anticipating for the two of them ended up awkward and tense. She dropped the baby talk. Jerry knew she would.

She was grateful when the Company sent her to South Africa for eight days to do nuclear security research during the beginning of February. She was back in Virginia just in time for Valentine's Day. Jerry took her out to dinner, gave her gifts of lingerie and roses, along with a card he'd written in his neat hand that spelled out the news that he'd had a vasectomy while she was in South Africa.

Dee had been injured in so many ways that night, she confessed to Poe in Don's Mixed Drinks, that she didn't know what ended up hurting most. Jerry's dashing of her dreams. His betrayal of her trust. His denial of her needs. Or his presentation of the surgical fait accompli as a *gift*. To her.

Poe fugued out momentarily as he was deluged by the memories of that night with Dee in Denver. It was a dark selection from his stash, one he'd never replayed before.

Sam had no way to know where Poe had traveled during the interlude of silence in the Copper Kitchen. When Poe finally looked his way again, Sam shrugged and said to him, "Your friend is pregnant. Trust me." Sam glanced at the adjacent table. "God, that bacon looks good. I should have gotten some. You know, since you're buying."

Poe swallowed a too big sip of coffee and looked at Sam. "Don't think so," he said. "She would have told me. We're kind of . . . close."

Sam said, "Maybe she doesn't know."

Dee returned to the table. Poe thought she looked pale. He tried to recall whether she'd looked pale when she left.

Sam caught Poe's eyes and nodded. Sam thought Poe was looking a little pale.

Before Dee could sit down, her BlackBerry sang a two-note alert.

She looked at the screen. Her jaw tensed. "There's news from the scene. Something about surveillance. I don't quite . . . get what this is saying."

Then Poe's BlackBerry buzzed.

A new video is posted on YouTube from a Yahoo.com account just before seven A.M. (eastern time). At about the same moment, the link to the clip arrives in the email inboxes of the New Haven Police Department and the Yale University Police.

At 7:03 the video begins playing for the first time in the Tactical Operations Center parked near Book & Snake.

The clip is three minutes and forty-one seconds long.

It is clear from the long shadows that the video was taken in the soft light before dusk. The time stamp indicates the previous evening. It is an aerial shot. The shadows obscure some detail, but the images are clear. To the local cops the landmarks are familiar.

"Is that from a balloon?" Jack Lobatini, asks after the first half minute of video. "Did anyone see one up there?"

The FBI IT specialist replies, "It's not from a balloon. A balloon wouldn't be able to move around like that."

"Sorry to interrupt," offers the New Haven patrol officer who is keeping the log at the door. "I'm pretty sure that was taken from an RC helicopter. I fly one on my days off. It's a . . . hobby. It's kind of geeky but it's . . . cool."

Jack turns away from the monitor and speaks to the patrol officer. "Lock that door, Officer Kroning. Tell us what you think you're seeing."

Hade Moody has not yet arrived on the scene. Jack has phoned him twice since he received word about the existence of the video.

Kroning is a six-year veteran of the New Haven PD. He locks the bolt on the door and steps closer to the group that is clustered around the monitor. "I'm almost certain it's taken from a camera mounted below a remote control helicopter. That's good resolution, considering the light. Better than a foot per pixel. Sweet setup—guy has a few grand in that equipment, easy. Not counting the camera. It may even be HD. To get shots like that, I mean that quality, those angles, I'd say the rig was flying three hundred fifty, maybe five hundred feet above the ground. No higher than that."

Everyone inside the command vehicle is looking at Kroning, the FBI guys included.

Jack says, "The music yesterday? This explains the damn music yesterday. No way we could have heard a little helicopter flying around during that."

Kroning shrugs. He wasn't on duty during the hip-hop intrusion the previous evening.

He continues, "When RC choppers are used for aerial photography, it usually involves two people. The pilot flies the chopper with one controller while the other guy remotely operates the camera, which is mounted on a rig below the helicopter. The camera operator has independent control of his camera—tilt, pan, zoom, whatever. But from the look of this video, it appears that the camera was installed in a fixed position below the chopper. See the delay in focus, right . . . there—" He points at the screen. "That delay is because the lens is on autofocus. Whoever's flying the chopper isn't doing anything more than adjusting the zoom on the camera. I'd say you're probably looking at a one-person operation. Basically, he's pointing the camera by flying the helicopter. Occasionally adjusts the zoom. Guy's not a bad pilot."

Jack asks Kroning, "Could the man inside the tomb have been flying it? Without an accomplice? I guess I'm asking—could someone fly a helicopter like that if he couldn't see it? If he was only able to track its flight based on the video he was getting on his monitor?"

"With practice? Probably. Usually the pilot can see the aircraft. But military pilots fly drones that are out of their sight all the time."

"What is the effective range of something like that? How far can it fly?"

"Depends on the equipment, of course. There's a new one every-body's talking about—it's called the Draganflyer X6—that could do this. One person can fly it and operate the camera. It has wireless HD video. The thing is even flight-stabilized—has gyros, accelerometers, magnetometers, GPS. Sweet package. If it loses radio contact with the pilot, it can even land itself safely. It's really a commercial-quality aircraft—way out of the reach of hobbyists like me. I'm talking megabucks."

Jack asks, "So it is possible—with the right equipment—that he was flying that thing himself? The guy inside the tomb?"

Someone pounds on the door.

Kroning says, "Sure," as he steps toward the door. "Depends on his transmitter and his antenna. If he can send it a signal, he can fly it. If it was something like a Draganflyer, he could also put it on autopilot temporarily if he had to." He unlocks the bolt. He stiffens his posture as Haden Moody bursts inside.

The lieutenant's face is as red as a baboon's butt. He stands behind Jack and joins everyone else in staring at the largest video monitor in the vehicle.

"Start it again," Moody says. "Somebody get me some coffee."

The IT tech looks at the SAC. The FBI commander looks at Jack. Jack raises his eyebrows. The commander nods.

The video is restarted.

The video from the helicopter is a concise aerial tour of the wide-ranging law enforcement response to the hostage situation in the Book & Snake tomb. There is no audio.

One by one, the camera clearly identifies each of the four FBI rooftop sniper positions. All the HRT activity in the tent city on the New Haven Green is highlighted. Every square yard of the Grove Street Cemetery is captured. SWAT's staging area behind the tomb is documented.

The Mobile Command vehicle gets a ten-second cameo.

After watching less than half of the restarted video, the FBI SAC says, "I can't fucking believe this."

He storms out of the vehicle and marches toward Commons to consult with his sniper and assault team leaders.

Twenty seconds after the commander leaves the vehicle, he rushes back in. His eyes are fire. He has been summoned back to deal with a fresh communication from the HRT sniper perched on the roof of Beinecke.

The Zulu sniper has just reported a fleeting visual of what he described as a "tube" moving quickly across the opening that's been created in the attic vent. He is estimating that when he spotted it, the tube was being moved around about one foot back inside the vent.

"Ask him the diameter of the tube," the commander says.

The question is relayed.

Seconds later the radio operator says, "Eight to ten centimeters. Estimated."

The SAC and the HRT hostage negotiator exchange glances. The commander blinks twice before he shakes his head almost imperceptibly.

"Whiskey? Any activity in the other vent?" he asks.

The Whiskey sniper responds to the query quickly. The comm officer relays the message. "Negative. His scope is on that vent. He reports his sector is unchanged."

The commander says, "Get Whiskey, Yankee, and X-ray snipers off their positions now. I want them redeployed to new FFPs immediately. I want the new FFPs invisible from the tomb, invisible from the ground, and invisible from the air. I want the redeployment to be completely undetectable. In fact, I want them invisible to God for the remainder of this mission. Am I making myself clear?"

The comm operator asks, "And Zulu, sir?"

The SAC says, "The Zulu sniper stays where he is until his backup is in place."

The orders are relayed to the snipers.

The SAC says, "Based on the YouTube video, we have to assume that the Zulu sniper has been made. Make sure he knows that."

The radio operator relays the information.

"What did he say?" asks the SAC.

"He said, 'Copy,' sir."

Moody turns to the agent closest to him. He whispers, "FFP? What's that?"

The agent says, "Forward firing position. The sniper's lair."

The SAC looks past Hade Moody toward the Yale campus physical plant liaison. He says, "That building is evacuated? The one the Zulu sniper is on?"

"Beinecke? Yes, sir. Completely. Yale Security inside only. We have armed personnel at the entrances."

"Good." The SAC looks around the inside of the command vehicle. "What about updates? Did we find those floor drains? Is the crap cam experiment dead?"

No one answers.

"Has the army shown up with the penetrating radar?"

Nothing.

"Well, is anyone prepared to brief me about the deployment plan for the radar? People?"

The space is silent.

The SAC's words grow crisper, not louder. "Does anybody know anything? I'm tired of being blind. I want some damn intel from inside that tomb. I want it now. And somebody locate that goddamned little helicopter he's using. I swear. God damn it." He takes a deep breath. "I want a briefing from intel and from the assault team leaders on planning and readiness in five minutes inside Woolsey."

The SAC calls Hade Moody over. They walk to the far end of the vehicle. "You see any reason your negotiator needs to know this?"

"What part?" Moody asks.

"The tube part."

"The unsub . . . the guy . . . may bring it up with her. We should maybe prepare her for that."

"I disagree. She may reveal something. We should keep her in the dark."

Moody says, "That shouldn't be hard. I'm in the dark."

"You'll know more when we know more," the SAC says. "In fact, you'll be first."

Moody isn't sure whether he's being patronized. "The helicopter? Should I tell her about that?" he asks.

"That's on fucking YouTube, Lieutenant. Jesus H. Christ. Her kids know about the damn helicopter."

Sam and Poe and Dee

Dee said, "I think I should make a call or two. Clarify what's going on." She marched toward the front door of the Copper Kitchen, her phone already in her hand.

Poe figured she was planning to talk to G.B. Jerry. She always walked away before she called G.B. Jerry.

Poe was involuntarily mesmerized by the arc of her hips as she walked toward the door. In his mind's flash memory he highlighted the image and hit SAVE. Then he turned back to Sam. "She almost always hears things before anybody else. It's annoying at first, but you'll get used to it."

Poe waited until that moment to check his BlackBerry. Sam noted that it was another text message.

Sam decided at that moment that the woman with Poe was CIA. Or NSA. Or DIA. Or some alphabet agency he'd never heard of that was even more clandestine than the ones he did know about. He'd done cases with the FBI before. This was the first one he knew about that involved intelligence, not law enforcement.

The waitress delivered their breakfast. The plates of food ran all the way up her left arm. The two men began to eat in silence.

Sam was considering all the various reasons Poe might be so reluctant to believe that the female fed was with child.

It wasn't a long list.

Dee returned after a few minutes.

Poe waited for her to announce what was up. She didn't. He said, "Hey? Pretty please? Throw me something?"

Dee bit the corner off the crust side of a piece of toast before she replied. She washed it down with some herbal tea.

She leaned forward slightly, dropping her voice to a hush above a whisper. "This much is public, probably too public: Late yesterday, the unsub apparently used some state-of-the-art remote controlled helicopter to do aerial surveillance of the HRT and SWAT preparations around the tomb. He succeeded in identifying the locations of all the HRT sniper teams and did successful reconnaissance of the entire law enforcement response on the ground, including the staging areas that are away from the tomb on the New Haven Green. He got HD video of one of the assault teams doing breach rehearsals on the Scroll & Key tomb. The video is now posted on YouTube for the world to see."

"Wow," Poe said.

Dee said, "HRT is redeploying assets. Everything they've done until now has been compromised."

Sam said, "The damn music yesterday. That was to cover the sound of the helicopter."

Dee nodded. "Probably. And there's something new going on in the attic of the tomb." She looked at Sam. "That part's not public. It isn't on YouTube."

Sam did a zipper motion across his lips. He thought he'd made it quite clear to both of them that he was a more-than-adequate keeper of secrets.

"What's going on in the attic?" Poe said warily to Dee. He narrowed his eyes.

Dee knew that Poe had a nose for things that blow up. She felt tension framing Poe's question.

Dee looked at Sam. He repeated the zipper motion.

Poe waited until Dee looked his way again. He was working to disguise his swelling apprehension about any number of things. He shrugged as he said, "In for a dime, you know?"

"Yesterday evening HRT began to detect activity in the attic. Someone removed a couple of the stone louvers from the rear attic vent."

Sam focused on the architecture. The gable ends on Book & Snake pointed in two directions only. He said, "The one facing the plaza?"

"Yes, that one. Since then they've been detecting intermittent infrared signatures. Someone has been moving in and out of the attic space. At times, two people. Last night a sniper detected a brief visual of a reflection. Initial read is that it was eyeglasses."

"But it might have been a scope," Poe said.

"I can't confirm that, Poe," Dee said.

Poe said, "That's it? That's all?" His tone announced his skepticism.

"That's all I know so far, Poe. But, no," she added ruefully, "I suspect that's not it." She puffed her cheeks in exasperation. "Intel reports that the only known hostage wearing eyeglasses is the son of the secretary of the army."

The men rushed to finish eating. Dee barely touched her food.

Poe sensed Sam's instinct to get himself to the action as fast as his feet could carry him. He admired the reflex, but he knew it presaged disaster. He said, "You can't go back over to the tomb, Purdy. I'm not making the stuff up about SSG. They catch you on that perimeter again they'll pull you in. Once the interrogation team has you, they won't be as understanding as I've been. Your career? History. The kid you're trying to help? An afterthought."

Sam looked at Poe's face, then at Dee's. She nodded her agreement. He settled his eyes back on Poe. "I have to do something. I have to. Get a disguise maybe? I don't know. There's too much . . . I can't just . . . I promised to help that . . ."

"Girl," Poe said.

Dee leaned forward. "You're not the only one, Sam. Poe's at risk near the tomb, too." She glanced at Poe, expecting him to squawk at her assessment. "There are undoubtedly a few people over there who know him from . . . previous cases. But they don't know me. Here's what I propose: Sam? You should go back to the hotel and stay glued to the television and the computer. Keep us posted about things we're not in position to see. Poe, you watch my back. From a distance. We all stay in touch."

"How?"

"Cell phone. Text."

Poe turned to Dee. He said, "And your back will be where?"

"I'm going inside the perimeter."

Dee was on her feet already. Her BlackBerry sang two notes. She lifted it and stared at the screen. "Shit," she said.

The Victor sniper checks in with the TOC from a new forward firing position in the tower in Sterling Library. The new lair is much farther from the roof vent in Book & Snake than was the Zulu position on Beinecke. He reports that wind has started gusting off Long Island Sound at ten to twelve knots. The HRT commanders know that means that if he's asked to take a rifle shot into that attic vent, it will be a more technical shot than the one Zulu had from Beinecke.

The SAC says, "Put the Zulu sniper on speaker."

The communications officer switches the open comm line to speaker.

The Zulu sniper, the one in the original blind on Beinecke Library, adds to the conversation in a hushed voice. His whisper belies no anxiety whatsoever. He is a golf announcer describing a twenty-inch gimme on the twelfth green in the middle of the second round of a third-rate tournament. "TOC, I have visual confirmation of the tube in the roof vent. Repeat, confirm. Diameter ten centimeters. Length approximately one meter. It now appears to be in a fixed position, recessed approximately fifteen inches behind the opening. Two infra-red signatures present. One is static. One is . . . moving."

The SAC asks, "Weapon signature?"

Moody is lost. He is waiting for someone to tell him what is going on. "Tube? What does he mean, 'tube'?" he asks. "What weapon? Somebody?" He also wants to know how big ten centimeters is, but knows he can't get away with asking that.

No one answers him. Jack would answer his questions, but Jack doesn't know what the presence of a ten-centimeter tube might indicate, either.

"Does anybody fucking know?" Moody blurts out. His face is getting red again. He thinks he's the only one in the room who doesn't know what's going on.

The SAC says, "Repeat. Do you have a weapon confirmation?"

The Zulu sniper says, "Negative on signature—the tube may be the barrel of a Russian Vampir. At ten c-m, size is right. I am attempting to get a visual on an optical sight or a night scope. Insufficient natural light."

To the room, the SAC says, "Vampir is the RPG-Twenty-nine, right?"

"Affirmative."

"Zulu sniper, can you tell where the tube is pointed?"

Hade Moody stuffs his hands into his pockets. He spreads his feet a good twenty inches apart. It's a posture he adopts when he's trying to restrain himself from a tantrum.

The sniper's tone stays as flat as a lake at dawn. He says, "Ninety degrees from the attic vent, parallel to the ground." The sniper adds that one of the infrared signatures has just disappeared from his scope. The other one is stationary.

Everyone who can does the geometry. The tube is aimed at the sniper's position on Beinecke.

The HRT hostage negotiator says, "Static infrared may mean a hostage."

The SAC poses a question to the room. "Does anyone know if the RPG-Twenty-nine can be operated remotely?"

Someone says, "Checking Jane's."

The SAC looks past Hade Moody. His eyes lock on the Yale campus physical plant liaison who is standing by. He says, "Before? You said that building is evacuated, right? The one the Zulu sniper is on?"

"Beinecke? Yes, sir."

The SAC orders the Zulu sniper off the roof of Beinecke.

He turns back to the Yale rep. "Is there anything in that building to be concerned about? Hazardous material? Radioactivity? Biohazards?"

The Yale representative says, "Uh, no. Not at all. That's a rare book library. I mean, there's a . . . Gutenberg Bible in the lobby. There are four Shakespeare folios inside. Beinecke is one of the premier collections of old books and manuscripts and literary artifacts in the world. It is a treasure to . . . humanity. You name it, if it has to do with literature and it's really old, or unique, or even if it's just rare, it's in that building. That's all that's in there. Nothing else."

The SAC says, "Well, that probably explains the RPG. I'm afraid this is bad news for Yale and, you know, humanity. You should inform the university administrators that the unsub has an RPG-Twenty-nine—" He stops himself, exhales. "The subject has an armor-piercing rocket-propelled grenade pointed at their rare book collection."

"What?" the Yale representative says. "I don't . . . understand. What does that mean? He's planning to blow up Beinecke? Can a grenade—that's what you called it? Can a grenade . . . go through stone? The building is . . . stone. Can it do that?"

The SAC has turned his attention back to the monitor. He says, "He's not going to blow it up. The building is way too big to be blown up with an RPG."

"I don't—"

"I'm not talking the kind of hand grenade an infantry soldier might toss in combat. The Vampir isn't technically a grenade launcher. It's an anti-tank weapon. It fires a roughly thirteen-pound, one hundred five-millimeter rocket that is designed to penetrate armor. Will it go through stone? How thick?"

"Those squares you see on the library? Here?" The Yale rep steps forward. He points at the exterior wall detail on the closest monitor. "The exterior of the building is constructed of special marble panels that are less than an inch thick. They're translucent, but they block light from the ultraviolet spectrum to protect the books inside. All the old paper and ink? It's a remarkable design. Secure. Practical."

The SAC sighs. "It would be a lot more secure and a lot more re-markable if those marble panels were a foot thick, not an inch thick. An inch of marble isn't going to stop a round from an RPG." He snaps his fingers. "First round'll bust right through a thin slice of stone like it's not even there. There will be an explosion, possibly a fire. If he is able to get off a second round and it goes through the opening that was created by the first one? You could see serious damage inside. Another explosion, more fire. What are we talking? Value-wise? For the books? Millions? Tens of millions?"

The Yale rep is almost speechless. "Millions? No . . . More like . . . Much more than . . . The collection is priceless. It's . . . one of the best there is . . . anywhere. Completely irreplaceable. There are original manuscripts from the greatest . . . I mean, one of a kind. . . It's hard to exaggerate the importance of . . . There's not a . . . comparable collection anywhere . . . Even a small fire . . . It would be a catastrophe."

"Inform the university that it appears that their building full of old books is officially being held hostage."

The Yale rep moves from bewilderment to bargaining. "Wait. No. Inside that building is another building, an interior building, if you will. A cube within a cube. The library's collection is contained inside the interior building. The interior cube is a sealed environment. It has a state-of-the-art fire-suppression system. Because of the fragility of the old paper, no water can be used to extinguish fire. If any smoke or unusual heat is detected in the inner cube, the fire suppression system kicks in. The oxygen in the inner cube is vented and largely replaced by inert gases. There isn't enough oxygen left behind to permit a fire to continue, so the flames are suppressed. The gas mixture itself doesn't damage the paper in the collection. It's . . . elegant."

"There you go," the SAC says optimistically. "What's the inside cube made of?"

"Glass."

"Glass?" He returns his attention to the monitor. "Sorry. You should start making arrangements to move the best stuff some place safe."

"But . . . It's . . . It *is* the best stuff. Beinecke *is* the some place safe. It would take a week—a month—to move it out."

"That's your call. If you decide to move anything, I will require you use an entry that's not exposed to Book & Snake. Coordinate with Special Agent Farmer in Commons."

The Yale rep's mouth is fixed in the universal *O*-sign of the flabbergasted.

The SAC says, "What do you want to risk? The old books? Or the people you have to send in there to try to save the old books?"

The Yale rep is frozen in place.

The SAC says, "Look, I'm sorry. The building is, literally, in the unsub's sights. The marble won't stop his rocket. And the glass inside . . . well, it won't stop shit. Frankly, I'm more interested in trying to save the students still stuck inside that tomb."

"What does he want? How do we keep him from—"

"We don't know that until he tells us." The SAC leans in closer toward the Yale rep. "This is need-to-know. You will have one of my men with you as you consult with your superiors. He will determine who can learn this information. He will determine what steps can be taken to mitigate the risk to the library. If this gets out, hostages die. Do you understand me?"

The rep tries to speak, but can't. He swallows. And nods.

Sam and Dee and Poe

Dee sat back down.

She raised her BlackBerry, started reading. The message was long enough that she had to scroll to finish it. She lowered her voice. "HRT is confirming that there is small artillery aimed at the Beinecke Library from the attic vent."

Poe shook his head slowly. He asked, "What's the weapon?"

"A 'Vampir'? I'm not familiar."

"It's an RPG-Twenty-nine," Poe said. "The library is the target?"

"Currently."

"Isn't the library made of stone?" Sam asked.

Dee said, "Very thin stone, apparently."

Poe intuitively sensed where she was going. He asked, "Target value?"

She scrolled and read from her BlackBerry. "Quote: 'The library contains a remarkable collection. One of the finest in the world.' Let's see . . . It lists two Gutenberg Bibles. Four Shakespeare folios. Thousands of original manuscripts. Tens of thousands of ancient texts. Total? Countless billions of dollars."

Poe said, "Having an armor-piercing rocket that will destroy it all?"

Dee took another bite of her dry toast. She closed her eyes.

Sam watched their faces. But he didn't volunteer the answer to Poe's question.

Poe sat back. He's the one who said, "Priceless."

*　　*　　*

Dee said, "I'm going to the tomb."

Poe said, "With how you're feeling? You're sure you're up for this?"

She stood up, grabbed her bag. She gave him a quizzical look. She said, "My stomach's upset. That's a disqualifier?"

"Wait a second," Poe said.

She paused. Poe reached into his back pocket. He handed her one of the throwaway maps from the Omni. He pointed at the area in front of the power plant. "I'll be over here. You can probably get as close as you want with your ID. You need to keep me informed of what's happening in front of you. I will let you know what's happening behind you."

Dee nodded. "I don't want to be seen with you. I'm leaving now. Give me a minute or two."

Sam said, "I should have your phone number."

Dee said, "What's yours?"

Sam told her. Her fingers flew on her BlackBerry. "I sent you mine."

She was up on her toes as she rushed from the restaurant.

Sam drained his coffee. He said, "Your friend doesn't eat much. She needs the calories. It's important for her, for the baby. I can't believe I know these things, but I do."

"Give it up," Poe said as he stood. "I got this," he said, grabbing the check. He threw way too much money on the table. "Stay in touch, Sam. I'm counting on you."

Sam waited in front of the café until he could no longer see Poe. He spotted a campus souvenir shop on the far corner. He would spend the last of his money on a baseball cap and a Yale hoodie that was just like Poe's. Sam was praying that SSG had better things to do than follow him.

His phone vibrated before he made it to the corner. PRIVATE CALLER. He opened the phone. He said, "Yeah."

"My name is Deirdre, by the way. Is Poe gone? If he's right next to you just tell me I have the wrong number."

Sam said, "He's gone."

"I have this sense—I pick it up from Poe, really; I swear the man's contagious—that we're heading into a combat zone this morning. Right now, any minute. There's something you need to know about Poe before anything else happens."

"Okay."

"I first met Poe on the job in Oklahoma City in April 1995."

Sam said, "McVeigh. The Federal Building. Wow. Okay. Enough said. Got it."

"It's not enough. I met him in the hospital. Poe was one of the victims. He was on the phone at his desk in the FBI office in the Murrah Building when the truck bomb went off. He—"

"God, I'm so sorry. I didn't know. I—"

Sam imagined Poe's little prison. The box he walked.

"Don't," Deirdre said. "Don't interrupt me. I'm almost at the perimeter. I need to finish this, please. Poe was injured that day. Badly. But it was the kind of injured that people recover from. Do you understand what I'm saying?"

"I think so."

"Poe was also . . . hurt that day. It was the kind of hurt that people don't ever recover from."

Sam said, "I have a friend . . . He's a marine. Three tours. Two Purple Hearts. Fallujah, Afghanistan. I think I understand."

"No. No, no. You don't. You may think you do, but you don't. In Afghanistan and Iraq—after the incoming mortar rounds, or after the IED exploded—your friend didn't crawl around in the rubble shredding his skin to the bone searching for his wife or his three-year-old daughter. Did he, Sam? Did your friend do that?"

"In Oklahoma City? Poe lost his family?"

"He did. His wife worked in the Social Security office. His daughter was in the day-care center on the second floor."

Sam remembered Poe's words in the Omni the night before.

"Moot. Don't have a kid."

Sam said, "God."

"Yeah, God. Poe has a problem with . . . explosions. It's a PTSD thing. He reacts. It can be violent. It takes him time to . . . reorient, come back. Okay? If you're next to him or around him or are talking to him when . . . there's another explosion. You have to stay with him. Keep in touch with him. Physically, your voice. Something. Retrieve him, lead him back. Can you do that?"

He said, "Yes."

"I'm at the perimeter. I'm going in." Deirdre hung up.

Sam tried to imagine Poe's world since 1995. He couldn't.

He made it to the souvenir shop on autopilot. He was standing at the cash register, his almost useless Discover card in hand, when his phone vibrated. He didn't recognize the name or the area code.

"Yeah," he said.

"It's Ann. I borrowed this phone from my cousin. She's from South Carolina."

The geographic trivia Ann tacked on was meant to inform Sam that she wanted to be certain that the call she was making wouldn't be within law enforcement's surveillance reach. At least from her end. He walked away from the counter, leaving the sweatshirt and the hat behind.

"I was about to call you, Ann. You need to stay in front of a computer and a TV. Keep a phone line open for me. There's a lot going on here. This time you're my eyes and ears. I'll explain later. This could be it."

Ann said, "Sam, do you trust me?"

"What?"

"Do you trust me?"

Sam covered his other ear. He said, "I do."

"I haven't been completely honest with you, Sam."

Yeah? "Yeah?"

"There are things I couldn't tell you. For Jane's sake. Her . . . safety."

What the fuck? "Okay."

The silence between them extended for seconds that felt infinite to Sam.

"Should I still trust you, Ann?" he asked.

"You should, Sam. I need you to."

"Okay. What's next?"

"Do you have your gun? Your police . . . pistol?"

"I'm not traveling with it. The suspension."

"But your luggage arrived at the hotel?"

"Yes."

"Did you pack a white shirt, Sam? For the engagement party?"

"Yes."

"Get the shirt. And a tie. Then find a taxi."

"Where am I going, Ann?"

"To save my baby."

"I'm three blocks from the tomb, Ann. I don't need a cab. I can be there in minutes."

"Trust me, Sam, please. Will you do what I ask?"

Sam hesitated for a heartbeat. He already knew what he had to do next. It was something he couldn't tell Ann. "Goes both ways, Ann. Do you trust me?"

"I do, Sam."

He thought, *You trust me, but I'm not deserving of your honesty back. What am I supposed to make of that?*

Sam said, "Okay, here's the thing. I'm broke. How far am I going? How much do you think the taxi will be?"

APRIL 20, SUNDAY MORNING
NEW HAVEN

Joey Blanks returns to Christine's side outside the tomb as soon as the first pale light peeks over the Connecticut hills.

Christine doesn't know if or where the deep-voiced cop slept. She doesn't know if anyone ordered him to assist her. She only knows she is grateful for his presence.

Christine is facing away from the tomb when Joey Blanks says, "We have company, Sergeant."

The dull background murmur outside Book & Snake rolls to a stop over the next three to four seconds.

The latest hostage has stepped outside the door. All eyes turn toward him.

The young man stops his advance on the same line as the four pillars.

Everyone in the know is checking him for orange. And trying not to react visibly or audibly with either horror or relief.

Although each member of law enforcement at the scene is beginning to assume the man in the tomb is eerily omniscient, no one wants to reveal any awareness of the color thing.

This student is a male, five-ten. His pronounced eyebrows protrude from beneath a knit mask. Unlike the others, he is not barefoot. He's wearing a pair of beat-up sneakers. His arms are not shackled. His ankles are not tethered. He is wearing a baseball cap that is pointed backward. His ears aren't visible. They are covered by the ski mask.

He is blinking away the effects of a just-removed blindfold or hood.

Christine feels her wounded leg beginning to stiffen. She shakes it once. Pain shoots to her toes.

The pain focuses her.

She introduces herself to the hostage.

He doesn't reply.

See, don't look, she reminds herself.

This hostage is displaying a confidence that Christine finds reassuring. His feet are planted shoulder-width apart, his left foot slightly forward of the right. Her impression is that he has not been defeated by whatever he has been through.

She asks him to hold his arms out to his sides and rotate three hundred and sixty degrees. After a delay of about five seconds, he does.

Christine is shocked.

As he spins—the pirouette is graceful—she sees no orange. No apparent bomb on his body. No apparent bulge that could be a weapon.

Wait, is there something in his right hand? Between his index finger and his thumb? What is that? What the hell is going on now?

Joey Blanks steps back a few feet and grabs a sheet of paper offered to him by another officer. He returns to his position behind Christine's right shoulder. He says, "We think this kid is . . . Markos Xanthis. Hope I'm saying that right. People call him 'Marko.' He's from London. In England. His family has controlling interest in a company that lays undersea cable. Internet backbone, it says. I don't know what that means. I can find out. Primarily in the developing world, it says. Office in Manhattan, Midtown, and Hong Kong. China. Parents live on Park Avenue. Sister is married to a guy in Parliament, House of Lords, if that means anything to you. Got lots more here if you want it."

Christine holds her fingers in front of her mouth. She says, "Was Marko on the ATL list?"

"No, ma'am. He was not."

"Do you see any orange on him, Officer?"

"I don't."

"Get me an enlargement of his right hand as he was turning around. As fast as you can. I think he has something between his fingers. Maybe a wire. Some electronics of some kind."

Joey passes along Christine's request to an officer behind him. Joey Blanks now has his own Joey Blanks. Seconds later Joey's voice moves into an even lower range. "Heads up, fed talker walking, Sarge. Coming from your five—the bus . . . right now."

"Thank you, Joey."

Before the fed gets any closer, Marko interrupts. In a booming voice, he says, "I have something to say."

Christine opens her eyes wide.

Oh, shit, she thinks.

Dee

Deirdre is hung up at the perimeter on College Street. She is unable to get permission to enter the secure area around the tomb.

She can tell from the tension she senses from the law enforcement personnel on the other side of the barricade that something is going on.

The massive form of Commons is blocking her view of the front of the tomb.

She leans forward toward the New Haven cop who is refusing to recognize her Company ID. In a saccharine voice she says, "I'm fucking CIA. Read it. Please."

Marko's voice carries. His native accent is subdued.

Joey Blanks pokes at the paper in his hands. He says to Carmody, "Kid does theater. It says here he's good. Shakespeare and stuff."

Christine waves Joey quiet. She says, "Marko? Is that your name? May I call you Marko? I'm eager to hear what you have to say."

The hostage turns his head and narrows his eyes. His mouth, framed by the fabric of the ski mask, forms a querulous "What?"

Christine guesses he's taking instructions through an earpiece. She will wait him out. She doesn't want Marko to get any of his directions confused.

Marko looks toward Christine. Directly at Christine. He exhales visibly. He inhales. He nods as though he's an actor indicating that he's ready to begin his audition.

She is ready, too.

He says, "Here is what is about to happen. Nothing . . . is negotiable."

Been there, Christine thinks. She waits.

"A helicopter . . . ," he says.

Christine thinks, *Oh God, here come the getaway demands. He wants a helicopter.*

". . . is currently approaching New Haven from Long Island Sound. It will land . . ."

He has his own helicopter?

". . . on Beinecke Plaza in . . . less than three minutes. Do not . . . interfere with it. Do not . . . approach it. Do not . . . scramble aircraft to intercept it. Do not . . . attempt any . . . contact with it. If you do . . ."

I will die. And I will not die . . . What? . . . Got it. Alone. I will not die alone. In my right hand I am holding a wireless closed-contact— Yeah? Okay. Kill switch. A kill switch. If I release the pressure on the switch, two hostages inside the tomb will die. Instantaneously."

Christine covers her mouth. She says, "Joey, I need that photo of his hand."

Joey Blanks says, "Sir." He hustles away. The HRT hostage nego-tiator is right behind Joey as he heads to the command vehicle for the photograph.

Marko briefly closes his eyes.

Christine thinks he's concentrating on the voice that is speaking in his ear.

Marko says, "Next. The tomb—behind me—is wired to . . . sur-prise you. He says . . . that when you enter, and he knows you will enter soon, if you are careful . . . if you are deliberate . . . and if you are lucky . . . you might be able to reach the remaining hostages. Eventually. But . . . if you choose a less deliberate, or rapid, or . . . explosive breach, many people will die.

"All the detonators and explosives are under his control via the Internet. Do not disable the network. The system checks for an oper-ating broadband connection every five seconds. If it fails to detect one, the detonators are activated . . . immediately."

Christine is staring at Marko's face. She is convinced that he is nod-ding almost imperceptibly, maybe even unconsciously.

He is telling her that what he just said is true.

A cell phone behind Christine begins to play a ringtone that sounds like a calliope. One of the police videographers fumbles to quiet it.

Marko waits out the interruption the way a stage actor might out-last an audience member's coughing jag.

"Next," he says. "There are also dangers, unseen, outside Book & Snake. Interfere in any manner, and those threats will become . . ." Marko pauses. It's apparent he's not understanding, or hearing, clearly. Finally, he says, ". . . unfor— Unfortunate . . . Realities. Those threats will become unfortunate realities."

Christine is in the dark about those external threats. She suspects that HRT is not. She curses silently as she turns her head to find Joey Blanks. He is just stepping back into position. He is holding the photograph.

He says, "Confirmation on the contact switch, Sarge." She takes the photograph. With a quick, dispirited glance she confirms the presence of the device in Marko's hand.

To Joey, she says, "Get the Sun out here. Not the Moon. And not my HRT shadow. No fucking liasing. I want Moody. I want him now."

Joey jogs away once more.

The wind blowing in from the Sound is carrying the distinctive *fwtt fwtt fwtt fwtt* of an approaching helicopter. The rhythmic pounding punctures the stillness of the morning air.

Okay, Christine thinks, *and there's my confirmation on the helicopter.*

The HRT special agent in charge is staring out the window of the command vehicle. He turns his head to look at his hostage negotiator. "Can you tell me one time—one—when a hostage taker has arranged his own transportation away from a multiday siege?"

The HRT hostage negotiator says, "Can't."

Hade Moody intrudes. He says, "You going to let it land?"

The comm officer says, "X-ray sniper has a visual on the chopper from the Payne Whitney tower. ETA . . . imminent. It is in his sights, sir."

"What's the status of Little Bird? Is it in the air?" The SAC is asking about the small helicopter that accompanied HRT to New Haven.

"Crew is mobilizing, sir. It will be up in . . . minutes. Air Force F-Sixteens are scrambled. They should be in position to intercept the chopper if it goes back in the air. Echo and Hotel assault teams are preparing to move toward the plaza from College Street, on your order."

The SAC says, "Jesus." His mouth is dry. "ID on the incoming chopper. Anything?"

"Only that it's been spotted, sir."

Law enforcement video cameras have picked up the approaching chopper. The people in the TOC are able to watch its maneuvers on one of the monitors. The landing gear is down. The pilot is swooping in, quickly adjusting to the wind, rotating the tail, and preparing to land the helicopter in the risky confines of Beinecke Plaza.

A large section of the plaza is a sunken sculpture garden attached to the Beinecke Library at the basement level. That portion of the plaza is unusable for a helicopter landing.

The SAC is conjuring all that can go wrong in the next few seconds. It's a long list.

"You going to let it land?" Moody asks again.

The SAC ignores him again. He says, "We have an ID on that aircraft yet?"

"It's a Sikorsky . . . an S-Seventy-six . . . uh, C-plus. November-four-two-six-one-Romeo." The IT officer's fingers dance on the keyboard. "U.S. Registration to . . . Black Swan Holding Company in . . . Hong Kong. Let me . . . Wait. Sir, that's a company that's connected to the parents of one of the kids."

The SAC says, "No way. What kind of company?"

"Undersea cable, sir. Telecommunication . . . infrastructure. It's a company chopper. U.S. offices based in . . . Newark."

"Is it this kid? The one on the steps right now? My God. The unsub is planning to escape on a helicopter belonging to the company of the parents of one of his hostages."

"It appears so, sir."

"Get me those parents. On the line. Now!"

"We are letting it land, sir? That's an affirmative?"

"We can't shoot it down where it is now. God knows how many people would die. Let it land."

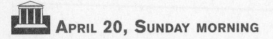

Poe and Dee

Poe's phone vibrates seconds after he finds his familiar perch outside the power facility down the block from the tomb.

It's Purdy.

"Write down this address. Don't argue with me, Poe." Sam dictates the address. He continues, "There's been a change in plans. Get a cab. Steal a car. I don't care. Meet me there as fast as you can." He hangs up before Poe can challenge him.

Poe tries to call him back. Once. Twice. Both calls go straight to voice mail.

Poe calls Sam back for the third time.

Sam doesn't answer for the third time.

Poe texts Dee.

Have you heard from our guy?

No.

He types, **Where r u d?**

He waits half a minute for a reply that doesn't come. He is assuming that Deirdre is inside the law enforcement perimeter. She does not have the privacy to respond.

He thumbs, **Barbara Lou?**

Poe starts looking around, trying to decide what to do. He doesn't know whether to stay outside the perimeter to support Dee or to chase after Purdy.

A taxi pulls up outside the law school to drop off a passenger.

Poe wonders if it's an omen.

He hears a distant, deep, rumbling *fwtt, fwtt, fwtt, fwtt* beginning to fill the air.

Instinctively, he checks the sky for the sudden stain of an assault helicopter. He figures the approaching chopper will mark the advent of the HRT breach. A tricky, dangerous final descent to the target. A roof drop. Agents on ropes. Explosive penetration. Top-down breach.

A simultaneous entry will be happening somewhere else along the ground floor. Front doors? Probably.

More explosives.

Poe's gut says that it's the wrong time and the wrong tactic.

Wrong, wrong, wrong.

He begins to feel like he's floating. In his mind's eye he is able to observe New Haven as though he's become an astronaut in Google Earth.

Nice view, but a bad sign.

The burn of acid is infiltrating his long bones.

He knows he needs to reach out for a toehold on reality before it's too late.

His eyes find the cabdriver just as the man is slamming the trunk of his car. Poe watches as the tall cabbie begins to fold his long body back onto the driver's seat.

All of Poe's instincts tell him he should not be heading away from the breach. Away from the tomb. Away from Deirdre.

The pounding blade chop grows louder. More insistent.

Poe finally spots the dark form of the helicopter as it appears just above the trees and rooftops, swooping gracefully over Cross Campus toward Beinecke Plaza. The chopper slows to hover. It is less than a hundred feet in the air. It appears to be rotating into the wind, preparing to land.

Poe can't tell for certain, but he doesn't think the helicopter is directly over Book & Snake.

When he sees the helicopter in profile, he is certain of even less.

It's too small for an HRT assault. Not enough capacity.

It's not a . . . It's a civilian chopper.
What the hell's with that?
He throws his right arm in the air. He yells, "Taxi!"
He's thinking, *Purdy, you had better be right.*

Dee hears the helicopter, too. She sees it swoop down over the plaza.

She recognizes that it's not a government aircraft. She doesn't know what that means.

Four different cops from three different jurisdictions are huddling on the other side of the barricade trying to decide if she is going to be permitted to enter the secure zone. Two others are on mobile phones trying to answer the same question.

I'm missing everything, she says to herself. *Everything.*

The HRT SAC is standing two feet from the largest monitor. He watches the helicopter edge into its final approach. He watches it land.

But not on Beinecke Plaza.

Just before touchdown, the pilot stops his descent and adjusts the approach to bring the craft down softly onto the roof of the Beinecke Rare Book and Manuscript Library.

The SAC mumbles, "The fucking roof. He just landed on the roof of the fucking library. Give me a break."

The comm officer says, "Those parents are not answering, sir. Straight to voice mail."

The FBI videographer with responsibility for the rear exposure of Book & Snake captures the landing. The aircraft is a deep, charcoal gray Sikorsky six-passenger helicopter. Luxury accommodations.

The camera reveals three people inside. The pilot is wearing a helmet and goggles. In back are two passengers. One adult, one child. They, too, are wearing helmets and goggles.

The photographic images of the interior, and of the two newest hostages huddled in the back, are displayed on the largest monitor in the command vehicle.

"That's a child in there. Jesus," the HRT hostage negotiator says.

"A child? What the . . . ," says Hade Moody. "What does that mean?"

"It means that the family is doubling down," says the HRT SAC, amazement clear in his tone. "Unbelievable."

The hostage negotiator explains, "The family had one child at risk in the tomb. Now they've bet the life of yet another one of their children to try to get the first one back safely. I can't imagine making that decision. It's like a reverse Sophie's Choice."

Even after touchdown the helicopter engine continues to roar. The blades continue to spin.

"Capacity of that thing?" the SAC asks.

Someone says, "Six passengers, plus pilot. But I don't think this guy is too worried about FAA regs."

Hade Moody says, "Is that the getaway car? Is that what's happening?"

"I don't know," the SAC says. "I don't know what the hell it is." He tightens his hands into fists. "Other than unanticipated. For the record, I'm not fond of unanticipated. Tell intel I want hypotheses. I want scenarios. I want containment strategies. I want them immediately."

The comm officer says, "Whiskey and Zulu snipers report they have shots of the pilot, sir."

"Steady," says the commander. "We don't know enough. Too risky. Story of this whole damn weekend."

"Whiskey sniper reports a paper sign has just been held up to the pilot's side window. It reads: BLU-One-ten JDAM."

"What? Say again," demands the SAC. His breath catches in his throat.

"The sign reads Bravo-Lima-Uniform dash one-one-zero, Juliet-Delta-Alpha-Mike."

The hostage negotiator sits down at the nearest laptop. He says, "I'm checking Jane's."

The commander asks, "Don't bother. I know what it is. Get me DOD. Is it feasible—is it fucking feasible—that the unsub really has a thousand-pound bomb on board that helicopter?"

The comm officer's voice is cool. "Snipers report no visual confirmation of that munition, sir."

Once the helicopter has touched down, Joey Blanks is finally permitted to pass along Christine's message to Haden Moody.

He steps inside the command vehicle. He says, "Lieutenant Moody? Sergeant Carmody would like to see you, sir. Outside. Now, sir. She says it's urgent, sir."

Moody doesn't even look at Joey Blanks. He says, "Jack's liaising."

"Sergeant Carmody specifically requested no liaising, sir."

Moody says, "Jack, take care of this. That's all, Officer."

Jack Lobatini glares at Joey Blanks.

Joey Blanks glares right back.

Christine steps forward from her usual position on Grove Street. She has advanced almost to the curb in front of the tomb. She chances a glance toward the command vehicle. Joey is stepping outside the door. He is followed by Jack Lobatini.

Christine recognizes that Moody is in full eclipse. *Damn him.*

Marko speaks again. Despite his powerful voice, he is forced to almost yell to be heard above the roar of the helicopter engines and blades.

He says, "He wants the plaza entrance to the library unlocked. Now."

Of course he does, Christine thinks.

Behind Marko, the door of the tomb opens. Two people exit, one right behind the other.

The first one is wearing a wedding dress.

What the—? Christine thinks.

She—if it is a woman—is also wearing a white head covering that wraps her entire upper body. Only her eyes are exposed.

Even though Christine knows a gown was carried into the tomb, the presence of the dress on a released hostage is completely discomfiting to her.

She feels some relief when she realizes she is seeing no orange.

The other person who exits along with the costumed bride is dressed identically to Marko.

The three of them begin to descend the stairs in unison.

Christine turns to Jack Lobatini, who is at her side. "He wants the library door open. I think you better do it." She hands Jack the photograph of Marko's right hand. "It appears he does have that contact switch between his index finger and thumb. It looks like the two that are dressed identically both have switches."

At the bottom of the stairs the three hostages exit the gate and turn left. They are following the approximate path that Michael Smith III took on Saturday after he jumped the fence—toward the stairs between Book & Snake and Beinecke Library that lead from the sidewalk down to the plaza.

Once they get to the plaza, the trio will be only yards from the entrance to Beinecke Library.

Jack uses his radio to communicate with the command vehicle. He recommends unlocking the library door.

He is told that the SAC has ordered no interference with the three people who just exited the tomb.

Seconds later he receives word that the library doors are open.

Christine thinks, *Well, there goes contain.*

Hade Moody is staring at the monitor, and at the progress of the three people as they step through the gate outside the tomb. He didn't understand the latest discussion about munitions and JDAMs. Despite the earlier witness statement about a white dress in a bag, he has no idea why a hostage is wearing a wedding gown. He says, "What the fuck? Who are those three?"

The SAC asks, "Is that a *hijab*? Is that woman wearing a *hijab*?"

Moody says, "What's a *hijab*?"

The SAC is talking to the room. "And why the wedding dress on a hostage? Is that a secret society thing? Is the hijab symbolic? Is he telling us this is about Islam? Thoughts, anyone? Intel? Come on. Some imagination please." No one proffers an opinion. The SAC says, "Am I talking to myself here? Wait a second. Are those really hostages at all? Do we know that? Is it possible that one of those two—"

"One of those three," says the HRT hostage negotiator. "Or more than one of those three. The unsub could be a woman. We don't know it's a man. There could be more than one unsub. Any or all of these people could be unsubs."

"Or hostages."

"Or hostages."

The comm officer interjects, "Victor sniper reports visual confirmation of an optical scope on the tube in the attic vent. Repeat, confirmed. Weapon is an RPG-Twenty-nine Vampir. He reports that the target has been adjusted up slightly. It is now aimed at the helicopter. There are now three—repeat, three—infrared signatures in the attic. Two static, one moving. Reflection off a glass surface spotted once again."

The commander says, "So it's possible, maybe even likely, that there is at least one unsub still inside the tomb. It's also highly likely that one of the three people in that attic is the son of the secretary of the army."

"I read it the same way," the HRT hostage negotiator says. He adds, "And, sir, according to DOD, it may be technically feasible to fit a half-ton munition on board that model chopper."

The commander says, "Son of a— Make sure DHS and DOD are aware that there may be a BLU-One-ten on board that helicopter." He takes a deep breath. He says, "Everyone?"

The room stills.

"Here's what I'm seeing. We have a helicopter full of jet fuel that may also be carrying a thousand-pound bomb. The chopper has just landed on top of a gazillion dollars' worth of one-of-a-kind books. In the back of the helicopter are two new hostages, including a child—a *goddamn* child. If we interfere with the three people the unsub has just released from the tomb, we have to assume that he'll kill the three civilians in the chopper by firing the RPG. The Vampir is a heat seeker, by the way, in case any of you don't know that. The rocket will blow up the helicopter, of course. Which will ignite the jet fuel. Which may set off the bomb. Which will destroy the library. And all those damn books. And God only knows what else.

"If he's telling the truth about the contact switch in that hostage's hand—and none of you is giving me a reason to believe he's not—if we do anything that causes physical harm to any of the three newly released individuals, explosive charges will kill the hostages remaining in the tomb. If we attempt to take out the RPG position, we have to assume he will voluntarily open the contact switch, and the tomb will explode. With either intervention, we lose the hostages that are still inside the damn tomb. With either intervention, we will likely lose the helicopter, the new hostages, the current hostages, the library, and some unknown number of public safety officers."

The HRT hostage negotiator says, "I'm afraid you've covered it."

The SAC grimaces as though he's just taken a physical blow to his gut. "Am I missing anything here?"

The sniper team leader says, "Whiskey or Yankee sniper might be able to take out the contact switch. Could work."

The hostage negotiator says, "It could be 'switches.' Plural. We won't get off two perfect shots at the same point in time."

"Even if we could, it might not work. The impact might set the switches off. We can't risk it." The SAC says, "The unsub knows we're not going to shoot at that chopper while it's sitting on top of that library. The repercussions are too severe. Too many civilians. Too much collateral damage. Too much media exposure. Too many . . . goddamn Gutenbergs." He rubs his forehead with his open palm. "Ideas? Anybody? This is fucking infuriating."

The hostage negotiator asks, "Do we let it take off, sir?"

Everyone in the room recognizes that there is no good answer to that question.

Sam and Dee and Poe

The taxi has a GPS. Sam has the address that Ann Calderón texted to him.

The driver almost plows into the back end of a city bus while he's simultaneously driving away from the Omni Hotel and plugging the destination into the device.

"Oh, jus' the airport?" he says to his passenger once the device responds. "Why didn't you say so? Airport's easy. Do it five times a day. Do it wi' my eyes closed."

The driver is a young black man. His eyes glisten like rock candy. He has a black tattoo on the side of his neck that looks like some kind of deformed tree. His teeth are as white as typing paper. Sam is thinking he may be addicted to tooth whiteners.

"How long?" Sam asks.

"Ten. Fifteen. Depends on traffic. You want this address? This one?" The cabbie pokes at the GPS. "Or you want the terminal? They be different."

Sam says, "The address I gave you. You mind if I change my shirt back here?"

"Makes me no difference. Keep your pants on. Then I don't care."

The driver punches the accelerator to beat a light that is turning red. Sam notices. He says, "Thank you."

"Hey," the driver mumbles. "I always say, thank me later."

Traffic is light. After some serious contortion in the narrow space, Sam gets the white shirt on. He gets his tie tied. Tucking in will have to wait until he's out of the car.

The cab pulls off I-95, approaching New Haven's airport.

Sam thinks about calling Poe again. If Poe isn't already on the way, though, it's probably too late. He calls Dee instead. He says, "It's your friend from breakfast. Something's up."

"I know. I take it the chopper's on TV?"

"What chopper?"

"The networks don't have it? Really? A civilian chopper appears to have just touched down near Beinecke. I couldn't see the landing from where I am. I'm still waiting to get inside the perimeter. I don't have a visual on it because of the buildings. I assumed it's all on TV."

Sam tries to make sense of what he is hearing from her. He can't.

"Where did it land? On the plaza? Is there room? Are any hostages getting on the helicopter? Tell me that," he pleads. "Have any hostages left the tomb? Are any hostages boarding the chopper? Any . . . female hostages?"

Dee turns her back to the uniforms who are guarding the perimeter barricades. She lowers her voice to a whisper. She says, "I can't see from here. I overheard a local cop say something about . . . three people . . . total, I think. Hostages or unsubs? I don't know. But they were heading toward the chopper. I can't tell where it landed. The engine is still on—I can hear it. I thought the guy said something about twins and a dress. I don't know what that means. Same cop said there are two additional family members of one of the hostages already on board."

A dress? "A girl?" Sam asks.

"Maybe, I'm not certain."

Sam is thinking, *Could be Jane. She's one of the girls left inside.*

Sam says, "Three in total? And there's family already on board the chopper? They were in it when it landed?" He moves pieces around in his head so he can try to get them to fit together. *Something about twins?* He spins them. *A dress?* Shoves them. Twists them. He says, "Damn. I'm having the hardest time figuring this out. You talked to Poe?"

"Not yet."

"I'll be back to you soon. Wait for my call."

"Are you at the Omni, Sam? You're not, are you? Wait! Wait!"

Sam closes his phone. The driver catches Sam's eyes in his mirror. "Motherfu— This is secret agent shit. Idn' it? That stuff goin' down at Yale? That crazy-ass secret society thing? Dang. Well . . . dang." He almost takes the cab onto two wheels as he screeches around the corner. "Man, you look nothin' like double-oh-seven." He switches into a posh British accent. "And there, straight ahead, is your hangar, Mr. Bond."

Sam jumps out of the car. He says, "Wait for me. I'm sending somebody out with your money."

"Man! Shit! James Bond don't— My money? Man! Don't you—"

Dee texts Poe. **I just got inside. I think we lost Sam.**

She is texting while she jogs, weaving her way toward the command vehicle.

You can't find him? Poe replies.

Poe still doesn't know if this blind quest he is on is taking him toward Sam, or away from him. He knows it is taking him away from Dee. He hates that.

Dee replies, **He's not answering.**

Poe types, **Let me know.**

After waiting for a reply from Deirdre for half a minute, Poe pulls his eyes from his BlackBerry. He slides a couple of twenties onto the front seat of the cab. He has already looked up the destination on Google Maps. He knows he's going to Robinson Aviation, a private plane facility at the New Haven airport. He still doesn't know why.

Poe is silently preparing speeches that will either praise Sam or curse his ashes. He's putting more rehearsal time into the curses.

"That's hurry money," he says to the driver.

"Yeah," says the driver. "Is there more?"

A young woman in a tailored white blouse and a black pencil skirt is waiting for Sam in the lobby of the Robinson Aviation building. In three-inch heels, she is two inches taller than Sam. She says, "Mr. Purdy? Right this way."

She leads him down a narrow hall, through two sets of doors, and into a spacious airplane hangar that is much cleaner than Sam's house. Sam almost has to jog to keep up with her long strides. He's busy tucking in his white shirt the whole time.

He follows her past two small business jets toward a door that leads outside.

A man emerges from a small office. "It just touched down," he says. "We'll make the switch during refueling." The man throws Sam some coveralls. "Put this on."

"What switch?" Sam asks as he struggles into the suit.

"Mrs. Calderón said you would be getting aboard the plane."

Do you trust me, Sam? . . . I haven't been completely honest with you, Sam.

"That green pickup truck right there is running. Drive it toward the fuel truck on the other side of the field. See it? There—at ten o'clock. Park between the fuel truck and the field. Got it? Go."

Sam says, "Someone named Poe may be showing up soon. Tell him what's going on. Tell him no cavalry."

"No cavalry, got it."

Sam climbs into the Ford and starts to drive toward the stubby fuel tanker. He tries to call Poe. It goes straight to voice mail.

Less than a minute after Sam gets to the tanker, a gleaming jet rolls up.

The door opens. At the top of a set of stairs that extend down from the jet is Ronaldo Angel Calderón. He is wearing a jumpsuit not unlike Sam's.

"So good to see you again, Sam. Please come up."

"And you, Mr. Calderón." They meet near the top of the stairs.

"Time is tight. You will be in the copilot's seat. It's where I've been. We expect that Jane and her captor will be boarding this aircraft soon. Any minute. We don't know how. We don't know the circumstances."

"This is your jet, Mr. Calderón?"

"Yes."

"This is the . . . ransom for your daughter?"

"It's a complicated arrangement, Sam. There are agreements in place."

Sam is wondering where the Canary Islands fit into those agreements. He says, "What happens next?"

"Ann and I are not naïve, Sam. We have no illusions that an aircraft of this size carrying this much fuel with someone like . . . that man . . . on board is going to be permitted to fly. If this jet gets airborne, it will be shot from the sky. We know."

Sam says, "What would you like me to do?"

"Save my family. That's it. Save my family, please, before this plane takes off. I don't know how. You can trust Carlos. I promise you that. And Sam, you should know I am proud of my son, and that I am proud of Dulce. She wanted to come. We wouldn't allow it."

Sam doesn't know what Mr. Calderón means. He is about to ask when the pilot steps out of the cabin. "Señor, I think it's time."

Ronaldo Calderón says, "Ditch that jumpsuit. Good luck, Sam."

"We both know I can't fly, right?" Sam says as he struggles to get out of the suit.

"Ann says you can do this. She knows you can. Trust, Sam. Trust."

Not quite, Sam thinks.

Calderón hands Sam a Glock. "This okay?"

Sam checks the gun. "It's fine." They pass each other on the narrow stairs. Sam says, "One thing, Mr. Calderón. There's a taxi driver out front. Could you take care of him, please? I'm busted."

Sam turns around inside the jet.

In the back of the cabin is Andrew Calderón. Alone, without his fiancé, Dulce.

Sam realizes exactly what Ronaldo meant with his comments about his son and future daughter-in-law. *And Dulce wanted to come?* he thinks. *To be part of this?*

Sam recognizes that the new hostage on board is an additional guarantee. The Calderóns have a child at risk at both ends of this transfer.

Andrew's eyes are blindfolded. His ears are covered by headphones. His ankles and wrists are restrained. Somehow, he senses that something is going on in the plane. His hands are both giving the thumbs-up sign.

Sam says a silent prayer. He watches Ronaldo Calderón drive away in the fuel truck.

The pilot says, "I'm Carlos. Once the chopper gets here we need to be ready to roll."

Carlos is a husky man in his forties with wide swaths of gray at his temples. Sam says, "Carlos? You know I don't know shit about any of this?"

"I know that."

"You have a weapon, Carlos?"

"Beretta."

"You know how to use it?"

"I'm okay. I admit I'm better with a Maverick." He taps his chest. "Navy pilot. Carriers. First Gulf War."

"You don't need a real copilot? You can fly this by yourself?"

"Two pilots are better than one, but sure, I'm fine. It's not relevant. We're too close to New York. They're not going to let us take off."

Sam knows it's true. He doesn't like hearing it out loud.

"So we improvise?" Sam says.

"Sí. These people are my family," Carlos says. "The Calderóns." Again, he taps a fist to his heart.

Sam looks back at Andrew. He thinks about Dulce. "Mine, too," Sam says.

Sam pulls out his phone. He calls Deirdre.

Sam says, "Don't talk, listen. Think twins. Go back and check the video of the first hostage, before he was blown up. Watch his eyes and his fingers before he dies. I think he was signaling to us that the hostage takers are twins. I don't know if that's important, but it's . . . something."

Dee says, "Got it. Where are you?"

"You'll know soon enough."

Sam closes his phone. To Carlos, he says, "I think she's a spook."

Carlos says, "You're connected that way? Señor Calderón said the feds didn't know about this trip."

Sam smiles at Carlos. "Officially, they don't. You know . . . if you rewind three days, I'm the least connected man on this planet. Life is funny."

"*La verdad,*" Carlos says.

The word is beyond Sam's Spanish comprehension. He hears the distant chop of helicopter blades. He texts Deirdre.

I'm in the jet. I assume you know about the jet.

Then he texts Carmen, his girlfriend, and Simon, his son. The texts are identical.

Love you.

The roar of an approaching helicopter precedes a swirling cloud of dust by about five seconds.

APRIL 20, SUNDAY MORNING
NEW HAVEN

The helicopter that landed on the roof of Beinecke Library is back in the air less than six minutes after it touched down.

It departs campus on almost the same flight path on which it arrived. In seconds it has cleared Old Campus and is crossing downtown New Haven.

Its altitude never exceeds one hundred feet.

Three new passengers are on board.

The sign is absent from the pilot's window.

The SAC stares at the monitor as the helicopter lifts off from the roof.

"Range? Fuel capacity?" he asks. He knows it doesn't really matter. The helicopter is no longer his problem.

Hade Moody asks, "You going to shoot it down?"

The SAC decides to answer one of Moody's questions. "It's no longer my call. It's now a military problem. We need to focus on getting the rest of the kids out of that tomb." He raises his voice. "I'm still waiting for some intel from you people."

The second man to exit Book & Snake that morning is sitting on the front passenger seat of the helicopter, next to the pilot. As soon as they are airborne, he hands the pilot a note indicating he wants private communications between his headset and the pilot's headset. The pilot toggles some switches and gives him a thumbs-up.

The man says, "You're flying directly to Tweed New Haven on heading one-five-zero. You'll see the airport soon enough, it's on the Sound just on the other side of I-Ninety-five. You are looking for a white Gulfstream on a taxiway adjacent to runway oh-two. Do not adjust your route for traffic. Fly directly there. No contact with the tower. Do not ask for clearances. Ignore warnings. Stay at this altitude or lower. You will be landing on the taxiway adjacent to the jet. Understood? Land on the runway side of the jet. Do not hesitate. Once I give you the signal, move the helicopter away from the jet. Land it elsewhere on the field. Wait."

The pilot says, "Roger."

"Keep this channel active. I want to hear all incoming radio communication. Do not respond to any of them."

"Deirdre Drake, CIA," Dee says as she hands her identification to the New Haven cop at the door of the Mobile Command vehicle.

He examines her ID. Nods. She enters the vehicle. She immediately spots the two FBI power centers in the room. By default, she approaches the HRT hostage negotiator. He is the one of the two agents without a phone at each ear.

"Deirdre Drake," she repeats. "CIA. Is there someone who can show me the video of the first hostage who was released?"

"Why?"

"No time. You'll see in a moment. Just get it on the screen. I may have something for you."

The negotiator instructs the IT guy to play the clip of hostage one's release.

The comm officer turns to the SAC. He says, "Air Force assets are almost in position to remove the target helicopter, sir. DHS wants you to stand by to advise."

The HRT commander says, "The chopper is over civilian populations. Tell Homeland Security if it poses an imminent threat, yes. Until then, not yet." He pauses. "And pray that I'm right."

The comm officer says, "Destination appears to be Tweed New Haven, sir. It's flying just above the rooftops."

"Do we have assault teams on the way to the airport?"

"Charlie and Golf. ETA ten minutes."

"The unsub has gotten us to split our assets." The SAC stares out the window toward the tomb. "Let me guess—the asshole has a jet waiting for him at the airport."

"Tweed Ground Control reports two possibilities, sir. A Cessna Three-ten . . . or a Gulfstream Two hundred. Both have landed in the last few minutes. Should airport security approach?"

"Not until our assault teams arrive. The locals are not equipped for this. I don't want them near those planes. I can't run the risk of friendly fire casualties if the air force decides to take out the jet or the helicopter with a missile. Run the registration numbers on both planes. Do the Gulfstream first. It will belong to the parents of another hostage."

"Sir."

"Get photographs of the interiors of those planes. There will be family members inside one of them. New hostages. More hostages."

"Sir."

"I want data on the range of the jet. And ground speed after take-off. Get me a list of nearby targets vulnerable to assault by that jet. I'm talking within minutes, right after takeoff. I know there's an oil storage facility on the Sound. Get me a list of bridges. Important buildings. Military installations. Assume the unsub is a trained pilot. What else? What am I missing? Anybody?"

"Include New York City?" asks the hostage negotiator.

"If he turns toward the city, he's dead. He knows he'll never make it that far. Inform DOD and DHS that I do not advise permitting the Gulfstream to fly. If there is any attempt to transfer munitions from the helicopter to the jet, both should be taken out on the ground, immediately."

"Sir. Victor sniper reports that the RPG's target has been readjusted—it is now aimed at the side of the library."

The HRT hostage negotiator states the obvious: "If he manages to get off two quick rounds from that RPG, the library is toast."

The SAC asks, "Rate of fire on an RPG-Twenty-nine?"

The negotiator is ready with the answer. "According to Jane's, ten to fifteen seconds, depending on operator skill."

The IT specialist chimes in, "High-value target, sir. Submarine Base New London is forty miles east. It's a . . . nuclear base."

"By air, that's—"

"Shortly after takeoff? Five to ten minutes, plus/minus."

The SAC says, "Get DOD to alert the base commander. Close all major bridges within fifty miles. Is there a demand on the table? What does this asshole want for the library?"

Christine Carmody steps past Deirdre. She looks at the HRT hostage negotiator. It's the guy from overnight. She asks, "Is that zip line ready?"

Her HRT counterpart says, "You should not be in here, Sergeant."

"Do you have the zip line ready?"

Deirdre asks, "What zip line?"

The HRT hostage negotiator says, "We are . . . preparing to deploy a zip line above the tomb tonight . . . for some reconnaissance."

Carmody interjects, "It could be used right now for preemptive strike on the grenade launcher, or later before it can fire a second round."

Deirdre doesn't get it. "That's important? The second round? Explain."

The HRT negotiator says, "Given the penetration capacity of the RPG-Twenty-nine shell, we think he'll need to use the first round to pierce the stone panels on the side of the library. We assume he'll then fire a second round through the hole created by the first. The second rocket will shatter the glass wall of the inner airlock of the library."

Dee says, "And that will destroy the books?"

"Yes. With the glass compromised, fire alone will do it."

Dee sees the dilemma. "How long to deploy the zip line?"

The negotiator says, "We could be ready to shoot the line in . . . ten minutes, maybe less. Five more minutes to secure it and get personnel in place."

Deirdre says, "You don't have fifteen minutes. This will be over."

"Ideas?" asks the SAC. "Anyone?" He waits two seconds. "Shit."

"I have a question," Deirdre says. "Why is your unsub waiting? Why doesn't he just take out the library?"

The HRT negotiator looks up from the monitor. He says, "You know, that's a good question."

The SAC raises his voice to a decibel less than a shout. "Anyone?"

Dee reads a text from Sam. **I'm in the jet. I assume you know about the jet.**

She thinks, *I underestimated you.*

The IT officer turns to Deirdre. He says, "Got that video, ma'am."

Deirdre steps toward that monitor. She watches for a few moments before she says, "Stop it right there. See those fingers. One in each hand. He was telling us there were two hostage takers. He used his two index fingers. Same finger, twice. Twins."

Carmody recognizes the clue. "Twins. I missed it."

Dee says, "We all did. But what does it mean?"

The HRT negotiator says, "It could be the two who just boarded the helicopter. They were dressed almost identically."

Dee says, "Maybe, but twins doesn't mean identical."

Carmody says, "But it might."

Dee says, "Let's deal with what we know. The unsub is going over our heads—leaving us out of the loop. He's bartering hostages for transportation—but he's trading directly with the hostages' families, not with our negotiator. One of the three people who got on board is a hostage in trade for the helicopter. Another has to be a hostage in trade for the plane at the airport. That leaves one unidentified. The one might—might—be an unsub. That means that if we're dealing with twins, at least one unsub remains inside the tomb."

"He could be operating the RPG," Christine Carmody adds.

Deirdre says, "But, again, why hasn't he fired? Why not take out the library before we're set to retaliate? What do they want that they haven't demanded yet?"

The hostage negotiator says, "What about the thousand-pound bomb? How the hell did he get that?"

Dee is about to ask, *What thousand-pound bomb?* as her eyes drift to an adjacent monitor. The video of the three hostages moving from the tomb to the helicopter atop Beinecke Library is being replayed on the screen.

Dee is startled. She says, "Wait! No! One of the three who was just released is wearing a wedding dress? What the hell is . . . ?"

None of the men responds. For them, the wedding dress is old news.

Christine says, "A wit saw them carry the dress into the tomb on Thursday."

Dee's eyes open wide. Her brain churns the new data. Dee says, "That is symbolism. Symbolism. Not tactics." She exhales. Thinks. She allows her shoulders to drop. "You know what? I think this means he may be . . . done. He's not going to destroy the library. He's not going to use the jet as a weapon. Commander, you need to stand down. You need to tell the military to stand down. Now!"

"Stand down? What? Are you nuts?" says the HRT negotiator. "He has a thousand-pound bomb in that chopper."

Dee can't make sense of the bomb. "What kind of bomb?"

"A BLU-One-ten JDAM."

"Yeah?" she says. "I know that . . . weapon designation. Where have I seen that before?"

She's frustrated that she can't fit the bomb into the puzzle, but she thinks she understands the dress. "That's what this is about. . . . The weddings. The damn . . . weddings. This isn't about Iraq, it's about Afghanistan. Oh God. Commander, you have to stand down. He's trying to get you to respond. No—no, he's trying to get you to over-respond. He's being intentionally provocative right now. He wants you to fire on the jet, or open up on the library, or even on the tomb. All three if he can get you to do it. He wants you to start killing civilians. Out in the open. In front of the cameras. He's not going to blow things up. He wants *us* to start blowing things up. You have to hold your fire."

The HRT hostage negotiator says, "Why would he be doing that?"

"To prove a point," Dee says.

"What point?"

Her brain is desperately trying to make sense of the hijab and the half-ton bomb. "I'm thinking this all has to do with a wedding in Afghanistan," she says. She's recalling the intel reports that had crossed her desk with a thousand others. "A mistake . . . A terrible mistake we made in Afghanistan. Twice, I think. We made it twice. Two different weddings.

"Holy. That's where I've seen that bomb designation. I think both bombing errors were made with thousand-pound JDAMs."

The HRT SAC has been listening to Dee's theory take shape. He doesn't get it. He says, "Who the hell is this woman? What the fuck is she doing in my TOC?"

Sam and Poe

Sam asks Carlos, "What would I be doing right now? I mean, if I were a real copilot?"

"We don't have cabin crew. One of us would greet the new passengers."

"That should probably be you, Carlos. If they talk to me, I'll say something stupid and give everything away."

"That's your chair on the right. Act busy checking things. Probably best not to, you know, change any settings."

Sam likes Carlos's sense of the absurd.

Sam says, "Either of us gets a clear shot, we take it. Yes?"

Carlos nods.

Sam is peering out the windshield of the jet. He watches the helicopter touch down nearby. Two people scramble out. The helicopter immediately pops back up off the tarmac. It tilts nose-down before it hops a couple of hundred yards across the airfield like a grasshopper, never gaining much altitude. It touches down again.

The pilot kills the engine.

Three more passengers run out of the helicopter in the new location. One is dressed exactly like the man who had already climbed out of the helicopter. The others are a middle-aged woman and a young child. All three are running as fast as they can away from the chopper.

The pilot's feet hit the macadam ten seconds behind them.

Sam recognizes that another hostage has been released. Or . . . the first unsub has escaped. He hopes Poe saw what just happened.

* * *

The first person up the stairs of the jet is wearing a wedding dress. A white fabric veil circles her head. Not even her eyes are exposed. She stops at the top of the stairs.

The second new passenger is wearing a ski mask. The man is right behind the woman. Close enough that they could be dancing. Together they move inside the jet.

The man in the ski mask faces Carlos. The cockpit door is open. Sam is visible over Carlos's shoulder.

"First thing? I have a dead man's switch, a contact switch, between my fingers. My waist is wrapped with explosives. Kill me, we all die. Including that one in the back. If I'm dead, no message is sent back to the tomb. If that happens, those hostages die. We understand each other?"

That's the voice, Sam thinks. *The guy on the phone call.*

The man is holding the woman in the wedding dress as though she is a hostage. Her body shields almost all of his body. The man says, "I was hoping it was clear by now that I'm not stupid. I saw the personnel switch you did as we were approaching the airport." He shakes his head. "Binoculars?"

He waits a moment for the men to deny it. Neither does.

"Which one of you is the cop?" the man asks.

"That would be me," Sam says from the cockpit.

He looks at Carlos again. Then once more at me. "Are you both armed? Or only you, Mr. Cop?"

Before Carlos can make the mistake of being valiant, and lying, Sam answers for him. "We're both armed. Handguns."

The man nods. "On the floor. Slide them this way."

Sam and Carlos produce their guns. They push them in the direction of the man. He leaves them where they stop. He is confident no one will shoot him while he's holding a dead man's switch.

The moment his fingers relax, the switch would open, and everyone would die.

"You FBI?"

Sam says, "No. Local."

The man looks at Carlos. "You ready to fly?"

Sam thinks it's an interesting question.

Carlos says, "Yes. Airport security is staging over there, near the terminal. You can see." He points out the open door. "I would guess that they are awaiting reinforcements. I can get us moving and . . . up in the air pretty fast, if that's what you want. But you should know I don't think they will—"

"Close the door. Roll into position for takeoff beginning in one minute. Check your watch. One minute."

Carlos sets his stopwatch. He secures the door, hurries to his chair. Sets his controls.

Why one minute? Sam wonders. As surreptitiously as he can, he texts Dee.

He types, **Guy is stalling, I think.**

Almost immediately she replies, **Yes, hold fire.**

Poe greets the four people who ran from the helicopter.

His handgun is in his hands. He forces all four to their knees and then onto the tarmac. Prone. Even the kid, a girl who is no more than seven.

There are a lot of tears.

"Somebody talk to me," he says as he pats each of them down.

The pilot says, "We dropped two off at the jet. One is a girl in a wedding dress. One is . . . one of them, I think."

Poe says, "You know it's a girl, or you think it's a girl?"

"I think."

Poe taps the foot of the young man in the ski mask. "You agree?"

The kid doesn't answer.

"What's your name?"

The kid doesn't answer.

Poe is thinking, *You don't want to see any more of your friends murdered.*

Poe tells the pilot to get up. "Lead them over to that building. Sit against that wall, wait for the FBI. These people are your responsibility."

Poe doesn't wait for a response. He takes off in full sprint toward the distant jet.

Sam

Carlos is staring at his watch to time the beginning of the jet's roll to the moment his watch finishes ticking off the proscribed minute. He says, "And we're taxiing."

"Roll straight into position for takeoff. Hold there, at the end of the runway."

Hold there? What?

I text Dee again. **Still stalling.**

I am considering making a charge for the man in the mask. He is sitting across the aisle from the person in the wedding gown. I am thinking that has to be Jane, that she was offered to the Calderóns in trade for the jet. The white veil continues to completely cover her eyes. It is held in place by headphones that cover her ears. She has no idea what is going on inside the plane.

My plan would be to use my body to cover the explosives that are on the man's waist. My effort might be enough to save Jane and her brother. If I don't try, we will all die. I am certain of that. If I do try, I will die, but the others might not.

I'm thinking United 93. A lesser-of-two-evils strategy. Active hero versus passive victim.

Problem is, I can't figure out how to get out of the damn harness that I'm in fast enough to make a charge at anything or anyone.

I'm afraid it would take me two minutes just to get out of my chair.

Other than a desperate charge at the man, I'm unable to think of an additional thing I can do that might be helpful. I'm saying my prayers.

And I'm already thinking about how I'm going to try to explain this whole thing to Carmen when she joins me in heaven.

Dee responds to my text. **Got it. Don't provoke him do not.**

I wonder what she knows. Why she is so certain that we are not seconds away from catastrophe.

I am at least that certain that we are.

Carlos points the jet straight down the long runway. I feel him pressure the brakes. He says, "Holding. Ready for throttle."

I unlatch the big clip on the harness. I turn to see if the killer is watching me.

I see him send a quick text with his cell phone.

I send one, too. Mine is to Dee: **Wtf?**

The man speaks to Carlos. "Throttle for takeoff. Count down to rotation. Loudly. Got it? Go. Now."

Carlos says, "There's a man charging onto the runway. See him?"

"Ignore him. Full power."

I've been watching the man approach the runway, too. It's Poe.

"Power for takeoff," Carlos says. Carlos pushes some big levers.

The jet jumps. I feel the g's hit me like the gale of a chinook as I'm forced against the back of my seat.

In almost any other circumstance I think I'd really be enjoying this.

The comm officer says, "Two passengers departed the helicopter and boarded the Gulfstream. One of the men. And the person in the wedding dress."

"I knew it," says the SAC. "An unsub and a hostage. Likely female."

"We have no visuals on the interior of the aircraft."

"Registration?"

"Checking Nancy-six-four-nine-three-Victor."

Deirdre is in the SAC's face. She says, "This is a trap, Commander. Stand down. This equation is not about whether the hostages are more valuable than the library or the submarine base. Don't fire. Don't be provoked."

"I shouldn't be provoked by a mass murderer with a big plane full of jet fuel and a helicopter possibly carrying a thousand-pound bomb? Why on earth wouldn't I consider that provocative?"

"Jet door closed," monotones the comm officer. "No munitions transfer."

Dee's BlackBerry vibrates. A text from Sam. **Guy is stalling, I think.**

Yes, of course he is, she thinks. *He's giving us time to screw this up.*

As fast as she can thumb, she replies, **Yes, hold fire.**

"Keep me posted in real time," says the SAC to the comm officer.

He replies, "RPG tube has just been moved forward. It is within inches of the opening in the vent and is visible to the naked eye. Aim is steady at the wall of the library."

Dee says, "He's making sure you can't miss the weapon. He has no reason to move it into the open other than to be provocative. He's trying to get you to fire on the RPG position. If you do, the hostages inside the tomb die. This is a trap."

The comm officer says, "We have reports of a solitary individual running across the airfield toward the G-Two hundred. No visual. Correction, we do have a visual. Monitor five."

A long shot showing the man sprinting across the tarmac pops up on a small monitor.

Under her breath, Dee says, "Poe."

She gets another text. Sam. **Still stalling.**

Dee suddenly understands what is happening.

The whole scenario comes into focus in her head. She sees the bad version. She sees the awful version. She raises her voice so that everyone in the vehicle understands her position. "Commander, your unsub is provoking you. He wants you to fire. Do not shoot at the RPG position. Do not allow the military to fire at that jet on the ground. Or on the helicopter. Stand . . . fucking . . . down."

Her thumbs fly. **Got it. Don't provoke him do not**

The SAC looks at her. With condescension coating his tone, he says, "Yeah? What if the jet starts to take off? We have a submarine base minutes from that airport. SUBASE New London is nuclear. And what if he fires round one from the RPG? What about the library? I just let them take the second shot?

"You're telling me I'm supposed to let this asshole start destroying national treasures, like the library, and vital national assets, like a nuclear sub base, because you don't want me to fire on hostages? Where exactly does that ball stop rolling? Do we let him take off and head toward the White House? Or just give him clearance to fly that jet into the George Washington Bridge? UN? Empire State Building? What?

"No, ma'am. No. We do *not* negotiate with terrorists. We will *not* be blackmailed by terrorists. It is unfortunate, but sometimes civilians perish in the national interest."

Dee says, "And sometimes civilians perish unnecessarily. This isn't about the library being more valuable than the hostages, or the sub base being more valuable than the hostages. This guy is begging you to start sacrificing civilians. You don't have to go along. You have margin. The first RPG round won't destroy the library. Right? What is the rounds-per-minute for that thing?"

The HRT hostage negotiator answers, "Four to six, depending on the operator."

"Commander, after he fires once you have fifteen seconds until he can fire again. Maybe more. You'll have time to assess and respond. The air force is scrambled and has assets ready to take out the jet. Five minutes is a lifetime for an F-Sixteen—the Gulfstream can be shot down long before it reaches New London. Be smart, use your margin. This is about our overreaction right now. Don't fall for his feints."

"Feints? We have intel. Hard intel."

Deirdre remembers reading the reports on the wedding bombings in Afghanistan. The officers who ordered those strikes thought they had hard intel, too. She says, "You only think you do, Commander. What you definitely have is time."

"I have no idea what you're talking about, lady. Victor sniper? On my order."

Victor sniper replies, "Copy."

Another text from Sam: **Wtf?** Dee moves close to the SAC. She whispers in his ear. "Sir, I have a man in that jet. It will not hit a target. Got it?"

The commander spins to look at her. His tone is faux-whisper. He wants everyone to hear it. "You have a man in that attic, too?"

There is an audible communal gasp in the command center as the first RPG round blows out of the gable vent of the tomb. The *whoooosh* of the little rocket is audible through the speakers. The explosion is instantaneous and sharp.

One of the stone panels in the side of Beinecke Library disintegrates in a cloud of smoke and dust and debris.

Dee barks, "Don't retaliate. Do not."

The comm officer says, "Jet is . . . rolling. Monitor three."

All eyes shift to monitor three. The Gulfstream is roaring down the runway.

The HRT hostage negotiator says, "We are nine seconds to reload on the RPG. Eight . . . seven . . ."

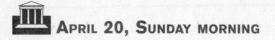

Sam

Carlos calls out, "I will rotate in five . . . four . . ."

I don't know what "rotate" means. I figure that I will find out in five . . . four . . .

My cheeks, the ones on my face, are quivering from the mounting g forces.

Outside the side window the world is flying by.

Beyond the glass of the windshield I see Poe standing as tranquil as a statue. He's on the centerline of the runway, staring a big-ass jet in the face.

He's not walking his box. He's not locked in his prison.

Poe is serene.

He actually thinks he can stop us from taking off. I have no idea if he's right. Will colliding with a solitary man keep a jet from . . . rotating?

I think I'm about to find out.

Carlos says, ". . . three . . ."

I brace myself for something.

Carlos doesn't wait for "two" or "one." I watch him pull back on the yoke. The nose tilts up.

I'm thinking we just rotated.

I lose sight of Poe.

I wait for a *thunk*.

In a pressured voice, the man says to Carlos, "Abort takeoff. Now! Do not go round. Back down! Down!"

Carlos says, "Shit."

His hands jump on the controls. I'm thinking maybe Carlos is wishing he had a real copilot sitting beside him.

He says, "Not possible. We can't stop in time."

I'm processing so many stimuli that I'm on complete overload.

Fear is clear, though. I'm scared shitless.

As my body tries to adjust to the rapid deceleration, I'm also wondering what the hell happened to Poe.

Dee sees the perfect coordination of the timing of the takeoff with the firing of the first RPG round as confirmation of her theory.

"Do not fire a shot you'll want back, Commander," she says. "You can't recall it."

The SAC doesn't reply.

"Jet is wheels-up," says the comm officer.

Dee says, "Don't. Do not. You have margin. Five minutes is a lot of margin."

The SAC says, "Advise DOD to take down the G-Two hundred the moment it is over Long Island Sound."

"Copy."

"Don't do it," Dee implores. "Use your margin."

The HRT hostage negotiator says, "We are four seconds to RPG reload . . . three . . ."

The commander says, "Victor sniper, take out the RPG position on my order—"

The comm officer interrupts. "Uh . . . Rear wheels are back down on the jet. Hard braking. Nose coming down. Aborted takeoff. Aborted takeoff."

Heads swivel to the monitor that is displaying the Tweed runway.

The SAC says, "Hold fire. Victor, hold your fire."

Victor sniper says, "Copy."

The HRT hostage negotiator says, "Reload window is complete for the RPG. Second round can fire at any time."

All eyes are on the small monitors.

One shows the jet careening down the runway, smoke popping in bursts from its superheated tires. One shows the smoldering damage on the side of Beinecke Library. The third is a close-up on the gable vent and the RPG position in the tomb.

The big monitor highlights the hole in the wall of the library. The first rocket has obliterated an entire marble panel. The hole is large. A second shot from the RPG will have an unimpeded path to the interior glass containment cube that protects the priceless collection in Beinecke.

The jet is in obvious trouble. It is rocking side to side on its rear wheels. The nose is not yet down on the runway. The plane has way too much speed.

Someone in the back of the room is focusing all his attention on the RPG. He is praying aloud, "Don't fire it, don't fire it, don't fire it."

The SAC says, "Victor sniper, remain at ready."

"Copy."

Five more seconds pass. Ten.

The nose of the Gulfstream comes down just as the plane blows off the end of the concrete.

It's apparent that the pilot has been trying valiantly to keep the jet on the runway after he aborted the takeoff. But the laws of physics are against him.

He fails. The front gear collapses a split second after the wheel goes from concrete to the soft earth that's intended to retard a speeding plane. The jet comes to rest after overshooting the runway by more than a hundred yards and spinning two hundred and seventy degrees.

Dee says, "What about the man on the runway? Where is he?"

The camera has followed the jet as it aborted its takeoff. The location where Poe was standing on the runway is not visible in the frame.

The IT guy says, "We don't have that visual."

Dee says, "Anybody? Please?"

"Waiting on a report."

Dee's BlackBerry sings two notes. She lifts it. Looks at the screen.

Where r u d?

She says, "Holy."

Christine Carmody is back in position on Grove Street when the front door of the tomb opens. Joey Blanks is at her side.

She has already told Jack Lobatini to get his liaising face out of her face.

Almost four minutes have passed since the RPG blew the hole in the side of Beinecke.

A long stream of young men and women are walking out the door of Book & Snake in single file. Their hands are in the air. They take seats next to each other on the top step of the staircase that leads to the tomb.

Every one of them looks shocked at the spectacle in front of them.

None of them is wearing orange.

After all are seated, a solitary man follows them out the door. His hands are in the air. In his left hand is a mobile phone. In his right hand is a closed contact switch.

He walks down the steps to the first landing before he stops.

He lowers one hand, glances at his mobile phone. With his thumb, he hits SEND.

The text reads, **I was right. We live. End of part one.**

He removes the contact switch—the dead man's switch—from the fingers of his right hand. He locks the device into a closed position. He holds it up for all to see before he places it on the stone at his feet.

In a loud, heavily accented voice, the man says, "I would like to speak to my attorney. Check your phones. I've sent you all his number."

Sam

Poe is standing on the soft dirt beside the jet. He is not patient. He is walking his box. It's been only a few minutes since the plane came to a stop.

I've done a lot with my few minutes.

The first thing that happened was that the man in the mask told me to keep the FBI away from the plane while we worked out his surrender.

I really liked the sound of that. I texted Poe. **Be patient. Keep HRT far away. It's almost over.** I didn't call him with the news because I didn't want to argue with him.

I then stepped in front of Carlos, who was on his way to release Andrew and Jane. I said, "Once this guy is in the custody of the FBI, we can free the kids, Carlos. Not now. The less Andrew sees and hears, the better. Neither of them needs to know I was here or who I am. It's much better for Jane, in the long run. Think about it. The danger for the Calderón family isn't over."

Carlos covered the necessary ground in seconds. He said, "I got it."

"And later, please give this to Mr. Calderón, not to Andrew." I wiped my prints from Andrew's iPhone, just in case, before I handed it to Carlos.

Everything I told him was true. What I didn't say was also true: If Andrew or Jane knew I was in New Haven, Dulce would know. If Dulce knew, Carmen would know.

Carmen would be furious with me, possibly even homicidal.

Being that rageful wouldn't be good for her, given her condition.

Once I had dealt with Poe, and with Andrew and Jane, and with Carlos, I did what I thought I was never supposed to do: I negotiated with the terrorist.

It didn't take long to come to an understanding. He was ready to give up.

I was so friggin' ready for him to give up.

Carlos, however, was having trouble getting the door of the damaged jet open. "This could take a while, Sam," he said.

"I got no place else to be, Carlos," I said.

While Carlos struggled with the door, I stood less than three feet from the murderer near the front of the luxurious jet. The man continued to keep the contact switch compressed between his thumb and index finger.

I couldn't resist asking. I said, "Why?"

In almost accent-free English, he said, "I thought you would want to know where I'm from."

"Really?" I said. "Where you're from?"

"'Where are you from?' is a thousand questions," he said. "'Where are you from?' is 'What motivates you?' 'Where are you from?' is 'Why are you so angry?' 'Where are you from?' is 'Who is your God?' 'Where are you from?' is 'What do you want?' 'Where are you from?' is 'How could you do this?'"

I wasn't in the mood. I said, "Just tell me why you did it."

"To get what I want, of course. I learned my lessons from your government. Ask them."

"We slaughtered innocent people to get what we want?" I said.

Immediately, I wanted my question back. I knew we had killed innocent people. At some point. Probably recently. My retort had been defensive and juvenile. I tried to dilute it. I added, "You just murdered six kids in two days."

He shrugged. "Yes, I did. Relevance? You killed six of my friends to get what you want."

"This was revenge?" I said, in disbelief. I couldn't accept that the motive was that simple. "Retribution?"

"Not at all," he said in a snarky tone that made me want to put my fist through his face. "Revenge would have been easy. I could have had my revenge with a truck bomb in Baghdad or Mosul. Could have given money to the Taliban or al Qaeda or Hezbollah. What we did was difficult. Expensive. Risky to me, to my brother. To the few who helped us. Retribution would have been cowardly. This was brave. Smart. Like America."

"'I am America'? That's what that meant? We killed, so you killed?"

He shook his head. "I released many more hostages than I killed. If I were after retribution, that tomb would be full of the corpses of your precious youth. The sniper in the tower would have been real. The campus lawns would be littered with his victims. The library of treasures would be nothing but embers and ash."

"I still don't get it. What were you after?"

"We had only one goal. To make certain that the United States knows that in the future she will suffer consequences for her acts of callousness. My brother and I now have the capacity to poison the well from which the monster drinks."

"What well is that?"

"The well of hubris. Of invincibility."

I didn't know what to say. I said, "What on earth did we do to you?"

I didn't think he planned to tell me.

But in a few seconds the man began speaking again, his voice suddenly bitter. His words started slowly, but the cadence accelerated as he continued. "You—your government—killed my older brother, two aunts, three uncles, my mother, my sister, four nieces, two nephews, three of my four grandparents, my brother-in-law, his family. And . . . nine of my friends. Not six. Nine."

I didn't like the instantaneous reflex I felt to dismiss his pain, his grief, his anger. But that's what I felt.

My instinctive thought was, *We had a reason. We must have had a reason.*

Then I looked over at Andrew and at Jane and, for an involuntary moment, imagined how catastrophic the man's loss would feel.

"War?" I said. I was hoping that learning the context would provide an explanation for me. Whatever it was my government had done to his family, I was sure we had a rationale. An explanation.

We had to.

"A wedding," he said. "A celebration. You bombed my sister's wedding."

I said, "That's her dress?" pointing at Jane.

"My sister was married in that dress. Moments later, she died in that dress."

Carlos said, "I think I'm getting it. Almost there."

Carlos was talking about the door of the jet.

"We bombed her wedding?" I said. I really, really needed some context.

"Yes" is all the man said.

"An accident?" I asked. It had to be.

"The bomb was a thousand pounds. A BLU-One-ten. A JDAM. That means it had precision guidance. It hit its intended target. Your government has acknowledged that. Killing my family cannot be called an accident.

"Two things came together that day. Faulty intelligence? Probably. That's one. The second? The absolute belief of the United States of America that its strategic interests supersede all other interests. Including any interest my family might have had in staying alive.

"From the ground, in villages like ours, the world looks like this: When America is threatened, she loses her capacity, or at least her desire, to weigh the plight of others. To see the lives of others.

"To see us. Our lives. Our rights. Our humanity.

"That's what I did here, in New Haven. Because I felt threatened, I determined that the wounds I had suffered were more important, and that my strategic interests were more important, than any U.S. interest. Even any civilian U.S. interest. To do what I did, I had to decide to be as ruthless as your government was the day my family died.

"For these few days, I had to be America."

I wanted to scream in his face.

I wanted to kill him. With my hands.

"Where are you from?" I asked finally.

"A village outside Kandahar," he said. "I am not al Qaeda. I am not Taliban. I am an Afghan. From this day forward, I am the protector of all innocent Afghans."

Carlos said, "Okay, here goes." He took a full step back, lowered his shoulder, and put all his substantial weight into the door. It creaked open a few inches. "Got it," he said. He forced it open the rest of the way.

I looked at the man's eyes. It was all I could see of his face.

I wanted to tell the man I was sorry. I didn't.

I wanted him to tell me he was sorry. He didn't.

All I said was "Okay. Let's do this."

I switched places with Carlos. My big ass body almost filled the doorway.

Poe has stopped pacing. He, of course, has his gun pointed squarely at my chest.

I swallow my instinctive fear. I know Poe is aiming the weapon at whomever or whatever he is thinking is behind me. I use my calm cop voice with him. I say, "You got those cuffs of yours, Poe? I have a prisoner for you."

Poe's left hand is balled into a fist. His right hand is gripping his pistol. I assess it. It's a Goldilocks grip. Not too tight. Not too loose. Just right.

That's good news for me.

He says, "I want to kill him, Sam. Just put him in the doorway. I'll do it. I don't care what happens after that."

"Hey, I'm with you on that, Poe. A thousand percent. But I'm not going to let you shoot him. Let me give you three quick reasons. First is, well, it's just not right. Though I admit that argument's pretty debatable. Second, there are witnesses on board the plane here. Once again though, I admit there's a big part of me that says *so what?* Third? The guy? Your unsub? Small problem there. He has a contact switch in his hand. If I let you kill him, the switch opens, and a chunk of my new family dies right along with him. Including the head of household. That would be me.

"So, all things considered, I think the best plan is for you to stay right where you are and for you to let me know when your homicidal urge passes."

I count silently as Poe considers his options. I get all the way to twenty-seven before he reaches behind his back with his left hand. He produces the cuffs. Tosses them up to me.

Poe asks, "Anybody hurt in there?"

I say, "Nothing serious. Frankly, my nerves are kind of shot. Pilot's brokenhearted about busting up his airplane, but . . . we're good here. Oh yeah, the guy—your unsub—he wants to talk to a lawyer. Has one picked out. He's already sent out a press release, or something. Says it includes his bio. Wants to make sure there's no confusion about him and his brother."

Poe sighs. He says, "Why am I not surprised?"

I turn around to face the man in the ski mask. I say, "All done. Did what I said I'd do."

The man shows me the screen on his phone before he hits SEND. Aloud, he says, "My brother." His final message reads: **You were right. They showed restraint. We live for now. End of part one.**

I watch him lock the contact switch closed. He removes the device from his fingers. He hands it to me. I hand it to Carlos, who cradles it like it is his firstborn.

Then the man holds out his wrists for the cuffs.

My final words to the murderer as I spin him around and bust him as hard as I can against the wall of the cabin are "Behind your back, asshole."

Sirens fill the air.

Poe begins to climb the stairs.

I am still wanting some damn context.

Sam

By the time darkness fell that Sunday night, word had leaked out that the government had managed to place an agent on board the Calderóns' company Gulfstream at Tweed New Haven airport.

I learned about the leak from one of the taciturn government employees with whom I was having an extended unpleasant conversation at an undisclosed location in Virginia.

I assumed that the leak had been self-serving. I didn't see any benefit for either Dee or Poe in revealing my role. The Calderóns certainly had no interest that would be served by outing me. The only other leak suspects I could identify were the cabdriver who had taken me to the airport or the employees of the aviation company at Tweed New Haven. But since the leak had come through an outlet that didn't pay for news tips, I didn't consider either the cabbie or the aviation folks to be likely suspects. Anyway, I was confident that all of them had been well taken care of by Señor Ronaldo Angel Calderón, and that he had encouraged their silence with some of his many fastener dollars.

It never crossed my mind that Carlos was the source of the leak. That wasn't him. Unless I had misread him badly, he was most definitely a fall-on-his-sword kind of guy.

I ended up deciding that someone in Homeland Security or Hostage Rescue was guilty of spilling the beans. Whoever had spawned the leak wanted to encourage the perception that the government alphabet agencies had been much more on top of the events in New Haven than they really were.

If that helped the public digest the tragedy at Book & Snake, I was okay with it. If it encouraged the public to have unwarranted confidence in the government's capacity to handle tragedies like the one at Book & Snake, I was definitely not okay with it.

No one at Homeland Security, or at FBI headquarters, or at Langley, was commenting publicly about the government agent on the jet. Nor did they endeavor to correct the mistake in the record.

See, technically the leak was in error. On the day the siege ended I wasn't a cop, let alone an agent.

I was not the special kind of agent—that would be FBI. Like Poe.

Nor was I the secret kind of agent—that would be CIA. Like Dee.

What was I? Despite the vague sense of betrayal I felt at the end, I was a friend of the Calderón family. I thought I would be that for a long, long time.

I turned the suspect over to Poe in the cabin of the Gulfstream. Poe informed me that the siege at the tomb had ended, too, and that the surviving hostages were free and safe.

Seconds later, a Black Suburban carrying an HRT assault team arrived to whisk me away from the crippled jet. The HRT guys wore matching black suits. They carried a lot of weapons. The weapons seemed superfluous. Each one of them looked like he could kill me with his teeth.

It was over, just like that. I embraced Poe and Carlos and saluted the still-blindfolded kids.

The Suburban dropped three of us at a building on the far side of the airport where I was led into an almost empty warehouse, and placed under guard. When I inquired, they called my status "protective custody," just before they told me to shut the fuck up.

I was leaking unused adrenaline.

I had a choice of two magazines to help me pass the time. One was from 2007 and was obsessed with Oprah's favorite things from the time before the world had been forced to refocus its acquisitive attention on essential things, not favorite things.

I chose to read the other magazine. It was a copy of *Forbes* from the late spring of 2008, a few months before the worldwide financial meltdown really picked up momentum. The experts writing in the magazine didn't look too smart, in retrospect.

Somehow I didn't feel so fat and out of shape after I read that old magazine. I'd already come to the conclusion that if our nation's rocket scientists were as incompetent as our economic gurus, those terrific little rovers we sent to Mars would have ended up scooting around somebody's backyard in a suburb of Des Moines, and their batteries would have died after about two weeks.

The next stop in my itinerary was a small jet that wasn't as nice as the Calderóns' Gulfstream. No meal service. Once we were airborne, an agent offered me a can of Mountain Dew or a bottle of water. I needed neither the high-fructose corn syrup nor the caffeine. I took the water. Poland Spring.

I thought it was fancy, imported stuff from Warsaw until I got bored enough to read the label. I laughed at myself. Sometimes my ignorance seems as big as the world.

The jet landed at a military base in Virginia. Another black Suburban carried me to my debriefing, which lasted an entire day.

The best part of my twenty-four hours as a guest of the government was that I missed all the news coverage that was pretending to make sense of what had happened at Book & Snake. I wasn't forced to see any of the kids get murdered again. I didn't have to listen to any of the speculation from the talking heads or the faux experts on Fox or CNN.

There were a lot of worst parts of being a guest of my government.

I was allowed only one brief, monitored telephone conversation with my son, and one with Carmen. With them, I pretended all was normal.

I didn't ask to call Ann Calderón. Too risky.

I quickly grew frustrated with the debriefing process. But I did my best to make sure that the government employees who were hanging with me also grew frustrated with the debriefing process.

I told them what I could. But I didn't include anything that might put Jane Calderón at further risk. Despite some heavy-handed attempts at persuasion on the part of my interrogators, I was retaining the right to be the sole arbiter of what information might put Jane at further risk.

Of course, the stuff I withheld was the stuff the alphabet agency guys were most interested in knowing.

In addition to my determination to protect Jane's safety, I had a personal reason to keep my own counsel. I didn't yet understand what had happened between me and Ann Summers Calderón. Her words just before she'd sent me off to the New Haven airport in the cab still reverberated in my head.

I haven't been completely honest with you, Sam. And *There are things I couldn't tell you. For Jane's sake.*

I didn't know what Ann had meant. Telling the feds a story that made no sense to me made, well, no sense to me.

I was not tortured by the interrogators, not even close. The ones playing good cops said nice things to me, called me a hero. The ones playing the bad cops made a lot of oblique threats I knew they wouldn't carry out.

Each time they went over the top with their pressure, I would inquire if their video equipment was working well. If I could maybe get a copy for my Facebook page.

I moved around the room as much as I could during the interview in order to make later video editing more difficult for them. They repeatedly told me to sit still. I repeatedly told them I had a condition. I was daring them to restrain me.

At those moments the feds would make it even clearer they weren't happy with me. That's when I would look directly at the pane of glass that I thought was concealing the camera lens and I would ask if I was free to leave or if I was in their official custody. I probably asked that question ten times.

A few times I initiated discussions about whether or not it might be prudent for me to involve a lawyer.

I'm a big guy who likes to dance. What we were doing was a dance.

We worked it out. I knew I wasn't the key to understanding the siege. At some point the FBI and the CIA and the DIA would realize it, too.

At the end of the day, what were they going to do? If they weren't planning to kill me or lock me up in Guantánamo's successor, they knew I could eventually spin this story any way I chose. Or not.

I made it clear to them that no matter how many times they asked, I wasn't planning to get all chummy with them.

Frankly, all things considered, I thought a little more gratitude was in order. Just my opinion. But what do I know? I'm just a schlub from the Iron Range.

Late Monday, I was told I was booked on a commercial flight back to California. By then I was no longer worthy of black Suburbans. I was driven to the airport in a Ford sedan by a solitary agent in a business suit. No automatic weapons that I could see.

I was wearing my three-season sport coat from Macy's. Late April in Virginia, it turned out, was one of its seasons. If I could have told Carmen, which I couldn't, she would have been pleased.

My luggage from the Omni was in the trunk of the Ford. When we got close to the airport, the agent handed me a manila envelope with my cell phone and my keys. He pulled my previously empty wallet from his inside pocket. I was pleased to see that it had been refreshed with one hundred taxpayer dollars. Five twenties.

I felt a little bit like a felon getting out of the pen after completing ten-to-twelve for something I hadn't done.

At the curb of the terminal he said, "Thank you for your service." I thought he'd meant it. He shook my hand. That was cool.

I had a couple of hours to kill before boarding.

I called Carmen and told her I was on my way. I called Simon and told him I'd see him soon.

I didn't call Ann Calderón. My cell phone indicated I hadn't missed any attempts Ann might have made to contact me while I was in federal custody. There was a lot I didn't understand about the end. But I understood that the next move between us was Ann's, not mine.

I did not want to insert myself into whatever charade she was trying to maintain. That would be reckless, and recklessness might not be good for Jane Calderón's continued well-being. I was not entertaining the delusion that the terrorists' threats had expired simply because they were in custody.

One of the other things I discovered before I meandered through Airport Security was that my new friends, Deirdre and Poe, were no longer taking my calls. That disappointed me. I had come to like them both.

I flipped through a couple of newspapers and watched a little TV while I drank a decompression pint in a Washington Dulles Airport bar. Compared to MIA, Dulles is, well, dull. All in all, I would have been much happier to be flying back out of Miami. I could have used a dose of pan-cultural Latin verve right about then.

Some Cuban food, too. Some of that. And a café Cubano or two.

I read the Afghan twins' biographies for the first time while I nursed my beer.

The narrative they'd written and sent to the press was long and rambling, but I found the story of their lives, until the end, oddly American in terms of hopefulness and opportunity.

They were raised in a small, impoverished village outside Kandahar. Their father was a teacher. Their uncle, who emigrated to Paris, had become an engineer. He paid for the education of his three nephews. The twin I met in the Gulfstream was educated in England and, later, in the United States, at Yale. His brother, the one who surrendered outside the tomb, was educated in Egypt and Germany.

The twins returned to Afghanistan, to Kabul, after the fall of the Taliban in 2003. Using the entrepreneurial and engineering skills they'd acquired in the West, they started a company that constructed mobile phone towers. In 2005 they sold their business to one of the mobile phone operating companies and returned to Kandahar. With the profits from their business sale, they became investors, primarily in the Chinese stock market.

They were successful investors. The day their sister was married in the village where they were born, the twins were wealthy young men, even by Western standards.

The twins maintained that they had been unaware of a firefight between the Taliban and U.S. and Afghan government forces that had taken place the night before the wedding a few kilometers outside the village. They had no idea that the United States government had developed intelligence overnight, human and electronic, indicating that after the skirmish, Taliban fighters had retreated into hiding in the compound where the wedding celebration was scheduled.

On direct order from Command, a single one-thousand-pound BLU-110 was dropped on the compound.

The twins survived the bombing without serious injury.

By their own report, they began planning the siege at Book & Snake one month later.

They did their own research. Used their own funds. They involved a "handful" of other Afghans for specific tasks, bringing them into the plot for only a few days right before the siege began. They made certain that everyone who assisted them was safely back out of the country before the ongoing siege was discovered by the authorities.

The country was already ripping into the open wounds of the tragedy. Columnists and pundits and bloggers were demanding to know what the parents of the surviving hostages had revealed to save their children.

Why was the secretary of the army's kid spared while the son of a bus driver from Fargo was murdered? What did they want from the Supreme Court nominee?

Why had the twin terrorists surrendered? Was that their plan all along?

I had some personal thoughts on that one—my bias was that the two brothers saw pluses and minuses to the alternative outcomes. From a terrorism point of view, a final conflagration would have had a clichéd finality to it. But surviving gave the men access to a big microphone in a society that until recently had prided itself on judicial transparency.

Terrorists exploit vulnerabilities. The transparency of our justice system was one of our nation's great strengths. And the transparency of our justice system made it one of our most explicit vulnerabilities. I thought the surrender was evidence of an overtly political motive. The murderous twins were doing what Karl Rove had always preached: Go after the strength.

The public was acting as though there were simple answers to all the complexities of the siege in New Haven. All I knew for sure was that the speculation would be endless and that it would cause more division.

That was true because we, as a country, would let it divide us. We actually seemed to welcome the chasms. I didn't get that.

The photographs I found in the newspapers from the quasi-crash of the jet at the airport in New Haven were overexposed and grainy. I guessed they were cell phone shots from hundreds of yards away. I saw myself in one picture. I only knew it was me because I knew it was me. Standing in the open door of the jet, with my white shirt and tie, I looked like a ticket agent who had snuck on board the plane to have his picture taken.

Although the photo had been snapped while I was asking Poe if he had those handcuffs of his, a government official identified the person in the shot as Carlos.

I couldn't imagine Carlos was thrilled. The pic wasn't flattering.

I promised myself I really would lose those twenty pounds.

Deirdre and Poe had managed to stay out of the news. The photograph I saw at the crash site included Poe, but he was smart enough to keep the hood of his sweatshirt up while he was pacing outside the Gulfstream. Not even his mother would have recognized him.

Deirdre never drew any attention to herself. She was that kind of lady.

I was beginning to think I was going to come out of the weekend with my anonymity preserved. That was the way the U.S. government preferred it, and it was the way that I preferred it.

*　　*　　*

It turned out I had a middle seat near the rear lavatory on the flight to LAX. I crossed my arms, yielding the armrests to my seatmates. I was okay with all of it.

The Calderón kids were alive.

I didn't think anything I'd done over the weekend had cost any other kid his or her life.

Maybe I'd been duped by Ann Calderón in some way I didn't understand. I could live with that. It was the proverbial end of the day, and I was feeling good about myself.

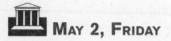 **MAY 2, FRIDAY**

Sam

A week and a half after the end of the siege, it was becoming clearer and clearer to me that the damn economic collapse had truly changed almost everything for everyone who wasn't sick rich. That included me and Carmen.

Once my suspension was over in Boulder, the plan was for Carmen to look for a law enforcement gig along the Front Range in Colorado and for me to look for one along the South Coast in California. We'd weigh our offers and decide whether to live with our new baby in the Coastal West or the Mountain West.

Carmen knew I wanted to be in Colorado because it would be less disruptive to Simon. If all things ended up looking equal, the where-we-would-live decision would tilt toward the eastern slope of the Continental Divide.

But every jurisdiction we contacted in both states was cutting back on hiring. I couldn't get an interview in California, let alone a job offer. Carmen's doctor-ordered bed rest had been extended—her pregnancy had been officially reclassified as high-risk—so she couldn't come to Colorado to interview for anything.

Her sick pay was rapidly running out. We needed money.

I went back to work at my old job with the department in Boulder. Both my boss and my partner were happy to have me. My captain helped me arrange my schedule so that I could fly to the coast to be with Carmen on my days off.

Carmen's sister had lost her job as a bookkeeper with a big box retailer in San Juan Capistrano. She was keeping an eye on Carmen between my visits to California. Carmen and I were helping pay her mortgage so she wouldn't lose her condo in El Toro.

The value of the condo was dropping like a rock. Someday soon, she would swallow hard and walk away from it. Until then, we'd help.

Being separated from my pregnant girlfriend wasn't an ideal arrangement, but I had serious financial and parental responsibilities in two states and no other way to meet them. Having jobs in difficult circumstances was better than not having jobs at all.

Carmen and I knew plenty of people in worse situations than us. Some were poor.

Some had been rich.

The Calderóns had contacted Carmen and extended us both job offers—security gigs with their company, or positions in some new field if we were willing to train. The offers were contingent on us moving to Florida. Or Argentina.

Carmen, of course, didn't understand the reason for her daughter's future in-laws' generosity. She assumed it was a family gesture, with a capital *F*.

When I let my gaze settle over the economic horizon, I knew that a time might come when we would have to consider the opportunity. One night back home, after comparing our likely income with our joint expenses, I did some serious examination of our employment options. I sat on my son's bed in my beat-up little house in North Boulder, spinning his cheap plastic globe.

I was amazed at the geography of it all. Buenos Aires was as far east as Greenland. As far south as the Cape of Good Hope.

I knew Argentina was far away. But damn . . . I had no idea it was that far away. I began to get intrigued. I wondered if my brain could actually learn Spanish.

A whispered voice was telling me I would like Buenos Aires.

I had gone back to work in Boulder during the week after the siege. From my first minute back on the job, I kept my head down. I tried my best to be a good cop. I knew I had smart enemies in my own police department, and damn smart enemies in the Boulder DA's office. I had to be vigilant.

I wasn't sleeping well. I took no comfort in the fact that I wasn't alone in my insomnia. As a nation, we had just watched a slow parade of tortured parents bury their murdered children. Day by day. One by one. Tear by tear.

Some New Haven police lieutenant named Haden Moody seemed to show up on every damn news program on television. He became the color commentator of our despair.

I got tired of the guy fast.

The fate of the two terrorists, and their unnamed comrades, became a national obsession. That was an obsession I didn't share. Through their attorneys, the terrorists made clear they were seeking a public trial. To ensure justice? Hardly. A big show would provide an opportunity for them to exploit our democratic system for their propaganda goals.

As difficult as it was for me, I tried to stay cognizant of the fact that what had happened at Book & Snake had little to do with the two killers. And I knew that whatever happened to them next would have little to do with justice. The national focus on the Afghan twins was, in truth, a distraction. Unfortunately, it was one that I feared my government welcomed.

There was plenty of speculation in the media, of course. I read everything I could find online regarding the theories—not to mention the accusations—about all the damaging information that the parents of the kids in Book & Snake might or might not have traded for their children's safety. The consensus seemed to be that, whether the government was willing to admit it or not, a lot of potential ammunition had changed hands.

The parents' ethics during the siege were debated by strangers who felt that in the parents' shoes they would have acted more honorably. The parents' patriotism, or lack thereof, was attacked by people paid to have opinions about such things. The local cops and the FBI were criticized by somebody for just about everything they'd done.

I canceled my cable package just so I would never again have to watch cable news. Also because I could no longer afford it. The money I saved on the monthly cable bill was helping to fund my trips to see Carmen in California.

I missed *SportsCenter* pretty much immediately. Although I also cut down my stool time at the West End Tavern, I was going to have to find a sports bars if I wanted to watch the Stanley Cup. That was a bummer.

I was thinking that if the Pioneers from DU and the Bulldogs from Yale ever scheduled a hockey game at the Whale in New Haven, I would figure out a way to get there before they dropped the first puck. That would be one game I wanted both teams to win.

Simon showed me how to set Google to alert me if any reporter on the entire planet wrote the words "Book & Snake" and "Canary Islands" in the same single news story. I hadn't known Google would do that. I thought it was nice of them until I realized, too late, that Google knew my secret: I was someone who cared if the words "Book & Snake" and "Canary Islands" showed up in the same news story.

I had a new worry. Could Google be trusted?

For my taste, there was far too little debate about how vulnerable we as a nation remained to inventive forms of terrorism. Or about how many inadvertent enemies we created, not through the military moves we made that were essential to guarantee our national safety, but through the occasional carelessness with which we projected our might, and the often unnecessary way we packaged arrogance along with our power.

On the second Friday after the siege, I decided to run a hypothetical I couldn't get out of my head by my friend Alan Gregory. He's the psychologist.

I was waiting for him in downtown Boulder when he finished his last appointment late on Friday afternoon. He'd offered to drive me to DIA for my Southwest flight to John Wayne for a couple of days with Carmen.

She'd already let me know the weekend plans: I was apparently going to be giving her a lot of foot rubs. That was going to be a new activity for me. She'd asked me if I knew my pressure points. I didn't, but I told her I did. On the way to Alan's office, I stopped at the main library and got a book on it. I learned something immediately: I hadn't known that rubbing feet was called "reflexology."

Or at least it was in Boulder. I would study my pressure point technique on the plane.

Once I had Carmen's feet as relaxed as I could make them, I planned to tell her about my weekend in New Haven and the reason we were being offered fine jobs in Argentina.

I'd gone early to meet Alan so that we would have some time to talk before we headed to the airport. The weather was glorious. The West End of Pearl was beginning to fall into the shadows of the Rockies and the streets had just enough life on them to be urban and interesting.

I suggested a beer. Alan and I walked the short distance from his office on Walnut to Pearl Street. He thought I was on the way to visit my favorite stool at the West End Tavern, but I kept on going until we got to another restaurant nearby. Centro. The place was lively and, more to the point, Latin. Not Miami Airport lively, and not Miami neighborhood Latin, but it had enough of the right vibe to meet my simple needs that evening. The happy hour crowd hadn't had quite enough time to get drunk, which also was good news. We found two seats at the bar. Alan bought me a Red Stripe. He ordered some Mexican soda he said he liked.

I didn't believe him. He was drinking soda because he was driving.

I downed half my beer before I said, "Let's say a patient of yours tells you that she may have just, you know, inadvertently revealed an important government secret to someone. She tells you there's a slight chance—one in a gazillion—that somebody, a bad guy, could use the secret to do major damage to our country. With me?"

"So far," Alan said.

"Do you break your code—the doctor/patient privilege thing—and tell the government what your patient said?"

"Depends," he said. "Is the danger imminent?"

"No, not at all. But the potential damage is catastrophic, you know, if the stars line up just the wrong way."

He didn't ponder the nuances of my hypothetical as long as I was thinking he should. He said, "I keep my mouth shut, Sam." He looked at me hard, his eyes suddenly all earnest. "What's this about?"

Something to know about my friend: Alan has never once in his life come across a sleeping dog he has ever allowed to just frigging nap.

I let him see a sliver of my truth. I said, "I can't get that thing in New Haven out of my head. The corner those parents were in."

He shook his head in parental empathy and overall despair about the Book & Snake siege. "I know what you mean," he said.

He didn't, of course. Know, that is.

He wasn't even aware that I'd been to Connecticut.

I had already decided I wasn't going to go any further with Alan about what had happened in Florida and in New Haven. It's not that I didn't trust him with the truth. He was as good at secrets as anyone I'd ever met. But he and I already shared one seriously toxic confidence. I felt the weight of it hanging around my neck in some way, shape, or form almost every day. I was sure he did, too.

I wasn't going to burden him with another one that he would have to lug around indefinitely.

Anyway, he had his hands full with events in his own life.

A woman walked up behind us at the Centro bar. I didn't turn to look at her; I thought she was a happy hour patron hoping to earn the bartender's attention so she could score a cocktail and get working on her buzz.

She spoke to Alan. "Do you mind if I borrow your friend?"

I recognized the voice. I turned my head. Deirdre.

I smiled, well, like an idiot. I hopped to my feet. I introduced them while I tried to comprehend what was happening. Deirdre, Alan. Alan,

Deirdre. For Alan's benefit, I added, "Deirdre's somebody I met back East. That engagement . . . weekend."

She shook his hand. Then she gestured to me with her eyes, indicating she wanted to talk outside.

I said, "Excuse me, Alan. Just for a minute. This is . . ."

"We won't be long," Deirdre said, rescuing me from my stammer. "Would you please order me one of whatever you're drinking?"

"It's . . . pop," Alan said in that befuddled way he has.

"Perfect," she said.

She took my hand and led me out onto Pearl Street. We turned right. We were heading in the direction of the Mall, a block away.

I was wondering if Alan had closed his mouth yet.

Deirdre said, "How are you, Sam Purdy?"

"Better than some," I said. "What about you?"

"Is the weather always this nice here?" she asked.

"More often than you'd think," I said.

"Damn pretty," she said.

"Shhh," I said. "Don't tell."

Whatever Deirdre and I were doing together while we strolled the Downtown Mall in Boulder, we were apparently easing into it.

We jaywalked 11th and crossed onto the herringboned path of the Mall. I was very aware she was leading me somewhere. I suspected the destination wasn't made of bricks.

I said, "This an official visit? I'll admit I'm thrilled to see you, Deirdre. Everything ended so abruptly, but . . ."

She squeezed my hand. "I have a question," she said.

"You know, I do, too," I said. I surprised myself with my eagerness to ask it.

"You go first," she said in a way that felt generous. With no lives hanging in the balance, I found myself liking her even more than I had that morning at breakfast in New Haven.

I said, "At the very end, when you were texting me, you seemed to know that all the destruction was going to stop. How did you know?"

We walked halfway to Broadway before she answered. She looked up at me. "I didn't know anything. Okay? I'm not in covert ops, Sam. I'm an analyst. I believe that during a crisis, a good analyst has to be willing to get off the fence. What you saw was me jumping off the fence. What you got from me was my . . . take—my best shot at the truth. That day my conclusion wasn't"—she paused—"a slam dunk. Not even close."

She was dissing one of her old bosses. *Take that, George Tenet.*

"Okay" was what I said to Dee.

In the months since Forty-three moved back to Texas, but prior to the siege, I'd been having the hardest time burying my instinct to give him and his incompetent friends the benefit of the doubt. After the siege, though, I'd discovered that my residual impulse to defend politicians of all stripes had dissipated considerably.

She said, "The library situation is what made me suspicious. If what the unsubs wanted was to go out in a blaze of destructive glory, they would have taken out the library when they had the chance. The country was watching. The RPG was in place. They had a prominent hostage next to the weapon. The moment the helicopter took off from the roof of Beinecke, the guy still inside could have fired off two quick rounds at the library. Would have taken fifteen, maybe twenty seconds. And they still had other hostages—both in the tomb and in the helicopter—to keep us from retaliating with overwhelming force. They didn't need to wait."

For a moment, I thought she was done. She wasn't.

"I knew when they didn't fire on the library that, whatever they were up to, it wasn't just about casualties and destruction. To me, the hesitation meant they had a bigger plan that I wasn't seeing, or that they had a point to make. The bigger plan option? I couldn't make that work. Didn't make sense to me. The moment one of them exited the protection of the tomb, they had to know we could overwhelm that person with superior force. So . . . I concluded they wanted to make a point. I just happened to see the wedding dress on a monitor in the command vehicle. It hit me right then that maybe they wanted us to make their point for them."

"Us?"

"Us as a country. They wanted us to cross some final line. To misread the clues. To overreact to what they were doing. Had done." She squeezed my hand again. "When I saw the wedding dress that hostage was wearing, that's when all the pieces came together for me. The suicide bomb, the sniper, the IED, the throat slashing. I'd been thinking all along that the siege was about Iraq, some sick retaliatory reenactment of all the damage that had been done to the civilians in Iraq during the war. But the wedding dress said Afghanistan to me. There was dried blood on the dress. I saw it as a symbol of one of the weddings we mistakenly bombed there. I made the connection with the thousand-pound bomb. I felt certain then. I jumped off the fence.

"I also knew that the girl wearing that dress would become the signature photographic image of the end of the siege."

"You were right about that," I said. Photograhs of Jane Calderón exiting the tomb wearing the wedding dress and the *hijab* were on the covers of the next issues of *Time* and *Newsweek*. It became one of the iconic images of the siege at Book & Snake.

"I concluded that the terrorists wanted us to duplicate our mistake at the wedding in Afghanistan right there in New Haven, but this time do it in front of the world."

She was making sense.

She paused. "When it turned out that there was a jet waiting at the airport, I knew it would push all our Nine/eleven buttons. The terrorists knew that, too. I think the unsubs expected us to overreact to that, of course. To blow up that jet. Either during takeoff, or just after. They knew we'd have fighters above them, waiting. Ready.

"So . . . that's how I knew, Sam. Or thought I knew."

"Huh," I said. I would chew on it some more during breaks from studying reflexology. "Your turn, Deirdre. What's your question?"

She smiled at me first. She waited for me to look at her face. She wanted to make sure I saw her smile before she started.

"I've been tasked with compiling an inventory of what strategic information the siege parents might have revealed to keep their children alive. It's been difficult. By and large, the parents remain . . . recalcitrant witnesses. But we have responsibilities—we have mitigation efforts . . . to prepare, and to enforce."

"Tough job," I said.

"Yes, it is. I'm here to see you because of the Calderóns."

"Okay." I had never mentioned the Calderóns to Deirdre or Poe. That she had connected those dots was no surprise at all. The government had been in possession of my cell phone for those twenty-four

hours I spent in Virginia. Though, if there had ever been a warrant is-
sued for it, it was from some court that didn't make its records public.
Let's just say I hadn't been offered a copy for my scrapbook.

We took two more steps before Deirdre spoke again.

"Canary Islands," she said next. She allowed that to sink in before
she added, "La Palma. Cumbre Vieja."

Her Spanish accent was comfortable. Practiced. She was someone
who would know whether it was cerveza más or más cerveza.

I wasn't going to lie to Deirdre. It's not who I am. If she'd solved
for x, she'd solved for x. "So how did you get there?" I asked.

"Just did what he would have done once he discovered he had
the Calderóns' daughter as a hostage. I searched the public record.
Looked for vulnerability I could exploit. Information I could use."
She stopped walking, let go of my hand, and reached into her shoulder
bag. She pulled out a magazine.

Actually, it was a journal.

"*Geophysical Research*," she said.

I nodded. It might have been a good place for me to tell a white lie.
But I just nodded.

"Dr. Ann Summers Calderón has a letter in here. This issue. It's
about Cumbre Vieja. You know anything about that?"

"It's a volcano," I said, not really answering her question.

"Yes, it's a volcano. Her letter is about how much raw force it
would take to cause a huge chunk of the west side of La Palma—
that's the island the volcano is on—to slide into the Atlantic Ocean.
It's a long, complicated letter. For a scientist, she writes well. Have
you read it?"

I gestured at the journal. I said, "You know, with the economy the
way it is, I had to let my subscription expire. I was only reading it for
the pictures, anyway."

She smiled. "That's a no?"

"That's a no."

"How about I summarize it for you? Dr. Calderón offers her
support for the prevailing scientific contention that the most likely
scenario for the geologic future of La Palma is that the volcano will re-

main intermittently active and that volcanic activity will cause the island to grow both larger and higher over time. Bottom line? La Palma has a high probability of staying intact for the next several thousand years, at least."

"That's nice to hear," I said. I was waiting for a "but."

The "but" would include the words "landslide" and "tsunami."

"Dr. Calderón discusses some recent controversy regarding the odds of a possible catastrophic landslide on La Palma. She concludes, as have others, that any future major landslide would require a confluence of events that are highly improbable. There would need to be a major increase in groundwater on the island, something that would first require a sustained, unexpected alteration in the regional climate. That's a big, big *if*.

"During any period of heightened volcanic activity, magma rising within the volcano would, of course, increase pressure along the fault. After a prolonged rainy period, the rising magma would also heat the additional groundwater, and the internal geological pressure within La Palma would rise exponentially as a result.

"That combination—pressure from fresh magma and drastically increased underground water pressure and temperature—could put tremendous stress on the existing fault network at the island's ridge-line. And, who knows? Eventually . . . *Craaack*. Landslide."

I didn't respond.

She said, "For the record, Sam? Although there is plenty of controversy about this as well, if a major eruption of the Cumbre Vieja volcano did trigger a landslide along the primary ridge fault on La Palma, it could, theoretically, cause a tidal wave of astonishing proportions. Some argue it would be an immense tidal push, a phenomenon that scientists call a mega-tsunami. Krakatoa? We might be talking that kind of wave. The mega-tsunami from La Palma would head west, sweeping the Atlantic before it impacted the eastern seaboard of North America. It would cross the Atlantic within hours. The tidal surge would be measured in tens of meters. Atlantic islands from Canada to the Caribbean would be decimated. Damage estimates along the coast of the United States and Canada? A thousand Katrinas. There would be neither time nor resources to evacuate major coastal population centers. Worst-case casualty estimates range from a million or two to as high as thirty million. Thirty million. Imagine that."

I looked at Deirdre for about three seconds. It was all I could tolerate.

"Poe said you mentioned something about that number in one of your talks with him. Thirty million. Casualties. Familiar?"

I said, "Yeah. It's familiar." Like I said, if Deirdre had solved for x . . .

"Volcano experts—are they called 'volcanologists' or am I making that up?—and earthquake scientists seem to agree that the island may indeed cleave at some point in the future. Way off in the future, Sam. Five thousand years. Ten."

"Didn't know that," I said. It was true. I didn't know that.

"Dr. Calderón doesn't dispute that contention.

"But her letter addresses a side controversy that's been raging for most of a decade in the popular media about whether the sheer force necessary to trigger the landslide could, alternatively, be precipitated by man. Unlike some of her colleagues, who completely disregard the possibility, Dr. Calderón argues that a nuclear device of a specific size, placed in one certain location that is currently accessible within an existing cave network that runs along the primary ridge fault, might—might, under just the right circumstances—be able to generate sufficient force to trigger the aforementioned landslide. She presents a mathematical argument to support her conclusion. Truth is, the math is way over my head."

"I'm sure it would be over mine, too," I said.

In my mathematically challenged head, I was traveling back in time. I was outside that Indian restaurant in New Haven, smelling the aromas of naan and curry. I was on the plaza near Morse College and Stiles College, listening to Ann Calderón describe the potential devastation of a landslide on La Palma.

The awful potential consequences of what she would have to reveal in order to save her daughter.

Dee said, "In her letter in the journal, Dr. Calderón doesn't identify the specific location within the mountain—precisely where in the cave network along the fault she believes a nuclear explosion would be most likely to precipitate the catastrophic landslide. I've been in touch with the journal editors. They tell me that her letter originally included that information, but that they asked her to excise it. For security reasons. In a post-Nine/eleven world. She agreed to their suggestion."

I was looking at my feet. Deirdre was looking in my eyes. I could feel the burn.

From the corner of my eye, I could see her tilt her head to try to hook my gaze. I didn't let it work.

She took my hand once more. We reversed course and started walking west. Back toward the setting sun, toward Centro, and toward Alan, sitting bewildered at the bar, trying to save us seats.

Alan wouldn't be happy with me. People in Boulder tend to lose their high-altitude cool when they catch someone trying to save seats at a popular bar during happy hour on a perfect Friday evening.

Deirdre put her arm around me for a few steps. "Dr. Calderón concludes her letter with her estimate of the statistical odds that the confluence of events—geologic and meteorologic—could ever come together so that a perfectly sized, perfectly situated, and perfectly timed nuclear explosion would be able to trigger a sudden, catastrophic landslide on La Palma.

"Want to make a guess about the number?"

Ann had used a number with me. I tried that one. "One in ten million," I said.

She laced her fingers in mine. "Don't lose any sleep about the Canary Islands, Sam. Even if she did give it up to the assholes, it's a long, long, long, long shot. Of all my worries after the siege, this one is near the bottom of the list."

Wow.

Ann Calderón hadn't trusted me.

The story she had told me about La Palma and Cumbre Vieja and mega-tsunamis had nothing to do with the ammunition that the unsubs wanted from her in trade for Jane Calderón's safety. Ann had sold me the Canary Islands tale so that she wouldn't have to tell me what the hostage takers really wanted from the Calderóns in exchange for Jane's safety.

I'd fallen for it like a rube.

Sometime on the Friday of the crisis, Ann had learned that what the unsubs wanted from her in exchange for Jane's safety was temporary custody of her son and access to the Calderóns' Gulfstream 200. But Ann didn't want me to know that. She was afraid that I might end up divulging the information to someone who might be in a position to betray both her children.

Ann Calderón treated me exactly like a hostage negotiator is treated by his or her superior officer. Ann never entrusted me with information that she didn't think I needed to know.

It was hard for me to admit, but it had turned out that Ann's caution was warranted, and that her judgment about me was correct. The reality was that, with motives as pure as a father's love, I had indeed tipped off the feds—first Poe, and then Deirdre—about the scope of the purported dangers of Cumbre Vieja. If I had known in advance about the unsubs' escape plans with the Gulfstream 200, I might well have revealed that information to Poe and Deirdre, too.

The consequences of that betrayal might have been catastrophic.

Was I angry that Ann had deceived me?

No. I felt chastened.

Deirdre had gotten what she wanted from me—confirmation about the La Palma story. Did she realize how well I'd been played over the siege weekend by Ann Calderón? I couldn't tell. I doubted I would ever know the answer to that question.

If I had to guess, I would guess that Deirdre did recognize the residue of Ann's finesse moves with me, and that part of the motivation for her trip to Boulder was to let me off the hook. Gently. I thought it kind of her.

She said, "If Poe or I can ever do anything for you, Sam, we'll be there. You need to know that."

"Thank you," I said.

We walked another half a block. I said, "How is Poe, Deirdre? Is he doing okay?"

She was ready for my question. "Poe's a survivor, Sam. Kind of like you, but . . . well . . . more damaged. What happened in New Haven has given him a lifetime of fresh investigations. He's invigorated. He has dragons to slay. Real dragons that he knows are breathing real fire. He's interviewing to bring a couple of new agents on board his little posse."

I glanced at Deirdre's belly. "What about you, Deirdre? How are you?"

She smiled and placed her right hand on her still-flat abdomen. "Poe said you knew." She made a puzzled face. "Still can't figure out how you do that. I'd known for only a day or two. I did the first pregnancy test on the Friday of the siege. I didn't really believe it, you know? So I peed on another stick in the lavatory of the Amtrak train on my way to New Haven the evening before I met you. You're dead-rabbit good, Sam Purdy."

I tipped an imaginary cap to her.

Dead-rabbit good. I liked the sound of it.

"I've gained a couple of pounds. Can you tell?" She raised her left hand and waggled her naked ring finger. "Lost some weight, too."

I touched her naked finger. "It's good?" I asked, in my best Alan Gregory therapy voice.

"It's good," she said.

She suddenly smiled, and waved at something in the distance. I looked down the Mall. On the other side of Broadway I saw Poe wearing his Yale hoodie and a pair of aviator shades. He looked a little like the Unabomber. He was near the hot dog cart, a big smile on his face. The sun had set behind him. A halo of striated oranges and pinks framed the Front Range.

I waved.

Deirdre said, "He insisted on hanging back while we talked so he could check for surveillance. You know, just in case."

"SSG?" I said. I still wasn't convinced they existed. "They're real?"

"They are," she said. She reached up and touched my neck with tenderness that took me by surprise. "His latest obsession. Poe needs his obsessions."

We were quiet until the light changed so we could cross Broadway. Deirdre broke the silence when we were still thirty feet from Poe. She said, "Do you know how many loose nukes there are in the world, Sam? Unaccounted-for nuclear weapons?"

I didn't have to think long. "No," I said. "I don't."

We made it to within a couple of steps of Christopher Poe before she said, "We don't either."

ACKNOWLEDGMENTS

This book gives me cause to remind that I make stuff up.

Although *The Siege* takes unconcealed advantage of real locales, legendary buildings, and revered institutions, I altered them whenever reality proved inconvenient. I adjusted the timing of actual events so that things that had already occurred and events that are planned for the future all take place during the story. I have also taken liberties with the geography of the Yale campus and with the architectural details of prominent buildings in order to describe perspectives that, well, don't exist.

The gestation of this concept took place over a period of five years. I'm particularly grateful to Brian Tart at Dutton for his guidance and encouragement as I searched for a way to tell the story. I could not have written a book like *The Siege* without the editorial fortitude Brian displays. Jessica Horvath provided crucial support and was invaluable in convincing all of us that the structure of the book didn't break any of the laws of physics. Claire Zion is everything a writer could want in an editor. Robert Barnett and Bonnie Nathan continue to advocate for me with remarkable grace. Jane Davis does so many things to help keep me afloat. I am grateful to all.

I thank Christopher Whitcomb, again. His captivating memoir of life on the FBI's Hostage Rescue Team, *Cold Zero*, was an essential resource.

Years back, Jeffery Deaver helped convince me that this idea had promise. After I began sharing pages I relied on a handful of trusted early readers for counsel. At various stages Francine Mathews, Alexander White, Rose Kauffman, Jane Davis, Elyse Morgan, Judy Pomerantz, Maureen Guilfoile, Kevin Guilfoile, and Nancy Hall let me know what was and wasn't working. Al Silverman's eye proved as sharp as ever. For everyone's help, I'm more grateful than I'm able to say. I also thank Patricia Limerick, and hope Jeff Limerick finds some heavenly amusement in the cameo-time in New Haven.

I had a sleeping dog by my side almost every day that I wrote. Writing without Abbey beside me is theoretically possible, but I'm not anxious to try.

Xan White provided indispensable research. Officer Joseph Avery answered my questions about the New Haven Police Department. Scott Meacham generously permitted the use of his evocative photograph of Book & Snake in the front matter. Killeen Hanson mapped New Haven and Yale to my peculiar specifications. Any variation from reality in her work is my responsibility.